More praise for *H*

"*High Hand* is a masterful political thriller, full of great characters performing noble and ignoble deeds in the wake of an attempted assassination of a presidential candidate. Reporter Frank Adams wants the truth, but the truth is costly, and ugly, for all. You won't be able to put it down."
— Nancy Barnes, Executive Editor, *Houston Chronicle*

"Beyond the enormously thrilling plot and pace of Curtis J. James's *High Hand*, the storyline's richly detailed use of spy tradecraft is a delight to read for those of us in the business. Move over, Tom Clancy; make room for Curtis J. James."
— Kevin Giblin, first Director,
NATO Counterterrorism Office,
and FBI senior counterterrorism investigator

"Reminiscent of the best of Ken Follett and Tom Clancy, *High Hand* is a taut page-turner packed with great writing, meticulous detail, and a fascinating view of the dovetailed worlds of international diplomacy and espionage. Insider knowledge of journalism, post–Cold War Russia, and the Washington, DC, power game makes this an irresistible read."
— Darryl McGrath, author of *Flight Paths*

"*High Hand* is a thriller in which all the players are bluffing, but someone holds the killer card. It mixes the high stakes of a US presidential race with the calculation of Russian intrigue. It's a whodunit enriched by who did it—a creative conspiracy of three very talented authors."
— Ned Barnett, Editorial Page Editor,
The (Raleigh) News & Observer

"A fantastic read! A contemporary political thriller with all the good, the bad, and the ugly you would expect, but it all comes at you in ways you never imagined."
—Paul Mattera, Senior Vice President,
Liberty Mutual Insurance

"*High Hand* is a page-turner with fast action and terrific internal conspiracies. Ominously but importantly, it reminds us that Russia is still a player in the Big Game."
—Charles Levenstein, economist and policy analyst,
University of Massachusetts

"*High Hand* embraces the subtle world of modern high-tech espionage and political intrigue.... This remarkable thriller builds to the point where you question the difference between reality and deception."
—John Darbyshire, Senior Scientific Consultant,
Iridessa Sarl, Switzerland

"*High Hand* has it all: political intrigue, sex, betrayal, terrorism, and espionage—all wrapped around a love story that spans the modern world's hot spots. A thriller not to be missed."
—Anders Gyllenhaal, Vice President for News,
The McClatchy Company

"*High Hand* is both a recreational and educational expedition through modern-day politics, business, and espionage. Featuring terrific historical and geographic realism..., it almost reads like a documentary—until some of our favorite characters start dropping. Then it's a screen-swiper until the end."
—David Rossetti, former Vice President
for Network Protocol Engineering, Cisco Systems

"Lisa Hawkes is a compelling new hero!"
—Juleen Zierath, Chairwoman,
Nobel Prize Committee for Physiology or Medicine

HIGH
HAND

HIGH
HAND

A NOVEL

Curtis J. James

COPPER PEAK PRESS
WASHINGTON, DC

Copper Peak Press
1220 L Street NW Suite 100-528
Washington, DC 20005-4018
www.copperpeakpress.com

Quantity sales. Special discounts are available on quantity purchases by corporations, associations, and others. For details, contact the "Special Sales Department" at the address above.

Orders by US trade bookstores and wholesalers. Please contact BCH: (800) 431-1579 or visit www.bookch.com for details.

Printed in the United States of America

Cataloging-in-Publication
    James, Curtis J., author.
        High hand / Curtis J. James. -- First edition.
        pages cm
        LCCN 2015959068
        ISBN 978-0-9864303-0-5
        1. Assassination--Fiction. 2. Petroleum industry and
    trade--Fiction. 3. International relations--Fiction.
    4. Detective and mystery fiction. 5. Thrillers (Fiction)
    6. Spy fiction. I. Title.
    PS3610.A4287H54 2016   813'.6
    QBI15-600237

First Edition

20 19 18 17 16   10 9 8 7 6 5 4 3 2

For Tance Harris, Barbara Ellenberger and Anne Salladin

I: CUT THE DECK

*In politics, strangely enough, the best way to play
your cards is to lay them face upwards on the table.*

H. G. Wells

CHAPTER 1

LOS ANGELES

FRANK ADAMS STRUGGLED to maintain focus. Focus had served him well as lead political reporter for the *Los Angeles Register*. He had been covering the campaign of Senator Stuart Roberts, the presumptive Republican presidential nominee, for a year. This stop afforded Frank a rare return home to Los Angeles. The candidate was addressing the faithful at Pershing Square. Hearing Roberts's stump speech for the umpteenth time, Frank half-listened for a new nuance; with the other half of his brain, he was remembering his father's stories about the 1951 pennant collapse of "Dem Bums," the Brooklyn Dodgers, and their redemption four years later.

Frank was just behind Roberts with a dozen other reporters and as many TV crews, twenty yards away on the raised stage at the head of the plaza. Standing next to him was his good friend Bill Wilson of the *Chicago Tribune*.

Bill looked at Frank with a smirk.

"Geez, Adams. Why are you so dressed up? Nobody in L.A. wears a coat and tie."

Frank ignored the taunt. He still believed that an address by a presidential candidate, even in the summer at an outdoor venue, required more formal attire.

The afternoon sunlight filled the plaza. The crowd applauded as Roberts dove into his stump speech.

"As you know, I was the United States ambassador to Russia in the 1990s. I was also proud to serve as a young man under President Ronald Reagan! As the presidential nominee of our great Republican Party, I intend to carry his banner all the way to the White House!"

A man in the crowd yelled out, "God bless America!"

Amid raucous cheering, Roberts gave a thumbs-up with his right hand, forced his campaign smile and waited for the crowd to calm down.

"President Reagan deserves much of the credit for winning the Cold War. But even though Soviet Communism is in the dustbin of history, there are new threats from Russia. Now let me make clear that my concerns are not aimed at the Russian people. I have many Russian friends. But there is a growing danger to the United States and Europe coming from Moscow. Its leaders have rolled back—"

An explosion ripped through the stage. It reverberated in the concrete canyon of buildings surrounding the plaza. Frank was thrown off his feet. Dazed and entangled with his colleagues, he saw people running for safety, but a ringing in his ears muted their screams.

As he tried to stand, Frank realized that Wilson was sprawled across his legs. Frank rolled away from the motionless body, and as he stood he saw the crushed side of Bill's face.

Bill had borne the blunt of the blast—and unwittingly saved Frank's life.

Frank moved his arms and legs. He was intact but covered with Bill's blood. He had a wound in his left forearm. He removed a handkerchief from his back pocket, clinched a corner between his teeth, wrapped it above the wound and pulled it tight.

Chaos overtook the stage. Secret Service agents surrounded Roberts. Reporters, campaign aides and local supporters stumbled to their feet, some of them reaching for their cell phones. Others lay in tangles, moans rising from them. Ambulances with wailing sirens raced to the platform.

A medevac helicopter landed next to the stage. Police and Secret Service agents cleared the area. Roberts was strapped to a stretcher. Secret Service medical techs ran the stretcher to the chopper and loaded him briskly on board.

As the chopper took off, Frank reached into a hip holster and pulled out an edgy-looking device. He gave a voice command. "Office—Editor!"

Los Angeles Register Political Editor Don Hudson answered.

"Don! A bomb went off near Roberts! He's hurt—I don't know how badly! They just medevacked him! Let's get something up online! I'll call back when I know more!"

Frank ran up to a cop and flashed his press credentials. "How bad is Senator Roberts?"

"I'm not authorized to talk."

"How many people are dead?"

"I'm sorry—you have to call headquarters."

Frank saw Michelle Hayes, a Roberts campaign aide, and raced over to her. She'd also been cut. Blood covered her arms and spotted her cream-colored pantsuit.

"Christ, Michelle, are you okay?"

Michelle was teary-eyed but tough. "I think so. This is a nightmare."

"Roberts—how bad?"

"I don't know. Shit, I hope he's alive."

"Did you see him after the blast? Was he conscious?"

Michelle's eyes welled up. "I just can't believe this."

Frank gently grabbed her shoulders. "Michelle, was Roberts conscious before they took him away?"

"Yes, I saw him talking with Peter. I don't know what he said."

"Do you know where they took him?"

"UCLA Medical Center."

Frank dashed off to his car.

Ninety minutes later Frank waited in the media throng near the hospital's entrance.

Secret Service agents swept the emergency room, asking all but two gravely wounded gunshot victims to leave. Ambulances sped injured reporters to the Good Samaritan Hospital on Wilshire Boulevard three miles away.

Frank waved off a medic's attempt to dispatch him there for treatment of his arm. More reporters arrived in the roped-off area outside the hospital.

Looking up at UCLA's Ronald Reagan Medical Center, Frank made a mental note: Roberts had been rushed to the hospital named after his political hero when it opened in 2008, replacing an antiquated facility across the street that the 1994 Northridge earthquake had damaged.

Frank's cell phone vibrated. He pulled it from his shirt pocket, saw that the call was from Moscow, punched the green button and held the phone to his ear.

"*Privyet*, Frank, this is Viktor!"

Viktor Romanov was a Russian reporter and Frank's friend from his Moscow assignment at the turn of the century. Frank strained to listen over the noise of TV reporters doing live stand-ups and traffic streaming by on Gayley Avenue.

The two journalists spoke in Russian.

"Frank, I just read your online piece about the attack on Stuart Roberts. Are you alright?"

"I'm okay, thanks. I'm at the hospital, waiting to find out his condition. I might have to jump off, but we can talk for now."

Frank debated whether to tell Viktor of his arm wound. It occurred to him that when he'd called Hudson, his editor hadn't inquired of his condition.

"Frank, any attempted assassination of a White House candidate is a big story everywhere. But the hit on Roberts is especially huge here because he was the US ambassador—and because he's been criticizing the Kremlin."

Scanning the hospital entrance for the signal to start the briefing, Frank weighed his next question to Viktor. "You don't think the Kremlin could be involved with this, do you?"

A few seconds of silence across the Pacific.

"People here are whispering about that. You know how we Russians love conspiracies!"

Viktor hadn't answered Frank's question. He was trying to wrap a serious topic in good-humored banter—an old reporter's trick at which the Russian was particularly skilled.

Frank tried a different tack. "Are you looking into this?"

Seeing that his ruse hadn't worked with Frank, Viktor gave a more measured response. "I'm making some discreet inquiries. You know what happens to reporters who ask too many questions that offend the Kremlin."

Frank thought to himself: "They disappear." He continued listening.

"But the notion that Russia tried to take out Roberts could be a false flag."

"False flag—what's that?"

"It goes back to ancient times when armies hoisted an enemy's flag to deceive the opposing force. Both sides used it in World War II. Since then, intelligence agencies have found creative ways to extend it beyond the battlefield."

Keeping an eye on the reporters around him, Frank understood that personal concern wasn't the real reason for Viktor's call. He wanted to exchange information.

Viktor switched gears. "Stuart and I have stayed in touch since we became friends at your poker games."

Frank half-teased the Russian. "Viktor, are you working on a piece about Roberts?"

Viktor dodged the question. "We're a weekly, Frank. We don't publish until Friday."

Frank scoffed to himself: as if *Kapital,* the top Moscow business journal, didn't have a website where Viktor and its other reporters constantly blogged, updated their print stories, filed fresh articles—and broke exclusives.

Viktor had recently written a series about a Russian oil scandal. Billions of rubles in government royalties were missing. Why this sudden interest in American politics?

Frank had another question. "When did you see Stuart last?"

"I've covered his visits here with other senators, but he and I just had some brief chats. The last time we really sat down together was after his big Israel trip when he was running for Congress. He spent three days here in Moscow with friends. He had a private dinner at Gusov's flat. I helped arrange several high-level meetings for him. He was already worried about Russia moving away from democracy. He wanted—"

A hospital staffer summoned the reporters. Frank cut Viktor off.

"Viktor, gotta go."

Frank put the phone back in his pocket and followed his colleagues inside. They walked through a maze of hallways and into an auditorium. As the reporters took their seats and the camera crews set up their tripods, the hospital's director waited at the front with the physicians who were treating Roberts. The director approached the podium.

"Good afternoon, I am Dr. Ricardo Montemayor, head of the UCLA Medical Center. Joining me is my team of trauma care physicians who are attending to Senator Roberts. Before I take questions, I will provide a summary of the senator's condition. Our communications staff has prepared a more detailed report that is being distributed and will be available online."

Montemayor took a sip of water. "Senator Roberts was injured in an explosion at Pershing Square. He sustained serious but not life-threatening injuries and is resting in the ICU. I can take your questions now. Please state your name and affiliation."

A young reporter spoke first as TV cameras swirled toward her.

"Angela Jackson, *Boston Globe*. You say Senator Roberts's injuries aren't life threatening. Would you characterize his condition as critical? And is he able to communicate?"

Montemayor's face remained expressionless. "The senator underwent surgery for a significant leg injury. He is under light sedation, but he spoke with our staff before surgery."

Jackson almost cut Montemayor off in order to speak before another reporter could jump in. "Quick follow-up: what did Senator Roberts say before the surgery?"

Montemayor had a ready answer, which he delivered with the slightest of smiles. "He thanked our team for taking excellent care of him. And he assured us that he would be fine."

A popular local TV correspondent spoke next. "Zhi Peng, WZYT Los Angeles. In reviewing our video, it appears that Senator Roberts was bleeding from the head after the explosion. Did he suffer a head wound?"

"The senator was conscious when he arrived at the medical center. Our examination indicates that he suffered only a minor head injury."

Frank grew impatient. As often happened at news

conferences, he thought his colleagues weren't getting to the point. "Frank Adams, *Los Angeles Register*. Is there anything in Senator Roberts's condition that would prevent him from meeting the rigorous demands of campaigning for president or, if he is elected, serving in the White House?"

Montemayor cleared his throat. "I am a physician, not a political expert. I will leave that question for Senator Roberts and his advisers to answer."

CHAPTER 2

LOS ANGELES

A S IT APPROACHED eleven, Frank, Don Hudson and Thomas Hawkes sat in Thomas's cherry-wood-paneled office. Thomas walked over to his liquor cabinet and poured Knob Creek bourbon into two tumblers. Before closing the cabinet, the publisher saw the bottle of Stolichnaya that Frank had brought him from Moscow a few years ago. Normally the vodka would have been long gone, but Thomas kept it unopened in his cabinet. It stood as a symbol for all the grief Frank had caused him. The messy divorce from his daughter. The hard drinking that had contributed to the breakup. The disappearances from work. Frank's refusal to admit he was an alcoholic until Thomas threatened to fire him if he didn't get help. The failed rehabs before one last try took hold.

Hawkes sometimes wondered why he'd stuck with Adams. It was tied to a rare feeling for him—guilt. After their return from Moscow, Frank and Lisa bought a fixer-upper in Santa Monica, one of those pink-stucco shoeboxes that cost a couple grand when it was built in the 1930s. The couple paid a million dollars in 2001 and considered it a steal. Like so many of their professional peers, they gutted the house and doubled its size. At Lydia's insistence over Thomas's grumbling, Frank and Lisa had lived with them for nine months during the construction. How many nights had he and Frank sat up into the wee hours playing chess and downing one shot of Stoli after another?

To use one of those psychobabble words Thomas hated, he'd enabled his son-in-law. Frank hadn't been much of a drinker before the Moscow assignment. After almost three years there, tossing back Stoli to gain the trust of Russian sources who drank vodka like iced tea, he came home a different man. Thomas took pride in his ability to read people, but he had missed the signs with Frank. He himself was old school when it came to booze. Hell, not much different than the Russian men of his generation. He could drink all night, day after day for years, and never come close to becoming a drunk. Frank and the other kids were different. They weren't as tough overall—"more sensitive" in the current parlance. Not being able to handle their liquor was just one piece of it.

Thomas and other men his age weren't good at introspection. It took him a long time to realize he'd let Frank down. He'd been too pissed off to cut him any slack. Pissed off at him for squandering his considerable talents and slamming the doors Thomas had opened for him; for leaving his daughter (well, she'd left him, but same difference); and most of all, for failing to deliver a grandchild. Frank and Lisa had talked about having kids, but she was close to fifty now and hadn't remarried. She would never be a mother.

There was more: Thomas was responsible for bringing Lisa into the Agency. Not that she needed his help to succeed at Langley. She was so damn competent at everything. But he'd always thought she might have been an ambassador or a Fortune 50 executive or a tenured professor at one of the Ivys. She would never have been interested in the spy business if it hadn't been for him. Lisa led a double life the whole time she and Frank were married, one that Adams still didn't know about. Few marriages could survive that level of secrecy. It had been different with Thomas and Lydia—the CIA had made their union possible. There had never been that kind of deception between them.

The most important reason Thomas hadn't let Frank go was the simplest one. Adams was still the best damn reporter at the paper—when he was sober. As he had been for three-plus years and counting.

Thomas handed one of the bourbons to Don and took the other for himself. He gave Frank a glass of club soda. Their eyes caught for a second as Frank took the drink, an acknowledgment that the sober center still held.

Frank's print article had been put to bed. Before filing it, he'd posted a half-dozen updates on losangelesregister.com. They were decompressing, looking ahead to the next day's coverage. Frank transferred a file to his work PC from the wand-like device he'd used to call from the plaza.

Thomas frowned. "What the hell is that?"

Frank was amused. "A bioWave—the consumer gadget IntelliView is about to release."

Frank's beta-testing of the device had proven that it was more substantial than a mere gadget, but extolling its remarkable technical prowess would be lost on his boss.

"That's right," Thomas offered, "you're leading one of our efforts to score a breakthrough in digital news delivery. If you hurry up, perhaps we can stop hemorrhaging money and stay out of bankruptcy."

Thomas was a hard-driving newspaper publisher out of a 1940s B-grade movie, shirt-sleeves rolled up to his elbows and an unbuttoned vest with its flaps hanging loosely on a surprisingly fit man in his early seventies. He loved the clatter and mess of the old Linotype presses at the papers where he'd started out, but his industry's harsh economic lessons of the last decade had forced him to regard the emerging technologies, what the kids called I-T, with a wary respect.

Thomas addressed the two men across from him. "It looks like Roberts is going to pull through. Where do we go next?"

Don spoke up. "I've got the entire National staff working on this, and I've pulled some of the Metro reporters. We're planning to get at least three stories up on the web early tomorrow, with another five articles online by three p.m."

Thomas drew on his cigar. The whole newsroom—hell, the whole fucking building—was legally smoke-free, thanks to the damn county, but Hawkes broke the law from time to time at night or on a Sunday morning.

"What are the mainbars?" Thomas asked.

"One article will focus on Roberts, his condition and medical treatment," Don replied. "Another will look at what this does to the White House race. The third mainbar will track the investigation. The feds won't talk about leads this early, but we'll interview former prosecutors and report on the theories already popping up online, who might have been behind the bomb blast, and why. Tied to this, we'll do a forensics sidebar exploring what type of explosives was used and where they might have come from."

Thomas peered at Frank. "You and Roberts go way back to Moscow. Played cards together, didn't you? Any idea who might have done this?"

Frank had some ideas about the hit on Roberts, but he wasn't prepared to share them with Hawkes.

Newspaper publishers traditionally ran the business operations while leaving the journalism to editors and reporters. Thomas, though, had a reputation in the newsroom for meddling in its coverage, especially on big stories.

Frank responded with a quip. "Maybe the Islamic State and the Kremlin are in cahoots. Hard to pick which one he hates more."

Hawkes pursed his lips: a typical wisecrack from Adams. He knew his ace reporter was hoping he'd rise to the bait, so he saved his thoughts for later.

The three men sipped their drinks. Thomas admired his cigar and spoke with a wry tone. "You and Lisa had your problems, but I'm glad my former son-in-law is still alive."

Thomas shook his ice and took a handful of cashews. "Roberts was the ambassador back when the two of you met in

Moscow. Any chance the attack on him was tied to his posting there? He's been jabbing the Kremlin strongman pretty hard, accusing him of bringing back the Soviet empire."

Watching Hawkes and Hudson drink their bourbon, Frank felt the familiar pang of desire for a taste of booze. But it was fainter now.

Duly noted.

That was what they taught you at rehab: note your desire, and then move on.

Frank picked up the thread. "America and Russia became friendly after 9/11 because they needed each other. But then we went into Afghanistan and invaded Iraq. Russia got rich when speculators drove up oil prices. The Kremlin got greedy in Ukraine. Our national interests don't coincide now as neatly as they did right after September 11th."

Thomas puffed on his cigar. "So the last thing Moscow wants is an anti-Russia hard-liner like Roberts in the White House."

Hawkes stirred his drink and looked at Hudson. "Don, let's start thinking outside the box. I'd like you to set up a file in the G-drive that everyone can access. Send out an all-points e-mail inviting story suggestions. Make it clear that you're casting a wide net. Sometimes even the strangest ideas contain a nugget of truth. We want to encourage the whole staff to give us their best thoughts."

As his editor and publisher talked, their voices receded from Frank, and his phone chat with Viktor outside the hospital unspooled in his mind. There was something odd about it . . . something important he'd overlooked. Just as he sometimes replayed his digital recorder to catch a crucial word, Frank retraced his talk with Viktor in his mind.

It was something Viktor said at the end of their conversation, just before the reporters got called into the hospital for the briefing on Roberts.

What was he missing?

Then it came to him: Roberts's stop in Moscow after his trip to Israel.

His 2006 visit to Tel Aviv and Jerusalem had been widely covered at the time. On his way to winning a Senate seat from California and already considered a future White House candidate, Roberts had met with Prime Minister Ehud Olmert and other Israeli leaders at photo ops that were nevertheless important props for winning the Jewish vote, padding his campaign coffers and establishing his foreign policy bona fides.

Frank had accompanied the candidate and filed articles from Israel. But he and other reporters were told that Roberts's travels had concluded there. When Stuart left Israel, Frank had spent an extra day in Tel Aviv to complete a Sunday piece before returning to Los Angeles.

In the last year, as Roberts pursued the presidency, Frank had researched the candidate's past exhaustively while writing substantive campaign profiles. He also had stayed on top of his competitors' reporting, reading hundreds of blogs and articles about Stuart.

As the major newspaper from Roberts's home state, the *Los Angeles Register* was determined to be the leading authority on him. And as its top political reporter, Frank was determined to know more about him than any other journalist.

Now, gazing out the window in his boss's office, Frank was certain that Roberts's three-day stopover in Moscow at the threshold of his political career had never been reported. For a candidate eager to bolster his standing on national security issues, the omission was curious.

Why hadn't Viktor reported on the visit? And why today, two hours after a bomb blast that almost killed Roberts, had Viktor disclosed the trip to Frank in their brief phone talk?

Don and Thomas were trying to pull Frank back into their conversation. Hudson was waiting expectantly. "Any thoughts before we close up shop for the night?"

Frank instantly made up his mind. "I need to go to Moscow."

It was hard to tell which of his two bosses was more astounded. Hudson let Hawkes speak. "Moscow? Are you out of your mind? It's one thing for us to bandy about Kremlin conspiracies over booze. But this is one of the biggest political stories in years! I need you here to lead our coverage."

Frank responded calmly. "There might be a better story in Moscow, Thomas. Don has other reporters covering the presidential campaign. Roberts's doctors say he won't be back out on the trail for a while. Why not make use of my Russian skills and Moscow connections?"

Hawkes scoffed. "Have you forgotten how your Moscow posting ended? The Kremlin kicked your ass out of there! And now you think you're just going to saunter back into town right after someone tried to knock off the most anti-Russian White House candidate since Reagan?"

Frank held his ground. This was typical harrumphing from the gruff publisher. "I didn't get kicked out. The Kremlin told me they could no longer guarantee my safety. Besides, I've made three trips to Moscow since then."

Frank knew these were pretty thin defenses. He wasn't surprised that Thomas tore through them.

"'No longer guarantee your safety?' That's Kremlin-speak for get the hell out of Dodge! And as for your so-called return trips, they've been with the president or with congressional delegations. You've been inside the bubble. You haven't gone back alone."

Frank still didn't know just what the Kremlin had meant. His reporting on post-Soviet corruption had fingered so many culprits, it was hard to calculate who he'd offended the most: the old Communists who'd rigged the rules to acquire capitalist riches; the bureaucrats at every level of government who were always on the take; the oligarchs with their billions of rubles tied up in webs of indecipherable business dealings; the shady oil dealers transforming Russia into a force in the world crude market; the criminal syndicates rooted in the ancient Caucasus enmities of Georgia, Armenia and beyond; the Chechen rebels who, like the Afghan mujahedeen, used the opium trade to finance jihad.

More recently, the *Register* had sent Frank to Ukraine, where his reporting on Russian aggression in the Crimea had angered senior officials in Moscow.

The Kremlin's claim that it couldn't protect his safety could have been a veiled threat, an honest admission—or both.

Hawkes was speaking again. "You can't even be sure you'd get a visa. Let alone in a day or two."

"A former source of mine works at the Russian Consulate

in San Francisco. We usually have dinner when I go to the Bay Area. I think he could come through."

"And not tell his superiors in Moscow?"

"He was one of my best confidential sources. Let's just say there are things he wouldn't want me to share with his bosses."

Hawkes laughed. Adams always had worked all the angles. "But it's still too risky for you to go in with a journalist's visa."

Frank paused. "I'll get a tourist visa. An old squash partner manages the Hotel National now. I don't need to tell him why I'm coming. He'll reserve a room for me and wire the consulate in San Francisco. I'll tell my consulate source to watch for the wire."

Don entered the fray. "Do you have any concrete leads there?"

Frank caught his editor's eye. This was their signal. He'd share some details with Hudson later when Hawkes was beyond earshot.

Frank spoke to Thomas. "You need to trust me. I can't give you any guarantees, but there's a good chance that it will prove worthwhile for me to go to Moscow."

Thomas had learned over the years that Frank's hunches sometimes panned out. Unwilling to grant verbal consent to this gambit, however, he merely nodded and drained the remaining bourbon in his tumbler.

Frank and Don got up to leave the office. As Frank opened the door, Thomas gave the reporter his marching orders. "One week and then you get your ass back here!"

Adams and Hudson left Hawkes's office and entered the darkened newsroom. A couple of unfortunate souls on the graveyard shift sat before lit computer screens.

Hudson nudged Frank's elbow. "You didn't tell Hawkes about your call from Romanov."

"Come on, you know we never tell Thomas everything. It's risky to give him too much information."

"I assume Romanov must have told you something to make this trip worthwhile?"

All playfulness disappeared from Frank's gaze. "I don't know, Don. Let's just say I have a feeling that Roberts left some clues in Moscow."

CHAPTER 3

MONTEREY, CALIFORNIA

L ISA AND THOMAS sat on the balcony of their family's "cottage" overlooking the Pacific. They savored the beauty of Monterey Bay, where the Spanish landed in 1602. When John Steinbeck wrote about Cannery Row, it had been a rough street of sardine fisheries, hookers and bums. Now, like so much of Old California that had disappeared, it was a must stop for tourists visiting its restaurants, nightclubs, hotels and boutiques.

A few hundred feet out in the bay, otters lay on their backs in the kelp, using rocks to break open clams that they put on their chests for a late-afternoon snack. Scuba divers in wetsuits emerged from the cold Pacific water. A couple in a kayak slid past them to watch the otters and their pups cavorting.

The Hawkes family retreat was California rustic with redwood and cedar inside and out. Steam wafted from the hot tub built into the deck. The sun neared the horizon.

Lisa was enjoying her visit, recalling the family's summer vacations here and the few years she had lived in this natural oasis while teaching Russian at the Defense Language Institute. A select group of military and intelligence personnel, with the occasional civilian interloper, attended the DLI. There they learned to speak, write, read and think like natives of Russia, France, China, Egypt and other lands where the US government believed it had important interests.

Lisa stood and walked into the large, open great room with skylights and towering slanted ceilings. A collection of rare, signed Ansel Adams photographs of Yosemite's Big Walls, El Capitan and Half Dome were interspersed with photos of a teenage Lisa swinging on the uneven bars and doing a backflip on the balance beam. There were also telephoto shots of her traverse via the King Swing pendulum on the Nose of El Capitan and her high-lining across a thirteen hundred foot abyss. The photographs hung above a roll-top desk. Knowing how much Yosemite meant to her, Frank had let her keep five of his family's photographs after their divorce. Together, they were worth tens of thousands of dollars, but for Lisa their value lay in their transcendent views of El Capitan rising above the Merced River and of other high cliffs in the great park.

Russian was Lisa's second language from childhood. While Thomas was studying in Paris, he'd met Lydia Karpovich, a beautiful translator for Soviet leader Nikita Khrushchev, who was being hosted by President Charles de Gaulle in March 1960. De Gaulle angered the Americans by stressing France's independence from the United States. Less worldly than he would later become, Thomas failed to realize that as one of the

Kremlin's official translators, Lydia was run by the KGB. His sudden romance with her attracted the attention of the CIA, which in short order approached him with an employment offer the Agency made clear Thomas shouldn't turn down.

Once Thomas was on board, CIA director Allen Dulles personally signed off on a plan to secret Lydia from the Soviet Union: a feigned illness by Lydia; a phony set of X-rays switched out by a CIA operative whose cover as an embassy doctor gave him access to the Moscow Central Clinical Hospital where the Communist elite got Western-quality care; an "emergency" medical flight to Finland, with Lydia accompanied by a Russian mole who'd infiltrated the Kremlin's elite Physicians Corps; an ambulance that somehow took a wrong turn speeding from the airport to the Helsinki hospital and ended up at the US Embassy; a trans-Atlantic flight to Washington; a debrief at Langley; a final flight to California; the release to Moscow by the Americans of a second-tier Soviet spy.

Deeply in love, Thomas and Lydia settled in San Francisco. They moved into the Hawkes family's three-story stone mansion on Columbus Avenue overlooking Washington Square in the North Beach section of town. Thomas joined the family's newspaper dynasty as a reporter while beginning his covert career with the CIA.

Turning sixteen had been a landmark for Lisa. She graduated high school two years early and was the youngest member of the Olympic gymnastics team. Being the youngest would become a feature of her life. She was the youngest woman to climb El Cap and to highline without a safety leash across the

Lost Arrow Spire Gap. Chongo, the legendary Yosemite dirt-bag and Big Wall climber, taught her slacklining, a close-to-the-ground version of highlining in which the same one-inch flexible nylon webbing is used.

Lisa was also the youngest person to graduate from "The Farm," the elite CIA training site outside Richmond, Virginia, and the youngest to be selected from this class of future spies to be a NOC—Non-Official Cover—working abroad as an operative with no protection from the US government and limited contact.

Whether climbing or sleuthing, the absence of a safety net riveted the mind. Lisa craved such clarity. High-lining, Big Wall climbing and a dangerous job infused her spiritual hunger.

All the furniture in the cottage, including a pair of comfortable oak rockers, was handcrafted. Lisa opened a cabinet and took out two crystal goblets. She walked by a shelf displaying back-lit pieces of Chihuly glassware. One piece from his Signature Sea Foam collection was missing. Lisa returned to the deck to find it on a stand next to her father.

"That better be a damn good cigar."

"Why, my dear?"

"You're using the most valuable piece in my Chihuly collection."

"Well, now it's an ashtray too."

Lisa smiled and handed him an ashtray. He placed his cigar in it.

Thomas sat down on a redwood recliner. Lisa went over

to the outdoor bar, poured two glasses of Pinot Noir and gave one to her father. "Daddy, this is from the boutique vineyard one of my friends from the Russian River Inn started a few years ago."

"It's nice to know that you still stay in touch with your former colleagues at Stanford and the DLI."

Thomas tasted the wine. "Nice nose, earthy blackberry finish. Not bad for amateurs."

Lisa laughed. For all her professional toughness, her father could still make her feel like a little girl.

"Speaking of the DLI, I had a chat last night with one of your former students."

"Who would that be?"

"Your ex-husband."

"Yes, I read Frank's article on the assassination attempt on my BlackBerry this morning. It was excellent."

"Always is. He's the best I've got."

Lisa made no attempt to hide her slight smile. "Do you think the Russians tried to kill Roberts?"

"Well, you've come in from the cold. You're the new head of energy security at Langley. What are you hearing there?"

Lisa swirled the wine. "This is the most obvious possibility, but it could be a false flag." Lisa purposely floated the same idea that Viktor Romanov had broached in his phone chat with Frank. She had decided not to tell her father that she knew about the call and had heard a recording of it.

Thomas took a handful of smoked almonds from a dish on the side table. "Let's keep our focus on protecting Roberts. It's taken me many years to get us this close to the presidency.

We need to find out who's trying to stop us, and why. And whatever we learn, Roberts has to come out clean. He needs to get back on his feet and into the White House."

Lisa had never been in favor of this longstanding operation. She felt compelled to remind her father, who still fancied himself the daredevil he'd been in his youth, of its outlandish risks.

Lisa's misgivings about Operation Long Shadow—Thomas's name for the secret plan—started with its rogue status within the CIA. Her father had correctly assessed that the Agency as an institution could never be involved in a plot to place an operative in the White House. If something similar were to happen in Chile or Greece or the Philippines, State Department officials and journalists would brand it a coup. Yet the operation couldn't be done completely outside the CIA. It required the Agency's intelligence capabilities to help Roberts with IntelliView's expanding overseas business, to monitor his rivals once he entered politics and to keep tabs on the senator himself.

For his inside man, Thomas had chosen Russell Talbert, a New Englander who at sixty-two was a decade younger than Hawkes. That made him old enough to have the critical judgment borne of espionage experience and to know how markedly the CIA's inner workings departed from its flow chart. Yet Talbert was young enough not to have completely missed the IT revolution, and he had availed himself of midcareer training to narrow the digital gap with the younger agents. Talbert now worked as the CIA's director of science and technology, a key post that placed him at the crossroads of emerging technologies and traditional spy craft. The position was proving useful in making sure that all the moving parts of Operation Long Shadow didn't collide.

The most important thing was that Hawkes trusted Talbert. They'd first met when Talbert was selected at nineteen as a Hawkes Family Foundation scholar in a program set up to identify future leaders. Sixteen years later they worked together on a covert job in Nicaragua. Aiding the Contras against the Sandinistas required a series of delicate, unorthodox maneuvers after Congress and then Reagan himself disowned the mission. Talbert's ability to go dark and get the work done had impressed Hawkes, and they'd formed a brotherhood of two since then.

It wasn't just the rogue nature of Operation Long Shadow that bothered Lisa. There was something about Stuart Roberts she'd never completely trusted. To his wide circle of acquaintances, especially women, he was a Boy Scout: handsome, debonair, smart, cool under pressure, devoted to his wife and children. Lisa, who never took adult Boy Scouts at face value, had always found Roberts too perfect by half. She'd watched him closely during the poker games at their Moscow flat. His reticence struck others as the appropriate diffidence of a diplomat. Lisa thought he played his cards closer to his vest than he needed to, and not just in poker. In her cover job as AmeriCon Energy's Russia analyst, she'd come to know a wide range of people tied to Moscow's oil interests, both within the vast country's territory and beyond in the booming Caucasus region where the Kremlin controlled an extensive network of pipelines. Over time, it had struck Lisa how often she heard Stuart's name mentioned among her oil contacts. With Russia becoming a major player in world energy markets, it was natural that the US envoy would closely follow its oil and natural gas industry. Yet Roberts's interest seemed excessive to Lisa.

Lisa returned to the conversation with her father. She reminded him that his desire to protect Roberts was secondary. "Even more important than keeping Roberts clean is safeguarding the Agency."

"You don't need to tell me that. I'm as committed to it as you are."

"Daddy, I know you still keep your hand in, but you're out of touch with daily operations."

"That's why I rely on you, Sweetie."

On his most instinctive level, Thomas used such terms of endearment for his daughter because he'd been using them since Lisa was a little girl, and his feelings for her, through all the years and all her remarkable accomplishments, were unchanged. She was for him what she'd been since birth: an angel with a glimmering nature who could send a wave of emotion through him with one shining glance or her clever-girl grin.

Yet, on a more calculating level that Thomas was perhaps unaware of, his pet names for her reinforced a chain of authority he was loath to relinquish: that he was her father, of course; that he was a wise elder, no doubt; and with a certain melancholy muffled deep within him, that he still had custody of secrets critical to the nation's future.

In ways that would have embarrassed him to admit, this extraordinary subterfuge with Stuart Roberts was Thomas's last grasp at the brass ring. He had started the operation when he was still in his prime. Now, with the passage of time, the energy and bullheaded confidence that had always defined him sometimes flagged, and every so often, in the hour just before dawn, he would wonder if he was still up to the task.

Thomas rose, walked to the balcony's edge and exhaled as he looked out at the sun setting over the Pacific. As Lisa joined her father at the rail, she felt a sudden foreboding that all her concerns about the Roberts operation had been justified. But having learned the need to conceal certain thoughts from her father, she redirected the conversation.

"What's Frank working on today?"

"He's on his way to Moscow."

Thomas noted the tremor in Lisa's hand as she lifted her glass and drank the remainder of her wine.

"Moscow? That's interesting." Lisa didn't let on that she knew about Frank's reporting assignment and had already taken steps to support it. But she switched gears and decided now was the time to tell her father about Viktor's call to Frank.

"How so?"

"He got a call from there yesterday."

Thomas disliked being surprised. "He didn't tell me about that. Are you sure?"

"NSA intercepted the call. It came from a Russian journalist named Viktor Romanov. He worked at the Oil Ministry when we lived in Moscow. He used to play cards at our flat."

Thomas snorted. "Another fucking poker player! Did the whole damn city play cards at your joint?"

Lisa laughed. She liked that her father used profanities

with her. It made her feel like one of the guys. There were few other women at the CIA whose rank matched hers.

"Why is NSA intercepting Frank's calls?" Thomas asked.

"It's not Frank's calls that are being intercepted, it's Romanov's. He's been investigating a major oil scandal in Russia."

"What did this Romanov fellow tell Frank?"

"We only got a partial, and some of that is hard to make out. My techies are trying to tease out more and work up a transcript for me."

In fact, the full conversation had been captured, and Lisa had heard the recording. Frank's trip to Russia would be dangerous. Romanov had been an SVR agent when they were based in Moscow, and there was no guarantee that he wasn't still an intelligence operative. Several prominent journalists who'd poked around in the Kremlin's business had been killed, and their murders were unsolved. Frank himself had to leave the country under an ominous cloud when the Foreign Ministry spooks had told him they could no longer guarantee his safety. On top of all this, he would be arriving in Moscow just a few days after Roberts's attempted assassination.

The surge of feeling for her ex-husband didn't entirely surprise Lisa. She knew that she'd never stopped loving him—not completely. Early in their courtship, he'd told her that they were soul mates. Although she hadn't thought she believed in such a romantic notion, over the years she had come to rely on it as the cornerstone of their marriage. Her guilt over their breakup came from knowing that her necessary daily deception—the double life she led—had violated the core commitments of being soul mates: honesty and openness and trust.

Lisa had assigned her two best Russian assets to tail Frank. But looking after him would do more than keep him safe. It might enable him to get to the bottom of a story that she believed could protect her father as well. If her suspicions about Roberts were on target, they might be tied to the hit on him at Pershing Square. Beyond providing security for Frank, Lisa wanted to help his reporting. She'd briefed Sergei Yemelin on Frank's assignment and instructed him to provide assistance. Yemelin was a former Soviet Oil Ministry analyst whom Lisa had put on the CIA payroll after he'd become a successful private consultant in Russia's burgeoning energy sector. When they lived in Moscow, Yemelin had been a source for Frank and a key contact for Roberts, yet Lisa was certain that neither suspected his CIA employment.

Yemelin knew all the players in Russia's oil and gas business. If there was something to be discovered about Roberts's dealings there, he could direct Frank to the best sources.

Gazing out at the sun's fading glow, Thomas noted that Lisa hadn't answered his question. Her dutiful-daughter routine didn't fool him. She was brilliant, tough as nails and not above deceiving her own father if it suited her purposes. He knew that she'd always had misgivings about Operation Long Shadow.

Thomas put his arm around Lisa. "Will you provide your old man with a transcript of Frank and Viktor's call?"

Lisa kissed his cheek. "That depends on what it says, Daddy."

CHAPTER 4

LOS ALTOS, CALIFORNIA

FRANK SAT IN a chocolate-colored leather armchair at an airport departure gate, sipping from a coffee cup and typing on his laptop. He was at Los Angeles International Airport, but he wasn't in a commercial terminal. He was at the Atlantic Aviation FBO, the private terminal on the south side of LAX, just west of the cargo airfield where Imperial Highway ends.

Frank looked out at the general aviation runway through the glass-and-aluminum grid windows. A Gulfstream 550 taxied to a stop, the name "IntelliView" sweeping along its side against a muted background view of the ocean with the sun breaking over it. Frank's most valuable contact at IntelliView, senior executive Ken Nishimura, had arranged the flight.

The pilot and a crewman deplaned and entered the terminal. Frank rose to meet them. He extended his hand to the pilot. "Frank Adams."

The pilot shook his hand. "Good to see you, sir. Give me a few minutes to sign in and use the facilities. Then we'll get you boarded and be on our way."

Starting in a small business mall in 1982, IntelliView grew over the next decade into a high-tech campus on 150 wooded acres in Cupertino. The company now occupied the most prestigious zip code in Silicon Valley, near the headquarters of Apple, Hewlett-Packard and other corporate stars of the computer age.

In 2005, as he prepared for his maiden Senate run, Roberts had replaced the aging Challenger 604s in his company air fleet with three Gulfstream 550s, the sleek dual–Rolls Royce–engine planes used by the Pentagon to ferry senators, ambassadors and other dignitaries around the globe. He had decided to upgrade to the 550 in the autumn of 2004 when the Israeli Air Force flew him on the luxury jet for a tour of Tel Meggido, Hazor and other biblical ruins in the Jewish state.

Roberts's guide, an undercover Mossad agent working as an Israeli colonel, described the plane's range of seventy-two hundred miles. That was far enough for it to ferry Roberts to most of the rapidly growing number of IntelliView's foreign customers and partners.

Today, one of the planes would transport a reporter Roberts had come to know well, although the wounded senator hadn't been informed of this trip.

Normally it would be an ethical conflict for a journalist to fly on a corporate jet. But Frank's circumstances were unusual. The clock was ticking on a big story. He was flying to Moscow that night and had to meet with an important source before leaving the country.

The pilot returned from the terminal's reception desk and beckoned Frank to accompany him to the runway. Frank boarded the plane and sat on a wide gray leather recliner at the front of the fourteen-seat cabin. He put his laptop case on the parquet wood table in front of him. On the wall across from him hung a fifty-inch plasma TV screen with a satellite-enhanced map of the United States. The Gulfstream 550 taxied down the runway. Shortly after takeoff a crewman approached Frank.

"Would you like breakfast, sir?"

"Sure. What do you have?"

"Many of our guests enjoy an omelet made with our organic eggs, accompanied by hormone-free ham and fresh-baked whole-grain croissants."

"That would be fine."

Ten minutes later the crewman delivered the meal on a bone china plate with a silver knife and fork with the InTLV logo etched on their handles.

The flight took fifty minutes. On a private runway at Norman Mineta Airport in San Jose, a BMW E70 X5 waited. Frank loped down the Gulfstream 550's steps and walked toward the car. Its driver put Frank's garment bag and well-worn, copper-colored leather grip in the trunk and held the back door open for him.

As they left the airport, Frank noticed that the driver was taking an unfamiliar route to IntelliView's office, which he'd visited before. "You must have a short-cut to IntelliView that I'm not aware of."

The driver, an attractive Latina who wore smart tan slacks and a crisp long-sleeve blue poplin shirt sporting the IntelliView logo, laughed. "Mr. Nishimura is working at his home in Los Altos. Although, I'll tell you, he rarely invites business visitors there."

"I feel honored."

"Mr. Nishimura speaks highly of you. He made it clear to his staff that he was not to be interrupted during your meeting."

It was a twenty-minute ride to Nishimura's home, a short distance on Route 17 and then north on I-280 into the foothills of the Santa Cruz Mountains.

As they neared their destination, Frank whistled. "Jeez, these houses are incredible!"

"Los Altos and its neighbor Los Altos Hills have some of the most expensive real estate in the country. Even small tract homes start at three million. Steve Jobs of Apple lived here and Yahoo founder Jerry Yang has a mansion near Mr. Nishimura."

The driver pulled into a circular driveway where the electronic gate stood open.

Ken Nishimura stepped out of a beautiful entryway and greeted Frank as he emerged from the car. "I trust your trip was enjoyable."

"I could get used to this."

"Come on in, Frank, I'm anxious to hear more about the attempt on Stuart's life. I can't believe that the *Register* is sending you off to Moscow. And I can't wait to hear how the bio-Wave has been performing."

Ken Nishimura, a third-generation Japanese American, was among Stuart Roberts's original employees. Now one of the highest-ranking officers at IntelliView, he headed the classified research and production division that worked with US military and intelligence agencies. He fit the image of the Silicon Valley high-tech entrepreneur: razorblade thin and dressed in designer jeans and a blue turtleneck jersey with the sleeves rolled up below the elbow. His jet-black hair was pulled back into a short ponytail.

Ken showed Frank into a large study with four oversized brown chairs arranged around an antique carved rosewood coffee table.

"Would you care for tea or coffee, perhaps a soft drink?" Ken asked, aware of Frank's aversion to alcohol.

"A cup of tea would be fine."

Ken must have pressed a button somewhere. A maid came into the room with two cups of tea and sweeteners, milk and biscuits. She placed the tray on the table and left.

"Stuart's family and doctors report that he is going to be alright. What can you tell me?"

"You probably have more information than I do, Ken. I couldn't get anywhere near his family, and the hospital was only giving out the most basic information about his injuries. What can you share with me?"

"His leg was badly injured, but he's in good spirits considering everything. You still haven't told me what you know about the forces behind this. Could it be connected to the war on terrorism, or do you think it has domestic roots?"

"I don't think anyone knows at this point. Stuart's friendship with Israel may be a factor. Homeland Security is looking at militant Islamic possibilities. Stuart's criticism of Russia's anti-democratic trends and its Ukraine gambit has raised questions about how far the Kremlin might go. Hawkes thinks it might be a good idea for me to do a little snooping around in Moscow while Stuart is laid up."

Frank didn't want Ken to know that the Russian trip was his idea.

"Are you at liberty to tell me about your assignment?"

Frank smiled. Ken was one of his most important sources. "Our usual rules apply?"

"Of course, Frank. You've never burned me."

"There's an oil scandal in Russia. The American oil companies are among Stuart's major campaign contributors. Some suspect the SVR—successor to the KGB's First Chief Directorate—was behind yesterday's assassination attempt."

"And your job is to connect the dots?"

"Find the dots. Then connect them."

Ken chuckled. "You brought the bioWave?"

Frank unzipped a pocket on his laptop case and took out the wand-like device. He handed it to Ken.

"How's it been working?"

"It's an amazing tool. I'm still getting the hang of some of the functions."

Ken looked at the object. "This bioWave you've been beta-testing is the commercial model that will be sold at our retail stores. The release date is the last day of the Republican National Convention."

Ken pointed to a similar-looking device on the table. "I

want to show you something new. This is our classified model of the bioWave. We call it the xWave. We're making it for DIA under a black-budget contract."

"For the Defense Intelligence Agency? Funding for it doesn't appear in congressional appropriations bills."

"Right. The money comes directly from the president's discretionary off-ledger account for the highest priority national security projects."

"So as far as Congress knows, the xWave doesn't exist," Frank said.

While he had come to trust Frank, Ken wasn't about to reveal the xWave's clandestine history. Nor would he mention other advanced devices under development by IntelliView that had been secretly underwritten by DARPA (Defense Advanced Research Projects Agency) and the CIA Quality Technology Fund for more than fifteen years. Thought-transfer, brain emulation, "mind meld" (a phrase originally coined in the *Star Trek* TV series)—these powers at the distant intersection of prodigious human cunning and ultra-extreme technology had long been grist for the science-fiction writers and conspiracy theorists. Reality had not quite caught up, but advances in the diverse fields of science, technology, medicine and the video-gaming industry were converging nicely in the xWave research program at IntelliView.

Despite his personal regard for Frank, Ken would observe the same protocol with the reporter that he used with members of Congress during their closed-door fact-finding sessions. That protocol was followed after staff was asked to leave and the pneumatically sealed doors closed at the classified briefing room in the US Capitol. This secure room was a few steps down a narrow hallway from the vice president's hideaway study, in a fourth-floor vault behind a tight spiral staircase up to the cupola.

Ken responded to Frank's question. "Only the chairmen and ranking members of the House and Senate intelligence committees have been told."

"I assume it has enhanced functions beyond the bioWave?"

Ken picked up the xWave and handed it to Frank. "See for yourself."

Frank studied the device as Ken described some of its features. "The xWave uses advanced neuroinformatics to identify individuals and measure the veracity of their statements. It will enable our intelligence agencies to create a far more extensive database of security threats than any that now exist."

"How does it do that?"

"The xWave employs iris-recognition technology that records 266 unique eye characteristics, three times more than the ninety qualities in a fingerprint. It adds a retinal scan that records each eye's blood-vessel patterns and calculates minute increases in blood pressure that indicate when a person is being untruthful."

"And the other lie-detection capability you just mentioned?"

"For this, the targeted individual must be holding the xWave. It will be most effective during interrogations in which the target is unaware of this function. But this capability delivers actionable data even when the target is aware of it."

"Impressive."

"We developed this function from the most advanced

computer-gaming technologies. It uses ultrasensitive sensors in the xWave handle to measure electrical skin resistance and chemical secretions. The sensors produce single-frequency audio tones five hundred times per second with internal buffers to minimize extraneous electrical noise, or hum. The tones are simultaneously recorded on an implanted computer chip, which is the fastest ever produced."

Since the discovery of brainwaves a century ago, the use of these bursts of electrical activity from neurons in the brain had generated speculation and research on how to capture them and decode their meanings. Technology had initially measured the four major types of brainwaves—alpha, beta, theta and delta—with forty-eight electrodes pasted on the scalp and connected by wires to a machine tracing the wavelike electrical activity on paper. It had advanced to large functional magnetic resonance imaging (fMRI) scanners used in hospitals. Most recently minuscule nanotechnology machines self-powered by body heat were developed to sense and transmit brainwaves. These nanomachines could adhere to the scalp through static electricity or be implanted directly into the brain to gain more precise readings with less "chatter," or background interference.

It fascinated Ken that scientists and spies used the same word—"chatter"—but with opposite meanings. For scientists, it was useless noise that interfered with the focus of their research and which they did everything possible to block out. For spies, chatter was the cacophonous global din of every manner of modern telecommunications among presumed terrorists hatching their plots, and so it was captured and slowed down and taken apart and "re-aggregated" and listened to and examined from every perspective to glean the one word, the single clue, that might prevent the next catastrophe.

"That's impressive, Ken. But what if a skilled target tries to evade it?"

"Shall we do a demonstration? I will have to ask you some personal questions."

"That's fine."

Ken looked to make sure Frank was holding the xWave by its handle.

"When were you based in Moscow?"

"From early 1999 to the fall of 2002."

"Who was your employer?"

"The *Los Angeles Register*."

"Were you married at the time?"

"Yes."

"What was your wife's name?"

"Lisa Hawkes."

"Did your wife work while the two of you were in Moscow?"

"Yes."

"What was her job?"

"She was head of AmeriCon Energy's Russian oil and gas division."

"I know that the two of you subsequently divorced. Was your marriage still good while you were in Moscow?"

"Yes."

"Did either of you have an extramarital affair in Moscow?"

Frank hesitated. "I can't speak for her. I did not have an affair . . . not then."

"How long after you left Moscow did your marriage end?"

Frank searched his memory. "Four years."

Ken smiled and reached for the xWave. He laid it on a table near a laptop. After a few key strokes, Ken looked intently at the computer screen and turned it toward Frank.

IntelliView was currently developing the xWave as an external sensor that could decipher brainwaves several feet away from the person under surveillance. This area of research had become the topic of excited speculation on the Internet. Some bloggers were certain that the day was not far away when spy satellites would be deployed to read people's minds. While satellites could already detect body heat, radio signals, electrical activities and mobile phone transmissions, the ability to capture brainwaves from outer space remained the domain of science fiction.

But in the real world, at IntelliView, Ken and an elite core of workers were refining this technology to detect brainwaves from humans at close range.

The screen that Ken turned toward Frank showed a multi-colored graph with a bright red line zigzagging up and down. It had a steep rise at the right end of the graph.

"Frank, I'm afraid the spike indicates that you were not faithful to your wife in Moscow."

Frank shook his head. "Wow. I wanted to make one false statement, but I was intent on remaining calm as I said it."

Ken smiled broadly. "No matter, Frank. The amount of electrical resistance on our skin surfaces and its chemical secretions change when we are lying. Our brainwave patterns are also altered. It turns out that truth resides in a different part of our brains than falsehood. The changes are subtle but measurable. It is beyond our control."

"So, the xWave is a lie detector on steroids."

"Precisely. It does everything a lie detector does and much more. Your data from our demonstration were transferred wirelessly from the xWave to my computer. A special program in the laptop then displayed the data in graphic form."

Ken turned off the laptop and snapped it shut.

"We believe that the xWave can prove more effective than the so-called enhanced interrogation techniques that were so discredited under the Bush administration."

"So, technology trumps torture."

"You might say that," Ken replied.

Like most of Frank's important sources, Ken had mixed motives for endangering his career and even his personal life by providing Frank such sensitive material. For one, the exchange gave Ken leverage with Stuart Roberts, his former boss who now stood on the verge of holding the world's most powerful office. At the same time, though no reporter would ever admit it, there was an unstated quid pro quo that Ken believed would produce more positive coverage of Roberts, however subtle the difference.

And Ken had motives beyond the presidential campaign. The grandson of Japanese American immigrants who'd been held in an internment camp outside San Francisco during World War II, Ken had been prodding Frank to write an investigative series on the Soviets' refusal—now perpetuated by the post-Communist Russian government—to return to Japan the four southernmost Kuril Islands. Called the Northern Territories by the Japanese, Red Army troops had seized them as the long war wound down. A portion of these four islands—Etorofu, Kunashiri, Shikotan and Habomai— could even be seen from the coast of the largest Japanese island, Hokkaido. California was home to tens of thousands of Japanese Americans and Russian émigrés. They would love to read such a series.

Frank would have offered a different explanation for Ken's willingness to share closely guarded secrets. His sources always had complicated, often contradictory, reasons for opening up to him, but in the end they were little more than dramatized rationalizations. For Frank, the motives were rooted in ego. Successful, driven people in key posts with access to valuable information seemed compelled to divulge secrets and then watch the earthquakes they set off.

Frank Adams and Ken Nishimura, reporter and source, had the same reason for engaging in this enterprise that, were it to be exposed, might put them in prison: they wanted to learn who had tried to assassinate Stuart Roberts. That knowl- edge would land Frank a major exclusive and maybe a Pulitzer Prize. For Ken, it would show whether the near-murder was tied to his mentor's political ambitions or business dealings.

Ken had decided to push the envelope with Frank. "I have a request for you."

Frank waited.

"I want you to beta-test the xWave as you've been testing the bioWave."

"Why?"

"We've determined that the xWave functions well in controlled circumstances in our lab and at other sites in the United States. We need to know how it will perform during foreign fieldwork. Russia would be a perfect testing ground."

"I assume you want me to use the functions you've just demonstrated?"

Ken nodded. "I haven't shown you its most advanced capability."

Ken handed the device back to Frank. "The xWave can receive and respond to telepathic commands."

Frank raised his eyebrows.

"The final product for the intelligence community will have a brainwave transmitter in a nanochip implanted in the head."

He gave Frank a dot-sized, paper-thin soft disc. "This is a test-phase substitute for the chip. Place it on your scalp, hidden behind your ear."

"You've got to be joking." Frank stuck the tiny disc behind his right ear.

Ken gave him instructions. "Turn on your laptop and put the xWave near it. As soon as the computer boots up, the xWave will sync with it."

Frank did as he was told.

"Now use telepathic commands to access a file. Simply go through the same series of thoughts you use when you are manually opening a computer file. All you need to remember is the name of each directory and subdirectory."

Frank centered his attention on the xWave lying next to

his laptop. In a few moments, a file of his background notes about Roberts's time in Moscow was displayed on the screen.

"Holy shit! This is science fiction."

Ken had anticipated Frank's reaction, but it still pleased him. "Not any longer. This technology was initially developed to aid tetraplegics. We have taken it several steps farther."

Frank picked up the xWave again. A quiver of apprehension stirred in the journalist: their crime had been compounded.

Frank put the xWave in the holster and placed it inside his laptop case. "You realize that in exchange for my help with the xWave, you're going to have to get me more background details about Roberts."

"There's always some sort of deal with you reporters."

"It's in our DNA." Frank glanced at his watch. "I need to pick up my visa in the City and then catch my flight to Moscow."

They got up and walked out a side door into a garden and down a manicured path to the front driveway. The BMW E70 was waiting. The driver opened the door for Frank. Ken motioned for her to get back behind the wheel. When she was out of hearing range, Ken leaned in and spoke in a soft voice to Frank. "Handle the xWave with care—you're carrying a couple-hundred million dollars of our proprietary technology."

Frank nodded.

"There's one more thing."

"What's that?"

"The NATO intelligence chiefs are meeting in Brussels on August 22. We would like to demonstrate the xWave there."

Frank laughed. "No pressure, right?"

"Unlike the bioWave, the xWave links with the National Security Agency's constellation of satellites for phone and Internet communications. So you can use it anywhere in the world, even where there's no cellular or broadband coverage."

Ken put his hand on Frank's shoulder. "Good luck with your trip. I'll be eager to know what you find out."

Ken closed the door. Frank watched him standing in the sunlight as the BMW drove away. For the first time, the full impact of the trip Frank was embarking upon hit him: using classified technology embedded in the xWave; carrying the device out of the United States; sneaking into Russia under false pretenses with a fraudulent tourist visa. He was already breaking the law in two countries. Gazing through the car window, Frank wondered whether his unusual reporting assignment would force him to take still more risks.

CHAPTER 5

OVER THE NORTH POLE

F RANK LOOKED OUT the window of the Aeroflot
Boeing 777 jet on his sixteen-hour flight to Moscow.
He took a drink of bottled water and turned on
the xWave.

Frank read the classified briefing materials Ken had given
him to help understand the device. He was beta-testing an
advanced Version 2 of the bioWavIntel (BIWIT), its develop-
mental name. Version 1 would soon be available to the public.
One groundbreaking feature in the crowded consumer electronics industry would be image projection as avatar. Version
3, the most advanced, was in earlier stages of development in
consultation with a small circle of senior military and intelligence analysts.

Frank's xWave prototype fused the features of Version 2
with some being refined for Version 3. They included receive
and transmit functions using brainwave-pattern recognition

and electrical-magnetic signals from the thalamus to the Broca and Wernicke language regions of the cerebral cortex, which are connected to hearing circuits in the parietal-temporal lobes. Versions 2 and 3 were equipped with nanosensors to measure neuro-secreted chemical and biological agents that were integrated with the electromagnetic signals carrying pre-processed and stored data, and then relayed on command. Version 3 would be hard-wired with a brain implant that incorporated continuous monitoring and control by external commands. The modified Version 2, which Frank now held, required him to place a transdermal nanoreceiver and trans-mitter in a 5 mm neuromorphic disc in the crook behind the upper lobe of his right ear.

Using the hologram projection, Frank scanned headlines, reviewed background material on the Russian oil industry and read e-mails from Viktor Romanov.

A flight attendant passed Frank and doubled back. "Are you okay?"

"Sure. Why?"

"You've been staring at the seat in front of you for a half hour."

Frank grinned. "I haven't slept much lately. Just tired."

When the attendant walked away, Frank shut off the xWave, placed it in his grip, put his head back and closed his eyes. He began reminiscing about key turns in his life, starting with his graduation from the School of Journalism at the University of California in Berkeley . . .

The Greek Theatre was jammed with eight thousand people— graduates, family and friends. Looking out at the crowd lit by afternoon sun, Frank waited his turn to walk onto the stage of the outdoor amphitheater and receive his master's degree.

The Los Angeles Register *publisher moved to the podium. Fragments of Thomas Hawkes's opening remarks came back to Frank. The importance of a free press in a democratic society . . . the mark individuals can make in their chosen fields . . . .*

"Our award this year goes to Frank Adams. We anticipate that Frank will leave his own imprint in his chosen field of journalism. I am pleased to announce that in addition to this prestigious Promise Award, the Register *is offering Frank an opportunity as a summer intern."*

When he reached the podium, Frank expressed the privilege he felt in helping fulfill the responsibility of a free press. He accepted the award and shook the hand of the man who would soon hire him . . . and later become an even more central figure in his life.

The medal recipients each year were smart, driven young people who would go on to have fine careers. After the ceremony, Frank had been surprised when Hawkes walked over to his table at the reception in the Journalism School's garden courtyard and invited him to stop by his office when the summer internship began in a few weeks. Then instead of moving on, Hawkes had found an empty table and asked Frank to join him.

Hawkes had begun asking questions, but Frank was soon querying him in an unobtrusive way. Thomas detected a certain calculating shrewdness camouflaged by a deceptive opaqueness, an easy-going intensity, an apparent obliviousness to rank or station in life.

Hawkes asked his stock question: what did Frank think of the Register?

Frank surprised Thomas by offering a sophisticated critique. The Register *was beginning to fade. More and more, it was resting on its laurels. The great writing and storytelling of the past had been whittled away. The* Register's *lead political reporter, Brian Rappaport, was still good, but increasingly in need of a gifted editor. Lesley Rank, despite her Pulitzer, wrote predictable columns. The newspaper's narrative voice was white and middle-aged, while California grew younger and more multihued.*

As their talk drew to a close, Hawkes did something he had never done before with a Promise Award recipient: he offered Frank a permanent reporter's job instead of the summer internship.

Frank's reveries turned to his introduction to the Russian language and his future wife.

Hawkes had chosen Frank as the Register's *Moscow bureau chief after a decade of superlative work at the paper in Los Angeles. The publisher had pulled some strings for him to attend the intensive Russian language course at the Defense Language Institute in Monterey, California. His daughter, Lisa Hawkes, was lead instructor.*

Lisa stood before her eight students, who would band together into a close group over the next nine months. "This is an immersion course in Russian language and culture. You will speak, eat and sleep nothing but Russian starting now."

Frank smiled at his teacher, a fit, slender woman with dark brown hair neatly tied behind her neck. About his age, Lisa had large amber eyes that penetrated everything she held in her vision. She looked at him but did not acknowledge his smile.

Halfway through the program he and Lisa discovered that they shared a passion for mountaineering. It would bring them together and form a cornerstone of their love.

Frank was on the verge of dozing off.

Lisa and Frank were ascending the Nose, among the most difficult and technical climbs on Yosemite's El Capitan, the world's largest granite monolith at 3,280 feet. Following the faster but more dangerous Route A, they were shooting to beat their personal best of ten hours, not far off the record time of 9:17 set in 1986 by John Bachar and Peter Croft.

Lisa started to climb the big walls of Yosemite as a teenager and had made more clean ascents of the Nose of El Cap than he'd made. She had red-pointed this route (a term coined by the Germans to identify a new path) by leading the climb without falling or even weighting on the rope that would save her life if she fell. Lisa's passion for the walls was fueled by her friendship with Lynn Hill, one of the world's greatest free climbers who helped popularize the dangerous method of scaling cliff faces with only the holds that nature provides, inching upward simply with fingers and toes.

Frank was taking his turn ahead of her, climbing hammerless in order to preserve the rock by not driving in new pitons, using only a streamlined rack of removable chocks and cams. They quickly ascended to Pitch 7 and entered the Stoveleg Cracks, named after the custom-built pitons made from the legs of potbelly stoves. Jamming hands into the Stovelegs to hold their weight, they established a rhythm that powered them 700 feet in a half hour to Pitch 9. Instead of taking the Jardine traverse short-cut to Eagle Ledge at Pitch 13, they opted for the traditional route and combined Pitches 15 and 16 by linking about 140 feet from the base of Texas Flake to the top of Boot Flake. Appearing to float on the surface of the wall, Boot Flake is where the crack networks of the first half of the climb blank out. The next system of cracks is far to the left without natural holds to cross over. Earlier climbers had solved this problem by using a roped pendulum move now known as the King Swing.

A storm came over the summit. Hail battering them, Frank and Lisa smeared their feet on Boot Flake. As the sun reappeared, Lisa lowered herself 15 feet. Using her gymnastic skills, she ran a few steps to the right, turned to the left and launched herself across the 70 foot King Swing pendulum. Without warning, a cam wedged in a crack at the top of Boot Flake, which was hold-ing Lisa's support line, skated out as she made an aerial barrel roll. She fell 45 feet and screamed when a blade of rock lacerated her right arm and her helmet hit the granite before her safety line went taut. She dangled from the line tethered to a chock.

Frank, belaying Lisa from a small stance near the top of Boot Flake, lowered himself to a point just above her position. He wrapped the rope around his leg for purchase in order to reach down and grab her left wrist. Still dazed, Lisa regained a position on a sliver of ledge.

Frank consoled her. "Catch your breath. Let me stop the bleeding."

"Thank God you were here. I'll be alright."

After bandaging her arm wound, they decided to postpone their attempt at the Nose for another day.

Later, at Sunnyside campsite with a view of Half Dome and the full moon, Lisa and Frank sat next to a fire and talked in the quiet, almost reverential, tones they instinctively adopted amid such natural grandeur.

"Ansel Adams took his famous photograph Moon and Half Dome *in 1927," he said. "It was first made public in his wedding announcement the next year."*

Frank gently pulled Lisa up and slipped his hands into the back pockets of her canvas shorts. They slow-danced to the crackling fire. His lips brushed the nape of her neck, then the earlobe, as he made a whispered proposal.

"Will you marry me?"

Still in each other's arms, they reached the tent. Lisa pulled back the flap, slid down Frank's body and eased him into the tent.

"Yes," she whispered.

II: *A*NTE *U*P

Poker reveals to the frank observer something else of import—it will teach him about his own nature. Many bad players do not improve because they cannot bear self-knowledge.

David Mamet

CHAPTER 6

O N A BRILLIANT California fall day in 1998, Lisa
Adams received a cryptic e-mail via her classified
Internet system at the Defense Language Institute.
It came from CIA headquarters with no identified sender:
"Personal hq appointment Thursday 9 a.m. UA Flight 172
SFO-IAD Wednesday."

Lisa had never been summoned to Langley. The directive
came three years after her urgent reassignment to teach Russian
to US agents at the DLI. That job followed the February 1994
arrest of Aldrich Ames, the American traitor who'd exposed
fifty high-level CIA and allied moles to the Kremlin. The Ames
scandal finally persuaded the reluctant hawks in the Clinton
administration that Moscow had somehow missed the memo
saying the Cold War was over and that they might want to

slow down their "peace dividend" dismantling of the Agency's decades-old Russian espionage operation.

It wasn't until Lisa was ushered into the DCI's office two days later that she learned whom she was meeting at Langley. Harrison Jenkins sat on a black leather couch. He motioned for her to sit down in one of two matching chairs diagonally across from him in the conference alcove. In the second chair sat Scott Dennis, a key advisor on clandestine affairs.

Jenkins was ten months into a four-year tenure. He'd earned a reputation as a convivial director who got along well with Democrats and Republicans alike, but now he was all business.

"I apologize for the short notice and long journey, but it was important for us to meet in person. And I'm sorry, but my schedule today will only provide us ten minutes."

Lisa understood that her immediate task was to listen.

"I have a critical mission for you when you and Adams move to Moscow. You are to work in a NOC capacity there."

Lisa was stunned that her assignment was to be carried out in Non-Official Cover.

Frank's posting as the *Register*'s next Moscow bureau chief hadn't been announced. She and Frank had agreed not to make their engagement public until his intensive Russian course was over in December. The two secrets intersected at Thomas Hawkes. Her father was the only person who knew of both their engagement and Frank's Moscow assignment.

Beyond her personal thoughts, Lisa felt the weight of Jenkins's words. Acquiring the status of Non-Official Cover meant cutting off all but emergency contact with her bosses at Langley or any other intelligence personnel.

The agents called it going dark. Lisa pictured herself high-lining over Yosemite Falls, fourteen hundred feet above the valley floor without a safety leash.

She spoke for the first time. "If I were to accept this assignment, I assume I would have a cover job?"

Jenkins responded as if it were a done deal. "You'll be head of the Russian oil division for AmeriCon Energy out of Houston. Your boss will be Bud Johnson. He has close ties with the Bush family. We believe that Governor Bush will be the next president."

Jenkins looked at his watch. "I only have a few minutes. But you've come a long way, and I think you deserve a bit of explanation."

Lisa waited.

"Our analysts forecast that over the next decade, American reliance on foreign oil will increasingly become a national security threat. This is especially true of Middle East regimes hostile to the United States. During this period, Russia will become a major player in the international oil market. We've made significant investments in the Caspian Sea region where some of the world's largest untapped crude reserves are located."

Normally protective of her interests, Lisa felt oddly passive. Because of her father's prominence within the Agency, she'd grown up accustomed to having senior intelligence officials at their home for dinner parties. Some of the guests were foreign espionage agents from allied governments. Still, for all the success of her subsequent CIA career, Lisa had never received an assignment directly from the head of central intelligence.

She finally spoke again, deliberately using the conditional tense in an effort to show that her agreement was needed to take on the daunting NOC assignment.

"Where would I fit into this big geopolitical picture?"

Jenkins sensed her apprehension. "Lisa, you're one of our most capable agents. I personally chose you for this mission because I know you can handle it."

The director continued. "The Caspian oil fields are within the territories of Azerbaijan, Kazakhstan and other nominally independent former Soviet republics. Once the crude crosses their borders, it still must be conveyed through Russian pipelines. The Kremlin can open or close those lines at will. We don't want to become free of the Arab oil sheikhs only to end up dependent on the whims of Moscow. Your job will be to help us develop our relationships with the Caspian nations as a counterweight to Russia. We have plenty of analysts here and at our cooperating think tanks and universities who know the lay of the land from a distance. We need someone with your skills on the ground. You'll make contacts and identify key players. When the time comes for us to take advantage of your expertise, we'll let you know."

Jenkins rose. "I'm sorry, but I've got a stack of other meetings lined up."

Lisa would later find it strange that the director told her something that would prove to be so important almost in passing as he led her from his office. "One of our best Russian contacts will help you on this assignment. His name is Sergei Yemelin. He'll be in touch with you after you get settled in Moscow."

They paused in a small passageway between Jenkins's suite and his executive secretary's office. Lisa felt emboldened to ask a direct question. "Is he on payroll?"

"Not exactly. For now we consider him an agent of influence. He's a brilliant young surveyor in the Russian Oil Ministry, head and shoulders above his peers there. That puts him in a position to be of enormous benefit to us. So far he's been completely reliable. As you and he work together, one of your tasks will be to determine whether he's trustworthy enough to come fully aboard."

Jenkins started to turn away, but she stopped him with a question.

"Am I permitted to share the true nature of my work with my husband?"

Jenkins scoffed.

"Absolutely not. No offense, Lisa, but you can't trust reporters."

Lisa thought ahead to her life in Moscow with Frank.

"How am I supposed to pull that off?"

"Pull what off?"

"Frank is perceptive as hell. He makes his living figuring out what makes people tick. How am I supposed to prevent him from finding out that I'm a spy?"

Jenkins smiled. He liked Hawkes's spunk, among other things.

"Your Non-Official Cover will help. You will have no

contact with us except in the most extreme circumstances. Your cover job with AmeriCon will be the real deal. You will find the work quite challenging. And while you may not know it, I have followed your career closely. One of your many fine traits is discretion. I have full confidence you will be able to keep your husband from learning anything more than he needs to know."

With that, Jenkins gave Lisa a nod of confidence and walked briskly into the hallway. In a moment he had disappeared down the corridor.

True to Jenkins's promise, Yemelin had contacted Lisa a month after her arrival in Moscow with Frank in 1999. Over the next three years, she found that he came precisely as advertised by the DCI: smart, hard-working, resourceful, and straightforward. Most important, he knew the Russian energy sector better than anyone else, had the most contacts and saw how his country would fit into the changing world oil market.

When Yemelin left the Russian Oil Ministry and formed a consulting firm, AmeriCon Energy was among his first clients. Lisa was his contact. She had never told Sergei that his consulting fees weren't paid by AmeriCon, but rather from her covert account. More precisely, the money was wired from Langley to her account and then transferred to AmeriCon's Russian division ledgers, which she controlled. Lisa had decided on that procedure as a firewall against putting Yemelin directly on the CIA payroll. And it helped her maintain her NOC cover as an AmeriCon Energy executive. As much as she'd come to trust Sergei, she thought it risky to inform him of her Agency ties.

Besides, for all his intelligence and contemporary business

élan, Yemelin remained a product of the now-defunct Soviet propaganda apparatus. Like most Russians, he saw American capitalism as a corrupt system that was indistinguishable from the corrupt American government. The top executives at an oil giant like AmeriCon Energy were certainly in bed with top government officials, and all shared the goal of enriching themselves in any way possible. So even if Yemelin had been told that the ultimate source of the monthly stipends Lisa wired into his account was Langley instead of AmeriCon, he likely would have shrugged his shoulders and decided that such an arrangement confirmed his expectations.

CHAPTER 7

MOSCOW
TUESDAY, JULY 20, 1999

STUART ROBERTS WAS having another big night at the poker table as he raked in a pile of chips. Mikhail Gusov, an amiable emissary of the new breed of bright, young Russians who seemed mesmerized by money, ribbed the US ambassador.

"How is it that you capitalists always win?"

It was a warm, unusually humid, night in Moscow. Even in July, most evenings in the ancient Russian capital were quite pleasant.

The poker game was planned as a weekly event. New to his assignment as Moscow bureau chief for the *Los Angeles Register*, Frank wasn't a passionate card player. But a regular poker game—at his home, under his control—would provide some important benefits. It would allow them—the diplomats, entrepreneurs, journalists and academics who came from various nations and served several governments—to blow off steam.

In a vast country where many had recited Communist dogma by day but inhaled incense and prayed to gilded icons by night, the superficial shift to Western-style capitalistic democracy was still haunted by the ghosts of Stalin's gulags; by the millions of corpses rotting in the birch forests and pine groves; by the aging sons and daughters of the Bolsheviks who had spied on neighbors and betrayed friends only to be slaughtered themselves or sent away to labor camps.

The paranoia and terror that had gripped Moscow for decades were gone. In their place was something only somewhat less sinister—a superficial gaiety; a brittle self-confidence propped up by petro-rubles; the age-old machismo of Russian men always just a few shots of vodka away from their core selves as Slavic mama's boys.

Even as Frank developed relationships and covered his government's restored diplomatic ties with the Kremlin, he never trusted Russia, or Russians. On a gut level, he was sure that decades of servitude to an evil regime—Reagan had been right—couldn't be overcome in a few years. Centuries of subservience under the tsars couldn't be removed from the collective memory or sliced from the Russian gene pool like a tumor before it metastasized.

The poker players who gathered at Frank and Lisa Hawkes's flat were under no illusions. For all the sophisticated trappings of contemporary freedom that Moscow conveyed, the players knew they were kept under close tabs.

The country remained a land of double-dealing with all the

power still controlled at the top. Everything—all rewards and punishment, forgiveness and cruelty, payoffs and reprieves—still flowed from the Kremlin.

Had Moscow been a more typical assignment, Frank's poker game would have provided the opportunity to develop sources and make a few friends. But over time, the game grew into something more complicated and treacherous. It became a place where Frank chose his words with great care. He listened to the others intently and watched them closely from behind his welcoming veil of happy host and would-be card shark.

Soon after the initial game, Frank grew less interested in learning his guests' hands and betting strategies. He became more focused on figuring out who they were, what had brought them to Moscow—and what relationships they were developing with one another.

So far, no one had missed the opportunity to show up and try to win a few rubles or—more likely, when Stuart was hot—to lose a few. With all eight players there, the winner of each hand sat out the next round.

Their spacious, high-ceilinged flat near the center of the city belonged to the family of Lydia Karpovich—Lisa's mother. Lydia had spent her early childhood there before the Soviets commandeered the home for a series of uses—a community cultural center; a health clinic; a temporary abode for KGB agents visiting from overseas postings; a diplomatic annex for the nearby Nigerian Embassy.

Lydia was taken from her parents and sent to a *kolkhoz* outside Tyumen, an early Siberian outpost in the Ural

Mountains. There, she knitted stockings for the brave Soviet soldiers fighting the Nazis in faraway battles, sang Soviet patriotic songs and learned to operate farm machines with other children who had also been separated from their families and sent to the large agricultural collective.

After the collapse of the Soviet Union, Lisa's uncle Dmitry, her mother's older brother, returned from exile in Paris. Through a laborious process greased by the payment of one million rubles to the new bureaucrats who had replaced the old Soviet *nomenklatura*, Dmitry reclaimed the family's flat on Neglinnaya Ulitsa, a short walk from Red Square.

When Dmitry, now a wealthy pharmacist for the capital's political and business elite, heard that Lisa and Frank had drawn assignments there, he insisted that they live in the family flat. Over Lisa's protests, Dmitry assured her that he would be moving into an equally comfortable accommodation. A close friend, Boris Bogdanov, belonged to a group of venture capitalists who had funded construction of an exclusive highrise apartment complex overlooking Gorky Park. Boris had made a large, top-floor corner unit available to Dmitry at a discounted price, and it would be ready for him to inhabit by the time Lisa and Frank arrived.

That's how, on a summer night at the century's close, an eclectic group of men from different backgrounds and with different missions came to be playing cards in a Moscow flat where KGB operatives had once nervously shaved in the morning before walking a kilometer to the dreaded Lubyanka headquarters for briefings with their superiors.

As the American ambassador stacked his chips in front of him, he joked with Mikhail. "You're a good student, Mikhail. Winning is indeed the goal of capitalism. Whining is the Communist reaction."

Roberts was the boy wonder of the Silicon Valley crowd. He had made millions as a whiz in microcomputers and the nascent field of nanotechnology. His company, IntelliView, became a household word. In political circles, Roberts had established a name for himself as well by bankrolling Republican candidates. He developed powerful friends early in his career as head of a group he founded, Young Business Leaders for Ronald Reagan for President.

As far as Frank was concerned, the ambassador was the perfect addition to his poker group. Frank had come to know Stuart well, starting with an in-depth series he'd done on the business luminary in 1996. Ostensibly an examination of how Roberts had started IntelliView and become wealthy, the series shined a spotlight on an emerging figure in the Republican Party. Though it was far from mere puffery—for one thing, Frank exposed Roberts's secretive nature and his habit of excluding even his wife or close associates from important matters—the series helped launch Roberts into public service. Before long, it was a broadly held expectation that he would enter elective politics at a high level.

The two Californians, with an intertwined history, gravitated toward each other. The opportunity to play cards and drink vodka with a top American correspondent and a senior

US official was a strong magnet for other interesting figures to join the poker game.

It was the ambassador's turn to deal. "Ante up, boys!"

Zev Levi, a high-ranking Israeli diplomat whom Roberts had introduced to Frank, picked up on the American envoy's wry wit. "In Israel, we have another word for 'capitalism.'"

Several of those around the table raised their glasses of Stoli in a mock toast as Zev finished the joke. "We call it 'Judaism.'"

The players, with the exception of Rado Weinstien, the dour German physics professor playing for his first time, laughed at Zev's sly joke.

Viktor Romanov, the Russian Oil Ministry analyst Frank had met on an earlier trip to Moscow, jumped into the exchange. "In the old Soviet Union, we just shot the capitalists!"

More laughter as Ahmad Durrani pulled the string. "You didn't just shoot capitalists in the Soviet Union, my brother. You were shooting my comrades in Afghanistan as well."

Ahmad was the brilliant doctoral scholar in archaeology who Mikhail had introduced to Frank. Mikhail, an ambitious researcher and lecturer in petrochemical engineering, had collaborated with Ahmad on several field assignments.

Amid laughter and raised glasses, Frank put his finger to his lips and pointed with exaggeration to a light fixture in the ceiling. Though he whispered with stage effect, Frank barely made himself heard over the laughter. "They're listening. This place is bugged."

Another of Frank's diverse circle of poker players was Qin

Sun, a Chinese visiting fellow in nuclear physics. He spoke in a quiet, heavily accented voice. "Who cares about the KGB?"

It annoyed Mikhail when foreigners misunderstood the recent changes in his homeland. "It's no longer called the KGB, my friend; it's now the FSB."

Just then, Lisa and Viktor's girlfriend, Svetlana Lutrova, opened the door from the small kitchen and entered the room carrying trays of *zakuski*, Russian appetizers. Svetlana would have turned heads at a Paris fashion show, though it certainly wouldn't have been due to what she was wearing. Most men who saw her immediately began envisioning her without clothes. She was strikingly beautiful—a classic Slavic woman with high cheekbones, a thin nose, full lips, a soft chin, shoulder-length blond hair and a well-proportioned, firm body that emphasized her ample breasts.

Svetlana responded to Mikhail's rendering of post-Soviet reality. "You're right, Mikhail. The KGB is alive and well, just under a different name."

Viktor injected his razor sarcasm. "Don't forget about the new and improved SVR."

Russia's Foreign Intelligence Service, *Sluzhba Vneshney Razvedki*, had been formed from the ruins of the KGB's dreaded First Chief Directorate. While the Federal Security Service, or FSB, focused on domestic surveillance, like Britain's MI6, the SVR ran the Kremlin's external espionage. Almost a decade after the demise of Communism, it remained more aggressive than most people realized.

Rado shot Qin a withering glance. "I have an old German saying."

The room became quiet. Rado hadn't spoken before. His stiff demeanor befitted a former East German physics professor with a sad family history that would have earned him sympathy were he ever to share it.

Everyone looked at Rado expectantly.

"Wisdom abandoned China when Confucius died."

As the air seemed to leave the room, Frank felt obliged to jump in as host. He'd see if the newcomer to the game could handle the usual locker room banter. "Lighten up, Rado! You Germans have no sense of humor!"

The players laughed as Rado glared at Frank. Rado picked up a shot of vodka and downed it.

Lisa and Svetlana set down the trays of *zakuski*. Frank reached over and picked up a thin slice of rye bread topped with red caviar. He looked at Svetlana for a fleeting moment.

"Did you make these, Svetlana?"

Viktor, Mikhail and Stuart exchanged glances. Frank couldn't hide his infatuation with Svetlana. They assumed that Lisa had resigned herself to Frank's wandering eye. Svetlana came over and put her arm around the American's shoulder. "Just for you, Frank."

The apartment buzzer sounded. Lisa went over to the door and opened it.

Bud Johnson, Lisa's AmeriCon Energy boss from Houston, stood in the landing. Lisa beckoned Bud inside, embraced him and ushered him over to the poker table. "I'd like you all to meet Bud Johnson. He directs our overseas operations at AmeriCon in Houston. He's here because I've been sending him frantic dispatches about the new oil field discovered beneath the Caspian Sea."

Viktor carried the earlier jesting forward with the visitor. "Mr. Johnson, why have you come to Moscow? Why aren't you down in Baku or Astana where all the action is? That's where our newly free brothers and sisters in Azerbaijan and Kazakhstan are finding all the oil!"

With the poker players speaking Russian, Lisa began translating for Bud. His eyes twinkled as he responded in a thick South Texas drawl. "How right you are, my friend! Lisa and I are headed to Baku tomorrow. The negotiations over the Baku-Ceyhan pipeline are almost done, and we want to shake some hands and pass around some business cards."

Mikhail jumped in. "It's true that the so-called independent 'Stans and their Caucasus neighbors have their own constitutions and parliaments now. They even have their own armies, if that's what you call some battalions with tanks and grenades. But Russia's in charge. We built their pipelines and still control them. These nations are like adolescents—we give them just enough freedom to make them feel independent."

Viktor chuckled. "Aren't you Americans rich enough already? You have to come here to steal our black gold!"

The Russians' bravado delighted Bud, who hailed from a big frontier state built on bluff and swagger. "To begin with, comrades, I'm a Texan first, an American second. And I'm here to help you Russians get as rich as we are!"

This prompted hoots around the poker table. Viktor rose

and motioned for Bud to sit down. "Why don't you play a few hands so we can enjoy some of that Texas wealth?"

Bud sat down with a flourish. "Don't mind if I do. How 'bout a hand of Texas Hold 'Em?"

CHAPTER 8

MOSCOW
TUESDAY, JULY 20, 1999

THE NIGHTTIME VIEW of Red Square is like other iconic images of its time, raped by gawkers and robbed of its beauty. For Russians, the fairy tale that foreigners saw at Red Square was a nightmare, centuries in the making. The multihued cupolas of St. Basil's Cathedral glittered over the graves of Russian Orthodox priests who died defending their church against invading Mongols, plundering tsars and Soviet commissars. The Kremlin's red-brick walls still sheltered the embalmed remains of Vladimir Lenin, a mummified murderer in his granite mausoleum. The arched gables and bright towers of the GUM Department Store greeted tourists and the newly enriched natives. They browsed the arcades that once displayed the body of Stalin's wife, Nadezhda Alliluyeva, after her suicide and stored the propaganda banners for

Revolutionary Day parades across the cobblestone range of Red Square.

Lisa and Frank's guests were in too fine a mood to ponder the tragedies of Russian history. They stood on the flat's balcony, gazing out at the panoramic tableau of the Kremlin and St. Basil's illuminated under a crescent moon.

Lisa came onto the balcony with a bottle of Armenian brandy. "Frank brought this back from his last trip to Yerevan. The Armenians say they make the best cognac in the world."

Mikhail's reflexive Russian chauvinism inspired his laughter. "The Armenians like to think all kinds of crazy things."

The others laughed as Lisa poured the cognac into blue Russian shot glasses. Frank raised his glass and offered a toast in vodka-smoothed Russian. "To your health, our dear friends and highly skilled poker partners!"

As everyone cheered, Mikhail downed his brandy and leaned over to Bud. "Sorry, Mr. Johnson, just because it's called Texas Hold 'Em doesn't mean you Texans get to win!"

Frank and Mikhail laughed and clinked glasses while a puzzled Bud looked on. "What did that ole boy say? What are ya'll hooting about like a bunch of drunk owls?"

Frank and Lisa exchanged glances. "If you insist on knowing, Bud." She translated Mikhail's quip into English, but with a comically exaggerated Russian accent.

Bud roared with delight. He threw his arm around Mikhail's shoulder. "Son, your Mother Russia is gonna pay me back in spades with black gold!"

With a frown, Lisa watered down Bud's proclamation as she translated again from English into Russian. "My young friend, I trust that my company's investments here will more than cover my losses at the card table."

Mikhail, though a bit tipsy, was both jocular and serious. "Mr. Johnson, we Russians appreciate your company's interest in our petroleum and gas reserves. Not too many years in the future our oil is going to be bigger than you could ever imagine!"

Bud smiled broadly and leaned toward Mikhail. "Just what do you mean by that?"

Stuart interrupted. This booze-fueled banter was straying into uncomfortable territory for the American ambassador.

"I think what Mikhail is trying to say is that Russia has a lot of untapped potential and—"

Bud cut off Stuart with a wave. "I think this young man is doing just fine."

Bud turned back to Mikhail. "Son, I admire your ambition, but all that oil doesn't do you Russians any damn good unless you can get it to market. Here we are almost eight years after Communism collapsed, and your country still doesn't know squat about making money."

Mikhail ceded no ground. "Things have changed more than you think, Mr. Johnson. We've come a long way from Communism. No offense to my friend Ahmad here, but the Communists couldn't even defeat a band of rag-heads in Afghanistan. We were taught to hate capitalism, and now the capitalists are taking over Russia!"

Mikhail raised his glass. "I intend to be one of the most successful capitalists!"

Bud was delighted. He toasted Mikhail's success. "The

reason I'm here, son, is to help you and other ambitious young Russians realize your dreams."

Lisa teased her boss. "What you really mean, Bud, is you want to help them become good capitalists."

As others laughed, Stuart displayed the dry wit that he normally kept under wraps. "Of course, that's the secret basis of our diplomacy."

Everyone roared at the rare show of humor from Stuart.

Rubbing his chin, Bud turned toward Lisa. "What do you say we take Mikhail down with us to Baku?"

Stuart worried about a break in diplomatic protocol. "Bud, Mikhail is a lecturer at the Moscow Technological Institute. We don't want to interrupt his work."

Bud scoffed. "Hell, Stuart, we're only talking about a few days. This young man will learn more on a trip with us than he'd teach his students in a whole damn year!"

Away from the hidden bugs in the Americans' flat, out on the darkened streets of Moscow as the hour passed midnight, Svetlana Lutrova, Rado Weinstien and Viktor Romanov could speak freely.

The two Russians and the German-born transplant knew that Frank and Lisa weren't fools. They knew that Frank, as a successful journalist from the world's most powerful nation, was a well-trained skeptic. Unlike most of the other clueless "visitors" whose lives the three Kremlin agents had infiltrated, Frank knew enough to be dangerous.

Viktor, descended from the Romanov Dynasty that had produced Peter the Great to briefly turn Russia's trajectory toward the West, understood that Frank's rare ability to speak his country's language well gave the American a depth of knowledge few foreigners could claim.

When *Los Angeles Register* publisher Thomas Hawkes, whom the Kremlin suspected of having CIA connections, had applied to the Russian Foreign Ministry for the new bureau chief's visa, Viktor had read Frank's dossier carefully. Say what you will about the now-reviled KGB, but the old Soviet spy agency was thorough. Several years before the *Register* hired him, while he was still a student at Berkeley, the KGB had pegged Frank as someone worth watching, a journalist-in-training who showed every sign of becoming a future star.

As a political science/journalism major taking an honors graduate seminar, Frank wrote a paper on the cultural and psychological similarities between the tsars who had ruled Russia for half a millennium and the Soviet dictators who had claimed to "free the proletariat from their yoke." In an extraordinary feat for an undergraduate student, Frank's professor helped the paper get published in a prominent American journal, *Russian Studies*, where it caught the attention of KGB operatives at the Soviet Consulate in San Francisco. Within days, the operatives had assigned one of their undercover agents at Berkeley, a Russian visiting scholar named Anatoly, to shadow Frank. The two students became fast friends. Their friendship strengthened the reports that "Tony"—as Frank came to call him—filed regularly to his overseers across the Bay.

The Soviet Union may have fallen, seemingly overnight in the last few months of 1991, but the Kremlin's surveillance of Frank continued seamlessly through the nineties during the reporter's rapid rise at the *Register*. The Foreign Intelligence Service, run directly by the Russian president, oversaw the surveillance of Adams.

The Kremlin's interest in Frank increased when the *Register* sent him to learn Russian at the Defense Language Institute in Monterey, a Pentagon and CIA bastion they had never managed to infiltrate. It was rare for an American civilian to study there. Adams's enrollment in an intensive course didn't prove that he was a CIA agent, but the Kremlin operatives knew one thing: someone close to him, perhaps Thomas Hawkes or maybe others at Langley, was pulling strings and guiding his career as a journalist.

Was it a coincidence that Adams's Russian instructor in Monterey was Lisa Hawkes, the attractive daughter of the *Los Angeles Register* publisher? Did the two of them really fall deeply in love in a just a few months at the scenic California outpost? For the Soviet spymasters, their sudden romance eerily resembled the Parisian infatuation between Lisa's parents.

The Kremlin had been watching Lisa and her family for decades. The devious escape to America of Lisa's mother, Lydia Karpovich, was considered a traitorous act by a member of Khrushchev's inner circle. One of only three official translators permitted to accompany him abroad, she had embarrassed Moscow and contributed to "the silent coup" that would replace him with Brezhnev. Beyond Lydia Karpovich's treason, the Soviets also blamed Thomas Hawkes, the student who had somehow romanced her in Paris and then lured her away, certainly with the aid of powerful helpers. Within the limits of complex Cold War espionage, the KGB monitored the couple closely once Thomas and Lydia settled in San Francisco in 1961.

It seemed natural that Lisa would grow up speaking Russian like a native. And even if her parents' biographies hadn't come straight from a spy novel, she did plenty on her own to draw Moscow's attention. Her doctorate in Russian linguistics from Stanford at age twenty-two, her postdoctorate work in the Russian archives at the Library of Congress, her post as the youngest instructor at the Defense Language Institute—all of this kept Lisa on the Kremlin's radar screen.

And then, when Adams was assigned to Moscow for the *Register*, Lisa landed an important job with AmeriCon Energy, the Houston-based multinational that was extending its tentacles through the heart of Russia's newfound oil wealth. The conglomerate reached across the Ural Mountains and into the Caucasus to encircle the massive crude reserves under the Caspian Sea. How had that happened? As impressive as her resume was, had she really done it on her own? Nearly certain that her father was a senior CIA proxy using the publisher's post as cover, Russia's Foreign Intelligence Service, the SVR, wondered whether Lisa wasn't a mole as well. Who were her bosses at Langley? What was her real job? How much of her work did she share with her husband? What did Adams know—and how much, using his highly honed talents as an investigative reporter, could he surmise?

The Kremlin tracked every American correspondent in Moscow for a major newspaper or TV network. It assigned "minders"—agents planted at the Russian Foreign Ministry or one of the "independent" think tanks that had sprung up—to befriend the journalists over coffee, on reporting trips, indeed at card games.

As they walked along Moscow's shadowy streets, Viktor, Rado and Svetlana knew that the American couple understood they were under surveillance. But did they understand how closely they were being watched? Did they realize the intensity of interest in them? Did they know how high that interest reached within the Kremlin?

In his sensitive postings, Viktor had gotten to know a number of Americans, and he had come to believe they shared a trait that went beyond their religion, class or political ideology: they were romantics. Unlike his countrymen, unhappy heirs to centuries of tragedy, Americans still lived in a country young enough, and foolish enough, to hope. The "happy endings" that Hollywood brought to life on the big screen weren't just movie devices. They were real, part of the cultural DNA, a touchstone of the optimism that led these friendly and energetic people to think they could make the world a better place.

Viktor had no doubt that Frank and Lisa were tough and shrewd. But beneath their canny exteriors, he was counting on them retaining their countrymen's belief in the innate goodness of others. He was counting on their native inability to be as vigilant and mistrustful as every Russian was from birth. He was counting on them to be, in the end, Americans.

As they neared Rado's apartment on a sheltered sidestreet off Kutuzovsky Prospekt, Viktor, as the senior agent, probed his temperamental charge. "I don't envy your assignment, Rado. Whether he's a spy or in fact just an envoy, Stuart Roberts doesn't give away much."

Rado volleyed back. "Your assignment is not as easy as it might seem. I trust you're not taken in by Frank Adams's drinking act. He's much more clever than he lets on."

Rado gave Svetlana a dare. "Speaking of Frank, I saw him staring at you. I think it's time to make your move."

Rado, typically, was overstepping his bounds. But Viktor listened as Svetlana responded. "Is that necessary? It could ruin my assignment to befriend Lisa if she finds out."

Rado said, "Well, then, just make sure she doesn't find out."

Viktor smiled to himself in the dark. For all his coarseness, Rado was bright, but he had a short fuse that Viktor enjoyed igniting. "You former Stasi agents are always so ruthless."

"And you former KGB agents are so cold," Rado replied. "The Stasi was run from Moscow after what you Russians call the Great Patriotic War. We just took your lessons and perfected them."

Rado could never take a joke. Viktor couldn't resist one last jibe. "Yes, you Germans always strive for perfection."

Svetlana was the adult here. As usual, she mediated when Rado and Viktor acted like teenage boys. She turned their attention back to business. "Of course, Nikolai will have to approve this plan."

Nikolai Volkov was their superior officer at the Foreign Intelligence Service.

Finally, the three of them could share a laugh. Viktor jested before he and Svetlana bid Rado good night. "Nikolai is always amused when our surveillance turns sexual."

CHAPTER 9

MOSCOW
MONDAY, JUNE 5, 2000

FRANK WAITED AT the Kremlin for the news conference of Vladimir Putin and the visiting President Bill Clinton to start. He marveled at how fast his first year as the *Los Angeles Register*'s Moscow correspondent had passed. That was always how it had gone in his career when time and place and passion met and he'd reported on a fascinating, ongoing story. There had been the Rodney King riots; the long subsequent investigation of LAPD brutality against blacks and Hispanics by the Christopher Commission; the trial and acquittal of the four cops who'd flailed away at King in an ugly beating captured on videotape and broadcast around the world. There'd been the bloody murder of Nicole Brown Simpson and Ronald Goldman; the O. J. car chase broadcast live for a captivated nation glued to their TV sets—the first reality show; the trial of the disgraced former football star; Simpson struggling to pull on the black leather glove at his murder trial; Johnnie Cochran's brilliant closing admonition to the jury, "If it doesn't fit, you must acquit."

Now there was the historic transition of Russia—from its corruption-filled "cowboy capitalism" period after the collapse of Communism and the teetering, tipsy leadership of the burly Boris Yeltsin to the chilling, tightly controlled rule of the former KGB apparatchik Putin. The country's future still hung in the balance, and no one knew whether the vast land would truly break from its long, despotic past and join the small ranks of successful democracies. Frank was right where he and other reporters were sometimes lucky enough to land: in the front row for history-in-the-making, chronicling the rough draft for the later work of historians casting judgments on the fates of nations.

On this early summer night, the poker players at the weekly game gathered in the living room of Lisa and Frank's flat, sitting on their plush tan leather couch, matching love seat and beige canvas armchairs. They drank large bottles of Donya Russian beer and ate *zakuski,* red caviar on mini slices of pumpernickel, pickled herring with onions, and *stolichny salat* (capital salad) with chopped potatoes, peas, diced ham and tomatoes from the small balcony garden.

The group watched a TV news broadcast of the just-concluded meeting between Putin and Clinton. They listened to the *Pyervy Kanal*—Channel One—correspondent, Pavel Sidorov, deliver a live report from the Kremlin. "United States President Bill Clinton has just left Moscow after a successful first summit with President Vladimir Putin."

The screen showed a clip of Clinton before his departure, engaged in conversation with Muscovites as he strolled along Red Square, Secret Service agents scrambling to control the growing crowd, forming a protective circle around the affable American president.

Pavel Sidorov continued his report. "The Russia–United States relationship has come a long way since Ronald Reagan called the Soviet Union the Evil Empire. And President Putin has been the Russian leader for less than six months."

The report shifted to a segment from the news conference Clinton and Putin had held a few hours earlier. The two presidents took turns calling on reporters, each choosing one from his country. Clinton, who knew Frank from his 1996 campaign trips to California, nodded at the correspondent to ask a question.

"Presidents Clinton and Putin: do you really think that by destroying sixty-eight tons of weapons-grade plutonium, America and Russia will stop the arms race?"

The poker group broke into mock cheers. Viktor lifted his glass. The others joined the toast as he spoke in his typical mixture of sarcasm and humor. "Way to go, Frankie! Let's drink to the end of the Cold War and to Russian-American friendship!"

Qin Sun didn't seem to catch the humor. "Don't get carried away, comrades. It's merely a friendship of convenience."

Mikhail never missed a chance to take a dig at the solemn scientist from Beijing. "You Chinese are always jealous when we Russians improve our relations with America!"

Rado Weinstien didn't join in the laughter. "This arms

treaty means nothing. Mark my words: there will be wars fought over the so-called weapons of mass destruction."

Zev Levi spoke in an accented voice sprinkled with jest. "Who knows, Rado? Now that so many Russian Jews have returned to their homeland in Israel, maybe you will join them?"

On paper, Zev was one of three commercial attachés at the embassy. That post made him especially interested in Mikhail's activities helping capitalism take root in Russia. Zev was also following the assignment of Roberts as the United States envoy. Members of the diplomatic corps in Russia's capital, which had doubled in size since the collapse of Communism, always suspected one another of holding covert positions with their home countries' espionage agencies. In Zev's case, it was accurate. Ostensibly, he was a trade specialist within the Israeli Foreign Ministry who was dispatched for two or three years to the Jewish State's far-flung embassies and consulates. In fact, he was a senior agent for the Mossad, the almost mythical Israeli intelligence agency that had operatives planted within every government department. In 1990, Moscow and Tel Aviv moved to re-establish diplomatic ties that had been ruptured during the 1967 Six-Day War.

On an earlier assignment to Moscow, Zev had been given the covert task of overseeing the renovation of the shuttered embassy on Bolshaya Ordynka, only a few blocks from the former KGB Lubyanka headquarters and prison where the Kremlin's goons tortured Russian Jews seeking only to emigrate to their true homeland. Zev's top priority was to prevent the Russian carpenters and electricians who worked on the Israeli Embassy from planting bugs inside it.

For months, he engaged in a cat-and-mouse game with a constantly changing cast of Russian "inspectors" and craftsmen. A new shipment of drywall would arrive, and the Russian crew would hurry to install it. Zev would come by with his debugging equipment. Like electronic hound dogs, the devices would sniff out the miniature recorders embedded in the sheetrock, and Zev would gesture for the Russians to take out their power drills and remove the bugs.

On another morning, Zev would find that a large chandelier had mysteriously been hung overnight in one of the reception rooms. A Russian electrician would be showing a great deal of interest in the giant light's wiring, particularly at a certain spot among the crystal pendants. After waiting for him to leave the room, Zev would investigate and find a tiny camera nestled in the ornamental fixture. It brought him great pleasure to remove his Swiss Army knife from his pocket, pull out the small scissors and snip the wire leading to the mini camera.

Zev's Mossad bosses in Israel knew that it was impossible to end up with a bug-free embassy. Besides, the Russian Embassy in Tel Aviv was chock full of sophisticated Israeli electronic gadgetry. As the Israeli Embassy moved toward its highly publicized reopening on October 24, 1991, Zev's goal was to limit the prospective damage to Israel's security and commercial interests by reducing the number of bugs inside its revamped embassy. It also didn't hurt to let the Kremlin know that the Mossad was onto its tricks.

Now, not quite nine years later, Zev sat in Frank and

Lisa's living room. The American reporter had invited him to join their weekly poker game after the two of them shared a Hot Toddy, made with strong black Russian tea fortified by Glenlivet single malt Scotch whiskey, on a frigid winter day at the Shamrock Pub on Novy Arbat Street. The two men had met for the first time a month earlier when Frank had come to the Israeli Embassy to interview Zev for an article investigating whether the Kremlin was still blocking visas of Russian Jews. On this evening, with Frank covering Clinton and Putin at the Kremlin, Zev felt obliged to assume the absent host's duties. He rose from the corner armchair and gestured expansively at the other poker players.

"I feel lucky tonight—let's play some cards!"

As the group moved to the dining room and sat down around the poker table, Lisa's Palm Pilot vibrated in the pocket of her khaki slacks. She pulled out the device and looked at its small screen. It featured a cutting-edge technology not yet for sale to the general public: the screen displayed a text message asking her to check a file delivered to her laptop computer. The message hadn't come from AmeriCon Energy. Its source was a modest modern complex of whitewashed buildings housing a key US agency in an affluent Northern Virginia suburb across the Potomac from Washington.

Lisa read the message, left the living room and entered her study. She turned on her Dell Inspiron 7500 laptop. Glancing behind her, she closed the door of the study.

CHAPTER 10

Moscow

Saturday, August 12, 2000

MIKHAIL WOULD NEVER have dreamed of missing a night of fun and poker at Lisa and Frank's place. Even though he was working most every waking hour at his nascent oil business, he enjoyed the unusual mixture of intellect, culture and experience presented by the characters at the former Karpovich flat. Mikhail had benefited from the interest Bud Johnson had shown in him a year earlier, when the AmeriCon Energy executive had invited the Russian to accompany him and Lisa on their trip to the Azerbaijan capital of Baku. Even more valuable was his budding friendship with Stuart Roberts. Whether it was his personal encouragement, management hints or commonsense economic views, the ambassador had emerged as a mentor for Mikhail.

It was approaching midnight. Two empty Stolichnaya bottles adorned the side table near the host.

Ahmad Durrani shuffled the deck and passed it to Qin Sun. The Chinese physics doctoral candidate called the game, Seven-Card Stud, his favorite, and dealt the cards.

No one smoked indoors, but the bright lighting over the poker table and the dimness surrounding it created an atmosphere of intrigue that the players relished.

Viktor elbowed Zev Levi as the Israeli picked up the last of his dealt cards. "Stop looking at my cards, you schlemiel! Your Mossad assignment doesn't include monitoring my hand!"

In mock alarm, Zev waved his arm above his head. "Why should you care, Viktor? You know this place is rigged with SVR cameras. Your colleagues at Lubyanka Square can see all the cards."

"Frank doesn't need to worry," Ahmad piled on. "Russian spy equipment is worthless. That's why it was so easy for the Mujahedeen to defeat them in Afghanistan."

Rado added with more envy than he intended. "I'm sure the equipment Stuart's company manufactures in California is far superior to the garbage the Russians use."

Stuart said, "Well, we certainly make superior products, Rado, but we've never made spy equipment."

This deadpan comment from Stuart elicited peals of laughter around the table.

"Come on, Stuart!" Frank chortled. "What are you doing with all those Pentagon and CIA contracts? Making million-dollar toilet seats?"

Mikhail threw down his cards in feigned disgust as Viktor

pulled a large stack of chips from the middle of the table into his own pile.

"Look at that—Stuart actually lost a hand!"

Stuart stood up amid more laughter. "I'm going out to have a cigar."

Mikhail rose as well. "I think I'll join the ambassador in his sinful pleasure."

Stuart and Mikhail walked through the cramped kitchen where Lisa and Svetlana were deep in conversation. They had developed a close relationship in the year since Frank had launched the weekly poker game.

"So, Svetik, have you and Viktor thought about getting married?"

"Oh sure, Lisa, we've thought about it quite a bit, but we're not ready yet."

Svetlana pulled a tray of *pelmeni*, the delicious Siberian dumplings, from the oven. "Are you glad that you and Frank got married?"

"Of course! Well, at least most of the time. Frank and I both work so hard. We sometimes go weeks when we barely see each other."

"I envy you, Lisa. You must meet many attractive men in your work." Svetlana paused, and then resumed speaking. "Have you ever thought of having an affair?"

Lisa laughed and put her arm around Svetlana's waist. "My dear Svetik, every woman *thinks* about having an affair at some point in her marriage!"

Out on the balcony, it was another spectacular summer night. The Kremlin and Red Square were bathed in soft light against a black moonless sky. The sounds of the city could be heard in the still air.

Stuart pulled a cigar from his pocket and offered it to Mikhail. "This is a first-rate *Toraño* from Honduras. The Honduran ambassador sends them over to me."

Mikhail reached into his pocket. "I've got something even better."

Mikhail handed Stuart a dark, torpedo-shaped cigar.

Stuart looked at the label. "This is a Cuban cigar. You know I can't smoke this."

Mikhail spoke with his trademark light sarcasm. "Ah, yes, the enormously successful American economic embargo that has somehow managed to prop up the Castro brothers for almost sixty years!"

Mikhail took the cigar and removed the label. "Let's just call it a Dominican cigar."

With some misgiving, Stuart watched Mikhail clip and light the cigar. He handed it to Stuart and then clipped and lit his own.

Mikhail exhaled a trail of smoke. "You know, Stuart, I'm in debt to you for your invaluable advice while I get my feet on the ground as an entrepreneur. I'm so glad that capitalism has finally come to Russia. Now that my oil business is up and running, I'm amazed by all the decisions I have to make. You were so successful with IntelliView. What's the secret?"

Stuart was enjoying the Partagas. At fifteen dollars, it was one of the most expensive Cuban cigars. He took a slow draw before answering.

"A lot of business success is timing and good fortune. I started off working with IBM when they were building the first home computers. I learned a lot there. After a few years, I broke off to start my own company. We focused on miniaturization of computer components."

"How did you come up with that idea?"

"I always thought every home and company in America would end up having a computer. And I believed that the key was constantly making the computers smaller. In the end, I was lucky. I just happened to bet on the right horse."

Mikhail looked at the ash on the end of his cigar. "I'll never forget that you trusted me enough to place a bet on this long shot. I will always value your friendship."

The two men put their cigars in an ashtray on the balcony table and walked back through the kitchen to rejoin the poker group.

Later that night, after their friends had departed, Frank brought some glasses and plates into the kitchen where Lisa washed and dried them. Their flat was filled with character but lacked a dishwasher and other modern conveniences.

Frank placed a stack of dishes in the sink. As he started back for the living room, he felt a pair of warm hands reach around him, unbuckle his belt and open his trousers. Frank turned around to see that Lisa had removed her blouse and bra. As always, he was amazed that Lisa's nipples were already taut. He'd often joked with Lisa about her "talent" at making her nipples protrude without manipulation. She always told him that this forte of hers was unique to the spell he cast on her. In turn he invariably swore to her that no woman had ever given him such quick and hard erections.

Lisa whispered in Frank's ear. "Leave the dishes; we'll finish up in the morning. I've got a little something in store for you." She pulled her husband toward the bedroom.

Frank nearly tripped as he stepped out of his pants and followed her. Despite the considerable amount of vodka he'd consumed, he was more than ready to take Lisa in his arms and help the rest of her body reach her breasts' state of arousal.

By the time he removed his shirt, Lisa was already nude on their bed. Her arms and legs still had the fine muscle tone of the gymnast she'd once been. The only real discernable change was in the fullness of her breasts and the roundness of her hips.

Frank lay down, and she immediately took charge. She turned him on his back and climbed on top. Lisa lowered herself onto him and began riding him with fierce vigor. Normally they liked to draw things out and power through different positions, but now Lisa pumped furiously until she reached a shuddering climax, setting off his orgasm.

Keeping Frank inside her, Lisa stretched out on top of him. They lay together in silence. Embracing her husband and breathing softly, Lisa stroked his cheek and murmured her appreciation. "I needed that."

"Not as much as I did, darling."

Lisa rolled to the side and looked into Frank's eyes.

"You've seemed a little preoccupied lately. Do you have a big story brewing?"

"Nothing really major. I'm just working a couple of leads."

Frank turned on his side and put his hand on Lisa's shoulder. "You're more secretive about your work than I am. I know we agreed that it's for our own good, but you don't share any of your gossip with me. Sometimes I wonder who you really work for."

Lisa raised herself on an elbow. "Don't be silly. You know we need to protect each other. Besides, if I told you AmeriCon's secrets, my bosses would have my head."

Relaxing in Frank's arms, Lisa changed the subject. She spoke in a mischievous tone. "Svetlana and I had an interesting conversation tonight. She asked me if I've ever thought of having an affair."

Frank smiled. "So what did you tell her?"

Lisa caressed Frank. "I told her that as long as you can go all night, I don't need another man."

CHAPTER 11

Moscow
Friday, February 16, 2001

FRANK PUSHED A pile of chips from the middle of the poker table into the big stacks in front of Stuart. "Jesus Christ, Stuart, don't you ever lose?"

Stuart responded with his customary calm. "Simmer down, Frank. I'll remind you that I dropped a few hundred rubles just last month. I thought you peasants would damage your vocal cords with all of your cheering."

Frank raised his glass and downed what little vodka remained. "That's because you'd never lost a fucking ruble before."

Zev jumped in to defend his closest friend in the group. "*Oy gevalt*, Frankie. I've been trying to get *ein bissel* of Ambassador Roberts's *glyck* to rub off on me. You're spoiling our *gemutlich* atmosphere!"

Everyone laughed at Zev's transparent efforts, punctuated by his fractured injection of Yiddish into his heavily accented English, to ingratiate himself with Stuart. Everyone laughed, save Rado. Never enamored with those who wore their Judaism on their sleeves, Rado thought Zev insufficiently reserved for the important work he did on behalf of Israel in Russia's rapidly changing circumstances.

It was Ahmad's turn to select the next game. He chose Five Card Draw. One of the most traditional poker variations, it was decidedly second-tier among the players, well behind the beloved Texas Hold 'Em and several favored versions of Stud.

Stuart and Ahmad were the big winners that night with hefty piles of chips before them. Also doing well but with smaller winnings were Zev, Mikhail and Viktor. With few chips left, the clear losers were Frank, Rado and Qin Sun.

After the initial ante and deal, Zev, Ahmad, Stuart and Mikhail folded. Only Frank, Viktor and Rado remained alive. Ahmad dealt them new cards in exchange for their discards. Frank, Viktor and Rado looked at their hands. Viktor picked up three blue chips and tossed them into the pot.

Frank glanced at his dwindling stack of chips. "Thirty rubles, you joker! You'd better have a winning hand!"

Viktor was amused. "Just worry about your own hand, my friend!"

Frank tossed in five blue chips. "I'll see your bet and raise you twenty."

Viktor shrugged. "I always know when you're bluffing, Frankochka."

The Russian turned his gaze to Rado, who silently pushed all his chips into the pot. Frank and Viktor uttered exclamations of surprise tinged with derision. Frank egged him on.

"Whoa, going all in, Rado! You must have at least a straight flush."

Rado smirked. "Put in your chips, Herr Adams, and you will find out."

Frank and Viktor matched Rado's raise. With an uncharacteristic flourish, Rado laid down his hand. Zev and Ahmad whistled when they saw the pair of aces joined by two jacks.

Viktor kept a straight face as he turned over his cards one at a time. First came the king, then a five, a seven, another five and then the final card—yet another five.

Frank threw his cards facedown next to the deck by Ahmad. "Three fucking fives! Beats my ass!"

Rado turned his cards over and got up from the table. "I've reached my five-hundred-ruble limit."

Qin stood up. "I'm out of money also. Professor, can you drop me off at my flat?"

Rado beckoned Qin to follow him. They left the flat, walked down three flights of stairs and stepped into the parking lot. Two inches of fresh snow covered the lot and most of the cars. The evening scene evoked an earlier era as light glistened off the pure white snow from the 1950s-era side lamps hung on rusting poles. Rado took a pack of cheap Russian cigarettes from his coat pocket. He put one in his mouth, shook out another for Qin, produced a vintage Zippo and lit the cigarettes.

"I read your dissertation draft. With some work, I believe that your Beijing superiors in the General Armament Department at the Central Military Commission will be pleased."

Qin shrugged. "It's alright, I suppose. More importantly, I'm making progress on the equation you assigned me."

"Good. If we are to succeed in designing the key miniature components for a nuclear trigger, we must maintain our focus."

Rado changed the subject. "I have some important contacts for you to meet, but no one else can learn of this. There could be a lot of money in it for us."

"You have opened many doors for me, Professor Weinstien. You know that I have pledged my honor—indeed my life—to our endeavors."

"I will set up a private meeting for us with a visitor from Iran."

Qin waited for his mentor to speak again.

"I've been contacted by a senior officer in the Army of the Guardians of the Islamic Revolution. You may know them by their more popular name of the Iranian Revolutionary Guards. They are keenly interested in our products, and they are willing to make us very wealthy if the nuclear trigger proves successful."

The two men tossed their cigarettes on the ground. Rado unlocked the doors of his Lada, and they got in. Rado pulled out of the parking lot and turned right onto Kutuzovsky Prospekt, traveling away from Red Square. They drove in silence until the Lada coasted to a stop in front of Qin's wretched dormitory at Moscow State University.

"Thanks for the ride, Professor."

"I'll be waiting for you in my office after the lecture tomorrow."

III: DEAD HAND

*There are few things that are so unpardonably
neglected in our country as poker. The upper class
knows very little about it. Now and then you find
ambassadors who have sort of a general knowledge
of the game, but the ignorance of the people
is fearful.*

Mark Twain

CHAPTER 12

MOSCOW

FRANK'S PLANE BEGAN its descent. The reporter looked out his window and saw the familiar grimy haze above Moscow. As usual, the foreigners on the flight remained in their seats while the Russians ignored the captain's admonitions. Rising as one, they opened the overhead bins and began a boisterous competition to retrieve their belongings. The captain shouted over the intercom for them to sit down but gave up when they paid no heed. Frank was relieved that at least they no longer disobeyed the smoking ban. When the plane touched down on the runway and bumped a few times to a halt, some of the passengers tumbled into one another in a mixture of laughter and profanities. Frank chuckled as he gathered his gear. For all the quirks of its people and the frustrations of its daily life, he always liked coming back to Moscow.

Aeroflot hadn't changed its practice of making passengers

on even its biggest jets climb down the metal steps reserved in America for commuter puddle-jumpers. The travelers still had to trudge across the tarmac as Airbus 340s and Boeing 737s took off and landed around them. Frank had a pleasant surprise, though, when he saw that the ground shuttle wasn't the creaking bus he'd ridden so often to the terminal, black exhaust cascading behind it. Instead, the arriving passengers stepped onto a gleaming blue bus with ads for computers and cell phones on its sides. The vehicle rode smoothly along for a few minutes before delivering the group to the main terminal of Sheremetyevo I, one of Moscow's five commercial airports.

The scene inside the terminal was again familiar. Taking his place behind other foreigners, Frank looked across at the natives jostling noisily into three domestic lines. The Russian passports were still red, but their covers no longer bore the hammer-and-sickle insignia of Soviet days.

As Frank neared the front of the control line and took out his passport, his pulse quickened. He hadn't entered the country on his own since the Kremlin had "suggested" he leave more than a decade earlier. Nektor Khabalov, his source at the Russian Consulate in San Francisco, had issued him a tourist visa based on a Hotel National room reservation wired by Evgeny Aisenyev, Frank's former US Embassy squash partner who now managed the historic hotel across from Red Square. Although flashing your media credentials could get you out of a dangerous situation, Frank felt it was too risky to wear his pass around his neck or carry it in a pocket.

Frank nervously checked his documents while waiting for the green light to flash him forward to an open booth. He'd gotten a new passport since accompanying Obama to Moscow in 2009, so there were no customs entry stamps. The tourist visa folded inside the passport listed the Hotel National as his destination. On his customs declaration, he'd written that he had nothing to declare. Everything looked in order; there was no reason he should encounter difficulties. Yet Frank knew that all it would take was one Russian Interior Ministry agent having a bad day, one bureaucrat who was hung over or in a foul mood or who had just quarreled with his wife, and calls would be made, he would be told to step aside. Any attempt to research his status would reveal his past posting as a correspondent, the hazy circumstances of his departure, his recent reporting on the wounded presidential candidate who'd been slamming Russia so hard. And then the inquisition would begin.

The green light flashed at Booth No. 3. Frank approached it and slid his passport with the visa inside beneath the bulletproof glass divider. A man who looked younger than thirty, clean-shaven and somber, opened the passport, studied the first page and copied it with a scanner. He wore a teal tie on a white shirt under the dark gray-green military dress coat of the Russian Border Service with its wide lapels and black epaulets topped by the lieutenant colonel's insignia of two gold stars and two gold stripes.

The officer peered at Frank with an expressionless gaze. "This is a new passport. Have you visited Russia before with previous passports?"

Frank knew that he could not risk answering this question truthfully. He responded in a casual tone. "I came years ago as a high school exchange student. I've made two visits since then. The last one was a few years ago."

The officer stared through the glass for what felt like a minute. He rose from his chair. "Please wait here."

Frank watched the guard leave through the booth's back door and cross the entry hall before disappearing into an office along a side wall.

Inside his supervisor's office, the Border Service officer handed Frank's passport to Yuri Kostomarov. "I have an American with a tourist visa who claims he was an exchange student years ago and has made a couple of visits since then. But our records show that he was a reporter based here in the late 1990s."

Kostomarov was a senior administrator in the FSB, which previously had been part of the KGB. He typed Frank's name into his computer. "It looks like this fellow is an eminent journalist with the *Los Angeles Register*. He has written many articles about the presidential candidate who just escaped assassination. I need to call headquarters."

After the phone conversation, Kostomarov delivered instructions to the lieutenant colonel. "General Pronichev wants us to permit Mr. Adams to enter. You are to inform him that he is free to proceed through control. Arrangements are being made to keep close watch over him while he pursues his so-called tourist activities. We don't want to alert him, so maintain a calm voice and direct customs not to go through his belongings."

Outside, Frank waited. Five minutes passed, then ten. Other travelers moved quickly through the lines on either side of him. Convinced that his cover was about to be blown, Frank felt the sweat form along the back of his neck beneath his polo shirt.

Finally the lieutenant colonel returned and entered Booth No. 3. Without a hint of expression, he slid Frank's passport, visa and customs declaration back under the window. "I apologize for the delay, Mr. Adams. Our system is down, and I had to report the problem to our technicians. Please enjoy your stay in our country."

Frank took the documents, put them in a pants pocket and moved past the booth. He took a few strides and stopped. He was in Russia, on his own for the first time in almost fifteen years.

The reporter looked around the loud, cavernous hall. Young men in black leather jackets and blue jeans offered rides to the arriving passengers, picking out the foreign diplomats and businessmen.

One driver addressed Frank in broken English. "Mister, I give you ride, please?" Had it been a quarter-century earlier, Frank would have assumed that the driver worked for the KGB or at least reported to the spy agency. The delay at passport control had put him on edge. Sizing up the driver, Frank couldn't be sure he was just another ambitious young man hustling to make some extra cash or if he had other motives. It never occurred to him that the driver might be employed by a different country's intelligence service, much less his own.

Frank replied in Russian that was only a little rusty

from lack of recent practice. "Can you take me to the Hotel National?"

Frank's fluency caught the driver off guard. "You are from Estonia, I think?"

This was a typical question. Frank's Russian wasn't good enough for him to be mistaken for a native, but he was often tabbed as a citizen of one of the neighboring Baltic nations who had been forced to learn Russian under the Soviet yoke before his country regained its independence. Frank decided there was no harm in telling the driver the truth.

"No, the United States."

The driver's eyes widened. "Ah, Ceh-Sheh-Ah."

This was the Russian abbreviation of *Coedenyonye Shtahti Ameriki*—the United States of America.

"How much would you charge me for a ride to the National?"

"Four thousand rubles."

Frank did the math. Sixty dollars. He didn't want to make waves. "Agreed."

Frank's years as an overseas correspondent had taught him to pack lightly. He carried a spacious garment bag with large pockets, a battered copper-colored leather grip and a black computer case with his laptop. He let the driver take the garment bag as they walked through the airport.

"Your Russian is good. Did you live here?"

"In the late 1990s and early 2000s."

The driver's tone was bitter. "The end of the Yeltsin years when everything went to the devil. And the arrival of so-called President Putin."

Frank recognized the typical mix of idiom and sarcasm that Russians used for all manner of calamity, from broken elevators or long grocery lines, to the paranoia of the Stalin regime or the failed coup against Gorbachev in the summer of 1991.

The two of them halted their conversation as a woman's voice blared over the airport intercom, first in Russian, then in French, finally in English.

"Air France Flight 972 to Paris is ready for final boarding at Gate C-24."

Frank and the driver passed a bank of TV screens. Frank stopped to look up at one. Brian Stevens, a former ABC Moscow correspondent who had accompanied him on some trips inside Russia, was reporting from Washington. Frank looked at his watch. It was 10:00 a.m. on the East Coast. He watched his friend's broadcast.

"Two days after the attempt on his life, Republican presidential candidate Stuart Roberts has been moved from the intensive care unit at UCLA's Ronald Reagan Medical Center. At a just-concluded news conference, Roberts's doctors said he suffered second-degree burns from the explosion and a broken leg. The physicians said Roberts is expected to recover fully, but his injuries will keep him off the campaign trail for at least three weeks. They were uncertain whether he will be in good enough condition to receive the GOP's formal presidential nomination on the last night of the Republican Convention in just ten days."

Frank started walking again. He and the driver passed through the rest of the terminal. They resumed talking in

Russian. "The assassination attempt on the presidential candidate Roberts—it must be a big shock for you."

Now Frank decided to reveal little. "Of course."

The driver shook his head. "Already they are blaming our government."

Best to appear sympathetic, Frank thought.

"The Kremlin always gets blamed for everything."

The two men left the airport terminal and walked through a parking lot where gypsy cabbies stood by their cars and smoked cigarettes. The driver led Frank to his Lada C-5. He put Frank's garment bag and laptop in the trunk. Unseen by Frank, the driver unzipped the garment bag and sprayed a fine, dry mist from a small pressurized can onto Frank's clothes and the outside of the laptop bag. It was an odorless mist containing nanotaggats, a mixture of unique synthetic DNA and electromagnetic wave-transmitting smart dust that enabled both identification and tracking of subjects by intelligence units. Once sprayed on a surface, the mist was visible only under ultraviolet light. The driver sat down in the car, reached over and unlocked the front passenger door. Frank opened it, slid into the seat and placed the leather grip on the floor.

The driver pulled the Lada out of the parking lot and exited Sheremetyevo. He took out a pack of British Dunhills, shook a few cigarettes forward and offered one to his passenger. Scolding himself, Frank took the cigarette. The driver held a Ronson flame beneath it, then lit his own. Smoking for the first time in years, Frank took a slow drag and exhaled.

The driver switched from the Russian language's formal

mode to the informal style of speech and introduced himself. "I'm Sasha. What's your name?"

Frank saw no need to use an alias. "I'm Frank."

He gestured at the pack of Dunhills on the dashboard. "All the Moscow drivers used to smoke Marlboros."

Sasha responded with an edge. "We no longer believe that American products are the best in the world."

Frank didn't press the point. He took another long drag. "The last time I had a cigarette was when Obama first visited Russia in 2009."

"His first and only visit."

Frank let this dig go. To pursue it would lead to discussion of the recent deterioration in US-Russian relations, the Russian gambit in Ukraine and the Kremlin's military efforts to prop up Assad in Syria.

As the Lada approached Pushkin Square, Frank peered out the window at the Macho Grill. Now a Brazilian cabaret and churrasco restaurant, it had been the Shangri-La Casino, the city's gaudiest post-Communist gambling hub. It opened shortly after Frank arrived in 1999, becoming an overnight sensation and spawning many imitators. Frank's article the next year about the burgeoning casinos heralding the triumph of Russian capitalism was bannered atop a Sunday front of the *Register*. With newspapers belatedly pushing their online content, it attracted a record number of web hits. As part of Frank's preparation for the article, Viktor Romanov had led him on a riotous night of "reporting" at the Shangri-La, where Frank dropped a week's pay playing blackjack and drank a half dozen shots of Stoli with Viktor. Though Frank was always wary of befriending Russians, he'd viewed that evening as a fun and fairly innocent journalistic outing with a reasonably trustworthy chum.

Back then, the nighttime streets of Moscow were lined with hookers in sequined dresses and overpriced boutiques selling the latest fashions from Paris and Milan. With the global recession that started in 2008 and the squeeze on Russia's oil profits, its capital city retrenched from those early post-Communist days of ostentatious display. There were still plenty of prostitutes, still expensive shops, still "ruble billionaires," but their exuberant glitz had dimmed.

In July 2009, when Frank accompanied Obama to Russia, the American president's visit was overshadowed for many Muscovites. Putin had made good on his antigambling threats, and all the casinos had just been closed. In his interviews, Frank had difficulty persuading Russians to focus on Obama or their country's ties with America. All they wanted to talk about was the shuttered gaming spots abandoned like giant seashells strewn across the capital. During a short break in his work one afternoon, Frank had gone to see Mikhail Gusov. Normally affable, Mikhail met Frank in the darkened interior of the Samovar, the casino he had opened two years earlier to great success. Although Mikhail was transforming it into a fancy dinner club, he was bitter about the gambling ban. Even so, he'd given Frank no hint then of his emerging political activities—certainly nothing remotely suggesting that he would form a major opposition party and launch a long-shot campaign for the presidential election in March 2018.

Concurrent with the White House campaign back home,

the demonstrations over allegations of rigged Russian voting were in high gear. The election was almost two years away, but Gusov was already working hard, flying around the vast country, addressing rallies and running TV ads. In the media spots, still a rare practice in Russia, Gusov warned of a return to Soviet dictatorship.

Frank checked the time. Given Mikhail's hectic schedule and his own urgent tasks, he doubted that he and his old poker pal would manage to meet this trip; perhaps he'd try calling him for a quick hello.

Just a few blocks from the Hotel National, Frank used a reporting move that he thought of as a journalistic Hail Mary pass.

"What do you think of the rumors that the Russians had something to do with the assassination attempt on Stuart Roberts?"

Sasha pulled the Lada to the curb outside the National. For a moment, Frank thought he was going to ignore the question. Then he spoke. "Life has changed a lot on the surface since you lived here. But beneath the surface, things aren't so different."

Frank pushed the envelope. "The KGB simply changed its name to the FSB."

Sasha looked directly at Frank. "It's common knowledge that the Kremlin still controls the intelligence apparatus, not to mention the criminal investigative agencies."

Frank had nothing to lose. "Do you think your government would possibly try to take out an American presidential candidate?"

Sasha was out of patience. "Those are your words, not mine."

With that, Sasha left the car, opened the trunk and gave Frank his bags. Frank pulled 4,000 rubles from his wallet and handed them to Sasha.

As Frank took his bags and began to walk to the hotel entrance, Sasha abruptly said, "Be careful."

CHAPTER 13

MOSCOW

FRANK WOKE EARLY the next morning. His room in the Hotel National was more lavish than he'd expected. After a quick shower, he shaved and put on a grey polo shirt, a pair of khakis and a navy blue blazer. Viktor had told him to come straight to *Kapital's* offices, but Frank ordered breakfast from room service. He had some important calls to make.

Frank was going to have to do what he'd always done: go out and talk with as many people as possible, ask a hundred questions and hope that in one or two of the answers, there might be at least a hint of revelation. Only one person besides Stuart could provide a firsthand account of his 2006 meeting with Mikhail—Gusov himself.

Gusov, however, was traveling the vast country, leading campaign rallies for the 2018 elections. Putin had become prime minister in 2008, ostensibly bequeathing power to his hand-picked successor as president, Dmitry Medvedev, but their countrymen knew who really ruled the country. Their suspicions were confirmed in May 2012 when Putin reassumed the presidency after a fraud-filled election. Many Russians liked Putin's no-nonsense leadership, and he now controlled nearly all the levers of power.

While eating breakfast, Frank researched Mikhail's itinerary online. Gusov was holding a rally that day in southwestern Siberia, with an afternoon event in Novosibirsk, a regional capital not far from Mongolia. He would fly in the evening to Pyatigorsk and address a Wednesday morning rally in the northern Caucasus slice of southern Russia wedged between the Black and Caspian Seas. His schedule beyond Wednesday wasn't available "for security reasons," according to a report by Interfax, a Russian news agency that had been fearlessly independent in its early days under Gorbachev, but which now toed the Kremlin line.

Given Mikhail's frenetic travels, Frank wasn't optimistic about catching up with him. The reporter took the cell phone he'd rented at a telecommunications boutique in the National's lobby and punched in his last cell number for Mikhail. It was three years old, so Frank was happy when he heard his old friend's voice on the recording.

Frank spoke in Russian. "Misha, Comrade Adams reporting for duty. I am in Moscow on a minor journalistic mission. I have been following your recent activities with great interest. I know how busy you are, and I will not be offended in the least if your schedule doesn't afford us an opportunity to meet. I'll be in Moscow for the next week. My cell phone number while I'm here is 978-5801-3479. If you can find a few minutes, I would be delighted to talk with you."

His next call was to the most knowledgeable source Frank knew to find out what was really going on in Russia's rapidly changing oil industry.

Sergei Yemelin's phone rang as he sat at his desk in his office suite high above the streets of Moscow. The Russian oil consultant didn't recognize the incoming phone number, but he suspected who the caller might be. Lisa had told him that Frank was on his way to look into Stuart Roberts's activities in Russia. Thanks in large measure to Lisa, Yemelin had longstanding ties with Roberts and had been one of Frank's best sources in Moscow. Lisa had asked Yemelin to help Frank in his reporting but to keep her role secret from her ex-husband.

Yemelin flicked his finger across the screen to put his phone on speaker. "Seryozha, is that you?"

Yemelin pretended as if he didn't recognize Frank's voice. "Yes, who is this?"

"Sergei, it's Frank. Frank Adams. I've just arrived in Moscow."

Yemelin feigned surprise. "That's wonderful, Frank! I read your excellent coverage of the attempted assassination of Stuart. I feel so badly for him, but I'm glad it wasn't worse. What brings you here?"

"Can I tell you in person? I'd like to meet with you if you can fit me in."

Yemelin thought it would be wise to let Frank talk with others before meeting with him and was hoping to put him off for a few days. "Let me check my calendar. Give me a minute."

Yemelin placed Frank on hold and read some recent

e-mails on his desk PC. He resumed their conversation. "Can you come to my office at four tomorrow?"

"That is terrific, Seryozha, I am really looking forward to seeing you!"

After hanging up with Frank, Yemelin spent ten minutes answering an e-mail from a Chinese client seeking his advice on investing in a start-up oil dig near Mongolia in eastern Siberia. Yemelin told the client that if he didn't mind waiting five years for the project to begin producing oil and become profitable, the stock price was low and it would be smart to get in on the ground floor. Once the e-mail cleared his screen, Yemelin pressed a small button on the underside of his desk. A wall panel across his office slid open. He rose, walked through the opening and heard the panel close behind him.

The consultant stood in a bare space the size of a large walk-in closet with soundproof walls. He approached a security device and entered a ten-digit code. A green light flashed and the panel opened. Yemelin removed an Iridium secure phone from the safe. He punched in the number of Lisa's satellite phone.

Unknown to him, Lisa was sitting in the fortified underground bunker of the US Embassy on Novinsky Boulevard off the Garden Ring circle three kilometers west of the Kremlin. Her satellite phone received transmissions via a wire antenna along the edge of the embassy's roof.

Lisa linked Yemelin's call to a video conference program and saw his face on the fifty-two-inch screen embedded in a wall of the bunker.

"Sergei, it's good to talk with you again."

Seryozha, as Yemelin's friends called him, had worked in the Oil Ministry before the collapse of Communism and before Viktor Romanov or Svetlana Lutrova arrived for their covert assignments in the post-Soviet Ministry. During the chaos and corruption of the 1990s under the tumultuous rule of Boris Yeltsin, Yemelin had made a smooth transition on his country's bumpy road to bandit capitalism. He understood better than most that the staid days of the state-run Oil Ministry, with its five-year production plans and steady but unspectacular output of crude, were over. Foreign oil behemoths had lined up to pour billions into the world's biggest untapped reserves of crude. The epicenter of the action would be the Caspian Sea.

In the Soviet era's dying years, Yemelin had attended the Moscow State Geological Prospecting Academy, an elite university that was among the first in Russia to do joint research with American and European scientists, some of them employed by the Big Oil companies in the United States. In 1990, less than eighteen months before the Soviet red flag was lowered for the last time from above the Kremlin, Yemelin received a mechanical engineering degree with dual specializations in deep-well drilling and pipeline construction. After taking a job as a surveyor with the Ministry of Oil and Gas, he spent two years traveling widely among new oil fields.

Yemelin's work took him to the Timan-Pechora Basin eighteen hundred kilometers north of Moscow, above the Arctic Circle near the Barents Sea. He played a key role in preparing the basin's oil fields for their privatization, persuading foreign firms that they could eventually produce two billion barrels of crude. After Yeltsin privatized the country's entire oil sector in November 1992, Yemelin was the point man in a joint venture the Russian government launched to develop Timan-Pechora with Texaco, Exxon, Amoco and the Norwegian company Norsk Hydro. When Yeltsin and Bill Clinton met in Naples, Italy, on September 24, 1994, Yemelin and other members of the Russian delegation joined their American counterparts as the two leaders signed a joint statement of cooperation on the ambitious project.

With that feather in his cap, Yemelin directed similar oil and gas development initiatives in Siberia and the European Russia fields west of the Urals. Then, as the new millennium approached, he turned his focus to the Caspian Sea. His innovative surveying techniques led to the discovery of the massive Kashagan reserves in May 2000. Over the next few years, Yemelin made numerous trips between Moscow and the Caspian, earning a reputation as Russia's "oil diplomat." He worked with government scientists and private prospectors from around the globe, all of them eager to tap new energy sources and free themselves of the Arabs' stranglehold in the Middle East.

Yemelin turned down lucrative job offers from oil firms, Russian and foreign alike, as another plan took shape in his mind. Instead of tying his future to the fortunes of one company, he decided to leave the Oil Ministry in 2005 and market himself as an energy consultant. With few rivals who could match his combination of elite theoretical training and extensive field work, Yemelin became a leading authority on Russian oil and natural gas development. He enjoyed a particular expertise in the burgeoning Caspian market.

Stuart Roberts first met Yemelin in 2000, when the ambassador traveled to Baku, Azerbaijan, to greet senior managers of the American oil giants flooding into the Caspian region to exploit the newly discovered Kashagan reserves. Yemelin's deep knowledge impressed Roberts, and the two men became close professional associates. Until his departure from Moscow in 2002 and during return trips, Yemelin schooled Roberts in the technical aspects of oil production and in the dark political currents of the Caspian region split among seven countries ranging from Russia, Azerbaijan and Kazakhstan to Georgia and Iran. He helped Roberts navigate the ancient region's local governments with their shadowy ties to foreign agents and criminal syndicates.

Yemelin calculated that cultivating a relationship with one senior US diplomat would pay more dividends than befriending twenty American oil executives. Yemelin's faith was redeemed as Roberts became a director of ExxonMobil in 2003 and laid the groundwork for a high-level political career. By 2006, Roberts was running for the United States Senate when he arrived in Moscow on an unpublicized visit that followed his heavily covered trip to Israel.

Over the years, maintaining her NOC status, Lisa had infrequent contact with Langley and its agents.

One of the rare meetings was in 2006 when Harrison Jenkins had shown up unannounced in Los Angeles. They'd met at the reservoir in Elysian Park just west of I-5 near

Dodger Stadium. He was no longer DCI but maintained broad ties within the intelligence community. After a few pleasantries, he surprised her by saying he was sorry about her pending divorce. Jenkins then asked how her Russia work had gone since her relocation back home to California. When she mentioned that Yemelin had become a private oil consultant in 2005, he posed the same question to her that she had raised eight years earlier in his office: had the Russian been placed directly on Langley's payroll?

Lisa explained the hybrid arrangement she'd devised: Yemelin was getting paid by Langley; he just didn't know it.

Jenkins had nodded approvingly: hiring a Russian mole without the risk of exposing her covert status or even informing him that he was employed by US spymasters. It was just like Lisa Hawkes to come up with such an ingenious approach. Jenkins had made the right choice in choosing her for the NOC assignment.

Now, Lisa decided there was no need to tell Yemelin that she was back in country for the first time in more than a decade. He began the conversation. "Lisa, I thought I'd update you on our discussion yesterday. Frank called me a short while ago and requested a personal interview. We set it up for tomorrow in my office."

"Excellent, Sergei. Did he tell you why he wants to see you?"

"No. He said he preferred to tell me in person."

Lisa was glad that Frank was being careful. God knows how many governments had been listening in on his chat with

Sergei. Many people still labored under the misapprehension that intelligence agencies didn't have the capacity to tap cell phones. A new generation of satellite monitoring equipment had removed that barrier.

"Frank will undoubtedly grill you about Roberts. We would like you to cooperate fully. Answer his questions as completely and forthrightly as you can."

There was a pause. "Should I tell him everything I know?"

Lisa laughed. Yemelin was one of the few Russians who could handle American-style teasing. "Sergei, do you mean everything you've told me about Stuart's activities over there? Or are you including the things you haven't told me?"

Sergei gave as well as he took. "Lisa, I hold no secrets from you."

Yemelin asked a question he'd posed to her periodically. "Why are your bosses at AmeriCon so interested in Roberts?"

Lisa had decided she trusted Yemelin enough to share some sensitive background with him. "Well, Senator Roberts might be our next president, and it's always beneficial to have a thorough knowledge of a powerful person's background. Aside from politics, we suspect that Stuart is doing business with some of our foreign competitors. As plugged in as you are, you may not know all the deals he's involved in. Frank is a top-notch investigative reporter. If anyone can get to the bottom of Stuart's activities over there, he can. I'd like you to be of all possible assistance to him."

Yemelin knew nothing about Operation Long Shadow—though as audacious as it was, he might, as a Russian, have found nothing surprising in an undercover scheme to plant a man in the White House. That, too, would have fit neatly into his skewed understanding of how America operated at the highest levels. The attempted assassination of Roberts had coalesced in Lisa all her longstanding misgivings about her father's rogue operation. Even with the perfect stooge, the plan carried unfathomable risk. And the Roberts hit had compounded the suspicions Lisa always harbored about the smooth Californian. She wasn't about to allow a deeply flawed man to bring down her father—and possibly devastate the Agency as well, despite Thomas's efforts to insulate Langley.

Beyond coaching Yemelin, Lisa was intent on doing everything in her power to ensure Frank's reporting success in Russia.

If she'd stopped to reflect, Lisa would have known that she had other motives for helping Frank. She'd never stopped blaming herself for their breakup. Yes, he'd slept with Svetlana, and probably others. Far worse, though, she'd come to understand that her NOC status had doomed their marriage. It had required one deception that turned into a dozen falsehoods that became a hundred lies. Most of them would have been innocuous alone, but woven together over time they formed a damaging tapestry of deceit. As part of it, Lisa had tacitly accepted Frank's vodka binges with his sources because he inevitably shared details of his reporting that she found useful in her work with AmeriCon Energy—and in her undercover role.

Lisa didn't need to search inside herself to know the most important thing: she still had strong feelings for Frank. More than he realized, this reporting trip to Moscow put him at risk.

Lisa wanted to protect whatever Frank discovered about Roberts, and she wanted to safeguard her ex-husband. She had some means at her disposal to accomplish both tasks.

Yemelin posed a final question to Lisa. "Should I tell Frank that I am still on retainer with Roberts?"

Lisa had prepared her answer. "Make sure you tell him that."

CHAPTER 14

MOSCOW

EMERGING OUTDOORS FROM Hotel National, Frank enjoyed the bright sun on his face. Moscow didn't have the spectacular summertime "White Nights" of St. Petersburg, but it was far enough to the north, about the same latitude as Hudson Bay in Canada, so that on this July day the sun wouldn't set until ten o'clock. Like other businesses in the city, *Kapital* had adjusted its work hours to accommodate the summer skies. The staff arrived at the newspaper's downtown offices around noon and stayed late. The next day, Wednesday, was the weekly print publication day for *Kapital*, so the reporters and editors would be working furiously, but Viktor had insisted that Frank come anyway.

Frank headed off to the Komsomolskaya Metro station a few blocks away. He'd gotten to know the subway system well during his posting. Standing in a train car, holding one of the seat rails for balance, he'd found that he could learn a lot about Russians' everyday lives by listening to their chatter as the massive Soviet-era concrete apartment buildings and the newly emerging billboards sped by outside the dusty windows. He'd developed a type of audio shorthand: if he heard the same observation about life or government or personalities voiced in three conversations on three different trains, he took the perspective as broadly representative of public opinion and found places to include it in his articles. The method wasn't scientific, yet he thought it reliable enough as a rough gauge of how Russians felt.

Before boarding the Metro, Frank stopped at Komsomolskaya Square. Unlike so many other streets and places, this broad plaza had retained its Soviet name for "Young Pioneers." Frank studied the human tableau. Couples kissed on concrete benches. Mothers pushed baby carriages. A *babushka*—old lady—sold *pirozhki*, the savory warm buns filled with cabbage, mushrooms or meat.

Frank crossed the square and entered the Metro station. He was pleasantly surprised to find that he could now use his credit card in the ticket vending machine. Inserting his American Express card, he punched in 30,000 rubles, an amount that should cover his time in Moscow, and waited for the machine to dispense his ticket. Walking through the station, he was stunned once more by how Stalin, a dictator ruling a vast half-famished country in the 1930s, could have spent so many millions to build such impressive subway stations. Komsomolskaya was among the most magnificent. Frank savored the high vaulted ceiling painted a beautiful dark yellow with gold-and-crystal chandeliers and inlaid frescos of Cossacks on horses framed by ornate white molding. He shook his head and rode the steep elevator a hundred meters down to the tracks.

It was only when he reached the platform deep beneath the streets that Frank sensed he was being followed. A shabby-looking woman in her sixties stood to his left about fifty meters along the platform. Frank realized that he'd seen her twenty minutes earlier at Komsomolskaya Square, reading the *Izvestia* newspaper on a stone bench. It could be a coincidence that they'd entered the Metro station at the same time, descended on the same escalator and were now waiting for the same red Sokolnicheskaya Line train headed toward Lenin Hills. Frank did the math: two lines at Komsomolskaya station, each with trains moving in opposite directions; there were four options, and she'd chosen the same one he had, a 25 percent chance of it being coincidental. Frank decided to test the woman. When a train arrived, she got on the same car he boarded, two doors down at the rear. Frank rode the train four stops to the Teatralnaya station, got off and transferred to the green line; again she traversed the same route and boarded the other end of his car. Frank's pulse quickened as he weighed his next move. He traveled one long stretch to the Novokuznetskaya station. This was the stop closest to the *Kapital* offices, but instead of leaving the station Frank walked quickly through a long passageway to the connecting Tretyakovska station on the orange Kaluzhko-Rizhskaya line.

Growing more alarmed, Frank glanced to his left and saw the woman on the platform. It was time to lose her. The next train that arrived was northbound in the direction of

Medvedkovo, a worker-bee complex of apartments built in the 1960s on the city outskirts. Frank boarded it and sat at the end of the steel bench with brown leather back and rump pads. He purposely chose a seat near the doors. He opened his issue of *Kapital* and appeared to become engrossed in reading. Frank didn't look up as the train stopped at Kitai-Gorod station, then hurtled on to Turgenevskaya station. After two more stops, the train sped toward the Prospekt Mira hub station where travelers could connect to the brown circle line that ringed Moscow.

Frank was in luck. A throng of teenagers, jabbering excitedly with some Russian slang he didn't know, stood waiting to get off. When the train came to a stop, the doors opened. In typical fashion, the Russians on the platform didn't let the teens and other passengers leave the car before pummeling forward into the car. Frank waited a minute as the human gridlock eased amid shoves and shouts and grumbling. Just as the doors started to close, he sprang from his seat, lowered his head and pushed through a group of latecomers boarding the train. As the doors slid shut, Frank looked back and saw the woman who'd been tailing him through the window, still seated at the other end of his car. When their eyes caught for a moment, she seemed to give a slight nod before the train rumbled off.

Frank rode the escalator up to the Prospekt Mir station and hurried out to the street. Soon he stood on the busy boulevard, five kilometers away from the *Kapital* offices. He hailed a cab and directed the driver to take him to Bolshaya Ordynka Street. Leaving the taxi, he headed north along the crowded thoroughfare, toward the Vodootvodny Kanal, a small fork of the Moscow River. Following Viktor's directions, Frank reached a tobacco shop, turned right into an alley and walked to the back. There he saw a gold sign with *Kapital* in bold green letters. Later that night he would focus on who might be following him and why; for now, he told himself to be more careful.

Kapital, the weekly newspaper where Viktor was the top investigative reporter, had started publishing in December 1989, some forty months after Mikhail Gorbachev announced his policy of *glasnost*, or "openness," to great acclaim in the West and to great skepticism among Russians. It was a clever choice of names for a newspaper claiming to be the country's first independent business publication. The name was, first and foremost, an ironic echo of *Das Kapital*, Karl Marx's famous 1867 indictment of capitalism that every Soviet schoolchild was assigned in the eighth grade. As the oligarchs accumulated their billions in the 1990s, the weekly became a must read for Russia's newly emboldened businessmen eager to follow one another's exploits. Its circulation peaked at 700,000 in 1992 on the crest of public fascination with the grotesquely rich tycoons before settling at 300,000 readers by century's turn. It stayed at that level even with the encroachment of the Internet, while gaining 10 million online page views per month at www. kapital.ru. *Kapital's* core of bright, young reporters thought of the paper as their country's version of the *Wall Street Journal*. So well-connected were they that Berezovsky, Smolensky and the other Big Seven oligarchs often opened the pages of

Kapital to learn surprising secrets about their own sprawling enterprises.

By 2008, Russia had eighty-seven billionaires, more than any other country. Many became mere multimillionaires a year later after the global recession arrived, oil revenues plunged, the stock market tumbled and the ruble took a beating in world currency exchanges. Moscow fell behind New York and London as the cities with the most billionaires.

Viktor had the cell phone numbers of all but five of the Russian capital's thirty-two billionaires. As his reputation grew, he'd become an information broker. The tycoons had an insatiable curiosity about each other's activities, and they frequently called or texted Viktor to share tips or ask questions about a rival. Viktor walked a tightrope of trust, maintaining his pledges of confidentiality from off-the-record parts of these exchanges while passing on tidbits of information that didn't violate his word. He often called one of the billionaires in what appeared to be a casual conversation. Following his source's lead, he would inevitably field questions about a business competitor.

Had Viktor heard that Mikhail Fridman, a Ukrainian-born Jew whose Alfa Bank had the largest capital reserves, was considering joining other oligarchs in exile?

What about the rumors that steel magnate Roman Abramovich's ex-wife had dragged him back into divorce court, complaining that the $1 million a month she got from him wasn't enough to support her and their five children?

Was it true that Mikhail Prokhorov, the "bachelor billion-

aire" who'd made a fortune with stock trades, was weighing a bid to buy the New Jersey Nets basketball team in America?

Most of the time, Viktor could answer the inquiries while protecting his sources. He was careful not to ask too many questions of his own, lest he appear overly inquisitive. Russians, and rich Russians all the more so, loved to gossip and boast. Viktor knew that most of the time, if he was patient, he would get the answers to his queries without even having to ask them.

Frank entered *Kapital's* office to be greeted by a pretty receptionist with auburn hair falling to her shoulders and fashionable glasses with rectangular frames.

"I have an appointment with Viktor Romanov."

"Your name, sir?"

"Frank Adams."

As the receptionist dialed an extension on her phone and spoke into its wireless headset, Frank tucked in his shirt and wiped the sweat from his brow.

"Viktor Ivanovich, a gentleman by the name of Frank Adams is here to see you."

In a minute, Viktor came down the stairs. He embraced Frank, then stood back from him. "You're looking disheveled, Frank! Did you run here?"

Frank decided not to tell Viktor about the tail. "Just got a late start, so I had to rush a bit."

The two friends walked up three flights and went down a hallway to a large room with high windows. Frank recognized a newsroom on deadline: Reporters stared intently at their computer screens and pounded away on keyboards. Editors huddled in office doorways. One young journalist hollered across the room toward an editor's office.

"The Kremlin has arrested another political opponent!"

From a few desks over came a sardonic reply. "Is that still considered news?"

As Viktor joined his colleagues in laughter, he beckoned Frank to follow him. "Come, I want to introduce you to my editor."

They crossed the room and entered a corner office. The editor rose from his desk and walked toward them.

"Pyotor Maximovich, this is my friend Frank Adams—the *Los Angeles Register* reporter I told you about."

"Very pleased to meet you, Mr. Adams. I am sorry about the assassination attempt on Stuart Roberts. What brings you to Moscow?"

Frank and Viktor exchanged glances. Viktor interjected some humor before Frank could respond. "Frank has always had an exaggerated opinion of my capabilities as a journalist."

Pyotor nodded. He knew Viktor well enough to understand that if more details of the American's visit were to be forthcoming, they would have to wait until the editor and his reporter were alone.

Pyotor handed a business card to Frank. "Our newspapers do not compete. If I can help you while you are in Russia, feel free to contact me."

Frank wondered if in the Internet age the editor really believed that their papers didn't compete. But he kept his thoughts to himself, took a card from his wallet and gave it to Pyotor. "Thank you."

Frank and Viktor left the editor's office, crossed the newsroom and entered Viktor's smaller office.

Frank whistled. "You've really moved up in the world. You have your own office."

"It probably could fit in a corner of your office."

Viktor's English had become quite good during his three-year assignment to London, but he and Frank naturally spoke in Russian with each other.

Frank laughed. "I don't have an office. In America, only the top editors get them."

"Lenin was right! You see how much better we working-class stiffs have it in Russia than you poor slobs in America?"

Viktor clasped Frank on the shoulder. "When were you last in Moscow?"

"In 2009. Obama's first visit to Russia as president."

"Ah, right. 'Yes, we can!' Such a brilliant campaign slogan. It gave rise to a joke here in Moscow: what was Vladimir Putin's campaign slogan?"

Frank knew the answer just as Viktor provided it. "No, you can't!"

Frank laughed again. Viktor had always been a very funny fellow. "It's good to see you, Viktor. Unfortunately, we should get down to business."

Viktor sat at his desk and beckoned Frank toward the chair next to it. "Ah, you Americans—always working! So, I suppose you're too busy for a toast between old friends?"

Frank eyed the bottle of Stolichnaya that Viktor was

pulling out of a drawer. He filled two shot glasses with vodka. Frank raised his hand and shook his head when Viktor offered him one of the glasses.

"I would love to join you, Viktor, but I stopped drinking a few years ago."

"You—stopped drinking? What's that about?"

"I'll tell you later."

Viktor shrugged and raised his glass. "To friendship!"

Viktor threw back the vodka and put his glass aside. He teased Frank about having become a teetotaler. "I hope this doesn't mean that our friendship is over, Frankie."

"Not at all, comrade. I authorize you to drink my share of vodka."

Viktor switched to English. "So, shall we speak in the language of Queen Victoria or Czar Nicholas?"

Frank responded in kind. "I fear that your English has outstripped my Russian, so let's go with English."

"Yes, my London posting after you left Moscow did help me finally learn English. But you'll have to put up with my occasional queer British expressions."

Viktor's English was excellent, though he spoke with a hybrid Russian-British accent.

Frank adopted his best London brogue. "Jolly good show."

Viktor turned serious. "I'm glad you weren't hurt in the explosion at Roberts's speech."

"I was lucky. Several of my friends who were near me were seriously hurt. A *Chicago Tribune* reporter was killed. A *Newsweek* photographer had multiple wounds. Any one of us could have been hit."

"And here you are in Moscow just a few days later."

Frank and Viktor began a complex psychological dance. They wanted to learn what the other knew, but each withheld more than he shared. Frank knew a great deal about Stuart's life in the United States; Viktor knew about his work in Moscow as ambassador and his subsequent dealings in Russia. The two reporters felt they could help each other; neither wanted an equal exchange.

Using his customary light touch, Viktor spoke first. "When we were playing cards at your flat, who would have thought that two of our poker pals would become prominent politicians?"

Frank nodded. "I've been so busy covering the Roberts campaign, I haven't been able to follow Mikhail's presidential campaign very closely."

"I respect Misha, but this crusade of his won't go anywhere in the end."

Frank pondered Viktor's assessment. "Is it really that bad here? You make it sound like the democracy that's developed is just a shell game."

Viktor smiled. "Democracy? You mean democracy that resembles American democracy even remotely? That, my friend, has never existed in Russia."

"Mikhail must understand this. Why is he challenging the Kremlin?"

"We haven't talked in quite a while. But we had a long conversation early last year. He spoke at length about why he'd decided to enter politics and form the Free Russia Party. It was hard for me to tell whether his main motivation was moral—to save the cause of freedom in his homeland—or financial. He was still very upset about his casino getting shut down. He felt that if the Kremlin could do that, his oil business wasn't secure either. He believed that the 2012 election results were fraudulent. And he saw the 2014 invasion of Ukraine as the return of Soviet imperialism. Now in his campaign speeches, he is warning about Syria becoming another Afghanistan for Russia."

Mikhail had told Viktor other things as well, but he wouldn't share them with Frank.

The American, sensing his Russian friend's reluctance to provide more details about Mikhail's political activities, steered their talk in a new direction. "I apologize that I didn't read your investigative articles about the Russian Oil Ministry when they were published. I've been on the road with Roberts virtually nonstop the last year."

Viktor laughed. "No need to apologize! My own mother doesn't even read my articles!"

"Neither does mine!"

Frank had learned long ago that bylines were important only to journalists. Most readers never noticed them.

Frank pursued his new line of inquiry. "In preparing for my trip here, I was finally able to read your entire series on the Russian Oil Ministry. It's outstanding work."

"Thank you, comrade. Coming from you, that is high praise indeed."

Frank bored in. His ultimate target was Roberts, the then-Senate candidate's secret journey to Moscow in 2006 and his meeting with Gusov.

With as skilled a reporter as Viktor, Frank knew better

than to take a direct path to Roberts. "You've done a brilliant job of discovering the missing oil revenues, but I take it that the source of the diverted funds is still a mystery."

Viktor continued his strategy of partial disclosure. "I have some theories, but nothing I can publish yet."

Frank tacked again. "You worked at the Oil Ministry for a long time. You must still have some sources there."

Viktor shrugged. "A few. They're as perplexed as everyone else about the disappearance of so much money. Or so they say."

"I couldn't help but notice that none of your articles mention Mikhail. Yet the two of you became good friends at our poker games, and then he became a wealthy oilman. His omission from your articles makes me wonder."

Viktor parried back. "Why's that?"

"Sometimes the names of my best sources never see the light of day."

Viktor was silent. There was no harm in telling Frank a little more about his relationship with Gusov. "After you left Moscow, I remained at the Oil Ministry as an analyst for five years. During that period, Mikhail developed his first oil field in the Caucasus. Beyond our friendship, our relationship was mutually beneficial. It was helpful for him to know someone inside the Ministry. From time to time, he would call me for help getting past a bureaucratic snag or to seek my advice on a new venture he was considering. From my side, it was useful to know a prospering oilman on the front lines who could keep me abreast of the industry's new challenges. And it didn't hurt to be filled in on the latest inside rumors about his competitors."

"How did you make the switch to journalism?"

Viktor understood that Frank's interest in his biography wasn't solely personal. "Five years ago Sergei Zhukovsky, the publisher of *Kapital*, recruited me. He knew I'd been a source for Oleg Pavlov, the paper's top oil industry reporter. Pavlov had left *Kapital* to join a venture capital firm. My work at the Ministry had become less interesting to me as the explosive growth of our oil industry leveled off. When Zhukovsky offered to triple my salary and make me the lead investigative reporter, I couldn't refuse."

"So, you went from being an insider source to a reporter in need of sources. Mikhail must have become even more helpful to you."

Viktor stood up. He spoke with his trademark facetious tone. "You are doing a good job, my friend, but I'm afraid our interview is over for today." He gestured toward the newsroom still humming with activity. "I need to see if my services are needed by my colleagues. I trust you remember where I live?"

Frank nodded as he rose from the chair. "The small street off Tverskaya. Just around the corner from the Pushkin Café."

"Right. I should be home by ten-thirty. Why don't you come by and we can continue our conversation in a more comfortable setting?"

The two reporters left Viktor's office. The Russian shook the American's hand. "It's very good to see you, Frank. Can you find your way out?"

"Sure."

With that, Viktor released Frank's grip and headed off to join a group of reporters and editors huddled around Pyotor Maximovich in the center of the newsroom.

Frank left the office and went out to the street. He'd had enough excitement on the Metro for one day, so he hailed a cab. After a few blocks, Frank noticed a gold Volga that seemed to be following them. He leaned forward and instructed the driver, "Turn right at the next corner."

Frank watched through the back window of the cab as the Volga, two cars behind the taxi, executed a right and was now one car back. He told the driver, "I think we are being followed by a gold car. Could you please take the side streets to the Hotel National?"

With the meter running, the driver was happy to make numerous diversions on the trip to the hotel. After ten minutes they lost the Volga, but Frank spent the next twenty minutes nervously examining every vehicle in the cab's wake. When they arrived at the Hotel National, he quickly paid the driver and included a large tip. He jogged up the steps of the hotel, hurried through the lobby and went up to his room.

CHAPTER 15

MOSCOW

F RANK OPENED THE door to his hotel room and stepped in. He needed to decompress. He couldn't believe that he'd been so naïve to think that he could enter Russia simply as a tourist. Looking back at his encounter with the Border Service officers, Frank realized that he hadn't fooled anyone. They were watching him, following him, waiting for him to make a mistake. He poured himself a glass of sparkling water and gazed through the bay windows of his corner suite.

The view of the Kremlin's red-brick walls and tower rising over Lenin's Tomb never grew old for Frank. Russians mingled with tourists on Red Square outside the famous fortress. Marriott, Hilton and the other big chains had built or renovated hotels that catered to business travelers. Once inside them you may as well have been in New York or Chicago; their rooms, restaurants and fitness centers were interchangeable.

Frank preferred the National. It and the Metropol two blocks away were the only hotels left from the days of the czars. When Teddy Roosevelt visited Moscow in 1906 on a European tour to celebrate his receipt of the Nobel Peace Prize, Czar Nicholas II had placed him in the National's Imperial Suite, occupying the entire third floor. Twelve years later, after Vladimir Lenin's Bolshevik forces had executed Nicholas, the new Soviet leader moved into Room 107 of the hotel. He wanted his post-Revolution government to make a clean break from the czarist reign. Nothing would demonstrate the change more than moving the vast country's capital from Saint Petersburg—the "window to the West" built on marshes two centuries earlier by Peter the Great—back to Moscow. Lenin and his Bolshevik brothers lived at the National while the Kremlin's offices and living quarters underwent renovation to prepare it as the seat of Soviet power.

Normally Frank had little appetite for luxury, but the National, restored to its original ornate glory, appealed to him as a reflection of Russian royal taste that had survived the soulless Soviet rule. His suite featured parquet floors, embroidered crimson curtains and gold-trimmed mahogany furniture shined to a high gloss. The lobby had ruby rugs and runners beneath alabaster cherubs clinging to marble Roman columns.

Frank's suite carried an absurd rack price of 70,000 rubles per night—more than $1,000—but he was paying far less. Evgeny Aisenyev, a cook at the US Embassy during Frank's Moscow posting, had become a friend over their spirited games on the consulate's basement squash court. During the Cold War, the State Department never allowed Russians to work at the Moscow embassy, but the ban was lifted in 1996 and Russians joined "locals" in other world capitals who made good money employed at US consulates. After Frank left Russia, Evgeny obtained his master of business administration in hotel management, hired on as a concierge at the National and climbed the hotel's ranks to become its general manager. For Frank's trip, he'd arranged a business suite for 15,000 rubles a day in exchange for a promise that the American journalist would try to fit in a squash match.

Frank had three hours before meeting Viktor at the Russian's flat. That would give him plenty of time to take a long shower and let the hot water relax his sore back from the plane ride. Then he would read a few Russian newspapers over dinner at the Babochka restaurant on Bolshaya Ordynka Street, one of his favorite eateries.

In forty minutes Frank was freshly shaved and dressed. Before he left the suite earlier in the day, he'd discovered that the room safe was broken. He hadn't taken his briefcase with him to Viktor's office, but faithful to Ken Nishimura's admonitions he made sure the xWave was with him at all times. He wanted to take his laptop to Viktor's flat, so he removed the xWave from his coat and placed it next to the computer in his briefcase.

As Frank closed the bag, something caught his eye. The outside pocket was halfway unzipped. Since losing his passport on a trip to Iraq in 2006 when he'd left the pocket open, Frank had been assiduous about making sure it was always zipped. He replayed his arrival at Sheremetyevo the previous evening. No one had touched his things when he went through customs, and Frank was sure the pocket was closed during his ride from the airport to the hotel. Then he noticed something else. The straps that held his laptop inside the briefcase were wrapped loosely around the computer. This, too, defied a resolute habit he'd learned the hard way: ever since his poorly secured laptop had fallen on an airport floor, he was fanatical about pulling the support straps tight each time he put the computer back in its case.

Frank's pulse raced again. He might have somehow ignored an ingrained habit once, but the odds of him making two such mistakes on the same day were small. Someone had been in his hotel suite during the four hours he'd been away visiting Viktor.

Even as he searched his room for more clues, Frank knew that he would find none. The intruder had been careful, though as it turned out not careful enough. Or was it possible that he had wanted to leave traces of his trespass? Just enough signs to make Frank wonder whether he was being paranoid. Perhaps the real purpose of the hotel break-in had been to deliver the same message the Kremlin had provided at the end of his posting: we cannot guarantee your safety.

No matter the motive, this episode, combined with the tail on the train and the gold Volga following his taxi, made Frank understand that he would have to expend considerable effort looking over his shoulder as he tried to uncover the hidden past of Stuart Roberts.

Frank shut the door to his suite, walked through the hallway, jogged down two flights of stairs and emerged from the hotel onto Mokhovaya Street. Squinting at the evening sunlight, he donned his sunglasses, walked three blocks to the

Borovitskaya Metro stop, removed his shades and took the long escalator down to the subway station.

Forty-five minutes later, uneasily assured that he hadn't been followed this time, Frank sat in Babochka restaurant. He ate a bowl of solyanka, his favorite Russian soup, and read *Izvestia*. His cell phone rang. Answering it, he was happy to hear Mikhail's voice.

"Frank, I only have a minute to talk. I was so glad to get your message, and I'm delighted that you're back in Russia. I would love to see you. I've decided to take next Monday off, return to Moscow and spend the day with my family. I'll spend the evening at the Samovar with my guests and employees. If you can come to the supper club at ten p.m., I'll carve out some time to meet with you."

Frank was surprised that what he said carried little tone of irony or tease. "I'm honored, Misha—I know how busy you are."

Mikhail scoffed. "You're an old friend, Frank! You and I don't stand on ceremony. But I do need to go. I look forward to seeing you."

With his salary of 500,000 rubles a month, Viktor could have afforded to live in one of the gated condo developments that had sprung up near central Moscow to cater to the capital's expanding number of prosperous professionals. But just as Frank liked staying at a historic hotel in view of the Kremlin, Viktor chose a pre-Soviet, century-old wooden building with six spacious flats off Tverskaya Street in a gentrified neighborhood of Old Moscow. After moving to the apartment in 2007, he'd bought a USB modem and subscribed to 4G WiMAX service from Yota, a Moscow start-up that was among the first communications firms in Europe to provide broadband Internet connections via microwave frequency bands.

Viktor had poured himself a glass of Stoli while waiting for Frank to arrive. The Russian wanted to test the American's resolve in having sworn off booze. Viktor offered a tumbler of the vodka to Frank as soon as he entered the flat.

Frank chuckled and declined once more. "You can stop trying to tempt me."

Viktor laughed, set the tumbler down and handed him a bottle of water. He beckoned for Frank to follow him into the living room. Like most Russian men, Viktor was proud of his ability to imbibe large quantities of vodka. Unlike most other Russians, Viktor knew his limit. Sometimes he exploited this advantage. Viktor would wait patiently, sitting at a bar, while one of the oligarchs or another well-placed source drank enough vodka to loosen his lips. Viktor had secured a number of scoops by obtaining information that sober men would not have divulged.

Now that Frank wasn't drinking, Viktor would have to use other tactics. As much as he liked Frank, he was certain the American was withholding his real reasons for making the trip. The *Los Angeles Register* didn't need to send its political reporter to Moscow in the heat of an American presidential campaign just to chase wild rumors of Russian involvement in a clumsy assassination attempt. Viktor knew the ways of the Kremlin far better than Frank. He knew how many inquisitive journalists at home and exiled critics abroad had been killed, their murders left unsolved. If the Russian government had wanted to take out Roberts, Viktor was certain he would be dead.

For his part, Frank had a more high-tech approach to the late-night meeting. He made sure to take his briefcase into Viktor's living room. Following his host, he felt the outline of the xWave inside it.

At half past midnight, the 750-milliter bottle of Stoli that Viktor had pulled from his freezer just before Frank's arrival stood barely touched on the coffee table. Half a loaf of dark rye bread was on the brightly colored, lacquered cutting board found in most Russian households. Frank half-reclined on the green microfiber couch. Viktor sat in his matching armchair kitty-corner from the couch across the table, the chair tilted partway back. The men had spent the past two hours sharing memories of their escapades together and trading journalism war stories. Having gingerly circled each other in Viktor's office, neither reporter wanted to reveal his interest in learning the other's secrets.

Finally, Frank offered an innocuous comment about the wounded American politician from California who'd been their poker partner. "Roberts has come a long way since he was the US ambassador and we all played cards together."

Viktor couldn't quite manage to make his response sound entirely in jest. "Well, that was his official title."

"What do you mean?"

Viktor chortled in mock disbelief. "Come on, you know that the people your government sends over here in those kinds of posts always work for the CIA."

"Is this claim based on your expert reporting or is it just one of those crazy conspiracies that you Russians are always dreaming up?"

Viktor's eyes gleamed. "Sometimes conspiracies have a way of coming true."

Frank pushed the envelope. "Hell, if Roberts worked for the CIA, why stop there? Maybe you worked for the old KGB?"

Viktor considered confessing at least part of his covert past, then thought better of it. There was no need to muddy the waters.

Frank's laptop sat on Viktor's living room table. An icon for the Yota service appeared in the corner of the screen. Frank double-clicked on the icon. Viktor gave him Yota's encryption code, and Frank glided online. Now, he and Viktor sat in the living room in the dead of night, connected to the world via their computers.

Viktor paid close attention to his HP Pavilion laptop on the coffee table, leaning forward from time to time to tap a few keystrokes or use the built-in mouse. Frank's Dell Inspiron rested on his thighs. He monitored the news on losangelesregister.com, clicking on a headline every now and then to read the top of an article.

The journalists' absorption with their computers offended neither of them. As world-class reporters riding the ever-faster electronic roller coaster of news, blogs and digital ranting, they were like emergency room doctors—on call 24/7, always ready to pounce on the latest leak or innuendo, start making calls, work their sources and do everything possible to ensure that their competitors didn't get a jump on them. If such commitment harmed their personal lives, that was the price they paid for holding glamorous jobs.

In fact, their intense engagement with their work had cost Frank and Viktor their marriages. Frank and Lisa, who had her own demanding job, spent so much time away from each other—or, when together, in their own worlds—that they woke up one day to realize they'd become strangers. For Viktor's part, he'd chosen Vera Razin as his wife because she was a traditional Russian woman who would keep house, wait in the interminable market lines, cook for him and cater to his other needs. The arrangement worked fine until it dawned on Viktor that his wife failed to meet his biggest need: being his intellectual partner, someone who cared as passionately as he did about the future of their country and followed the pressing issues of the day as closely as he did.

As much as the Internet revolution had put whole libraries at journalists' disposal, it created problems for them as well. Until the new millennium, the traditional limits of beat and border provided ample protections for their turf. A business reporter didn't have to worry about a political correspondent scooping him. A journalist in Hong Kong needn't be concerned with the digging by one of her counterparts in Washington.

For decades, beat reporters from around the globe had kept a distasteful secret from their editors: Whether based in foreign countries, covering the financial markets in New York or working at the White House, they were often friendly competitors. They traveled together, ate together, chased the same stories. The unspoken rule of thumb was that if one of your competitors needed a quote or some background information, you would provide it because you might find yourself in the same fix.

A second implicit guideline was that no one should get too creative with his reporting or writing. If a dozen reporters traveled with the US secretary of state in Asia or with the British foreign minister in America, it caused problems if one of them ran a lead that differed markedly from the others' "tops," the key first few paragraphs of an article. The outlier's editor would ask why the Associated Press or CNN or other major outlets had a different take on the story; meanwhile, the outlier's competitors would get urgent calls from their bosses inquiring if they could match the lone ranger's lead.

Except for the biggest exclusives, it was in nobody's interests to wander too far off the reservation. So you often could see journalists on the same beat calling quick huddles on the plane or in the media filing center. Amid the good-natured trash-talking, they were comparing notes, tossing out trial headlines, ensuring that their stories would be roughly equivalent.

That was why the articles on the front pages of the *Chicago Tribune* or the *New York Times*, the reports on the networks' evening news, often read and sounded the same. It wasn't because of reporters' inherent genius to all zero in on the same salient facts. Rather, it was due to the same "band of brothers" mentality shared by cops walking the street or soldiers sharing bunks in a platoon. The outlook was "us against the world." Like the police desk jockeys or the military brass far removed from danger, the editors back home were not to be trusted.

The exploding world of online news, however, had blown up the longstanding boundaries that made such cooperation possible. The traditional news cycle kept getting shorter as it went from days to hours to minutes. The shelf life of a lead kept shrinking as other reports quickly eclipsed it. Bloggers writing in their pajamas at home were almost as likely to make a splash as established correspondents. Journalists no longer had the luxury of knowing that the economics reporter in San Francisco didn't threaten their work covering Congress. Reporters on the same beat couldn't afford to share even minor bits of news. Each tidbit now was broken off, hyped and blogged and tweeted about as if it mattered more than it did.

So it was that Frank and Viktor, based in cities with an ocean between them, were wary of each other even as they broke bread and engaged in banter to renew their friendship.

For all their genuine mutual fondness, the trust between them was ephemeral. Each respected the other's talents enough to know that he wouldn't divulge his ultimate reporting target or any key information gathered along the way. Yet Frank and Viktor were both confident enough to believe that they might pry away small clues from each other and piece them together to form a vital link they might not find on their own.

What the two journalists didn't yet appreciate was that they would soon find themselves together in a dangerous web of international deception, one in which much more than their next exclusive would be at stake.

CHAPTER 16

Moscow

VIKTOR GLANCED AT his watch. It was almost two in the morning. He and Frank had caught each other up on their lives. Viktor had learned as a child that sugarcoating his demands, whether of adults or his playmates, increased the likelihood they would be met. Jovial by nature, he'd become skilled at leveraging this personality trait in all manner of personal and professional settings. Women, in particular, were disarmed, and sometimes disrobed, if you could turn your desire to bed them into a lighthearted wish. Sources, especially well-sauced ones, seemed to feel less threatened by a question bathed in laughter.

As Viktor zeroed in on the American's real motives for coming to Moscow, it was thus second nature for him to start with a hearty chuckle. "Comrade, now that we've let our hair down a little, I thought you might share a bit more about your current assignment with an old friend."

Frank raised his eyebrows. "Why would you think there's more to share?"

"The big story in the United States is the Republican presidential nominee-in-waiting lying in the hospital after an attempt on his life. But you're here."

Frank parried back. "That's precisely why I'm here."

"Meaning?"

"Roberts will be laid up for the next couple of weeks. With him out of action, there's not much for me to do in Los Angeles."

Viktor laughed. "Oh, come now! You're being entirely too modest. Do you really expect me to believe that right after a bomb almost blows up a White House candidate, one of America's most important newspapers is going to send its top political reporter halfway around the world?"

Frank suppressed a smirk but didn't respond.

"You know more about Stuart than any other journalist, and you've been on the campaign trail with him for a year! The last thing your editors would do after an assassination attempt is ship you away from the scene of the crime. You yourself were almost killed!"

Frank wasn't surprised that Viktor's instincts were on the money, but he wasn't about to tell his friend that this Moscow trip was his idea. And he certainly couldn't let Viktor know that it was a comment by the Russian himself, during their phone conversation just after the assassination attempt, which had triggered the American's interest and led him to Moscow.

Viktor knew about the secret rendezvous between Roberts and Gusov, yet he'd failed to report it. Mikhail had become a

Russian oil tycoon, but a major investigative series by Viktor didn't once mention his name. Was it possible that Viktor, among the most perceptive people Frank knew, simply didn't realize the potential significance of a secret dinner by two prominent men, one American and the other Russian, both of them rabid Kremlin critics?

Why had Viktor never reported the meeting and then informed Frank of it almost casually in a phone conversation six years after the fact? Whatever Viktor's true motives, the last thing Frank wanted to disclose was his real quarry, particularly to the man who'd sent him on the hunt. He decided a lesson from American history was in order.

"Don't forget that Lee Harvey Oswald married a Russian woman and lived here."

Viktor chortled. "Come on, Frank! Talk about conspiracy theories!"

"Don't laugh, Viktor. JFK had humiliated Khrushchev in the Cuban missile crisis and forced him to back down. The year before that, Kennedy launched the Bay of Pigs invasion and tried to topple Castro, the Soviets' most important client, just ninety miles from Florida. Millions of Americans still believe that the Kremlin had a hand in the JFK assassination."

Viktor shook his head. "All of that was when the United States and the Soviet Union were sworn enemies at the height of the Cold War! Then they became partners in the war on terrorism. Now our two great countries are at loggerheads over Ukraine and trying to figure out if they are enemies or allies in Syria."

Frank reached for his briefcase before speaking. "I'm sorry

you're so disappointed by the truth, Viktor. My editors just want to make sure that any Russian connection to the hit on Roberts is as crazy as it seems. I was a natural to get the assignment because I speak the language and know the lay of the land over here."

Frank removed the xWave from his briefcase. He turned it on and discreetly placed the tiny soft disc on his head behind his right ear. The wand-like device caught Viktor's attention.

"What's that?"

"A gadget I'm trying out for my bosses. They're desperate to find ways to deliver news to the young twenty-somethings who don't read newspapers and are moving away from PCs or even laptops."

"Everything for them is mobile."

"Right."

"So your bosses' answer is to make high-tech toys for them."

In his joking way, Viktor didn't realize how accurately he'd described the xWave: its most remarkable features were based on ultra-advanced gaming technologies.

Frank decided it was time for the device's first field test. Viktor played into his hand. "Mind if I take a look?"

Frank handed Viktor the xWave. He leaned forward and gave a mental command. Viktor's eyes widened as he stared ahead into the space before him. "Magic! My article has become a ghost!"

Frank had planned on steering their conversation back to Roberts, but it took an unexpected turn. "I appreciate your help on my little reporting trip here."

Viktor gave a look of mock horror. "The CIA sent you—I need to watch you closely!"

Frank jabbed back. "Just like the old days, eh?"

Viktor feigned surprise. "What on earth do you mean?"

"The SVR planted minders with all the American correspondents. I always assumed you were my minder. Was I wrong?"

For a change, Viktor fell silent. He finally spoke. "There was an intelligence agent in our poker game, but it wasn't me."

"You're not going to tell me that Mikhail worked for the Kremlin."

"It wasn't a Russian."

Frank searched through the faces of the card players in his memory. "Zev Levi?"

Viktor shook his head. Frank tried again. "Rado Weinstien?"

Viktor nodded. Frank recalled part of Rado's past. "Before the Berlin Wall fell, he moved to Moscow from East Germany."

"The Stasi was more ruthless than the KGB. The two agencies worked closely together."

"But Rado is Jewish."

"There weren't many Jews left in Germany after the war. It wasn't hard for the Stasi to keep track of them. It served their purposes to have a few Jewish agents."

Frank followed the progression. "So when the Stasi disappeared after the Wall fell, Rado just switched to the KGB. Which then became the SVR. Rado, I assume, worked in the Foreign Intelligence Service."

Viktor nodded. "Yes, the SVR. I'm sure you remember that Putin had been based in Berlin when he ran the KGB's foreign operations. He was fluent in German. Few other Russians spoke it so well."

Frank waited for Viktor to continue. "There were rumors that Putin took Rado directly under his wing. Rumors even that after he became president, Putin wanted to keep up his German, so he would invite Rado to the Kremlin for private chats."

Frank whistled. "Not a bad guardian angel for Rado."

"And an important spy inside the SVR for Putin, or so the story goes. He employed Rado to keep tabs on the intelligence bosses."

Using one of Viktor's tricks, Frank tried to lighten his next question with a laugh. "How do you know all of this?"

"I have my sources."

Frank looked at the xWave. He wanted to make sure that Viktor was still holding its handle. "You didn't follow Rado over to the dark side, did you?"

Frank lowered his eyes and watched a graphic display on his laptop screen as Viktor spoke. "Rado tried to recruit me. He hinted that he had high connections in the Kremlin. He said I would be well compensated."

Viktor smiled wistfully. "I was tempted to work for our agencies. But my grandparents had died in Stalin's labor camps. I could never bring myself to take Rado up on his offer."

The red line on Frank's laptop graphic spiked upward. He had to force himself to show no reaction. Instead, he closed his computer programs, turned off the laptop and gestured for the xWave.

"Well, that's good, Viktor. I don't have to worry about our new gadget being a target of Russian industrial espionage."

Frank took the xWave and put it in his briefcase. "I'm afraid I need to go back to my hotel and get some sleep."

Viktor accompanied Frank to the door. The two men exchanged the traditional Russian bear hug before Frank headed out into the night. He was pleased with the xWave's first trial. He'd learned something important about Viktor.

Viktor's apparent hidden past as a Kremlin mole presented interesting possible explanations for why he had never reported Stuart's meeting with Mikhail in 2006.

Why was Viktor unwilling to share with Frank an important part of his past that the American reporter suspected anyway? Was Viktor still working undercover for the Kremlin?

As he walked back to the National along Moscow's deserted and darkened streets, Frank understood one thing. He would be even more careful with Viktor than his competitive drive already required him to be.

CHAPTER 17

MOSCOW

SVETLANA AND VIKTOR had met in 1997 at the Russian Oil Ministry, where they were analysts in the rapidly expanding foreign investment section. That official designation combined nicely with their covert assignments for the SVR. After recruiting them separately during Oil Ministry training retreats a year apart, the SVR directed Viktor to monitor the activities of Dutch, French and Italian oil companies. They had formed a consortium with a Kazakh government venture to develop the newly discovered Kashagan crude reserves beneath the Caspian Sea. The European firms' status as state-owned utilities suited the Kremlin spymasters. Viktor's portfolio grew when Exxon and Mobil joined the consortium, and he was assigned to get to know the on-site executives.

Then, in 1999, Svetlana and Viktor expanded their espionage with Frank and Lisa's arrival in Moscow. The Kremlin had been watching Frank since his Berkeley days, and Lisa's job as head of the Russian oil and gas division of AmeriCon only added to her intrigue. As did the Kremlin's near-certainty that her father, Thomas Hawkes, had long been a senior US intelligence official using his newspaper post as a cover. Frank, meanwhile, began traveling to the Caspian and writing exposés on the sprawling Russian and international oil exploration. The Kremlin wrongly assumed that Lisa was feeding her husband inside information for his investigative articles uncovering the corrupt deal-cutting in the crude-soaked region.

Their SVR bosses directed Viktor to shadow Frank—"mind" was the term of art—and instructed Svetlana to befriend Lisa. The assignment would work best if the Kremlin waived the prohibition on romantic ties between its agents. The easiest way for Svetlana and Viktor to gain the newcomers' trust would be to approach them socially as one couple interested in getting to know another. For Viktor, the assignment was a dream come true: Svetlana was ravishing, and he had exercised enormous willpower to refrain from pursuing her and being unfaithful to his wife. Now he had a get-out-of-jail card for infidelity: it was required by his job, his real job with the SVR. For her part, Svetlana, though less enamored of Viktor, found him attractive, certainly more virile than some of her past marks.

During their first bout of lovemaking, a tryst at Svetlana's flat that they jokingly called their practice session, the two went at each other with a wild passion that surprised them. Within days, all pretense of official duty disappeared, and they had sex whenever and wherever the urge hit them, at times in barely hidden public places where the risk of causing a scandal only heightened the excitement. Before long they had completely subsumed their cover roles as paramours-by-assignment, and whether consciously or not, found themselves half in love with each other.

Viktor and Svetlana formed an odd couple of the sort that the tumultuous waves of history sometimes produce. He was descended from the House of Romanov. As a great-great-nephew of Czar Nicholas II, Viktor would surely have been sent to a Siberian labor camp had he been born a generation earlier under Stalin's reign of terror. His parents had avoided that fate by becoming avid Communists and putting their full services at the party's behest. When others asked whether he was a descendant of the czars, Viktor would laugh, roll his eyes and quip: "If only it were so."

Svetlana's family history was quite another story. She was the great-granddaughter of Inessa Armand, Lenin's mistress who had lived with the Bolshevik leader and his wife, Nadezhda Krupskaya, during his pre-Revolution exile in Austria. By all accounts, Inessa was the love of Lenin's life, a singular woman who went on to fight for female equality and to chair the First International Conference of Communist Women in 1920. Unlike so many other early Soviet figures who fell into disfavor, Inessa was never discredited or airbrushed from photos in schoolchildren's textbooks. Most of Svetlana's acquaintances knew of the connection, and many noted that she had inherited Inessa's beauty, intelligence and headstrong determination to get whatever she set her sights on, whether man or mission.

Viktor and Svetlana, wrapped in each other's arms, would sometimes joke that their sexual union had fused the best elements of their country's Russian and Soviet pasts.

Viktor waited for Svetlana on a peeling green bench in Gorky Park. He felt uncharacteristically nervous.

In defiance of their spymasters' orders, Viktor and Svetlana had refused to end their sexual liaison after Frank and Lisa returned to Los Angeles. Carrying on a covert affair within their covert assignments, they'd continued to sleep together until Viktor left the Oil Ministry to become an investigative reporter at *Kapital*. At that point, Viktor's journalistic ethics became clear where his espionage morals had not: he couldn't have romantic ties with a woman who would become one of his most important sources.

The sexual magnetism between the two of them hadn't waned, however, and they knew that if they were to meet in person even for a platonic dinner or cup of coffee, they would be in bed in short order. So for six years, their only contact had been by phone, e-mail or text message.

Checking to make sure that the recorder in his pocket was running, Viktor steeled himself against Svetlana's almost unbearable allure. The rendezvous was at the Slavic beauty's request. Viktor had reluctantly agreed to meet only after she'd insisted that she had something urgent to tell him and that it must be conveyed in person.

Viktor had found himself hoping that the intervening years had aged Svetlana; perhaps she'd put on weight or otherwise lost her stunning figure. Now, as he watched her walking toward him, wearing a svelte, almost sheer light-blue dress on the hot summer day, Viktor saw that his hopes had been in vain. Svetlana was as gorgeous as ever. She sat down next to him.

Viktor spoke first in what he tried to make a firm voice that didn't expose his racing heart. "How are your colleagues at the Oil Ministry weathering the scandal?"

Svetlana's response was all business. She had long experience at tapping or sealing her sexuality as circumstances required. "They're hardly my colleagues. The Kremlin is pressuring me to get to the bottom of the scandal. Billions of rubles in royalties have gone missing. Mikhail's opposition rallies have really turned up the heat. There are more FSB agents than ever at the ministry now."

Viktor felt that if they remained next to each other on the bench, he would against all willpower reach over and embrace her. He rose and beckoned her to follow. They walked along a path through a birch grove.

When Viktor was certain they could not be overheard, he spoke. "You haven't forgotten the poker games at Frank and Lisa's flat?"

"Of course not. As you know, I came to know Frank rather well."

Viktor took a breath. He'd never told Svetlana that the vision of her in bed with the American journalist had tormented him. He took a dig at her. "All in the line of duty, of course."

Many women would have blushed; Svetlana did not. She

said nothing as Viktor continued. "Frank's in town. Did you know that he and Lisa are divorced?"

Now it was Svetlana's turn to feel her heartbeat quicken. During their numerous sexual trysts, she had come to like Frank much more than she wished. He was smart, witty and thoughtful. He was quite talented in bed. And he had fallen in love with her.

They walked down the path. She asked the obvious question. "Why is Frank here?"

"He's looking into the attempted assassination of Stuart Roberts."

Svetlana stopped. "What does that have to do with Russia?"

"Frank is chasing rumors that the Kremlin had a hand in the Roberts hit."

They resumed walking. Viktor couldn't know it, but Svetlana had prepared her next comment. "The Russian government is being unfairly blamed for the incident. You know as well as I do that the Kremlin would never botch such a high-profile wet operation so badly."

When Viktor didn't respond, Svetlana spoke again. "I have a different explanation."

Viktor looked into her eyes for the first time. "What's that?"

"An American oil company might be involved."

Viktor's investigative reporting interest was aroused. He kept his voice calm. "How so?"

"The Kremlin has learned that Mikhail and an American oilman cut a secret deal some years ago."

"What kind of a deal?"

Svetlana didn't answer Viktor's question. "I have a contact in Atyrau you should meet."

Viktor exhaled in exasperation. "Kazakhstan? That place is the pits!"

Svetlana smiled slightly at her former lover's barb. "It's also the new oil frontier. Our wells and pipelines there are bringing in billions of rubles."

Viktor couldn't help adding: "Except for the stray two or three billion rubles."

Svetlana laughed. He shrugged his shoulders and spoke again.

"I'll have to take Frank along."

Svetlana pretended to protest. "Why?"

Viktor wasn't about to share his real reasons for wanting the American to accompany him on the trip. He closed this unsettling conversation with Svetlana. "We're both famous reporters, my dear, and Russia and America are no longer enemies."

CHAPTER 18

MOSCOW

A FTER JUST A few hours' sleep, Frank meticulously mapped out his day. He decided not to call his sources in advance, but rather to simply appear unannounced at their offices or homes. Yemelin had told him to come in the late afternoon. There was a risk, of course, that he would miss some of the others. But the danger of arranging interviews in advance was greater. He didn't want word to spread that he was in Moscow and talking with Roberts's former acquaintances. He was certain that some of his contacts' phones were being monitored.

Using a map of the capital's Metro system, Frank had planned his stops in the most efficient order: nine contacts spread across the breadth of the city and its environs. The schedule would take all day and require a lot of legwork, but Frank knew that he had limited time left in Moscow. He had promised Evgeny Aisenyev to try and work in a squash match before he left the country. Although he would be tired after a full day of interviews, Frank always felt rejuvenated by physical exercise. On the way out of the hotel, he would drop by Evgeny's office and see if they could play that evening.

Frank's list included five Russians who'd belonged to Stuart's circle of friends when he served as envoy and four others who were always well-connected with Moscow's revolving corps of diplomats from around the globe. Frank knew better than to ask his sources directly about Roberts. He had crafted a cover story: with Stuart off the campaign trail, Frank had come to Moscow to do some reporting for an enterprise article on how American foreign policy might change with Roberts in the White House. To further deflect the spotlight from Stuart's dealings in Russia, Frank would tell his contacts that Moscow was one of three European capitals he was visiting for the story.

Five of Frank's sources were not at home or at the office when he arrived. A sixth contact was ill and unable to accept visitors. Frank declined to leave notes asking them to call. Fortunately, none of the family members or work assistants he encountered knew him by face. When they asked for his name to pass on, he said he was a friend from Estonia and would call in the next day or two.

The remaining three contacts were available. Two didn't realize he'd been covering Roberts's presidential campaign. He saw no need to tell them.

In each interview, Frank began asking questions about Stuart only after some broad queries about the state of US-Russian relations—he made sure to say "Russian-US relations"—designed to relax his sources and give them ample opportunity to expound on their perspectives. Not until a half hour into each interview did Frank zero in on Roberts. He steered clear of Stuart's well-known criticisms of the Kremlin. His interest, he assured them, was merely to ascertain how much Roberts had augmented his already considerable expertise in Russian-US ties since leaving his post as ambassador. The three men Frank interviewed provided fragmentary information that nevertheless would prove to be quite useful.

Maxim Menshchikov, an economist with the Russian Progress think tank, was certain that Roberts had visited Moscow a dozen times after his diplomatic assignment. Perhaps half the trips were before he entered politics. On one or two of the later journeys, he had come as part of a US Senate delegation. Menshchikov remembered having a detailed discussion with Stuart at a reception in 2008 or 2009 for the visiting senators in the VIP lounge of the Russian Foreign Ministry. The economist was reasonably sure that on at least one other occasion after joining Congress, as recently as two years ago, Roberts had arrived in Moscow alone. Menshchikov didn't recall any official receptions during that visit, and he himself hadn't met with Stuart; but one economist friend who was an expert on the oil industry had held extensive private sessions with the senator.

Vladislav Kapriyanov shared his memories. Now a professor in diplomatic studies at Russian State University, he had recently left his position as a Foreign Ministry senior analyst specializing in the United States. Kapriyanov also remembered Roberts's trips—he had helped host the visiting senators—but he thought he recalled an earlier solo visit by Stuart. The professor was almost positive that it came before Roberts's election to the Senate. When Frank asked him to name the year, he narrowed it down to 2005 or 2006.

Roberts and Kapriyanov had talked over a leisurely lunch. The former ambassador had made a few unusual requests. He'd asked that the two of them not dine at the Foreign Ministry's excellent restaurant, requesting instead a discreet eatery where they could be guaranteed privacy. Stuart had also asked Vladislav not to tell his Foreign Ministry colleagues of the Californian's pending arrival. Perhaps most surprising, Kapriyanov learned over lunch that Roberts had made plans to go to Atyrau the next day.

The Caspian headquarters of ExxonMobil, on whose board Roberts sat, was in the Azerbaijan capital port of Baku on the eastern shores of the Caspian Sea. Stuart, though, indicated no plans to go to Baku; he'd been vague about his itinerary, and Vladislav hadn't pressed him. Atyrau, on the sea's northern coast, was a smaller and more recent oil boomtown with less of a presence by American, European or other Western oil companies. It was dominated by a handful of Russian, Kazakh, Azerbaijani and Turkish firms. Most prominent among them was NeftKorp, a rapidly growing oil venture founded by Mikhail Gusov.

Frank's heart quickened when Kapriyanov mentioned Gusov. He didn't tell the Russian that he knew Gusov and was to meet with him before the week was up.

The journalist hadn't nailed down details of Stuart's clandestine meeting with Mikhail. But he had new indications that the two men had even more extensive contacts that went beyond the Russian capital. The mention of Atyrau added a new and interesting twist to the mystery.

CHAPTER 19

MOSCOW

FRANK'S MOST IMPORTANT interview of the day was with Sergei Yemelin. Roberts had introduced Adams to Yemelin in late 2000 with Baku newly dubbed "the Houston of the Caspian." Yemelin became an invaluable source for Frank, explaining the industry's technical challenges and opening doors for his reporting trips to Baku and beyond. Adams's value to Yemelin was more difficult to measure, yet it was significant. Over time, Frank became an important outlet for him to influence how America saw his country. He helped Frank appreciate that Russia retained legitimate interests in the oil-rich lands Moscow had controlled under Soviet rule. After the September 11 attacks, Yemelin took Adams beyond the charged rhetoric about the "war on terror" and the new US-Russian alliance against radical Islam. With Yemelin's help, Frank wrote the first major article showing that al Qaeda's roots dated to the Soviets' doomed occupation of Afghanistan—and to the fundamental-ist Muslim Mujahedeen that the CIA and Pakistan's ISI spy agency had funded to overthrow the Soviet yoke.

It went too far to say that Frank's subsequent reporting was more "pro-Russia" as a consequence of his evolving relationship with Yemelin. Instead, his perspective became more reflective, however slightly, of Russia's geopolitical perspectives.

Beyond their professional ties, Adams and Yemelin had developed a personal bond. They were the same age, thirty-four when they first met. Perhaps because he was younger than many of Frank's other Russian sources, Yemelin was bolder than most. He seemed comfortable in his skin and didn't evince the need of some Russian men to boast of his achievements or connections. Most important, he didn't speak in the maddening ideological patter or academic cant of his peers. To Frank's ears, he sounded more like an American—direct, unadorned, to the point.

So when the two men clasped hands, the journalist felt that he didn't need to be as circumspect about his real reason for returning to Russia. Yemelin, his instructions from Lisa on how to deal with her ex-husband fresh in his mind, could speak freely of his concern over the hit on Roberts, and his fear for the safety of a man he'd come to know well.

Yemelin looked at Adams from across his desk in his office on the sixty-fifth floor of One Capital City. Anchored on the Krasnopresnenskaya Embankment of the Moscow River, the office gave him a commanding view of the Kievsky Rail Station, an ornate Byzantine structure topped by a clock tower. In the distance, he could see the city's famed Arbat pedestrian street and, poking up its red masts at the horizon's end, the Kremlin.

Yemelin had moved his consulting firm into One Capital City in 2010. Offices were supposed to be limited to the bottom ten floors, with residential units on the other levels, but he had used a generous gift to the landlord to gain his loftier perch.

Yemelin smiled as he watched his guest gaze at the kaleidoscopic scene beyond his wall-length window.

"Not too shabby for stodgy old Moscow, is it?"

Frank shook his head. "When I lived here, I don't remember being in a building higher than twenty floors."

Yemelin laughed. "Since you left, we've built five of the world's two hundred tallest skyscrapers. None of them are quite as high as Freedom Tower or the Empire State Building, but we're making progress."

Adams and Yemelin fell silent. Yemelin spoke first. "I'm glad that my friend Stuart Roberts escaped the attempt on his life in your country."

Unlike in his interviews earlier in the day, Frank felt that he could take a direct tack. "I'm also glad that Stuart survived. But I'm beginning to suspect that I don't know as much about him as I thought I did."

Yemelin went back to the start of their relationship. "You and Stuart became friends over poker. He then brought you and me into contact."

Frank chose his next words with care. "Sergei, I wouldn't say Stuart and I were friends. Reporters and sources often become somewhat close, but there was a certain distance from Roberts that I had to maintain. Although after being with him on the campaign trail for the last year, I thought that I knew him well."

Sergei let Frank continue. "Of course, since I left Moscow, I've written many in-depth profiles of Stuart's political career, first with his Senate campaign and now with his White House run. Most of my reporting was focused on his activities in California and Washington. I knew that he'd maintained contacts in Russia, but that was normal for a former envoy."

Frank's voice trailed off before picking up again. "After Stuart became a senator, he was part of a few congressional delegations to Moscow. I accompanied him on his first one. And before that, he'd sat on ExxonMobil's board of directors and had some involvement in its oil exploration in Russia and Azerbaijan. But I've raked through his disclosure reports and campaign-finance documents over the last six years, and there's no mention of Russia."

Yemelin finally spoke. "You won't find any information about Stuart's trips here in those reports. Not his private trips."

Frank was surprised. "Private trips? Once you're elected to Congress, there is no such thing as a private trip abroad. Not only must senators disclose their foreign travel, they have to brief the State Department when they return to Washington."

Yemelin waved his hand. It was a gesture of impatient dismissal Russians liked to use. Frank interpreted the gesture in this case to mean that men accustomed to the business success Roberts had enjoyed weren't going to lose sleep over official requirements in the political realm.

Yemelin asked Frank a question he'd asked the journalist a number of times before. "Can we speak on background?"

The two men had traversed this territory in the past, but it was important to Frank that they spell out the rules once more. "Meaning?"

"What I tell you cannot be attributed to me. I will show you contracts and other documents that verify my account. But you must then confirm it independently. Otherwise, I will deny having told you anything of significance about Roberts."

Frank nodded. "Fair enough."

Frank watched a train leave the Kievsky Rail Station through the window. Yemelin leaned forward and spoke with new intensity. "Not to boast, but I know the Russian oil industry as well as anyone. I'm one of the few who under-stands the engineering, the geology and the physics, but who's also gotten his hands dirty in the field. Over time, Stuart came to appreciate my expertise."

Frank decided not to ask any questions for now.

"Of course, Stuart learned some things about the oil busi-ness as an ExxonMobil board member. But as we saw in the Enron scandal, the directors of these giant energy companies fly so high above the day-to-day operations, they never really know what's happening on the ground. For a long time, Stuart viewed the international oil trade the way the Americans and the Arabs, for all their cultural differences, see it: The oil axis ran from Houston to Riyadh, with some tributaries breaking off to Iran and Mexico. Russia was a side player at best. While it had large untapped crude reserves, its lack of infrastructure and supply chains would limit Moscow to being a regional supplier, content to sell mainly to the Eastern Europeans and to one or two of the paper tigers in Asia."

Yemelin drank from a glass of filtered water. "Over time, I helped Stuart update his geopolitical map of the oil world. I persuaded him that its epicenter for the next half-century would be the Caspian Sea region. He learned that while Azerbaijan, Kazakhstan, Georgia, Ukraine and the others had gained political independence, Moscow still controlled the oil and gas pipelines that run through them. No matter who was elected in those countries, no matter how much those leaders objected, Moscow could turn the energy spigot off at will. The Kremlin, quite literally, decided whether the Georgians would freeze in winter, whether the Kazakhs could buy gas for their cheap little cars, whether factories in Kiev or Baku would sit idle."

As Frank listened, he began to understand that all the attacks on the Kremlin he'd heard Stuart make in his campaign stump speeches perhaps had not been based solely on political ideology or abstract concepts of freedom.

"By 2008, Russia had become the largest exporter of oil and natural gas to the twenty-seven member nations of the European Union. It supplied one-third of their energy, and that share has gone up since then."

Yemelin glanced at his computer screen, opened an e-mail and read it before continuing. "All of this is prelude to the main event. So far, our major foreign oil markets have been on our western flank. That was our primary focus during the Cold War. But no more. For the next several decades, the big action in the energy sector will be to our east. As recently as

1993, China was completely self-sufficient. Now, thanks to its explosive economic growth, it's the world's second-largest oil importer behind the United States. By 2025, China is expected to rely on other countries for 85 percent of its energy. The same thing is occurring in India, and in Indonesia. Even Pakistan's economy is starting to take off. These nations are aggressively competing for foreign oil sources. Russia is just as aggressively positioning itself to be a major supplier. Even where it doesn't own the crude, as in the big oil fields discovered in Kazakhstan, Azerbaijan and other parts of the Caspian region, we are becoming an energy broker through the control of the pipelines and some of the big shipping lanes. While political ideology defined our relations with the world last century, economics will drive our international ties this century."

Frank wasn't about to reveal what Kapriyanov had just told him about Roberts's private visit to Kazakhstan in 2006 and his likely business dealings with Gusov.

"I appreciate your guidance on all of this, but what does it have to do with Stuart? His business background is in advanced computer electronics. Other than being a director of ExxonMobil, he had no direct involvement in the oil trade."

Yemelin pursed his lips. "That's not quite true."

Frank volleyed Yemelin's words. "Not quite true?"

"Stuart was hardly the first American envoy whose Moscow posting left him with a sense of personal investment in Russia's future—and a deep concern over its influence on world affairs. After he left in 2002, Stuart was increasingly dismayed by the reversal of democratic freedoms here and by the growing consolidation of power in the Kremlin. Events in

Georgia, and more recently in Ukraine and Syria, have amplified that concern. As he came to understand our exploding oil sector, his alarm increased. He feared that the control the Soviet Communists had exerted for decades over large parts of the world with military force and nuclear weapons would be replaced in the twenty-first century by the Kremlin's economic stranglehold based on its oil reserves and pipeline network. If rising powers like China and India came to rely on Moscow for their energy, that development would threaten the United States' national security as much as its longtime reliance on the Arab sheikhs for imported oil."

Yemelin took another sip of water. "Shortly after I started my firm in 2005, Stuart hired me as a consultant. My assignment was to help him strengthen US oil interests that could counter the Kremlin's growing dominance. He put me on a monthly retainer, with one condition."

Frank was too stunned to speak.

"Stuart demanded that our business relationship be kept secret. And not only our relationship. All of the contacts I arranged for him were to remain completely clandestine. As you know, Stuart has a wry sense of humor. He would joke that in the US intelligence community, our activity was called a 'black op,' a dangerous operation that must be untraceable to either of us as its principals."

As he found his tongue, Frank felt like he was treading water in a fierce current. "You spoke of a retainer. May I ask how much Stuart paid you?"

Yemelin issued a reminder before answering the question.

"You're a pro, Frank, but remember, nothing is attributed to me, and you'll have to verify everything."

Frank nodded his assent.

"Fifteen thousand dollars a month."

Frank whistled. "That was a nice piece of change. It must have helped you build your consulting firm."

Yemelin stared at Adams. He understood the significance of what he said next. "My contract with Stuart hasn't ended."

When Adams said nothing, Yemelin emphasized the point. "I'm still on retainer."

The revelation sent Frank's mind racing. He'd combed through Stuart's campaign financial statements and disclosure reports, first as a senator and then as a presidential candidate. Their disbursement sections itemized expenditures to hundreds of vendors, from printers, pollsters and direct-mail companies to media consultants and TV stations that ran campaign ads. There was no way Frank could have overlooked payments of more than a hundred grand a year, much less to a Russian firm. If Stuart had failed to disclose such payments, he had clearly violated federal election regulations.

It got worse.

Foreign lobbyists were required to register with the clerk of the Senate, detailing their ties to their governments and the nature of their work in Washington. Unlike their American counterparts along "Lobbyists' Row" on K Street, they were forbidden to make campaign contributions to members of Congress.

A sitting senator—and White House aspirant—making

covert payments to a Russian consultant? That would be a breach of law far more serious than violating campaign rules.

Frank had long taken Roberts to be a careful man who weighed every risk and always erred on the side of caution. Was it really possible that he had engaged in such reckless behavior? Behavior that could not only end his political career, but land him in prison?

Yemelin's cell phone jingled. He read the text and stood up. "I'm sorry, Frank, but I must leave now. My wife and I are hosting a dinner party tonight, and I'm already an hour late." He extended his hand. "I trust you've found our session useful. I also trust that you will protect me under the guidelines we've agreed to."

Frank was so flabbergasted, he could do little more than shake Yemelin's hand. "You have my word."

Frank reached the squash court at Moscow State University an hour later, still numb from his interview with Yemelin. He was looking forward to his game with Evgeny. The hard exercise might shake him from his stupor.

After their match, Frank and Evgeny went to a café across the quad in the university's student union. They sat at a small table, sipping espresso. For the first fifteen minutes, they exchanged pleasantries and caught each other up on their lives over the last few years.

Frank hadn't planned on interviewing Evgeny, but he now saw an opportunity to start verifying the astounding claims Yemelin had made about Roberts. Evgeny had been a cook at the US Embassy during Roberts's posting as ambassador.

Frank reverted to his strategy of not asking directly about Stuart. "So, what do you think of Mikhail Gusov's political activity?"

Evgeny frowned. "He became a marked man the day he formed his opposition party."

For the next few minutes, Evgeny delivered a familiar rant about Russian politics. It combined a passionate description of dark forces converging at the Kremlin with just enough historical fact to prevent the account from sliding into pure lunacy. Frank found his attention starting to wander when Evgeny said something that caught his ear. "I actually have a bit of a tie to Gusov."

Frank had never told Evgeny of his friendship with Mikhail. Now wasn't the time to do so. "What's that?"

"When you and I met, of course, I was a cook at the embassy. I became friends with another Russian cook there, Vitaly Kournikov. A few years after you left Moscow, he hired on as a personal chef to Gusov."

Evgeny laughed. "We were all jealous. Vitaly's salary increased tenfold. Gusov often hosted dignitaries in his luxurious flat off Red Square. From what Vitaly told us, it was incredibly opulent, but also tastefully appointed with imported furniture and paintings by famous artists."

Evgeny sat back. "About a year after he became Gusov's chef, Vitaly described an especially lavish dinner the oligarch had asked him to prepare for an important guest from America. The visitor was someone Vitaly and I had cooked for many times at the embassy—Stuart Roberts. I didn't think anything much about Roberts's visit until an American friend of mine at the embassy told me something odd."

"Who was your American friend?"

"A fellow named Paul Hayes. He was supposedly an economic analyst, but we Russians all assumed he was CIA. He and I played squash every few months. A week or two after Roberts's dinner with Gusov, he told me that as a former ambassador and current United States Senate candidate, Roberts should have been assigned a security detail from the American Marines based at the embassy. But he had turned down the chargé d'affaire's offer of protection, saying his visit was private and he didn't want to call attention to it."

Evgeny shook his head in wonderment. "I never imagined that Roberts would end up being the target of an assassination attempt."

Frank spoke in a matter-of-fact tone. "Do you recall when Roberts's visit was?"

"Late September 2006. I'm certain because it was just before I left my embassy job and returned to the university to get my MBA."

Frank finally had his answer to the riddle raised by Viktor's seemingly nonchalant comment during their initial phone conversation. In different circumstances, the confirmation might have elated him. Now he understood that it was one piece in an expanding puzzle.

CHAPTER 20

MOSCOW

FRANK AND VIKTOR had reached an undeclared truce in their unspoken competition to get to the bottom of the attempt on Roberts's life. Frank was trying to find out why Stuart had made an unannounced stop in Moscow following his trip to Israel; why he'd met with Mikhail for an undisclosed dinner; and why Viktor had chosen not to report it. Viktor, in turn, had delayed telling Frank about Svetlana's new source in Atyrau. He didn't want to get beat on the Roberts story, but his main target was still the billions of rubles in royalties missing from the Russian Oil Ministry's coffers. He thought that Frank's quarry and his own quest might overlap. Yet he hadn't compiled enough evidence for an article tying everything together. Normally, Viktor wouldn't want another reporter going with him to pursue a lead, but in this case that was preferable to leaving Frank behind in Moscow to work on his own.

Each reporter felt he needed to keep a close eye on the other; each believed that he could stay ahead of the game and learn more from the other than he might give up.

As the sunset's apricot glow bathed the Russian capital, Viktor and Frank shared a window table at City Space, a stylish bar atop the Swissotel Krasnye Holmy. Viktor drank a Russian Kamikaze, three shots of Stolichnaya colored with Chambord raspberry liqueur. Frank was enjoying one of his nonalcoholic favorites, freshly squeezed pomegranate juice with a splash of club soda. They ate from a plate of pumpernickel bread slices with pickled herring.

Viktor took a gulp of his Kamikaze and reached for the plate. "So, have you discovered the secret trail of Stuart Roberts's blood to the Kremlin?"

Frank laughed. "You know that the Kremlin contracts out its most important hits. I'm certain the best forensics scientists in the world wouldn't find the faintest trace of blood anywhere near Red Square."

"That's precisely why you and I should get out of Moscow for a little sojourn."

"A sojourn?"

"A reliable source of mine has put me in touch with a contact in Atyrau. I've arranged a meeting on Saturday. I'd like you to join me."

Frank was stunned at the mention of Atyrau after what he had learned earlier in the day. Frank struggled to maintain his reserve and to react with caution to Viktor's invitation. The xWave had shown that he was lying when he told Frank he'd never been a Russian intelligence agent. His almost cavalier disclosure of the secret Gusov-Roberts dinner seemed too casual for such an accomplished journalist. It occurred to Frank that Viktor's apparently accidental slip might have been deliberate. He might have wanted to lure Frank to Moscow.

Now Viktor was inviting the American to travel to Atyrau—in the heart of a semilawless Caspian Sea region rife with corruption, bulging with oil riches, home to competing mobsters of Russian, Kazakh and other national origins—and site of unknown intrigue involving Stuart Roberts, Mikhail Gusov and God knows who else. Was Viktor baiting Frank again?

Frank played dumb. "Couldn't you have chosen a better destination than Kazakhstan?"

Viktor laughed. "The best stories happen in the most sordid places, my friend."

Viktor considered telling Frank that his source for the Atyrau contact was Svetlana. But that might backfire—Frank had fallen hard for her, and then grown bitter when she said she wasn't in love with him.

Viktor played a different card. "You remember that Mikhail, Lisa and her boss from Houston made that trip to Baku shortly after your arrival in Moscow?"

Frank felt a pang as he recalled the period when he and Lisa were still happily married. "Of course. Lisa told me after the trip that Bud was in his element down there. He spent the three days carousing with oilmen from Azerbaijan, Kazakhstan and Russia. Their translator taught him how to say, 'A round of drinks for the boys!' in Russian, and he'd shout it out every time they met a new group."

Viktor tossed back the rest of his Kamikaze. "A big part of Stuart's portfolio as the US ambassador was the expanding involvement of American oil companies in the Caspian region. You wrote a number of articles about his visits there. In fact, didn't you go with him on one trip?"

Frank nodded. He was dissecting Viktor's words as he listened, parsing them for a clue to the Russian's intentions.

Viktor added something he knew would pique Frank's curiosity. "Stuart's interest in the Caspian didn't end with the completion of his Moscow assignment."

Frank chortled. "That's hardly news, Viktor. In my campaign profiles, I've reported that Stuart served on the ExxonMobil board of directors after leaving the diplomatic corps and before entering politics. He toured their Caspian operations several times."

Once more, Viktor couched his response in humor. "Ah, but you yourself haven't been back since you left Moscow. There are no doubt acquaintances of Stuart still down there. Don't you want to see whether this grand Russian conspiracy you're chasing has connections to the shadowy Caspian region that is so famous for intrigue?"

Frank tried to match Viktor's light touch. "Why are you suddenly being so helpful? You haven't exactly been a fount of information since I got here."

Viktor signaled for the waiter and gave a hearty laugh. "You're my friend, Frank! Besides, if I keep you by my side in Atyrau, I won't have to worry about you making mischief here in Moscow."

"I can't be away for long. This will be a short trip?"

"Less than three days. We'll fly down and meet my contact Saturday. You can look up some of Stuart's acquaintances. We'll return Monday."

The two journalists spent the rest of the night recalling old times and exchanging tales of sexual conquests since their divorces. As the bar began to shut down, they took the elevator to the lobby, left the hotel and hailed a cab. The taxi dropped off Viktor at his home and headed for the National.

Walking into the hotel, Frank felt certain that Viktor, for all his apparent good spirit, continued to withhold vital information. He was no doubt not telling the whole truth about their Atyrau trip. Frank entered his room and turned on his laptop.

If Viktor was still being less than fully forthcoming, there were some things Frank hadn't told him as well.

IV: WILD CARD

At gambling, the deadly sin is to mistake bad play for bad luck.

Ian Fleming

CHAPTER 21

LOS ANGELES

T HOMAS HAWKES HAD an aversion to hospitals, but it was imperative that he talk with Roberts. He wasn't about to let Adams dig up things in Stuart's past that took him by surprise. Hawkes drove from his Malibu home to the UCLA Medical Center. He left his Cadillac SRX with the hospital valet and headed for the elevators. He knew that Stuart would be in the "Gold Coast" section on the eighth floor, a wing of secluded suites reserved for celebrities and the super-rich.

Thomas turned left out of the elevator and saw that in addition to the hospital's own security detail at the entrance to the wing, there were three federal agents with earpieces and bulges under their jackets.

Hawkes took out his wallet and produced his *Los Angeles Register* photo ID along with his California driver's license.

The female Secret Service agent took his cards, scanned the list on her hand-held computer and found Thomas's name.

"Mr. Hawkes, Agent Sullivan will have to perform a body search. I apologize, but it's standard procedure for anyone entering Senator Roberts's room."

Thomas stepped to the side and raised his arms as the male agent performed the thorough pat-down. Hawkes was then directed to walk through the metal detector before the hospital's own security checked his credentials once more, logged his name and the time of his visit and opened the door.

Inside the suite, Thomas looked down the carpeted hallway. Another group of agents huddled with three doctors in white coats. As Thomas approached Stuart's room, one of the agents asked for his ID and put him through the same ordeal he'd just endured.

"I apologize, sir, but we're under strict orders to ensure that the senator's visitors have been properly screened."

Hawkes hid his annoyance. "Not a problem. I understand."

One of the agents finally ushered Hawkes into Roberts's room. The doctors remained outside the door.

Stuart looked up from a document he'd been reading and greeted his visitor. "Nice of you to drop by, Thomas."

Roberts addressed the agent. "Peter, I need to be alone with Mr. Hawkes."

The agent nodded and departed.

A nurse entered and gave Stuart a glass of water and two pills. "Thank you, Elizabeth. Would you please close the door on your way out."

No sooner had Thomas sat on a wooden chair by the bed

when Stuart lit into him. "Operation Long Shadow was your idea. You pulled me into it! I've done my part. Your job was to keep everything under control and get me into the White House. But I'm almost killed and you take five days to show up and visit me!"

Thomas had never seen Stuart so agitated. Hawkes ignored his accusations. He studied Roberts's bandages and cast. "How are you feeling, Stuart?"

Roberts settled down. "The burns hurt like hell, but the doctors say I'm fortunate that I only have a minor leg fracture. I'm in physical therapy and making good progress."

"That's good. We need to get you back out on the campaign trail. But things appear to be more complicated than we initially thought."

"How so?"

"We've come into possession of some communications between the Russian Oil Ministry and a reporter for the *Kapital* business journal about an American oil company."

Thomas raised his eyebrows and waited for a response. There was something vaguely accusatory in Thomas's tone that irritated Stuart.

"What does that have to do with the attempt on my life?"

"It's time you level with me about your activities in Russia after you left as ambassador."

Stuart set the glass down. "You've got to be kidding me."

They were alone in the room, but Thomas lowered his voice nonetheless.

"From the start, you and I had a very clear understanding about Operation Long Shadow. It could only succeed if you were completely transparent about your business dealings. I told you there was no margin for error. Anything less than full candor could threaten everything. We had to be certain there would be no surprises. In exchange, we would get you into the White House. Those were the terms you accepted."

"What are you suggesting, Thomas?"

Thomas leaned in to Stuart. "The Russian reporter who played poker with you in Moscow has obtained potentially compromising information."

Stuart lost his patience. "Are you saying the poker group was some sort of plot? Your former son-in-law hosted the card game! We played at his flat—also your daughter's flat, by the way. Why don't you run your crazy theories by Adams?"

Thomas suppressed his anger. "Did you stay in close contact with Mikhail Gusov after your Moscow posting?"

Stuart didn't answer directly. "I've seen some of the former poker players from time to time. Frank's covering my campaign, of course. We talk often out on the trail."

Thomas concealed his annoyance with Stuart's less-than-forthcoming answers. "What about the others?"

Visibly disturbed again, Stuart shifted his position in bed. "For Christ's sake, Thomas, isn't it your reporters' job to ask these questions? You and I are on the same side. You're treating me as if I'm the one under investigation."

Thomas kept his cool. "I'm not doubting you, Stuart. I want to protect you. Have you had any contact with Gusov or other Russians since you left Moscow in 2001?"

Stuart went back on the offensive. "I've worked hand-in-glove with you for years. You have a dossier on me ten feet high. I want to know who's trying to kill me."

Hawkes rose and put his hand on Roberts's shoulder. "That's precisely what we're trying to figure out. But perhaps our dossier on you isn't as complete as we thought it was."

Thomas went to the door and stopped before leaving. "Take care of yourself, Stuart."

CHAPTER 22

BEVERLY HILLS, CALIFORNIA

THE NIGHT WAS gorgeous for the gala event in a large ballroom opening to the huge pool at the Peninsula Hotel. Guests mingled in the garden around the pool and the lavishly decorated room with a large ice sculpture of two doves in flight surrounded by drink stations and beautiful young waitresses offering trays of *hors d'oeuvres.* Thomas Hawkes was being feted for his extensive philanthropic work providing educational opportunities for disadvantaged Latino and African American youths. A few hundred of California's rich and famous from business, politics and Hollywood had gathered to honor him at the annual awards gala of the California Givers Fund. Banners hanging on the walls proclaimed: "Thank you, Thomas Hawkes!"

Rotating among the prominent guests, Thomas noticed Ken Nishimura standing alone near the pool. He excused himself from a discussion with the chairwoman of the Los Angeles City Council and walked over to Nishimura.

Hawkes decided not to divulge his visit with Roberts. "Hello, Ken. How is Stuart doing?"

"He took a hell of a jolt, but he keeps himself in good shape and should be able to recover quickly."

Thomas sipped from his champagne flute. Ken asked a question of his own. "Does your paper have any idea who did it?"

"We're following a number of leads. I've got virtually the entire newsroom on the story. In addition to my political crew, our intelligence reporters are leaning hard on the FBI, Secret Service, DHS and CIA because of the rumors of Russian involvement. They've gotten a few leads, but it's difficult to catch a break in a case of this magnitude."

A waitress offered them fancy delicacies. They raised their hands, and she left.

Thomas looked around before continuing the conversation. "I want to thank you for meeting with Frank before he left for Moscow."

"I'm taking a big risk letting him leave the country with a prototype of the xWave. If it were to fall into the wrong hands, I would be toast. I'm just surprised that you'd pack him off halfway around the world right after the attack on Stuart."

"Frank is careful. If the xWave is half what you say it is, it might come in handy during his reporting. I wasn't entirely sold on the idea of the trip, but the more I think about it, the more sense it makes. How are things going at IntelliView?"

"The release date for the bioWave, as we agreed, is still

planned for the last day of the Republican Convention. We've done a good job priming the market. It's going to be difficult, however, to make a really big splash in your industry without some very compelling news that goes beyond Stuart's nomination for president."

Thomas half smiled. "Perhaps we'll finger the culprits behind the attack on Roberts."

Ken raised his eyebrows. "Nothing better than a blockbuster to launch the bioWave. As I've told you, this little machine could spark a communications revolution."

Thomas eyed Nishimura with cautious amusement. "I gave up on revolutions when I was a kid, Ken. All I know is that the current upheaval in journalism is killing us. What we need is something that will make money again."

Ken winked. "I've always rather liked a quotation from Emerson: 'Every revolution was first a thought in one man's mind.' We've adopted that as our motto at IntelliView."

CHAPTER 23

QUEENSTOWN, MARYLAND

THE WYE RIVER Plantation on Maryland's Eastern Shore, forty miles east of Annapolis across from Kent Island on the Chesapeake Bay, had a schizophrenic history. The tobacco estate and its classic Southern mansion with white pillars on the front porch were donated by the Houghton family to the Aspen Institute, a nonprofit think tank and conference foundation. It provided Aspen, headquartered in Colorado, an East Coast beachhead near the political heart of the United States. Wye first gained international recognition in October 1998 when President Bill Clinton, PLO leader Yasser Arafat and Israeli Prime Minister Benjamin Netanyahu reached an ill-fated peace accord on its secluded grounds. The Aspen Institute also hosted seminars for top thinkers from academia, government and the private sector to discuss weighty topics such as justice, leadership or the good society. Its conferences were housed in three buildings—Wye Woods, River House and Houghton House.

Wye River Plantation had another function that few visitors knew. The original mansion had been fitted with soundproof, windowless rooms. These secure rooms had a singular purpose: providing a venue for senior military and intelligence officials to hold sensitive talks.

A corporate-class Bell 429 twin-engine helicopter settled onto the landing pad one hundred yards from the mansion in a canopy of aged oak trees, surrounded by gardens of azaleas, roses, forsythia and magnolias. The helicopter door opened, and Russell Talbert, the CIA's director of science and technology, climbed out. Thomas, who had flown in earlier from Los Angeles on a chartered Gulfstream IV, strode onto the asphalt and shook Talbert's hand as the whirling chopper blades blew their thinning white hair. The sun was setting over the Wye River. Hawkes and Talbert walked through the red-brick mansion and out onto the veranda overlooking the water.

Adjutants in tuxedos brought gin and tonics, a bowl of nuts and two cigars. The aides placed the refreshments on the glass table between the two men and took their summer sport coats. Hawkes and Talbert sat under an extended porch roof and peered out at the gardens. A ceiling fan stirred the humid air. Thomas cut the tips of the cigars and handed one to Russell.

Talbert, who had set up the meeting, spoke first. "I understand you visited Roberts at the hospital yesterday. How is he?"

"His physical recovery is coming along fine. But I'm concerned about his state of mind. The assassination attempt seems to have unnerved him."

Talbert lit his cigar. "How so?"

"He became aggressive when I visited him. He started pushing me to find out who tried to kill him."

"Sounds pretty amateurish. Is he still reliable?"

Hawkes weighed what to share with Talbert. "I'm not sure he's told us everything about his Russian contacts and his time in Moscow, especially after his posting there."

Talbert had read the intelligence dossier on Roberts carefully. He knew a great deal more about his Russian ventures than Hawkes did, but he revealed nothing to Thomas. "That's unfortunate. We can't afford any surprises."

The two men's work together on past projects was legendary among those few in the know. They had long held similar views about the mission and leadership of the Agency. Hawkes had chosen Talbert to be his inside asset for Operation Long Shadow. It was crucial to Talbert that Hawkes continue to view him as an ally in the operation.

Russell finished his first gin and tonic. "Do you think Stuart might be involved in this Russian oil scandal that Frank Adams's friend Viktor Romanov has been investigating?"

"That's one of the leads that Frank's looking into over there. We've invested too much in Roberts for there to be any questions this late in the game. He needs to have clean hands."

Russell cut to the chase. "Or we need to fix it. Adams and Romanov might uncover particularly unpleasant aspects of Roberts's past. After we find out what they know, we may need to deal with them."

Thomas exhaled smoke. "Don't worry about Adams. I can handle him. But you're right about the Russian."

The dinner bell rang. Thomas and Russell moved into the high-ceilinged room that could have been in a scene from *Gone with the Wind*. They were joined at the table by a half-dozen Aspen Institute seminar participants. Hawkes and Talbert listened as the cutting-edge thinkers around them began discussing the pressing issues of the day. Leading off, of course, was the US presidential election and the attempted assassination of Roberts. Were al Qaeda or Islamic State terrorists behind it? Could the Russians be involved? Was it possibly the work of some madman operating alone?

Talbert was amused by such talk. It was common among these young people with the "Potomac Fever," which seemed to infect most of those who work in the nation's capital. Such far-fetched theories also filled spy novels. The espionage community was even known to feed the notion of conspiracies by employing false flag strategies that shifted apparent responsibility for mischief to an enemy government.

Conversation ebbed as the wait staff served the visitors their choice of Maryland crab cakes, Eastern Shore free-range chicken or a medley of farm-to-table seasonal vegetables. A chamber quartet of touring students from the Aspen Music Festival began playing Beethoven's Grosse Fugue in B flat major, Opus 133.

Ninety minutes later, as after-dinner drinks were served, chopper blades whirled in the distance. Talbert glanced at his watch and nodded at Hawkes. They rose from the table, walked outside and moved toward the landing pad lights.

The helicopter dropped slowly to the ground. As Talbert approached the aircraft, a steward held open its passenger door. Talbert boarded and sat down on the leather seat behind the pilot. The chopper lifted from the pad and leveled off.

Talbert opened the console next to his seat and took out the secure satellite phone. He punched in a number and waited a few moments.

The phone on Raz Gonan's desk in Tel Aviv beeped three times. On paper, the three-star general was in charge of Israel's Air Defense Command. His covert assignment was running counterintelligence operations for the Mossad.

"Good morning, Raz. I thought I'd brief you on my meeting with Hawkes."

"Go ahead."

"Thomas has his top reporter, Frank Adams, in Moscow investigating whether the Russians were involved with the attempt on Roberts's life. Adams has connected with a Russian reporter named Victor Romanov. Both of them are possible SVR targets. Hawkes's daughter, who used to be married to Adams, is the Agency's energy director. She has assigned several of her operatives to track Adams and Romanov."

Gonan interjected: "You and I should have independent means to protect our interests."

Talbert gauged the potential consequences before responding. "That's an excellent idea. But let's proceed cautiously before considering further action. We need to find out what Adams and Romanov learn in their reporting."

Gonan concluded the exchange.

"I have just the person in mind for this assignment."

V: FULL HOUSE

Life is like a game of cards. The hand you are dealt is determinism; the way you play it is free will.

Jawaharlal Nehru

CHAPTER 24

S INCE THE LAST poker game at Frank and Lisa's Moscow flat, Mikhail Gusov had realized his dream of becoming a rich oilman.

The Russian television film crew members were getting impatient. They'd agreed with Gusov to interview him in the oil capital of Baku in Azerbaijan. The segment would be featured in *The Oligarchs*, a popular documentary series about the lucky and ruthless ones who became the richest men in Russia after the collapse of Communism. While dealing with a succession of Gusov intermediaries, the TV crew had finally been told to meet the oil tycoon at the five-star Excelsior Hotel Baku in the grimy city on the western shore of the Caspian Sea. Lead correspondent Pavel Sidorov hoped to get Gusov to reveal how he'd emerged at the top of what had been a wasteful state-run oil monopoly. Sidorov even thought he might get Gusov to appear sheepish and uncertain on camera.

He was in for a surprise. Gusov happened to be in the right place at a good time. When the Soviet spoils were being divided in the rush to embrace enterprises, he had been fortunate to fall in with the right crowd. In fact, much of his success was due to his cutthroat competitiveness and keen attention to detail.

Gusov's trip to Baku with Lisa and Bud Johnson, courtesy of AmeriCon Energy in the summer of 1999, was one of those defining moments when an individual sees clearly what the future portends. Mikhail knew that he wanted to get into the oil business. That trip, plus his participation in a little-noticed international signing ceremony in Istanbul four months later, set him on his way.

The Turkish event was to seal a multilateral agreement, funded by British, Russian, American and European oil companies with World Bank support, to build a pipeline from Baku, through Georgia and Turkey, to the Mediterranean. The Baku-Tbilisi-Ceyhan pipeline would be the world's second-longest at 1,768 kilometers, eventually moving a million barrels of oil a day to feed the insatiable demand of developing nations. President Bill Clinton joined other world leaders in Istanbul on November 18, 1999. Lost in the ceremony was a side agreement with Kazakhstan to build a feeder trough to the main pipeline to move Kazakh oil along the same route to the Mediterranean.

Mikhail knew that the future wasn't just with the developed countries clamoring for oil and natural gas. The Russians,

Azerbaijanis and Kazakhs were already moving crude to China. Mikhail figured that Pakistan, India and other countries to the east with their huge populations were the ticket to success. Pipelines were essential to his vision of markets to come.

Mikhail's decision to conduct their interview in the lobby lounge of the Excelsior Hotel would help him control the tenor of the conversation. Although the surroundings were plush by most viewers' standards, there would be no TV panning of fancy offices, security guards or layers of functionaries. Sidorov wouldn't get to impress his viewers with his access to the inner sanctum of one of Russia's most secretive businessmen.

Mikhail was relaxed and smoking one of his perpetual cigars with a couple of beautiful Azerbaijani women at his side when the camera crew hustled into the hotel lounge. Waving the correspondent over while dismissing the sexy attendants, Mikhail stood and gestured at Sidorov to take a seat.

As his crew set up their cameras and lights, Sidorov wiped his brow with a handkerchief and thanked Gusov for the interview. When his crew gave the signal, he looked into the camera, gave a short introduction to Baku for his viewers and briefly described the history of oil production on the shores of the Caspian.

"We are here in Baku, site of the world's first oil wells dug eleven years before the Americans struck oil in 1859 in the state of Pennsylvania. According to historians, Baku was producing oil from surface pools as early as the third century. Legend even has it that before recorded history began, one of the world's oldest religions, Persian Zoroastrianism, had a fire temple in Baku fueled by oil."

Sidorov strode toward Mikhail and continued speaking. "But we have come here today because Baku is the headquarters of the huge oil and natural-gas empire Mikhail Gusov has built as the most successful of New Russia's second wave of oligarchs. Mr. Gusov has graciously permitted us to interview him and to follow him with our cameras so that we might get a taste of the incredible life he has built just fifteen years after the Soviet Union disintegrated."

Sidorov sat down next to Mikhail. "Mr. Gusov, thank you for inviting us into your domain. I hope you don't mind that part of my job as a reporter is to ask you difficult questions."

Gusov smiled. "Of course. I wouldn't have it any other way."

"Some Russians say that you and the other oligarchs got rich so fast by using your connections with powerful people to acquire state-owned enterprises for next to nothing. What is your response to such claims?"

Mikhail looked into the camera. "I disagree with such negative portrayals. This is the New Russia. There are opportunities for many people to be successful if they would only take the initiative. I've labored hard for my success, as have my workers and those who have invested their well-earned money in our enterprise. I would humbly suggest that all of us involved in this undertaking deserve whatever rewards it has provided."

"Sir, we Russians have all heard about the Italian Mafia in America. As I'm sure you know, some Russians point out that five of the original seven Russian oligarchs are Jewish. Are we seeing the birth of a Jewish Mafia in our homeland?"

Mikhail gave Sidorov a half-disgusted look. "People should be proud of their heritage, but it has nothing to do with their business endeavors. And I daresay that I view my fellow oligarchs as competitors rather than as members of some sort of Jewish dynasty."

Mikhail rose and beckoned for the others to follow him. "The best way for you to understand who I am and how I have built my oil business is to see it for yourselves."

Outside the hotel, Mikhail's driver rushed around the Mercedes-Benz and opened the front passenger door for him. Sidorov and his cameramen climbed into the backseat.

As they drove toward the Caspian oil fields, it was easy to see how crude had made Baku one of the world's filthiest cities. The pollution was unbearable. Its canals and streams were filled with sewage. While oil had provided the means to build skyscrapers and monuments, everything had a grungy tarnish.

Once they left the industrial outskirts of the city and approached Mikhail's oil fields, the driver lowered the windows so the crew could film the scene. Mikhail directed the driver to stop.

"I have a special fondness for this oil field because here was where we had our first big strike. It used to be that Baku oil was very close to the surface, but now we have to drill down to incredible depths and seek new reserves under the sea."

The Mercedes rode past more oil fields. Many workers took off their soiled caps and waved them at Mikhail.

Mikhail waved back. "You see? I take good care of these men. They are loyal to me, and I am loyal to them."

A phone rang in the front of the car. The driver handed it to Mikhail. After a short discussion, Mikhail gave the phone back to the driver. "I'm afraid that I will have to leave you. That was an important call from one of our foreign investors. I apologize, but I'm going to have to attend to some critical business."

Mikhail instructed his driver to drop him off at his field headquarters building four kilometers away and to take the television crew back to their hotel in Baku.

When Mikhail entered his ramshackle office, he found his friend from AmeriCon Energy standing there. Bud Johnson, wearing his traditional cowboy hat and bolo tie, embraced Mikhail and gave him a Texas bear hug.

"Damn, it's good to see you, Mikhail. Sorry I didn't let you know I was coming, but ever since Lisa moved back stateside, I've been like a bull without horns. I couldn't find my ass if I put a skirt on it."

Mikhail laughed. Though he now spoke English passably well, the Russian couldn't follow some of the Texan's colorful turns of speech. Yet he always enjoyed Bud's affable manner and wide smile.

"You're welcome at my oil fields anytime, my friend. Thanks to you, the BTC pipeline has just been completed and is now moving hundreds of thousands of barrels of my oil through Georgia and Turkey."

Mikhail led Bud from the building. "Why don't we take

a walk into the fields? There's some new drilling technology that the Azerbaijan Oil Academy has developed that I want to show you."

Bud nodded. "You know, oil flows through my veins, Mikhail. I'd love to see what you're using to increase production."

The two men walked down a dusty path that led to several rigs in full operation. Bud was in his element. He loved the smell and sounds of pumping crude. "Damned if this doesn't remind me of Texas when I started out as a wildcatter."

Mikhail nudged his friend. "I'm sure that even though the equipment is a lot more sophisticated than when you started, the thrill is just the same. As I look back at how you helped me get into this business and introduced me to some of the key figures behind the BTC pipeline, I still can't believe that things have turned out so well."

Mikhail looked out at his field. "Do you remember that night in Moscow after poker at Lisa and Frank's flat? You and I went out on the balcony with them and Stuart Roberts."

"Of course. That's when I saw the potential in you that I now realize I underestimated. Wasn't there an Afghan student on the balcony with us?"

"As a matter of fact, it was Ahmad Durrani, an archeologist who is now becoming well known internationally."

Mikhail thought of telling Bud about some of his current dealings with Ahmad but decided to divert the discussion. "Speaking of that night on the balcony, how is Stuart doing these days?"

"Quite well. We have a number of mutual friends and contacts. He's entered politics. Some of the big-money boys are financing his run for a United States Senate seat in California."

Mikhail wasn't surprised that Stuart had decided to run for office. He'd always suspected Stuart was aiming high. "He was a skillful diplomat. I would expect him to be as successful in politics as he has been in business. Russia has not yet evolved to the level of your country where a thriving business-man like Roberts can become an ambassador and then seek high political office. In our country, it's more like your Wild West a century ago. We become powerful by knowing the right people in the Kremlin. And we keep our competitors at bay with whatever means are necessary."

Bud laughed at Mikhail's take on the ties between business and politics in their two countries. "It looks like this Russian Wild West has worked out well for you!"

Mikhail smiled and shook his head. "We need to develop a political culture that is more sympathetic to the new capitalists. A culture that provides our oil companies with the kind of favorable laws and tax shelters Washington gives your oil industry."

Bud turned their conversation to the real reason for his visit. "You know, Mikhail, I've always believed that you Russians need a little encouragement once in a while. You and BP have hit a goldmine in the Azeri-Chirag-Guneshli oil fields out in the Caspian. But you need some good-old American know-how for getting it to market. My company would like to help you build another pipeline to move your oil and gas to other deep-water ports."

Mikhail decided to speak forthrightly. "I've already thought about that, Bud. But it's not the Black Sea or the Mediterranean that will bring in top dollar for oil. It's the growing demand in China, Pakistan and India that I want to serve from my oil fields in Kazakhstan." Mikhail removed his sunglasses and put his arm around Bud's shoulders. "I plan to build a pipeline to Pakistan. I could use some outside capital. And it would be nice for the two of us to have our own project without others interfering."

Bud was momentarily flummoxed, but he quickly recovered. As Mikhail waited for a response, Bud drew a map of the route in his mind. "Wouldn't such a pipeline have to go through Afghanistan?"

"Of course."

"Things are pretty dicey there with the Taliban and the other Muslim radicals."

"That's where Ahmad can help us. He's from Afghanistan and knows the territory well. He has a lot of contacts."

Bud did some quick calculations. It was a high-risk project with a potential for large yield. "We might be able to help, but it could get pretty expensive."

"Just how expensive?"

"If we build the pipeline, AmeriCon would be willing to go fifty-fifty."

"Fifty-fifty?"

"AmeriCon Energy gets half your oil royalties in exchange for financing the pipeline."

Mikhail remained calm. "It's my oil. I'll give you one-third of the royalties."

Bud slapped Mikhail on the back. "Well now, I see you

really have left Communism behind! How about settling on 40 percent of the royalties for AmeriCon?"

"Agreed."

The two oilmen walked along in silence until Mikhail stopped to ask a question. "Have you ever heard the Russian word 'blat'?"

"What does it mean?"

"It doesn't have a precise definition, but Russians understand it's how things get done."

This tickled Bud. "Oh, you're talking about greasing the wheels!"

"Just a little on the side for the two of us. After all, we're the ones who are making all of this happen."

Bud looked to the left and then to the right in a theatrical show of caution. "Damn, comrade, if you aren't a capitalist already! We've got ourselves a deal."

They walked back to the field office where Bud's car and driver were waiting. Just before the vehicle drove off, Mikhail leaned in.

"Next time you bump into Stuart, please give him my best regards. Those were good days back in Moscow." Mikhail added a final thought. "And who knows? Depending on how Stuart's political career develops, we all might be able to help one another."

CHAPTER 25

FIVE YEARS AFTER the last poker game at the Adams flat in Moscow, Stuart Roberts was running for the United States Senate. A pilgrimage to Israel was a required stop in a Senate election campaign. Political and cultural knowledge of the Middle East added to the candidates' credentials, while personal contacts with Israeli leaders bolstered their standing with the American Israel Public Affairs Committee and other powerful US lobbying groups for the Jewish state. An added benefit of an Israel tour was filling campaign chests and helping secure Jewish votes back home.

Roberts landed at Ben Gurion Airport near Tel Aviv on his first political journey to the Holy Land. He eschewed flying on IntelliView's Gulfstream 550 to make a political statement by traveling on El Al. Walking from the arrival gate to the terminal hub, he reflected on the stream of diversity among his fellow passengers. Many visitors shed joyful tears or wore expressions of happy anticipation. Their glee contrasted with the somber looks of returning Israelis as they steeled themselves against the chronic stress of living in a still-young country whose Jewish population was being outpaced by its Arab birthrate. Israel's confinement to a land the size of Vermont while surrounded by hostile neighbors hyped the stress.

Reaching the hub roundabout and joining the stream of humanity from the other arrival spokes, Roberts viewed the departure waiting area one floor below with its symbolic waterfall from a glass dome flowing into a ceramic-tiled pool. Surrounding the pool were shops selling mezuzahs, menorahs, tallit clips, silver Kiddish cups and tzedakah charity boxes. He left the roundabout and started down a ramp surrounded by a glass wall rising forty feet to the ceiling. At passport control, he received the same scrutiny as other arrivals did from the brown-uniformed border agents and the soldiers walking in pairs with their Uzi submachine guns.

Roberts collected his bag from the carousel and walked through the green "Nothing to Declare" exit. He spotted Zev Levi. Stuart smiled as he thought of Zev's poker "tell" of pursing his lips when he was bluffing. Levi was now a senior Israeli Foreign Ministry official who oversaw immigrants and helped them develop ties with Israeli businesses.

After embracing, the two men walked outside to a limousine driven by a Mossad agent who took them north on Highway 431 to Jerusalem. Sitting in the backseat, Levi and Roberts discussed the sordid state of Israeli politics. Zev, whose habitual sparkle in his eyes bespoke a connoisseur of mischief, gleefully informed Stuart of various scandals surrounding the new Prime Minister Ehud Olmert, a former Jerusalem mayor who headed the Kadima (Forward) Party. Former Prime Minister Ariel Sharon had formed the center-right party a year earlier before a severe cerebral hemorrhage left him incapacitated. Olmert, Sharon's key ally and hatchet man, vowed during his campaign to follow in the footsteps of his stricken mentor, a retired general who'd commanded an armored division on the Sinai front during the 1967 Six-Day War.

Stuart smiled to himself: he was employing a similar strategy back home by evoking Ronald Reagan's name at every campaign stop.

Zev expressed concern about Olmert's leadership of Operation Autumn Cloud, the recent movement of Israeli armed forces into the Beit Hanun area of the Gaza Strip to destroy rocket-launching sites aimed at Israeli settlements. Olmert had caused an international stir by refusing to rule out a military strike on Iran. Since Israel had nuclear weapons and the Iranian military was a substantial force, some world leaders accused Olmert of war-mongering.

After an hour-long ride from the airport, Zev and Stuart saw the Knesset, a square, white, five-story building perched on one of Jerusalem's seven hills. Levi and Roberts left the limo and passed through the perimeter security gate. They approached the entrance to the Great Assembly. Entering the parliament building, Zev shepherded Stuart through the internal security stop.

Stuart knew he was in good hands. "Zev, it's so good of you to introduce me to your colleagues here in the Knesset and to your Foreign Ministry contacts."

Zev winked and leaned into Stuart. "You're not only a personal friend, you're a good friend of Israel."

The two men walked down a corridor outside the Knesset chamber. They passed the body's members in all their glory: the Lubavitchers with long beards and curly sideburns, the bankers wearing bright blue yarmulkes, the Russian émigrés looking like Queens Mafia figures. One Hasidic member approached Zev and threw his arm around him. They exchanged traditional kisses on each other's cheeks.

"Omer, let me introduce you to an old American friend. This is Stuart Roberts, who founded the IntelliView telecommunications company in California."

Zev lowered his voice. "He's also running for the United States Senate."

Zev turned to Stuart. "Omer Aaronson is chairman of the finance committee here in the Knesset." Zev rubbed his thumb against his forefinger to signify that Omer controlled the government purse strings.

"It's a pleasure to meet you. How do you know my good friend Zev?"

Stuart flashed his politician's smile. "We were both stationed in Moscow in the late 1990s and into the new century."

Zev gently elbowed Stuart. "Who cares about our jobs? We played poker together!"

Zev leaned into Omer again, pointed to Stuart and spoke in a stage whisper. "He always won. And not only did he take my money, he took our friend Rado's money."

Stuart was surprised to hear this name. "Rado Weinstien?"

Zev smiled broadly. "The one and only."

Omer prepared to depart. "I'll be sure not to play cards with you, Mr. Roberts. But if you'll excuse me, I must go to a committee hearing." He hurried off.

Zev and Stuart walked down a corridor to a coffee bar. They approached the counter. Switching to Hebrew, Zev ordered. "Two double espressos."

They sat down. Zev took out a cigarette and lit it. "I know you Americans don't allow smoking in your government buildings, but I trust you will allow me."

As Zev inhaled, Stuart raised his eyebrows in feigned disapproval. "So, you're still in touch with Rado?"

Zev eyed Stuart with surprise. "Of course! My job with the Foreign Ministry entails looking after high-level immigrants from Russia and Eastern Europe."

"What is Rado up to these days?"

"A few years ago, he used his business success to get elected to the Knesset. After first arriving in Israel from Russia, he started a company called NanoTek that has become quite successful. Being in the high-tech field, you're no doubt familiar with nanotechnology. Rado's firm contracts with Israeli defense and intelligence agencies. His company specializes in making miniature components for sophisticated weapons and intelligence-gathering systems."

Stuart showed genuine interest. "My company provides equipment and software to the Pentagon and the Agency. It appears that Rado and I have more in common than one would have guessed. I'd be interested in seeing him."

Zev smiled again. "It just so happens that I've arranged for the three of us to have dinner tonight."

CHAPTER 26

SIX HOURS LATER, Zev, Stuart and Rado sat at a window table in Mishkenot Sha'ananim, Jerusalem's exclusive French restaurant whose prominent diners have ranged from the late Prime Minister Golda Meir to spy novelist John Le Carré. Through the window, a spectacular sunset cast pink and orange hues over the walls of Jerusalem's Old City, David's Tower and Mount Zion. Zev hosted his guests at an elegant table covered by a white cloth with silverware, crystal goblets and Fürstenberg porcelain china. The sommelier poured from a bottle of Mouton-Rothschild cabernet, 1986 vintage.

Zev welcomed his guests. "Moise Peer, the owner of this wonderful establishment, has become a good friend over the years. His wine cellar is one of the best in the world. He selected this wine in honor of our special dinner tonight." Zev spoke in a confidential tone. "Moise selected this particular cabernet from the private collection that he saves only for wines with a perfect 100 Parker score."

Zev could not resist one more boast. "It sells at auction for $800 a bottle! Moise is giving us a nice discount." Zev winked. "He wanted to make it a gift, but I told him we government types can't be on the take."

Zev lifted his glass; Stuart and Rado raised theirs. "To friendship that somehow survived many gambling losses at the poker table!"

The three men clinked glasses. Although they were a bit older now, their personalities were unchanged from the Moscow days. Zev was expansive and playful. Stuart was observant, as friendly as the moment required, but careful even among old acquaintances. Rado remained humorless. He was the first to speak after savoring the wine. "As I recall, Stuart did not lose at poker."

Zev and Stuart exchanged covert glances. Rado had always been difficult.

Zev lightened up the conversation. "Ah, come now, Rado. You know that we let him win!"

This actually elicited a rare half-chuckle from Rado. His glass was always half empty. He was torn between his insatiable greed for wealth and recognition as a leader of men within the Jewish homeland and his dark history as a Stasi agent for the Soviet puppets in the Democratic Republic of Germany. Rado was the only child of a rare Holocaust survivor who didn't leave Germany after the war. He'd always been tormented by the vagaries of what life might have been had his mother not remained in what would become East Germany, a place where anti-Semitism greeted him at every turn and eventually came to define his own life.

Rado looked across the table. "What brings you to Israel, Stuart?"

"I'm running for the United States Senate. I'm visiting Israel to broaden my foreign affairs portfolio. And who better to visit here than a senior official in the Israeli Foreign Ministry?"

Not stage whispering this time, Zev lowered his voice so other diners couldn't hear. He spoke to Rado. "Stuart will be going to Moscow from here to see our friend Mikhail Gusov. This is on a need-to-know basis. Stuart has asked that his meeting with Mikhail and his entire trip to Russia not be made public."

Rado frowned. "Gusov has profited handsomely from the corruption in Russia."

Stuart felt compelled to defend his Russian friend. "Mikhail has taken fair advantage of his opportunities."

Zev's glance darted from Rado to Stuart. It had always been his role to ensure a certain level of social comfort. "Speaking of opportunities, I thought the two of you might find it useful to explore a joint business venture. After all, your companies fulfill similar contracts for our governments' defense and intelligence agencies."

Rado and Stuart eyed each other warily. Each waited for the other to speak.

Stuart broke the silence. "IntelliView works with many federal agencies in Washington."

Rado followed. "The main focus of NanoTek is the high-end consumer market for advanced electronic devices."

Zev waved his hand in pretend annoyance. "Gentlemen, please, let's not stand on ceremony! We are old friends, and Israel and the United States are the closest of allies. There's no need for secrets among us!"

They laughed. All three men knew of the intergovernment spying and industrial espionage between the two countries. Stuart and Rado agreed to meet at NanoTek the next day.

When he returned home that evening, Rado retrieved his secure cell phone from the desk safe in his den. He placed a call to his principal contact at the Mossad, General Raz Gonan. Unknown to Zev, Rado and Gonan had worked closely together ever since the German had emigrated from Russia to Israel in 2003. Their relationship was a marriage of convenience. The leadership at the Mossad was keenly interested in Rado's experience as an intelligence operative in both Stasi and the SVR.

The general answered after the second ring. "Gonan."

Rado went right to the point. "I had dinner tonight with Levi and Stuart Roberts. As you no doubt remember, I was Roberts's minder when he was the US ambassador to Moscow. I'm meeting with him tomorrow to explore a joint venture between his company and mine. IntelliView is at the cutting edge of nanoelectronics. That could aid NanoTek enormously with our nuclear trigger project. His firm is a giant in US defense and intelligence contracting. It has a huge piece of the vast American investment called the National Nanotechnology

Initiative. This could be the breakthrough that we've been waiting for."

"What are the downsides to working with Roberts's company?" Gonan asked.

Rado's old resentment surfaced. "Everyone thinks he's so charming, but he's always been devious."

CHAPTER 27

DEH RAWUD VILLAGE, AFGHANISTAN
THURSDAY, JULY 17, 2008

AHMAD SAT IN a tent in the Afghan desert near Deh Rawud, the childhood village of Mullah Omar, the spiritual leader of the Taliban fundamentalists leading the insurgency against US forces. Four Taliban and Ahmad huddled around a frayed map spread across a large cardboard box turned upside down to serve as a table. The Taliban wore Muslim robes and Kufis on their heads. Ahmad was also covered in traditional religious garb. He had grown up speaking Farsi and learned Dari in school; but for this meeting he spoke Pashto, the language of the radical Taliban who dominated the southeastern region of Afghanistan along the Pakistani border.

The Taliban leader, Abdul Jabar, praised Ahmad. "For an intellectual from the city, you speak our language well. Where did you learn it?"

"My work has allowed me to see many parts of our country. It has introduced me to many servants of Allah."

The other three Taliban representatives recited in unison: *"La Illaha Ill Alla!"* ("There is no deity except God!")

Jabar sipped from his cup of tea and invited Ahmad to do the same. He tested the archaeologist from Kabul. "Do you know what my name means?"

Ahmad had researched his answer. "Servant of the mighty."

Jabar nodded in approval. "You work for the rich Russian. What is his name?"

"Mikhail Gusov."

"We do not like the Russians," Jabar said sternly. "When the heathen Soviet fools dared to invade our land, we drove them out like frightened dogs."

The other three Taliban again recited together. *"Hassana Hijrah!"* ("Good deeds committed in the path of God!")

Jabar looked intently at Ahmad. "The imperialist Americans will suffer the same fate as the Russians."

Despite the stifling heat outside, it was almost comfortable within the confines of the tent, especially when a soft breeze blew through the partially open entry flap.

"Why should we help the wealthy Russian increase his riches?" Jabar asked.

"Our pipeline will bring oil to the servants of Allah in Pakistan," Ahmad replied. "They will have less need to import oil from the Saudis and the Iranians."

This pleased the Taliban chieftain. "The Saudi royals have betrayed Allah with their Western ways! And the Shiites in

Iran observe a bastardized form of Islam." Jabar looked down at the map. "Show me the path of this pipeline."

Ahmad removed a laser pen from inside his robe. He traced the red beam from Mikhail's oil fields in Kazakhstan, through Turkmenistan, across southern Afghanistan and into Pakistan.

Jabar followed the route. "That is a great distance."

"Twenty-five hundred kilometers," Ahmad said.

Jabar focused on one part of the map. "You have secured passageway from our Sunni brothers in Turkmenistan?"

"Yes."

"What percentage of the royalties will this Russian Gusov pay them?"

Ahmad hesitated. With a jab of his head, the Taliban boss bade Ahmad to respond.

"One-third," Ahmad finally said.

Jabar rose and glanced at the others. "We will require more. Afghanistan is in the midst of war. The security provided by our jihadi will not come cheap."

Hearing voices outside the tent, Jabar and the other Taliban rose to their feet. Ahmad stood up with them.

Mohammad Nabi Omari, the Taliban's Minister of Communications, entered the tent, followed by a stocky man with a bushy beard and wide, piercing eyes. Omari waved his hand for Durrani and the Taliban to resume sitting.

"Our Iraqi brother, Abu Bakr al-Baghdadi, may Allah always protect him, will join us in this important discussion," the minister said.

Omari nodded toward the bearded visitor.

"Caliph Ibrahim, together with the esteemed al-Qaeda leader in Iraq who fought so well with us in the struggle against the Soviets, Abu Musab al-Zarqawi, may Allah continue to embrace him in paradise, were instrumental in fighting the American imperialists and their Shiite lackeys in Fallujah four years ago."

The Taliban shook their fists in appreciation of Baghdadi and the martyred Zarqawi.

Omari beckoned to Jabar to continue.

Jabar repeated his earlier question for the minister's benefit. "What percentage of the royalties will the Russian Gusov pay for the protection that we will provide?"

Ahmad, although flustered by the interruption of Omari and Baghdadi, followed his negotiating strategy. "Forty percent."

Omari interjected before Jabar could respond. "We will insist on half of all profits. A portion of that will go to Calib Ibrahim here for sending his revered warriors from Anbar in Iraq to help secure this pipeline."

Ahmad glanced at the visitor. He remembered the ferocious Battle of Fallujah but didn't recall Baghdadi's role in it. After searching his memory for a moment, he nodded in assent.

As Ahmad put the laser pen back into a pocket under his robe, Omari added another condition. "And while the pipeline is being built, we will need one million dollars a month to ensure that your workers are not attacked."

Ahmad responded carefully. "I will try to persuade Gusov to accept this arrangement."

Ahmad made his own demand. "For 50 percent of the royalties, we will expect complete protection and all necessary assistance in working with local authorities."

Omari smiled for the first time. "The Taliban will provide nothing less."

Omari motioned for the others to come toward him. He looked at Ahmad. "It is noon. Will you join us for Dhuhr prayer?"

"Of course."

The Taliban placed their prayer mats on the floor of hardened sand. All seven men got on their knees and faced Mecca. Prostrating themselves, they began to pray.

CHAPTER 28

THE ISRAELI KNESSET'S session was concluding for the day. Rado Weinstien reflected on the changes in his life since leaving Russia in 2003. His ruthless personality and expertise in nanotechnology were well suited for Israel's business environment. His financial success and connections with Russian immigrants had propelled his election to the Knesset and selection as the "attack" deputy leader of Yisrael Beiteinu, a conservative political party founded by Russian Jews who followed the teachings of Ze'ev Jabotinsky and now numbered more than one hundred thousand.

Meanwhile, Rado's company, NanoTek, made miniature spyware for the Mossad. As the Israeli legislature was ending its morning session, Knesset Speaker Reuven Rivlin rapped his gavel. The members rose from their seats at once, and the chamber exploded into noisy talk. While the other parliamentarians exchanged gossip and pleasantries, Rado walked briskly through the chamber and into the main hallway.

Waiting for him by a window off to the side was General Raz Gonan in his crisp, dark-green Israeli Defense Forces uniform. The two men stood near a window that looked out onto western Jerusalem from the hilltop neighborhood Givat Ram.

"Hello, Rado."

"Good afternoon, General."

Rado followed his Mossad boss away from the Knesset chamber. They entered an empty committee room and sat at a dark wood table in front of the semicircular long desk where Knesset members convened for hearings. "Bring me up to date on your company's business venture with IntelliView and Stuart Roberts."

"As a senator from California, Roberts publicly can't have anything to do with IntelliView."

"There are ways around that. When the Mossad recruited you in Moscow in the late 1990s, you were working for the SVR as Roberts's minder. I'm sure you have arranged to stay in close contact with him about our joint project with Washington to develop a nuclear grenade."

"Of course."

Rado eyed the general. The Israelis had less humor than his former Stasi colleagues.

Gonan spoke again. "Langley is asking whether we are still on schedule for the test phase of the nuclear grenade."

"Yes, we're on schedule. I have someone finalizing the nuclear trigger. And we're beginning to cast the miniature ceramic components."

Gonan nodded. "We need to get this done. Let's meet again in two weeks."

The two men left the committee room and went their separate ways.

Rado and Qin Sun entered the opulent Michael Andrew restaurant in west Jerusalem. The illuminated Wailing Wall and Temple Mount centered a spectacular view from their table. Qin was now a successful physicist with a senior post in China's top-secret Nuclear Forces Agency. Through Qin, Rado's company was providing nanotechnology for atomic weapons to the Chinese government. Unknown to Beijing, Qin was working for Rado on the side. Their illicit enterprise was making millions of dollars selling sophisticated weaponry on the international black market.

A waiter poured two glasses of Golan Heights Winery Cabernet Sauvignon, 1984 vintage. Rado tasted it. The finish was thin, and he set the glass on the table. "How was your flight from Beijing?"

Qin took out his cell phone. "It was very successful."

Rado pondered whether to return the wine. "Successful?"

Qin removed the cover on the back of the cell phone. He took out the battery and handed it to Rado.

Rado was annoyed. "Why are you giving me your cell phone battery?"

Qin smiled broadly. "It's not a battery. It's the nuclear nanotrigger. We now know it can pass through airport security."

Rado disliked being caught off guard. He didn't know how to react to this bombshell.

"Clever, but you risked everything without my approval."

"I'm no longer your research fellow, Rado. Besides, I bring good news from Beijing."

"What's that?"

"The Nuclear Forces Agency has approved payment of one billion dollars for delivery of the nuclear grenade technology. The first deposit of five hundred million will be made when the testing phase starts."

Rado's frown morphed into a smile. "That is good news indeed, but no more freelancing on your own. I need to maintain the absolute trust of the Mossad—not only for the sake of this deal with Beijing, but for future ventures with other parties in our weapons trade."

CHAPTER 29

MOSCOW
SATURDAY, APRIL 3, 2010

FOUR YEARS HAD passed since Mikhail Gusov and Bud Johnson had hatched their secret plan to build an oil pipeline across Afghanistan. Gusov's progression toward political engagement in Russia had been driven by, of all things, the fierce public debate over legalized gambling. When the Bolsheviks took power in 1917, they had banned gambling as a bourgeois scourge of the West. Russians knew better. The country's three literary giants—Pushkin, Tolstoy and Dostoevsky—were gambling addicts who had produced some of their major works under the lashing deadlines of large gaming debts. Mikhail didn't give much thought to his nation's triumvirate of literary titans as he laid plans to build a casino in Moscow. He would call it the Samovar, named after the beautiful water heater with a nest on top to hold the tea kettle, a hallmark of every Russian home.

Other than an occasional fling at one of the forty casinos that had sprung up in Moscow during the capitalist binge of the 1990s, Gusov wasn't a gambler himself; his oil and natural gas ventures in the Caspian provided enough risk. But he didn't trust Russia's topsy-turvy stock market, and bandits owned the banks, so Gusov was seeking other investments for his growing fortune. A casino seemed like a good choice. The newly rich *beezneesmyen* were profligates, flaunting their wealth and throwing their money in every direction.

Mikhail saw a niche for his casino as a classy alternative to all the carnival casinos. There would be no flame-breathing dragons like at the Shangri-La on Pushkin Square and none of the constant din of big bands in Jazz Town at Taganskaya Place. Most importantly, the mobsters, with guns tucked in their waistbands and high-heeled hookers on their arms, would not be welcome at the Samovar.

In 2006, Vladimir Putin had his parliamentary cronies introduce a bill to prohibit gambling as part of an "antivice program" that recalled the heavy-handed moralism of Soviet Communism. Like others, Gusov assumed the move was merely a symbolic shot across the bow meant to remind all the ostentatious tycoons that the Kremlin strongman still controlled their destinies. Surely in the New Russia, the government wasn't about to shut down a $6 billion industry that employed thousands while providing hundreds of millions of rubles in badly needed tax revenues.

As the Putin legislation gathered dust, Mikhail moved ahead with his plans. The Samovar opened in May 2007 and quickly became one of Moscow's most successful casinos, an elegant alternative to the capital's rowdy gaming spots. Gusov differed from his fellow casino owners in other ways: he refused to pay hush money to the shady extortionists boasting of their Kremlin connections and citing the consequences of ignoring their entreaties. The threats compelled Mikhail to hire a private security detail.

The intimidation tactics also drove Gusov inexorably into the political arena. He believed that the corruption would never cease until the casino owners put aside their economic rivalry and took a united stand against it. He and Michael Boettcher, a Brit who had opened the first big casinos in Moscow, formed the Association of Gaming Operators. They began negotiations with senior Putin aides to submit their industry to greater regulation and to pay more taxes. For a while their initiative appeared to be bearing fruit; the *apparatchiks* signaled a willingness to reach a deal that would allow the industry to survive. Mikhail became a frequent guest on TV talk shows, arguing for self-policing and putting a human face on the gambling parlors as legitimate businesses. Just as he began to think his efforts were succeeding, Putin lowered the ax: on April 1, 2009, the casino owners were given ninety days' notice that their operations would be shut down. Even then, Mikhail viewed the edict as a negotiating ploy, a show of strength intended to wring higher taxes and other concessions from the industry. But as the weeks passed and the clock ticked down, there was no sign of bluffing from the Kremlin.

Putin issued a decree limiting the location of legal casinos to four remote areas of the vast country: the Altai Republic in Siberia; an isolated strip of land near the Azov Sea, hard up against the Ukraine border in Southern Russia; Kaliningrad, a Russian outpost between Poland and Lithuania; and a coastal region along the Pacific Ocean near China and North Korea.

Such farce infuriated Gusov. Who would travel so far to play the slots or bet on the roulette wheel? The decree stank of Stalin's 1934 creation of "Socialist homelands" such as the Jewish Autonomous Oblast, heralded as a Zionist frontier in the Soviet Far East, a God-forsaken place whose Jewish population never reached twenty thousand. But there was nothing Mikhail could do. When the deadline came, he took down his roulette tables, removed the slot machines and transformed the Samovar into a private dining club. Every month, as he reviewed his ledgers and saw his profits fall, his reluctance to enter politics receded. Even if Putin was intent on quashing dissent, Mikhail had believed that, like the Communist Chinese in Beijing, he would allow capitalism to take root and permit at least the semblance of economic freedom. But if the Kremlin, by virtue of simple edict, could shutter a whole industry virtually overnight—what kind of capitalism was that? If Gusov could be forced to close his casinos, how safe were his oil pipelines? The whole notion of private property was a sham.

Mikhail realized that he had underestimated Vladimir Putin.

He decided to form an opposition party.

On a spring day in 2010, he summoned a dozen allies to a closed-door meeting at the Samovar. By then, any traces of naiveté had vanished; Mikhail realized the danger of his new ambitions. He directed his invitees to tell no one of the secret gathering, not even their spouses.

Gusov held the meeting in the executive conference room of his club on a Saturday evening. As his busiest night of the week, he could count on the club being filled with activity. He assigned the participants staggered arrival times. Some were instructed to enter the club through a rear door; others were told to use the main entrance. They were first seated in small groups at tables in the main dining room. Every few minutes, one of them would excuse himself, rise, go to the restroom in the back, emerge and instead of returning to the table walk down a corridor past the kitchen and enter the conference room.

In a half hour, eight men and four women were seated around the teak conference table. Gusov entered the room and took his place at the table's head.

Mikhail peered at the group. His most trusted lieutenants were Dmitry Kaslin, a former classmate in Moscow State University's MBA program who had built Russia's first fast-food chain; Alexander Razumsky, a wholesaler of heavy equipment for the oil and gas industry; and Natasha Alekseyeva, a physicist and the first female on the Russian Academy of Science's governing directorate. He had told the three of them that they would form his political inner circle, an unofficial presidium of confidants. He'd instructed them to let the others speak at the meeting, listen closely and then share their impressions afterward.

The heavy doors to the dining room opened. Waiters in white tuxedo vests delivered glasses of mineral water, plates of red caviar, pickled mushrooms and marinated herring, and baskets with thin slices of dark rye bread.

Mikhail gestured at the food. "Please, enjoy, my friends."

As the guests began to eat, Pavel Sidorov spoke. "Where is the vodka, Misha?"

Sidorov, the TV correspondent who'd filmed the well-received documentary about Gusov, had become a confidant of the oilman since that initial meeting in Baku.

Mikhail smiled. "I'm sorry—no alcohol. We must be clearheaded tonight."

Gusov spoke with deliberate formality. "Ladies and gentlemen, we are gathered here because none of us likes the direction our government is heading. None of us wants to see a rebirth of Soviet Communism. None of us wants to see the reestablishment of the Kremlin dictatorship that murdered, imprisoned and silenced our parents and grandparents. None of us wants to return to the past. That would mean an end to the opportunities we have enjoyed in recent years."

Igor Lebedev, leader of the Liberal Democratic Party in the Duma, nodded. "The Parliament is almost completely under the control of Putin. Whatever democracy remains is just for show."

Viktor Romanov described his experience as a prominent business reporter. "My newspaper is one of the few left that the Kremlin doesn't exert total censorship over."

Yuri Levada, founder of the first independent political polling firm, relayed his surveyors' mounting difficulties. "People are afraid to answer our polling questions honestly."

For the next twenty minutes, the guests exchanged stories

of their frustrations as they ate. Finally, Mikhail rapped the table with his knuckles and waited for the talking to subside. "It is because of disturbing developments like this that I have made an important decision."

The group waited.

"We are tonight forming a serious opposition party for the purpose of preventing Russia from sliding back into repressive Stalinist rule. As some of you know, I have been reluctant to embrace open political action. But I believe that now is the time for us to step forward and identify an alternative to the current leadership of our country."

Approving murmurs encircled the table. Lilia Shevtsova, a senior historian at the Carnegie Moscow Center, spoke first: "If we are forming a party, it must have a name."

The talented young painter Alexis Kalyakin, who had traveled from St. Petersburg, added: "A powerful name."

Gusov rose dramatically and stood before his friends. "Free Russia Party," he said, then raised his glass. "My friends, we are at a grave juncture in the history of our Motherland. After the promise of democracy, most political opposition has been silenced. Anna Politkovskaya and other journalists have been murdered, yet their killers go free. Russian businessmen now bow to the Kremlin."

Mikhail set his glass on the table. "I don't need to tell you that the step we are taking is a dangerous one. We must meet this challenge with courage."

Now the guests lifted their glasses and spoke in a single voice.

"Courage!"

Two hours later, Pavel Sidorov walked along the Arbat, the central pedestrian street where Moscow merchants and craftsmen sold their wares. It was past midnight. The Arbat was empty save for a drunk staggering home. Sidorov turned onto Plotnikov Lane and looked around to make sure he was alone. The TV correspondent took out his cell phone and dialed a number that few people would know.

A kilometer away, a solitary figure sat in a Kremlin study. Normally long asleep by now, the man in the study awaited the call. The only light in the room came from a Tiffany peacock lamp on the antique black walnut desk. The phone rang on his private line. He lifted it.

"Do you have something to report?"

A streetlight's ray fell on Sidorov. "They have formed a new political party."

"What is its name?"

"Free Russia Party."

The man in the Kremlin study hissed. "'Free Russia.' Indeed."

The line was silent for a moment. Sidorov spoke again. "Gusov is clearly the organizer."

Sidorov lit an Artika cigarette and inhaled as he listened. "You must bide your time. Let Gusov believe that his ambitions are moving forward. Allow him to feel powerful for a while. All that matters is that he is stopped before he becomes a real threat."

Sidorov exhaled the smoke and continued listening. "When the time comes, your sources will blame it on the others?"

"The other oligarchs," Sidorov replied.

The Kremlin man had the last word. "Gusov will learn the lesson these other obscenely rich men have learned: they can enjoy their wealth as long as they play by our rules."

CHAPTER 30

R USSELL TALBERT, CIA director of science and technology, parked his Porsche Boxster and crawled out from behind the steering wheel. Talbert was a bear of a man with a reddish, lived-in face and a pouch of fat overhanging a low-riding belt. He was occasionally taken for the politician and former history professor Newt Gingrich. He walked with a slight limp toward the entrance of Old Anglers Inn, a Washington landmark from the 1860s. He opened the wooden door with a cast-iron handle and entered the restaurant's dark interior lit by candles on wooden tables and a large stone fireplace with glowing embers. He spotted Scott Dennis, director of the CIA's National Clandestine Service (NCS), sitting at the bar. Talbert's suspicions from the earlier voice-altered phone message were confirmed.

Talbert and Dennis were in equivalent positions as heads

of two of the four directorates at the top of the CIA hierarchy. Although not friends, they had a collegial working relationship because of the need to translate advances in science and technology to NCS field work. Dennis headed the most secretive and deadly arm of the CIA with the stated mission "to strengthen national security and foreign policy objectives of the Agency through the clandestine collection of human intelligence (HUMINT) and covert action." He had a long history of HUMINT assignments in the Middle East and the former Soviet Union before moving into the Agency's upper strata. A slight man in his early fifties with gray hair, Dennis could be mistaken for an accountant, advantageous in his line of work.

Talbert sat down as Dennis ordered two Irish coffees. The Inn was one of the venues favored by agents when they wanted to get away from the constant surveillance at headquarters in Langley on the Virginia side of the Potomac. Talbert knew this was not the final destination when he had accessed his voice mail that morning and heard a digitally distorted voice instructing him to meet a contact at the Inn and to wear hiking boots and warm clothing. Talbert had traced the call to the phone bank in the arrival area outside customs at Dulles International Airport. The artificial voice sounded like the computer-generated voice of the theoretical physicist Stephen Hawking. Talbert was familiar with the now-outdated technology developed to aid Hawking and others with amyotrophic lateral sclerosis, known in the United States as Lou Gehrig's disease. Newer technology had been invented, which NCS field agents used through a smartphone app created for the intelligence community.

"I thought the call came from one of your colleagues, so I'm surprised to see you here," Talbert said.

"We have business to discuss," Dennis replied as he attended to his coffee. He wanted Talbert to stew over the meeting's purpose. Finally Dennis took the last sip of coffee. "Let's stretch our legs."

They walked out into the midday sun, crossed a two-lane road and entered the Angler spur of the C&O Canal tow path leading toward the Billy Goat Trail, a popular hiking route along the Potomac. They headed north across a boulder field, passing two abandoned gold mines and the Spitzbergen rock cliffs where teenagers jumped seventy feet into the river in the summertime. On this cold Monday in January, few hikers were on the trail.

They finally reached an overlook of Great Falls. The Potomac cascaded down one hundred feet over jagged rocks and gathered speed as it flowed through the Mather Gorge, the training course of US Olympic kayakers. Only the extreme kayakers would challenge going over Great Falls.

Talbert was winded, and his left leg with the artificial knee was throbbing. He knew that Dennis had him at a calculated physical and psychological disadvantage. He sat on a boulder and gazed at the icy water swirling past their vantage point. Catching his breath, he confronted Dennis. "You'd better have a goddamn good reason for hauling my ass out here."

Dennis chose his words carefully. "I didn't volunteer for the excursion. This is a bit bigger than your shop or mine."

"Just what the hell do you mean by that?"

"Your friendship with our old colleague Thomas Hawkes has ruffled some feathers."

Talbert stared at Dennis. "The Company approved my involvement with his family's foundation years ago and, as you know, has benefited enormously from the talent we've gathered as a result."

Thomas Hawkes's grandfather had created the foundation in the late 1800s with some of the fortune he'd made trading bullion during the California Gold Rush. The Hawkes America Foundation, on whose board Talbert served as a director, selected a small number of brilliant high school students as Hawkes Scholars and paid for them to attend the finest institutions of learning. The CIA had secretly funded the foundation beginning in the 1950s and recruited promising scholars to work for the Agency. Talbert himself had been a Hawkes Scholar at the California Institute of Technology, majoring in chemistry and physics, and then went to graduate school at MIT; there he completed a dctoral thesis on two deadly neurotoxins, erabutoxin in the venom of sea snakes and tetrodotoxin from the ovaries of pufferfish.

"It's not your work with the foundation that troubles the sixth floor," Dennis countered. "It's your collaboration with Hawkes's risky political agenda. He's always been a cowboy. That's why he was passed over for the directorship and left the Agency."

"That's ancient history," Talbert said. "Hawkes has been a valuable resource for us beyond his experience and connections. Hell, Lisa Hawkes is one of our shining stars, and she wouldn't be at the Agency if it wasn't for her old man. His ability to mine information for us through his newspaper is legend."

"You know better than that, Russell. Hawkes treats the flow of information like a permanent high tide in his direction. And his efforts to nurture direct relationships with second-tier leadership at the Farm, and even with field operatives, haven't escaped our attention."

Talbert rubbed the skin over his artificial knee. "So, you dragged me out here in the wind and cold just to dress me down about Hawkes?"

Dennis ignored the question. "The win that Hawkes's man racked up in Iowa last week was a wake-up call. We didn't expect Stuart Roberts to emerge as the Republican favorite in the presidential race. He's got some troublesome skeletons in his closet."

Dennis extracted a buff folder from his jacket. "This is a summary we've put together with some input from friends of ours. It's for your eyes only and is to be disposed of at the Pit." Dennis handed the folder to Talbert. "Read this carefully. We have every confidence that once you think things through, you'll reach the appropriate conclusions."

Without another word, Scott Dennis turned and trekked back toward the C&O towpath.

VI: BLIND MAN'S BLUFF

Fortune brings in some boats that are not steered.

William Shakespeare

CHAPTER 31

ATYRAU, KAZAKHSTAN

FRANK CHUCKLED AS the Air Astana 1970s-era Fokker 50 twin-prop plane made a rickety descent into the provincial capital of Atyrau on the northeastern coast of the Caspian Sea. Most Americans had never heard of Kazakhstan until the success of the movie *Borat*.

Atyrau's airport was compact but modern. Frank and Viktor collected their bags, zipped through customs and headed out into the bright sunlight. They hailed a cab and slid into the dusty backseat.

It had been years since Frank had made the journey to Kazakhstan, chasing an oil-strike story. Even though the country had substantial inland coastlines along the Caspian and Aral Seas, it was dominated by arid steppes and had the feel of a land-locked wasteland. Kazakhstan was huge, larger than all of Western Europe combined, stretching twelve thousand kilometers across half of Asia from the eastern edge of Europe at the Ural foothills.

The place had always been a downtrodden outpost in the Russian empire, long before it "joined" the Union of Soviet Socialist Republics in 1936. Nearly a quarter of its population was wiped out as the Soviets forced all agricultural activity into collectives. Deprived of any incentive to benefit from their own labor, farmers simply gave up. The results were mass starvation and ethnic violence. Thousands more lost their lives during the purges Stalin imposed to eliminate the followers of Leon Trotsky and Nicolai Bukharin and to ensure that party functionaries didn't stray from Moscow's dictates.

Not surprisingly, given its servility to the Kremlin, Kazakhstan was the last republic to declare independence after Communist rule ended in 1991. It was led then by Communist henchman Nursultan Nazarbayev, a rough-hewn petty despot who clung to power for years after his Soviet patrons had disappeared. Frank had profiled Nazarbayev in a 1999 article, spending a week in the renamed capital of Astana. He interviewed mid-level government functionaries in their dingy ministry offices and smoked cigarettes at cafés on the Ishim River with political dissidents who glanced over their shoulders as they complained of rigged elections, nepotism and bribery in the vast land's booming oil and natural gas sector.

Through it all, Nazarbayev remained in office. Always "elected" by huge margins, his countrymen—those who dared to whisper it—called him the ultimate oligarch.

In a return visit to Kazakhstan, Frank had come to Atyrau in the fall of 2000, just after the Kashagan oil field was discovered under the Caspian, seventy-five kilometers southeast of the boomtown. It was a smaller oil strike than the Tengiz field in 1979. Those reserves of twenty-five billion barrels had lured the American oil giants Chevron, Exxon and Mobil into the Caspian region's menacing web of political intrigue for the first time. But with a crude capacity of sixteen billion barrels, Kashagan was plenty big. Now, Exxon and Mobil had merged and were developing the underwater oil field as part of an international consortium with Dutch, French and Italian energy behemoths, plus a Kazakh government venture that was little more than a state-sanctioned Mob operation. Kashagan had been scheduled to start pumping crude in 2005, but a witch's brew of brutal offshore conditions, local power struggles and a fledgling regional environmental movement had caused delays. It still was not producing oil.

Viktor shared an odd historical note with Frank. "This place used to be called Guryev. It was named after a seventeenth-century merchant who got rich delivering caviar to the czars." He laughed. "We still have a czar, although that title has lost favor, and the Kazakhs are still delivering caviar to him. Only now the caviar is called crude. And the Kazakhs have gotten wise. They don't let us Russians have an oil monopoly anymore. They're making a killing selling crude and natural gas to Europe and China. And they got rid of all the Communist city names. 'Atyrau' comes from an old Kazakh phrase that means 'where the river goes into the sea.' It's where the Ural River empties into the Caspian Sea after its run from the mountains."

There was more that Viktor might have told Frank, information more relevant to their current mission.

Frank knew that Gusov had made his billions by building a well-chronicled natural gas pipeline to Europe. The fortune it brought Mikhail had transformed him into an oligarch, a status that carried both the admiration and disdain of his countrymen.

Yet, Viktor suspected something that Frank didn't know: Gusov might have been hatching a bigger megadeal. A reliable source from Viktor's Oil Ministry days had told him that Mikhail was preparing to build a new pipeline. It would follow a treacherous southeastern route, through Turkmenistan and Afghanistan, to Pakistan.

And there seemed to be more to the story. Another source, a Foreign Ministry functionary who Viktor believed to be an SVR agent, had dropped a bombshell over coffee a few weeks ago: Gusov's secret project was being funded in part by a big American oil company with close ties to powerful politicians in Washington.

His source's claim of an American energy firm's involvement in such a controversial venture could be just a typical unfounded Kremlin slur. The claim might also be true, or have at least a shred of truth to it. Fiction or fact, Viktor wasn't about to share his lead with Frank.

Viktor's editor, Pyotor Maximovich, had been off the mark back in their office last week. Like many older people, even smart professionals, Pyotor Maximovich didn't understand how much the ground beneath him had shifted.

The editorial offices of *Kapital* and the *Los Angeles Register* were eleven time zones apart, and their papers were published in different languages. But thanks to the Internet, the two newspapers were indeed competitors. A big story on losangelesregister.com became a huge international story in an instant. If that story had roots in Russia; if it purveyed big news about one of the country's richest men—that story would cut a swath straight across Viktor's beat as a top business reporter.

Viktor and Frank were friends, no doubt. But they were also rivals. As the taxi neared their hotel, Frank delivered a gentle reprimand. "You haven't briefed me on our interview here."

"My source didn't give up much. I was just told that a contact named Surum may have information about the Oil Ministry scandal and the hit on Roberts."

"Do you really think the Kremlin wasn't involved? We both know that those thugs never shed their KGB ways."

Viktor didn't need to hear lectures from Frank about his country's leaders. He understood them far better than Frank ever would. They were smoother and more finely groomed than Brezhnev or Stalin. They knew their way around a world-class wine list and could drop a French or German phrase when the occasion required. But the powerful men inside the Kremlin were no less capable than their predecessors, merely in a day's normal course, of unleashing swift violence against anyone who stood in their way.

Viktor was pursuing a different theory. Roberts had spent

a lot of time in Russia. He maintained a network of high-level contacts inside and beyond the government.

Viktor had no love for his country's rulers. But when he heard Stuart's daily denunciations of them out on the campaign trail, when he caught a TV news clip or an Internet video and listened to the bitter fervor of Stuart's self-righteous attacks, something about them didn't ring true.

Was Roberts, a man who'd always impressed Viktor as being complex and cunning, merely adopting the lazy role of a humdrum politician? Was he inspiring fear against an easy target and catering to his countrymen's crassest instincts? Or did Roberts have other motives? One might ask why Roberts was protesting about Russia so often and so shrilly. This train of thought, these leads—if, in fact, they turned out to be leads at all—Viktor would keep to himself as well.

Viktor suspected that Frank had some private leads of his own.

The two reporters, so warm in their affection for each other, were treading parallel tightropes of cooperation and competition on their unusual joint assignment.

CHAPTER 32

ATYRAU, KAZAKHSTAN

THE TAXI PULLED up to the Renaissance Atyrau Hotel, an architectural oasis surrounded by drab concrete buildings constructed in the dreary Socialist style of the old USSR. After checking into their fourth-floor rooms and cleaning up, Frank and Viktor took the elevator downstairs. They walked through the lobby and into the lounge, where they were supposed to meet a man named Surum.

Frank had no idea that his former lover, Svetlana Lutrova, the gorgeous Russian woman who had helped destroy his marriage, was the intermediary of the man they were to interview. This was one more detail Viktor hadn't shared with Frank. It was an omission the Russian would have come to regret were he to understand its consequences.

Frank and Viktor sat down at the bar. Frank checked his watch. "Do you know what this guy looks like?"

"No, but I've been assured that he will recognize us."

The concierge entered the lounge and approached Viktor. "Sir, are you Mr. Romanov?"

"Yes."

The concierge gave Viktor a sealed envelope and walked away. Viktor read the note inside and tucked it into a pocket as Frank watched expectantly.

"Well?"

"We have to go to another bar to meet Surum. This message has the directions."

Frank and Viktor left the hotel, walked over to the taxi stand and got into a cab. The driver took them through central Atyrau and then toward the edge of town. It was obvious that Atyrau was growing rapidly in haphazard fashion.

There was one sure sign that the Kazakh boomtown had become an important front in Big Oil's relentless search for new sources of crude: wireless Internet was available everywhere. As the cab drove along Albai Street, Frank saw a firm called Landmark Graphics. He took out the xWave and Googled the company name. The answer came in a moment: it designed and sold specialized computer software to oil companies.

After entering an industrial neighborhood with acres of oil equipment behind high fences topped by barbed wire, the taxi stopped outside a sleazy-looking, working-class tavern with a small sign over the door.

Viktor paid the driver. He and Frank left the car and entered the roustabout bar. They walked into a dark room, the air thick with stale smoke. The joint pulsed with prostitutes, rigworkers and a palpable feel of danger.

They stood by the bar, uncertain whether to sit on stools.

A man walked unsteadily up to them and held out his hand. "Viktor, I am Surum. I have a table for us in the corner."

The three of them walked across the room. Surum seemed to stumble as he navigated the route to the darkest corner. On the table sat a bottle of Snow Queen, a rot-gut local vodka. They took their seats. Surum poured the vodka into three glasses. He picked up one of them and drained it.

Frank studied the bottle's label. "I didn't know they made vodka in Kazakhstan."

Viktor spoke to Frank under his breath, switching to English so that Surum wouldn't understand. "It's awful, but we need to drink it."

Frank had spent years combating alcoholism. He could recite in his sleep the warning signs that led to a resumption of drinking. Frank also understood his duties as a reporter and the sometimes unpleasant requirements of the job. He would have to join Viktor in playing this game. Frank picked up his glass and downed the vodka.

Surum watched them eagerly as they tried the Snow Queen.

Viktor put his hand to his mouth and muffled a cough. "Quite distinctive."

Frank nearly gagged on the bitter liquid but managed not to cough. He kept a straight face. "A real treat."

The journalists exchanged glances. Frank waited for Viktor's lead.

Viktor eyed Surum. "Our Moscow contact says you have information to share with us."

"How much is it worth to you?"

Surum appeared to be on the verge of a drunken stupor. An alcoholic stench permeated his breath.

Viktor hid his disgust. "How can we know until you tell us the information?"

"Twenty thousand rubles now and twenty thousand rubles later."

Viktor took a wad of bills from his pocket, peeled off four 5,000-ruble notes and handed them to Surum. "We're all ears, *tovarisch*."

Surum broke into a ramble. "I'm from Atyrau. Long before the big Russian and international oil companies showed up, I used to play in the fields that are covered with rigs now. My father left us when I was twelve, and I had to quit school to get a job."

Viktor and Frank were surprised that Surum could put two sentences together.

Viktor, though, was impatient. "Get to the point."

"It will all make sense when you hear me out. My first job was on a—"

A cell phone chimed. Viktor pulled his phone from his pocket, put it to his ear and listened intently as Surum continued talking with Frank.

Viktor heard a female voice. "The drunk is a decoy. Your real contact is in a car in the alley behind the bar. Come alone."

"Understood."

Viktor put the phone back in his shirt and resumed listening to Surum.

Frank was trying to focus Surum. "Did you ever meet an American named Stuart Roberts?"

"You mean the guy who's running for president and just got shot? I'll get to him in a minute. But as I was saying, you need to understand how much this city has changed since they discovered oil here."

Viktor stood up. "Excuse me, I need to use the men's room."

After he entered a dark hallway at the rear of the bar, Viktor walked past the restroom, found the backdoor and stepped into an alley leading to the street.

CHAPTER 33

ATYRAU, KAZAKHSTAN

VIKTOR SAW AN overflowing dumpster with garbage strewn about the cobblestone alley. He walked toward the street. As was his habit before interviewing a source, he pulled out his recorder, turned it on and began speaking.

"Four p.m., Saturday, July 23. In Atyrau with Frank Adams. Just left him at the bar with Surum. Svetlana Lutrova's source. Got a call from her telling me to come alone and meet a contact outside in a car."

Letting the recorder run, Viktor tucked it back into his safari vest's pocket. As he left the alley and turned onto the street, a black Mercedes-Benz W126 S-Class sedan with tinted bulletproof glass pulled up. It was a 1991 model, the last year Mercedes made that luxury car, but it had been well maintained.

The door opened. A burly Kazakh emerged from the front passenger seat and approached Viktor. "Viktor Romanov?"

Viktor nodded. The functionary put his hand on Viktor's elbow and opened the door to the backseat for him.

Viktor climbed into the car and sat down next to a man he recognized at once. It was one of his former SVR colleagues from what agents still called the First Chief Directorate.

Viktor couldn't conceal his shock. "What the hell is going on?" The man ignored the question and poured two glasses of Johnny Walker Blue into thin crystal tumblers, a familiar custom from their previous meetings. He handed one glass to Viktor.

Viktor felt wary but he tipped back a small taste of the very good scotch. This was a routine both had grown accustomed to over their years in the spy business.

His ex-partner looked directly at Viktor for the first time. "I saw you on Alexander Zmeyov's TV show. You've done quite well since you left the Committee."

The use of the inside name of the Soviet-era's dreaded KGB—short for the Government Security Committee—was common among most former espionage officers, rather than "the Service," as younger agents called what had been renamed the Foreign Intelligence Service.

"To what do I owe the privilege of seeing you after all these years?"

"I'll be happy to explain."

As Viktor took another sip of whiskey, his lips tingled with numbness and stinging pain. He took out his handkerchief and wiped them.

With a look of betrayal, Viktor hissed. "You son-of-a-bitch, you've poisoned me!"

A smile crossed the man's face. "TTX cocktail. As I recall, you've served it yourself."

Viktor, barely able to move his lips, gasped in a faint voice. "Tetrodotoxin, the chemical compound from Fugu, the fatal Japanese pufferfish."

"Precisely. A thousand times more deadly than cyanide."

Viktor struggled to speak. "Why are you killing me?"

His former compatriot reached over and put his hand on Viktor's shoulder. The gesture was Judas-like, warm and evil at the same time. "I am sorry, Viktor. You were a capable agent, and now you are a good journalist. Unfortunately, your skills are bringing you too close to revealing awkward truths. My hands are tied. This goes beyond Russia."

Viktor, fully paralyzed, appeared to be conscious. His eyes were open but unblinking. There was no movement in the muscles of his face. He was dead. The neurotoxin had done its efficient work, asphyxiating him through total respiratory arrest.

The Mercedes moved forward and turned into the alley Viktor had come from. Directly behind the bar, the car slammed to a stop. The beefy Kazakh emerged from the front seat, opened the back door and grabbed Viktor's body.

The Kazakh deposited the corpse near the trash dumpster and jumped back into the car. The Mercedes peeled off.

CHAPTER 34

ATYRAU, KAZAKHSTAN

RANK WONDERED WHAT Viktor was doing. Surum's rambling had given him a headache. The bar had become even noisier and more smoke-filled. Surum had been doing almost all the talking. Most of what he said bordered on the inane. Frank played the empathetic journalist's role, trying to appear interested. He and Viktor needed to learn what Surum knew about Gusov. Surum slurred his words and spoke melodramatically.

"It's very difficult for outsiders—and pardon me, sir, no offense meant—to understand what's been happening here. Of course, we are no different from everyone else. Wherever there are great riches, people start behaving differently. But the behavior here has become quite strange—quite strange indeed! Let me remind you . . ."

As Surum droned on, Frank checked his watch again. It

had been twenty minutes since Viktor excused himself to go to the men's room.

Frank finally interrupted Surum. "I need to find my friend."

Frank stood up and started to walk toward the back of the bar. Surum trailed after him.

The last thing Frank needed was a drunk Kazakh meddling in his affairs. Frank placed his hand on Surum's shoulder and firmly guided him back into his chair. "I need to go alone."

Frank headed toward the back of the bar. He approached a door with the peeling letters "WC" painted at eye level and looked inside the wretched water closet. It was empty. Scanning the hallway, Frank noticed that the back door was ajar. He walked over, opened it and went out into the alley. There he saw a body on the ground, near a trash dumpster. The realization that it was Viktor stunned Frank. He rushed over to his friend and put two fingers on the side of his neck to check for a pulse. There was no blood or visible wound, no abrasion or other sign of struggle.

Trembling, Frank did what he had done before in the most upsetting moments of his personal life and during his encounters with danger on the job: in the worst days with Lisa when they traded barbs about their sexual affairs; while he dodged sniper fire in Bosnia; as he watched a roadside bomb blow apart the Humvee in front of his vehicle in Iraq, killing soldiers he was imbedded with in Combined Joint Task Force 41. In this squalid alley in a grimy oil boomtown halfway around the world from home, he issued directives to himself to still the shaking in his hands and force his eyes away from his dead friend's face.

Feeling exposed, Frank worked quickly. He opened Viktor's coat and checked his vest pockets. He found Viktor's wallet and passport and slipped them into his own jacket. He discovered the recorder in another of Viktor's pockets, its red light still lit. Holding the device in his left hand, he retrieved Viktor's cell phone with his right.

Suddenly the black Mercedes came barreling down the alley. Hidden behind tinted windows, the driver aimed the car at Frank. Whether propelled by his rock-climbing experience or simple self-preservation instincts, Frank moved before he was aware of having made a conscious decision. The Mercedes clipped him in the side as he dove behind the dumpster in a cutout space of the shop next door. As Frank landed, his hand hit the ground and Viktor's recorder went flying into the alley. The Mercedes's back right tire ran over the device and sent it skittering under the dumpster. The wind knocked out of him, Frank lay facedown on the ground.

Surum appeared in the alley. Holding a 9mm Glock, he moved quickly to where Frank was lying motionless. With his steady walk and unambiguous purpose, he put to rest any doubt that he was sober. He raised the Glock and aimed it downward at Frank.

His head sideways on the ground, Frank remained still. He opened his eyes, unaware that Surum stood directly over him with the Glock pointed at his head. As he regained his focus and looked down the alley, Frank saw someone on the street, pointing a gun at him.

With a groggy clarity, Frank realized that the gunman was the driver who had met him at the Moscow airport just a few days earlier. A shot rang out. Frank recoiled, expecting to be hit.

Surum, shot in the head, fell dead to the ground, nearly landing on top of Frank.

Hovering above was a small unmanned air vehicle that had been tracking Frank from the time he and Viktor had left the hotel. This microdrone, the latest version of the Lockheed Martin RQ-170, was fitted with nanosensors, a variable aperture TV camera, an infrared camera for night vision, and synthetic aperture radar to penetrate haze. These advanced surveillance tools had been developed by IntelliView with funding from the US Air Force's clandestine TTLI—Tagging, Tracking and Locating Initiative. Frank's clothes were still carrying advanced nanotaggats and the radio-transmitting smart dust that the driver had sprayed into his garment bag at the airport.

The shooter turned and walked down the street away from the alley. He pulled an electronic device from his satchel and spoke into it. "Urgent message for Black Star. Someone tried to kill Adams, but he's alive. Romanov wasn't so lucky. I'll circle back to make sure Adams gets out of this."

Black Star had been watching the unfolding events on a video screen fed by satellite from the high-resolution camera mounted in the microdrone.

Lisa breathed a sigh of relief. Sitting in the secure command center at the US Embassy in Moscow, she was glad that her field agent had saved Frank's life. But she knew he was still in danger.

Frank struggled to stand. He noticed Viktor's half-crushed recorder under the dumpster, walked over and picked it up. He started to leave but heard a car speeding down the alley again. It was the same Mercedes-Benz.

Frank jumped behind the dumpster and crouched down.

The Mercedes squealed to a stop. The functionary and the driver emerged from the sedan. They reached the lifeless Surum and turned him face-up with their boots.

"What the fuck? This is *our* guy. Where's the American?"

After hastily dumping the bodies of Surum and Viktor into the Mercedes's trunk, the henchmen returned to the front, climbed in and drove off.

Inside the moving Mercedes, a short, unpleasant conversation ensued.

The functionary, in the front seat, opened the sliding window to the back and delivered the news to his boss. "One of the bodies was our man. The American must have escaped."

The man's face turned dark. He squeezed his whiskey glass until it shattered. Blood and scotch splattered the glass divider in front of him.

CHAPTER 35

ATYRAU, KAZAKHSTAN

FRANK'S SIDE, WHERE the Mercedes had clipped him, hurt like hell. After the car had sped off, he ducked back into the bar. It was risky, but he'd learned in his career that going back to a place with new information brought it into sharper view.

Frank looked around, wondering if he'd missed something important. Most of the prostitutes were talking with men alone or in groups of two or three around tables in the dark room. Frank sat down at the table that he, Viktor and Surum had shared. Almost immediately, a shabby-looking Kazakh woman who appeared to be at least fifty approached him.

"You look very tired and lonely," she said in Russian. "I'm sure I could restore some color to those cheeks and get the blood flowing to your extremities."

Although tempted to chase her away, Frank recognized the opportunity to escape the bar and get back to the hotel.

Leaving with the whore might throw off whoever had killed Viktor and targeted him.

Frank responded to the prostitute's solicitation in the Russian language that was native to neither of them. He employed his best Snow Queen slur. "Why don't you grab us a taxi?"

Frank settled the tab. By the time he peered out the front door of the bar, his date had a cab waiting next to the curb. Once inside the taxi, Frank told the woman that he had to break off their engagement. He gave her 5,000 rubles and asked her not to return to the bar. Once she was out of the cab, Frank told the driver to take him to the Renaissance Hotel.

Back in his room, Frank removed his shirt and examined the dark bruise on his side. He took a quick shower and put on a clean pair of slacks and a fresh shirt.

His body aching, Frank did what he'd always done when he was baffled and dispirited. He went back to work in the reporter's stubborn faith that if he went down enough paths, looked under enough rocks, asked enough questions, he would find the solutions to his puzzles. It was an article of faith for Frank that every question had an answer. As a reporter, you just had to ask the right questions. And then drive yourself until you found the answers.

Frank went into the hallway and approached a maid. "I left my passport in my friend's room, and he's out to dinner. Could you please let me into his room?"

"I'm not permitted to do that, sir."

Frank reached into his wallet, pulled out a twenty-dollar

bill and discreetly handed it to her. She smiled slightly, tucked the money into her blouse, glanced down the hallway in both directions, led Frank to Viktor's room and opened the door.

After closing the door, Frank opened drawers, looked in the closet, lifted the mattress, searched under the bed. He found two reporter's notebooks in the desk drawer and put them in his pockets. Frank saw the message light blinking on the phone next to Viktor's bed. He picked up the handset and pushed the flashing button on the base. Frank recognized a voice he hadn't heard in years. It was another of their poker partners, Ahmad Durrani, the Afghan archeologist.

"Viktor, I tried to call your cell phone but couldn't get through. I have some new information on Gusov and the oil scandal. It's best for us to talk in person. Please come to Kabul as soon as possible. Call me when you arrive."

Frank hung up. He spotted Viktor's laptop on a table next to an armchair in the corner. After he turned on the computer, there was a soft knock. Before he could get up, the maid opened the door and leaned into the room. "Sir?"

Frank closed the laptop and put it into the canvas case he'd brought from his own room. "I found my passport. Thank you."

The maid stepped aside and let Frank out of Viktor's room.

Frank returned to his room. Next to a battered chest of drawers was a mini refrigerator. Frank stared at it and struggled with the demons that Viktor's murder and his own narrow escape from death had unleashed inside him. He felt a different kind of danger now, the existential threat of his weakened resolve. Badly shaken, he told himself that he needed a drink, just one, and just this one time. He took two miniature bottles of Stolichnaya from the mini fridge, paused momentarily and then opened them.

Frank poured the Stoli into a tall glass and downed it quickly. The vodka seemed to soften the throbbing in his side.

Viktor was dead, and Frank had no idea why. Frank himself would have been killed save for the mystery man who'd driven him from Sheremetyevo Airport to the Hotel National just five days ago.

What the hell was going on? Were the former poker players being targeted? First Stuart, then Viktor and Frank himself. That was the only pattern Frank could see in the violence unleashed a half world apart. And now, yet another poker player had emerged. What new information about the Russian oil scandal did Ahmad have?

CHAPTER 36

ATYRAU, KAZAKHSTAN

SITTING AT THE desk in his room, Frank removed Viktor's laptop from his briefcase. He turned it on, waited for it to boot up and inserted a USB flash drive. He tried to open Viktor's computer files. The laptop screen flashed a message: "ENTER ENCRYPTION KEY."

Frank turned on the xWave. He placed the soft nanodisk on his head behind his right ear, focused on the xWave and silently communicated his thoughts. The device quickly linked to the laptop. Frank deftly maneuvered it through a series of steps to bypass the computer's firewall and to unscramble the data. In a minute the screen displayed a better message: "FILES TRANSFERRED SUCCESSFULLY."

Frank opened a file named "Mikhail-USPolitics" and read Viktor's notes in Russian on the screen: "Mikhail suspected of giving money to US politician through AmeriCon Energy exec Bud Johnson. (Lisa Hawkes worked for ACE when she and Frank were in Moscow. Bud Johnson was her boss; she brought him to poker game. Can Frank be trusted?)"

Frank scrolled down the screen to read the end of Viktor's notes: "Could US politician be Stuart Roberts?"

Frank poured himself another glass of Stoli and mentally commanded the xWave to hack into Viktor's e-mail account. He found four e-mails from Svetlana Lutrova.

The e-mails rattled him. Frank knew that Viktor and Svetlana had been romantically involved years earlier, but he thought their affair was over. Viktor had never mentioned Svetlana during Frank's subsequent trips, and he'd assumed that their paths had parted for good.

Svetlana's e-mails unnerved Frank for other reasons. Before he could control it, her almost unbearable Slavic beauty tumbled back to Frank. The feel of her long, blond hair sweeping across his chest, her honeysuckle scent flooding over him, the soft skin inside her thighs sliding against his own, her voice murmuring Russian words he'd never heard, her hands cradling his head, her flashing green eyes slicing into him as he pushed into her.

A deep shiver shook Frank: Svetlana was Viktor's source. He scolded himself. How could he have been so naïve?

Frank opened the most recent e-mail from Svetlana and read it on the screen. "Have you met with my contact yet in Atyrau?"

Frank shook his head. Was Svetlana an unwitting accomplice? Or had she knowingly sent Viktor and Frank into a deadly trap?

Then he remembered Viktor's recorder. He pulled out

the half-crushed device and examined it. The mini screen was cracked but intact. Frank turned on the recorder and touched the play knob. The machine spewed out pieces of a garbled conversation in Russian.

Straining, Frank heard Viktor's voice. "What the hell . . ."

Another Russian voice was similarly jumbled. "—Alexander Zmeyov's TV—"

Viktor again, badly distorted, almost a whisper. "—poisoned—"

The rest of the recording was too corrupted to make out.

Frank tried to listen to the recording again but heard only a few mangled words.

Frank looked at his watch: 11:00 p.m.—noon in California. He picked up the xWave and gave a voice command: "Conference—Ken."

Shortly, in the air before him, Frank was viewing a projected avatar of Nishimura in his IntelliView office. Momentarily transfixed, Frank watched Ken greet him as if they were in the same room.

"Hello, Frank. It's nice to know that the xWave video-conference function operates from over there. I thought you'd be checking in from Moscow, but my virtual screen says you're somewhere in Kazakhstan."

Frank cut him off. "Ken, I don't have a lot of time. You've been a good source for me on Roberts, and I've protected you. I need to ask you an important question."

"Fire away."

"Do you know anything about a relationship between Roberts and a Russian oilman named Mikhail Gusov?"

Ken was his usual unflappable self. "Not offhand. I can make some inquiries."

Frank nodded. "Please do that. I need some technical help as well."

"With the xWave?"

"No. I've got a garbled digital recording that I can't decipher."

"Even if the voice file is corrupted, the xWave should be able to access the raw data directly from the chip in the device. I can walk you through that."

"Alright, go ahead."

"The personal voice qualities will be lost, but a simulation program will reproduce the conversation. I've transmitted the code to your xWave. It will take a minute for the conversation to be reconstructed. We'll need to disconnect for the voice-reproduction to operate."

"Thanks, Ken."

Ken's image faded from the air. Frank placed the xWave next to Viktor's recorder until they synced up. While he was waiting for the recording to be reconstructed, Frank paused for a moment of what he knew was futile resistance. He went over to the refrigerator, grabbed the last small bottle of Stoli, poured it into a glass and returned to the desk. After he had taken a few sips, the xWave beeped and a blue light flashed twice. Frank heard the reproduced conversation. He listened intently to two computer-generated voices speaking in Russian.

"What the hell is going on?"

Frank heard a glass being filled, then the response: "I saw

you on Alexander Zmeyov's TV show. You've done quite well since you left the Committee."

"To what do I owe the privilege of seeing you after all these years?"

"I'll be happy to explain."

The conversation paused, then resumed. "You son-of-a-bitch, you've poisoned me!"

"TTX cocktail. As I recall, you've served it yourself."

Viktor—an assassin? Frank couldn't believe it was true. Frank listened to the end of their exchange.

"Tetrodotoxin, the chemical compound from Fugu, the fatal Japanese pufferfish."

"Precisely. A thousand times more deadly than cyanide."

Frank strained to hear the gasping voice. "Why are you killing me?"

"I am sorry, Viktor. You were a capable agent, and now you are a good journalist. Unfortunately, your skills are bringing you too close to revealing awkward truths. My hands are tied. This goes beyond Russia."

Frank was stunned. The story he had come to Moscow to get—who had tried to assassinate Stuart Roberts—was metastasizing.

CHAPTER 37

ATYRAU, KAZAKHSTAN

F RANK PUT THE xWave back into its holster and placed it in his briefcase. He opened his wallet and found the business card Viktor's editor had given him five days earlier. Frank turned his attention again to Viktor's laptop and the slain journalist's still-open e-mail account. He clicked on "new message," waited for the template to appear and typed the editor's e-mail address from his business card. Posing as a virtual Viktor, Frank typed the message in Russian: "Pyotor Maximovich, I'm off to Kabul to follow leads. I'll be in touch in a few days. Viktor."

Frank sent the e-mail. He saw that a new message had arrived from Ahmad. He opened the e-mail and read it on the screen: "Viktor, did you get my cell phone message?"

He clicked on the "reply" icon and typed a response, once more as if from Viktor: "Ahmad, I received your message about new information. I will arrive in Kabul tomorrow. Please tell me via e-mail where and when we can meet."

Frank hit the send button and turned off Viktor's laptop. He sat back. The only obvious link connecting the startling events of the past week was the poker game he had hosted in Moscow. In his mind, he went around the poker table. Gone or injured were Viktor, Stuart and himself.

Left, he hoped, were Mikhail Gusov, Rado Weinstien, Ahmad Durrani, Zev Levi and Qin Sun. He had to contact them and warn them that they were in danger.

Frank would see Ahmad in Kabul and then Mikhail back in Moscow. He needed to talk to the other three, both to alert them and to learn if they knew any pieces, no matter how small, of this widening mystery. He went to his briefcase and pulled out the xWave. Realizing that he didn't have contact numbers, Frank hoped that the device would be able to find his former colleagues. He communicated his thoughts to the xWave and before him, in a hologram, appeared two names and telephone numbers.

He concentrated on the first name. The xWave dialed the number in Beijing. The phone rang and Frank heard a recorded message, first in Chinese and then in English. "This is Professor Qin Sun. I am not available. Please leave your message."

Frank left a message asking Qin to call him at the number of the cell phone he'd rented.

Frank concentrated on Zev. The xWave dialed the number it had found in Tel Aviv. After two rings, a pleasant female voice answered in English. "Mr. Levi's office. May I help you?"

"This is Frank Adams. I'm a friend of Zev's from his days in Moscow. I need to talk to him as soon as possible."

"Mr. Levi is away from the office, but I will relay your message to him. What number can he reach you at?"

Frank gave the secretary his cell phone number. "Please tell Zev that it's important."

Frank went through the same process to reach Rado. There was no answer.

Frank put the xWave back in its holster and stored it in his briefcase. He then put Viktor's computer to the side, pulled his own laptop forward and turned it on. A minute after launching his e-mail program, Frank saw a message from Thomas Hawkes that the publisher had copied to his editor, Don Hudson: "We haven't heard a word from you. It's been a week. Call me at once."

Frank closed Thomas's e-mail without replying. He opened the new message template, addressed it to himself and typed out a message: "Viktor Romanov was killed in Atyrau, Kazakhstan, apparently by a former colleague from the SVR. I barely escaped. Investigate the money link between Mikhail Gusov and Bud Johnson. Check if funds went to Roberts's campaign."

Frank reviewed what he had written with the odd feeling of a dead man reading through the eyes of someone left behind. He added a closing note before hitting the Send button: "Talk with Lisa about AmeriCon Energy."

CHAPTER 38

KABUL, AFGHANISTAN

FRANK WAS IN a stupor during his flight from Baku to Kabul. Viktor was dead. His murderers, with the SVR somehow involved, had tried to kill Frank. A mystery man wielding an automatic with a silencer had saved his life.

To reach Kabul, Frank had been forced to fly first from Atyrau to Baku on a relic plane that should have been hanging in the Air and Space Museum in Washington. The Anton-4 craft belonged to Scat Airlines, which operated a "fleet" of five planes from its "headquarters" in the Kazakh "regional capital" of Shymkent. Scat boasted on its website that the Anton-4 had been designed for "meteorological research," but with a single propeller on its nose, the double-wing craft looked like a Depression-era crop duster. In the tiny cabin behind the pilot's berth, the plane had four tattered seats. Frank was the only passenger. The flight took an hour over the full length of the Caspian Sea, providing him a beautiful view of the vast waterway through his cracked window.

In Baku, Frank boarded a Tupolev-154 designed by the Soviets. The jetliner seated 164 people in a single cabin that was half full. Compared with the Anton-4, it felt luxurious.

As the Azerbaijan Airlines plane sped toward Kabul, Frank wondered what secrets about Mikhail and the oil scandal Ahmad had referred to in the message he'd left for Viktor. Ahmad's request for a personal meeting could mean only one thing: the information was so sensitive, it must be shared face to face.

Viktor had clearly once worked for the SVR, something Frank suspected during his tenure in Moscow. But everything Frank knew about Viktor convinced him that was in the past. Viktor had become a legitimate journalist, and a damn good one.

The apparent involvement of Svetlana in setting up Viktor's meeting in Atyrau and, even worse, her possible complicity in his murder set Frank's mind spinning. Did she know that he had accompanied Viktor to Kazakhstan? Had she dispatched both of them to their deaths? Had she learned that Frank was still alive?

Frank's discovery that Viktor was onto a story linking donations from Gusov through AmeriCon Energy to a US politician was staggering. The hint that it could have been Roberts had been buttressed by his own recent investigations in Moscow, but it still needed to be nailed down. Frank wondered whether Ahmad Durrani could help close the deal.

Ahmad had been perhaps the most surprising of the poker

players. Living in Moscow while he finished his archaeology doctorate, he was one of the brightest people Frank had ever met. Quick-witted and self-effacing, Ahmad became one of the most popular members of the group. The other card players eventually pried from him that he was a distant descendant of the famous emirs of the Durrani Empire based in what is now Afghanistan. Believed by some historians to have been the founder of modern Afghanistan, Emir Ahmad Shah Durrani in the mid-eighteenth century started a dynasty that would grow to include Afghanistan, the northeastern region of present-day Iran, most of the area now known as Pakistan, and the Punjab region of India.

Frank had never forgotten Ahmad's reaction to the Taliban's decision to destroy the ancient Buddhas of Bamiyan 240 kilometers northwest of Kabul in March 2001. The statues, one 36 meters tall and the other 54 meters high, had been carved in the sandstone cliffs of the beautiful Bamiyan Valley between the years 507 and 554. Ahmad was shattered by the decision of Mullah Mohammed Omar to sanction the destruction of the world's largest standing Buddhas. At the poker game that month in Moscow, the archeologist had been inconsolable.

Normally a defender of everything Afghan, Ahmad's mood that night fluctuated between weeping and rage. He told the other card players a sad but fascinating tale: During a visit to Afghanistan almost two years earlier, he'd met with Mullah Omar and persuaded him to preserve the Buddhas. The next month Omar issued a decree pledging to protect the statues; there were no longer any Buddhists in Afghanistan, and the giant figures could be an important source of tourism revenue. But shortly afterward, with Ahmad back in Moscow, hundreds of radical clerics from across Afghanistan demanded a crackdown on "un-Islamic" manifestations in Afghan society. Their campaign, with Mullah Omar's cowardly acquiescence, provided the rationale for destroying the Buddhas.

While Frank and Ahmad had become friends over cards, they hadn't seen each other in a long time. Frank calculated that his only chance of learning what the Afghan archeologist knew was to convince him that he and Viktor were working together. Viktor's murder would soon become public knowledge, but Frank would have to withhold that shattering news from Ahmad.

Frank believed that Ahmad's life was threatened, but his need to extract information from the archeologist precluded him from warning his Afghan friend, at least for now. Although the moral morass troubled Frank, he'd grown accustomed to it over his years as a journalist.

Frank grabbed a taxi at the Kabul airport. A half hour later, the beat-up Indian Tata pulled up to a downtown cybercafe amid a row of battle-scarred buildings. Frank paid the fare, got out of the cab and entered the café. Even after fifteen years, he recognized Ahmad at once. He walked over to the table where Ahmad was working on a laptop and sat down. Ahmad looked up with a quizzical expression. As Frank sat down across from him, Ahmad's shock gave way to bewildered happiness.

"Hello, Ahmad."

"Frank! It's great to see you after so many years, but what is this about? I'm expecting Viktor Romanov any minute now."

Frank endeavored to speak in a relaxed tone. "Viktor and I are working together on this oil scandal. My editors in Los Angeles believe it might be connected with the assassination attempt on Stuart Roberts. Viktor and I arrived in Atyrau yesterday to talk with a source. Viktor's editors called him back to Moscow urgently this morning, so he asked me to fly here and meet you. He said you might have information for us."

Ahmad was stunned. He and Viktor had been careful to keep their communications to themselves. For all his friendship with Frank, Ahmad's confusion quickly yielded to wariness.

"Why did your editors send you to Moscow in the middle of the presidential campaign? I've read some of your articles. You're their lead political reporter."

Frank had prepared his cover story. "After the hit on Roberts last week, Viktor called and told me he was working on a big article. He hinted that it involved Stuart."

Caution filled Ahmad's voice. "Did Viktor tell you what I've shared with him?"

Frank removed the xWave from its belt holster. Ahmad, a computer geek despite his training in ancient ruins, stared at the strange-looking device. "What is that thing?"

"An electronic toy I'm beta-testing for my paper. Look at your laptop screen."

Ahmad was startled to read a copy of an e-mail from Viktor to Frank.

Frank:

I have to go to Moscow for an urgent meeting. Ahmad Durrani, our old poker pal, has become a valuable source for the oil project. He called and asked me to come to Kabul because he has new information.

Could you please go to Kabul and meet with him? His cell phone number is 178-43-205.

Viktor

Ahmad turned off his laptop, closed the computer and put it into his case. "Let's go for a walk."

CHAPTER 39

KABUL, AFGHANISTAN

AHMAD AND FRANK left the cybercafe and walked through Pashtunistan Square toward the main bazaar. The crowds of people, almost all men, were virtually suffocating. Kabul had grown enormously since the American occupation began with the launch of Operation Enduring Freedom in October 2001. It was now a teeming city of four million souls. Ahmad and Frank entered the bazaar and tried to keep together in the crush of humanity walking, shopping, talking, arguing and sightseeing along the narrow streets displaying an array of foods and products from around the world.

One stand caught Frank's eye with its exhibit of beautiful cobalt stones in all shapes and sizes. A glass case in the center of the stall contained some of the most stunning jewelry he'd ever seen.

"What is this, Ahmad?"

Ahmad stopped and smiled at Frank. He spoke with

evident pride. "That, my friend, is lapis lazuli from Kokcha Valley in the northeastern corner of Afghanistan. It has been mined there for over seven thousand years."

Frank walked over to the glass case. "I've never seen anything that has such a deep hue of blue. I'd love to buy a piece if I can afford it."

Ahmad laughed. "You don't need to worry! The merchants have been selling these gems for centuries. Their prices are quite reasonable. Which piece do you like?"

Frank pointed at a necklace with a large polished stone fixed to a silver chain. "How much does that one cost?"

Before Ahmad could ask the bazaari in Farsi what the price was, the trader spoke to Frank. "For you, Sahib, I charge just two hundred dollars."

Ahmad was about to counsel Frank on bargaining protocols when the American responded to the seller. "I wouldn't pay more than one hundred dollars for this trinket."

This pained the bazaari. "Sahib, I have family to feed. I cannot give necklace away."

Frank turned to Ahmad. "Are there other shops that sell these stones?"

Before Ahmad could answer, the merchant signaled with his hands his assent to Frank's offer. "For you, sahib, I take loss on stone. I want you to remember good people in Afghanistan."

Frank took a leather money clip from his trousers and pulled out a hundred dollar bill, which he handed to the vendor. The shopkeeper polished the necklace, wrapped the jewelry in cloth and folded it into a heavy piece of brown paper. He handed the package to Frank, who placed it in his pants pocket.

"Frank, you must have a special friend in mind for that exceptional stone. I'm sure her beauty will be enhanced when she wears it."

Frank grinned at Ahmad. "You might even know her."

Frank and Ahmad emerged from the bazaar and proceeded down a dusty, rubble-strewn street. Ahmad lit a cigarette. He returned to the last question Frank had asked him at the café. "Everyone knows that Mikhail became rich by building a pipeline to deliver oil and natural gas to Western Europe."

It wasn't Ahmad's nature to be dramatic, but he seemed to pause for effect before continuing. "There are plans for a second pipeline that hasn't been built yet."

"Another pipeline? Where would it go?"

"Pakistan."

"That's interesting. But how do you know this?"

Ahmad exhaled some smoke. "Do you remember that night on your balcony after one of the poker games?"

"Which one? There were a lot of nights out on our balcony. I had usually consumed a fair amount of Stoli by the time the poker ended."

"This was a night with you, Lisa, Mikhail, Stuart and me. Lisa's boss from Houston was with us. Mikhail talked of making a fortune in oil after the collapse of Communism."

Frank fastened on that particular night. "I remember now."

"After you and Lisa left Moscow, Mikhail and I stayed in touch. I finished my fellowship while Mikhail developed his business. He occasionally sought my advice on archaeological matters related to oil exploration."

"What does archaeology have to do with oil exploration?"

"In this part of the world, wells or pipelines must sometimes be drilled or built near ancient ruins. Archaeologists help devise ways of protecting such historical landmarks."

"That's where Mikhail thought you could be helpful?"

"Mikhail told me he wanted to build a pipeline through Turkmenistan and Afghanistan to Pakistan," Ahmad responded.

"Why Pakistan?"

"China and India were consuming so much energy as their economies boomed. Pakistan and India are long-time enemies. Islamabad seeks an energy source that it won't have to share with Delhi."

Frank thought aloud as they walked. "Mikhail's pipeline would meet that need."

Ahmad nodded. "Especially since the September 11 attacks, Azerbaijan, Uzbekistan, Kazakhstan, Turkmenistan and other oil-rich nations in Central Asia see themselves as providing an alternative to Arab crude. That would not only develop them economically, but also give them new status as political powerbrokers."

"I've researched Mikhail's past, and I've seen nothing about a second pipeline."

"There are reasons for that."

"Such as?"

"The war between your country and insurgents in my country," Ahmad replied.

"How does that tie in?"

"The pipeline must go through large parts of Afghanistan that are not controlled by the US-backed government in Kabul."

Frank was putting the pieces together as he listened.

The journalist stopped. "You're not doing business with the Taliban?"

Ahmad sighed before answering.

"It is worse than that."

"What do you mean?"

"We're also providing protection money to Baghdadi and ISIS."

"Holy Fucking Christ! You guys are in bed with the terrorists we're at war with in Syria and Iraq?"

"It wasn't that way at the start, but things change. Baghdadi was working with the Taliban when the deal was brokered."

At that moment, Frank knew that Stuart Roberts's presidential campaign was over. His political career was done. He could end up in prison—if Frank could return home safely to report the story.

He and Ahmad resumed walking. "Ahmad, if this is all such a big secret, why are you telling me?"

Ahmad looked at Frank. "Mikhail and I became close. I believe his life is in danger."

Frank's pulse quickened: another poker player in peril. He thought to tell Ahmad about Viktor's death but ignored the impulse. He had to put his professional needs as a journalist ahead of his personal feelings. He pulled the reporting string with the Afghan.

"Ahmad, it's obvious that Mikhail leading an opposition

movement against the Kremlin is risky business. Is that what you mean?"

The Afghan stopped once more and turned to face his visitor.

"I'm not talking about Mikhail's political career."

There was a brief silence. Frank nodded for Ahmad to continue.

"The Soviets occupied my country for ten years and withdrew in disgrace. The Americans were here even longer and also left in defeat."

Frank felt impatient.

"Why are you telling me things I know?"

Ahmad's eyes narrowed.

"Because there are things you don't know."

Frank absorbed the rebuke.

"Go ahead."

"For all his smarts, I'm afraid that Mikhail has gotten in over his head with his current oil dealings. And he is not alone."

"Who else?"

"AmeriCon Energy became the largest foreign investor in Mikhail's company and helped him finance the first pipeline to Europe."

Frank felt the adrenaline jolt that reporters get when a new door opens.

Lisa's ex-boss in Moscow.

"So Bud Johnson is involved with this new pipeline?"

"He and Mikhail were much closer than you may have realized. NeftKorp and AmeriCon are doing business worth billions of dollars in a cutthroat part of the world."

Frank mused for a moment. "So Mikhail's business deal-ings are as dangerous to him as his political activities."

"You can draw your own conclusions."

Frank considered asking how Roberts fit into this menac-ing picture, but he decided that for now he'd pushed Ahmad far enough. Even had Frank asked, the Afghan archaeologist wouldn't have been able to tell him much. As close as he and Mikhail had become, Gusov kept his own counsel regarding his most sensitive business ventures.

VII: ALL IN

A Smith and Wesson beats four aces.

American proverb

CHAPTER 40

Moscow

O N THE ADVICE of his security team, Mikhail hadn't publicized his itinerary for a rare visit home on this pleasant summer day. A ruthless Kremlin prone to silencing its foes needn't know that its most prominent critic had returned to the capital. The secrecy shrouding his arrival was so strict, even his family had no clue until he walked through the front door of their elegant home on Baltschug Ulitsa with its spectacular views of St. Basil's Cathedral across the Moscow River. Neither were any of his employees told that he would spend the evening at the supper club. He hired a separate security firm than the one he used to guard the Samovar.

Just after eight, Gusov entered his club via a back door. He crossed the kitchen to startled looks from cooks and dishwashers, stopping to shake hands and exchange greetings. Encircled by his security contingent, he walked into the rear of the dining hall. A buzz steadily swept the vast room, giving way to cheers that grew louder as he made his way. Mikhail waved to the delighted diners, squeezing past tables to embrace long-time customers. By the time he reached the front of the room, two hundred guests and employees were standing and giving him a boisterous ovation.

As cries of "welcome!" and "speak!" echoed, Gusov raised his clasped hands and smiled broadly. He waited a full minute before quieting the throng. "Thank you! Thank you so much, my dear friends! Please excuse me for barging in on your dinner!"

Laughter swept the room.

"It's a pleasure to see you, Misha!" one diner shouted.

"It's an honor!" another yelled.

A new round of applause began, but Mikhail motioned to cut it off. "Please sit down! Please. I can't tell you how deeply I appreciate your friendship!"

The excited patrons settled back into their seats. Gusov waited until silence had taken hold to begin speaking again. "Forgive me for not telling you in advance of my visit, but we all know that here in Moscow, even in the New Russia, it can be dangerous to advertise one's whereabouts. Especially if one has the temerity—the audacity that is a fundamental freedom in truly democratic nations—to criticize our country's leaders."

A knowing murmur crossed the tables.

"In America, when President Obama promised 'change you can believe in' during his historic campaign, tens of thousands roared his name. And the very government he was criticizing supplied Secret Service agents to protect him. Sadly, here in Russia, to speak of change still borders on treason. A rival presidential candidate is forced to hire private security!"

A mixed chorus of boos for the Kremlin and cheers for Mikhail rang out.

"You've heard one pundit after another say that my campaign has no chance of success. They say it's a mock campaign waged only to annoy the Kremlin. Nothing could be further from the truth! I'm here tonight to tell you that we are in this contest to win! And your support gives me the courage to keep fighting!"

As the diners leapt to their feet once more and roared their approval, Gusov raised his voice to be heard above the din. "Your support inspires me in this great initiative to replace our false freedoms with enduring rights that will finally, once and for all, make our Motherland a permanent member of the elite club of world democracies!"

With the cheering at fever pitch, Mikhail waded into the crowd and embraced one person after another. For the next hour, he roamed his club, sitting at tables for a few minutes, visiting with friends, basking in his homecoming.

At 9:30 p.m., after most diners had left and the hubbub had waned, Gusov stood in the near-empty dining room. He removed a Cohiba cigar from his shirt pocket. As he started to unwrap it, his mistress, Katrina Korneeva, embraced him from behind. She took the cigar and whispered into his right ear. "Let me do that. You know how much I love unwrapping things for you."

Katrina was a Slavic beauty who had rendered Mikhail helpless from the moment four months earlier she had introduced herself after a rally and, with a knowing glint, offered her full services to his campaign.

Gusov was immediately aroused. He spoke softly to her, desire in his voice. "Of course, my dear." He turned toward Katrina. "Let's go outside. I want to smoke my cigar. And be alone with you."

As the couple headed toward the main entrance, Katrina stopped. "Don't you want to summon your security crew?"

Mikhail stroked her hair. "No, my love. Every precaution was taken tonight."

The oligarch kissed his mistress. "Besides, I don't want any other company."

The lovers walked through the front entrance. Gusov asked the two doormen to give them a few minutes' privacy. The sentries crossed the parking lot and began smoking Belomorcanal cigarettes, a popular brand named after the canal Stalin had built to connect the Baltic Sea with the White Sea for Soviet naval ships.

Alone under the club's burgundy awning, Katrina placed the cigar in Mikhail's mouth, took her gold lighter and held the flame at its tip. As he drew on the cigar, a shot pierced the air, its deadly sound muffled by a silencer. Gusov fell to the ground.

Katrina gasped and plunged down to cradle his head. She held a handkerchief against the wound as blood stained her golden gown. She screamed for help. The doormen came running and began trying to revive Mikhail. One of them pulled a mobile phone from his pocket and called the chief of Gusov's security detail.

On the top floor of an office building a block away, a dark figure disassembled a Dragunov Sniper rifle, put it in a shoulder case and disappeared.

Hearing Katrina's sobs, employees and the few remaining diners ran from inside the Samovar. While she clasped the bleeding Mikhail, the guests and a growing crowd began shouting in an angry crescendo. Women and men alike joined Katrina in crying.

Within minutes, ambulances and police cars converged on the club, their sirens wailing and their lights piercing the night. Satellite TV trucks appeared from nowhere.

The crowd expanded as people dashed out from nearby flats to check on the commotion. Amid jostling and fearful shouts of "What happened?" from the back, police tried to control the mounting mob.

Russian One TV correspondent Pavel Sidorov broadcast live from amid the chaos. "Prominent opposition leader Mikhail Gusov, a rich oilman and leader of the second wave of oligarchs, has just been shot here outside the Samovar, his downtown dinner club."

At 9:45 p.m., Frank walked from the Hotel National to the Samovar. He was exhausted from Viktor's murder, his own narrow escape and his stop in Kabul, but he was looking forward to seeing Mikhail. He wanted to learn more about the secret dinner Gusov had hosted for Roberts, Stuart's subsequent private trips to Russia, and the senator's continued involvement in Russian oil schemes.

As Frank neared the Samovar, he heard sirens. An ambulance

hurled past him, its red lights flashing. Three police cars streamed by the street ahead of him. Frank broke into a trot. By the time he reached the dinner club, a large crowd had gathered outside. Police and Federal Protective Service agents rushed to the scene. Onlookers groaned in grief.

As Frank tried to move through the mob, police held him back. He flashed his media credentials, but they ignored him. All around Frank was bedlam, people weeping and moaning and pushing and screaming.

Frank found himself yelling to be heard. "What happened?" he shouted at a man.

The man looked at him in disbelief and cursed. "What happened? Mikhail Gusov has just been murdered in cold blood! That's what's happened!"

Frank tried to move forward but got nowhere. Finally, he gave up and ran away from the Samovar. He pulled the xWave from its holster and checked the time. Ten p.m.—noon in Los Angeles. Stopping on a corner a few blocks from his hotel, he called Don Hudson's direct work number.

"Hudson."

"Don, this is Frank. Mikhail Gusov has just been assassinated outside his dinner club! I'm running back to my hotel!"

"Holy shit, Frank! The head of the opposition movement? Are you fucking kidding me?"

"I wish I was. I'll call you from my room when I'm ready to roll."

CHAPTER 41

Moscow

FRANK WOKE BEFORE seven following a few hours of fitful sleep. After calling Hudson, he'd done a few quick interviews with shell-shocked Muscovites about Mikhail's murder, raced back to the National and filed two leads for losangelesregister.com. As he wrote the articles, he shipped a dozen tweets to his thirty thousand Twitter followers, filled with color and drama that showed he was on the scene: "Russian oligarch killed by sniper's bullets"; "Muscovites weep, curse at another political hit"; "Mikhail Gusov's just been murdered in cold blood!" With LA ten hours earlier than Moscow, he'd had time to do a write-through for the next day's paper, pulling in details from Russian TV news and the local online sites that started exploding within minutes of the gunshots. Finally, he'd gone into the Register's digital repository of three hundred obits-in-waiting—prewritten profiles of prominent people—and pulled up the one he himself had written for Gusov four years earlier. Adding to the basic biography of Mikhail as a billionaire oilman, Frank hammered out a section about his more recent leadership of the Kremlin opposition movement and filed the updated obit. He waited until the second web piece and the obit had been edited and posted online, read them quickly on his laptop and fell asleep after three.

Frank ordered coffee from room service, pulled on running shorts and a T-shirt, booted up his computer and went to the desk. Mikhail's murder had removed any doubt about whether the poker players were being targeted. If his trip to Moscow had been dangerous at the start, he was now a marked man. And with Viktor dead, he would have to use other means to learn more about Roberts's clandestine visits to Russia.

After showering, Frank turned on the television to catch the morning news. He used the remote to select Moscow's most popular station, Channel One. What he heard and saw on the screen jolted him.

"Prominent *Kapital* journalist Viktor Romanov was found murdered in Atyrau, Kazakhstan, late yesterday. Romanov, one of the top investigative reporters in Russia, had written extensively about the long-festering scandal over billions of rubles in missing royalties that the Oil Ministry has been unable to account for."

The TV picture showed file photos of Viktor and then cut to live shots of a dusty trash heap in an industrial area of Atyrau. The TV correspondent described a metal scrap yard where the bodies of Romanov and a yet-unidentified person had been found. "Romanov, according to his *Kapital* editor, had gone to Atyrau to meet someone connected to the oil scandal. Sources also tell us that Viktor Romanov was seen in Atyrau with another reporter, possibly an American. It is unknown whether the second body is that person."

Frank turned off the TV and stilled his racing thoughts. He understood that his time to find new leads and close the story on Stuart's oil dealings in Russia had run out.

One cold fact stood out: their former lover had sent him and Viktor to the trap in Atyrau. Frank picked up the phone and dialed the number for Svetlana Lutrova that he'd found in the digital Rolodex file on Viktor's computer.

Svetlana's voice hadn't changed. "Hello?"

Normally, her sultry greeting would have made Frank's knees buckle. Now his anger overrode his lust. They spoke in Russian. "*Privyet*, Svetlana. This is Frank."

Frank understood now why she sounded so flabbergasted to hear his voice. It wasn't because they hadn't talked in more than a decade. It was because he was still alive.

"Why are you calling me?"

"I thought you might know."

There were several seconds of silence before Svetlana responded. "Frank, it's important that we speak in person. Meet me today at three o'clock. I'll be in Gorky Park on one of the benches inside the entrance near your old flat."

Frank wanted answers. People he'd once trusted—Stuart and Viktor, to start with—had played him for a fool. Svetlana's affair with him and its role in his divorce—he had put all of that into the past. But dispatching Viktor to his death in Atyrau and no doubt intending for Frank to be ambushed as well? This deadly business was of a whole different magnitude than sexual traps or divorce. He was beyond Svetlana's seductive reach now.

Frank arrived early at Gorky Park. He sat on the green bench for a few minutes, felt restless and walked along a path through shrubs with brilliant white and pink French lilacs that Russians called Pride of Moscow. Just before three, he walked back out into the clearing and saw Svetlana sitting on the bench.

Frank hadn't seen her in years. The Slavic beauty still looked stunning. She wore a sheer, lime-and-white-striped sundress that showed off her striking figure with thin green bands crossed above ample cleavage and tied behind her neck. For all his anger and resolve, Frank had to catch his breath before approaching the bench. Despising his male weakness, he greeted Svetlana as he sat down next to her.

"You're as beautiful as you ever were."

Svetlana was startled, but she quickly recovered. "That was a long time ago, Frank."

Frank's fury returned. "Why did you send us to Atyrau to get killed?"

Svetlana flashed the intense, blue-eyed stare that had first captured him years ago. "I don't know what you're talking about. Did my contact not give you valuable information?"

"Your contact killed Viktor and tried to kill me."

Svetlana seemed genuinely stunned, but Frank had learned the hard way that she was a gifted actress.

"That's impossible."

"No one knew we were in Atyrau except you."

"I wouldn't be so sure."

"What is that supposed to mean?"

Svetlana reached over and grasped Frank's left arm. He shook her off and waited for her answer. She stared directly into his eyes. "Viktor feared he was being tailed. As I'm sure you know, many reporters here have been killed just for doing their jobs. The government investigations never go anywhere. Many Russians assume the SVR is hiring contract killers."

"Do you think the Kremlin killed Mikhail?"

"You need to come with me."

Svetlana started to rise from the bench. Frank remained seated. As she sat back down, he spoke with icy precision.

"Stuart Roberts, Viktor Romanov, myself and now Mikhail Gusov. I want to find out why the players in my poker game so long ago are being targeted, and who is going after them."

For the first time, Frank looked Svetlana directly in the eyes. Not a glimmer of romance was left. Their visual exchange was cold as he spoke to her.

"Every reporter's instinct in my body tells me that you have some answers."

Frank almost recoiled when Svetlana touched him on the shoulder.

"If you want answers, there's someone you must meet."

Frank continued looking at her. He thought of Danny Pearl, the *Wall Street Journal* reporter who'd pursued dangerous leads to his ultimate beheading in Pakistan by the 9/11 thug Khalid Sheikh Mohammed. Frank wasn't in the hands of terrorists now, but he knew he was in peril. Still, as Pearl had done in the back alleys of Karachi, Frank knew what he must do here on the familiar streets of Moscow—chase what could be the story of his career. He had to keep reporting. When Svetlana rose again from the bench, he stood up too. He followed her along a path and through a thick glade.

CHAPTER 42

MOSCOW

FRANK TRAILED SVETLANA out of Gorky Park. She walked briskly; he nearly had to trot to keep pace. They emerged onto Krymsky Val Street. Svetlana hailed a gypsy cab. In Moscow, as in all world capitals, gorgeous women never stood long by a curb. The possibility that she had made prior arrangements with the driver didn't occur to Frank.

The couple climbed into the car. Svetlana directed the driver to proceed to a destination Frank didn't recognize on the city's outskirts. He was being led to a remote location by a dangerous woman who, the evidence indicated, had already tried to have him killed. Frank forced himself to appear confident. He was doing what his job as a reporter had always demanded—following the story, even at his own risk.

The cabbie drove parallel to Gorky Park until he reached

Leninsky Prospekt, where he executed a right turn and headed south away from central Moscow.

Frank looked at Svetlana across the backseat they shared. "Where are you taking me?"

Ignoring his question, she spoke with a trembling voice. "Frank, I can't believe that Viktor is dead! How did that happen?"

Frank wasn't buying Svetlana's act. He responded with cool detachment. "You tell me, Svetlana. Viktor was my friend. Until you convince me otherwise, I think you set him up to be killed—and me as well. I don't know why, but I'm going to find out. What can you tell me about the SVR agent who killed Viktor?"

Svetlana didn't take the bait. "SVR agent? I don't know what you're talking about."

Frank controlled his anger. "I think you know. An SVR agent gave Viktor a poisoned drink in Atyrau, and then his goons tried to run me over in an alley. One of them was about to finish me off with his Uzi when he was killed by a gunman firing from the street."

Frank's voice rose. "You were Viktor's Oil Ministry source. It was you who sent us to Atyrau. I want to know what the hell is going on!"

Svetlana responded with equal force. "Frank, I'm afraid that the tragic deaths of Mikhail and Viktor have unhinged you!"

When Frank said nothing, Svetlana spoke again. "I believe that the person we're going to meet will help lay to rest these wild accusations."

The taxi pulled up to a large abandoned industrial complex.

Windows were missing their glass panes. Walls leaned away from the perpendicular. Blank holes gaped where bricks once resided. Rusting steel beams protruded at odd angles from a former factory. Grass and brush had overgrown the surrounding grounds to cover any semblance of paths.

Svetlana told the driver to wait. She beckoned Frank to follow her out of the car and toward the rear of the large building in front of them.

The one-time lovers walked in silence around the building and came to a large area overgrown with weeds and strewn with garbage. It had once been a courtyard. In the center of the square were the remains of a low, brick circular wall that sheltered a well.

His sense of danger heightened, Frank was on full alert. Why would Svetlana bring him to such a desolate place? His answer arrived. Rado Weinstien emerged from the shadows. Frank saw them exchange glances.

Frank had let Svetlana lead him into another trap, but this time he wasn't caught off guard. Since Svetlana had provided nothing but lies, he now addressed the German who'd played cards at his Moscow flat.

"Rado, what an unexpected surprise."

"The pleasure is mine, Frank. It's too bad we won't have time to play poker."

Rado pulled out a Glock 19 9mm semi automatic pistol. "I'm going to have to use more conventional means of getting rid of you than I used to kill Viktor."

Forcing himself to control his fear, Frank spoke in measured words. "We were all friends. Why are you doing this?"

Rado nearly spat out his reply. "All of you thought you were so clever with your digs at our poker games. Everyone thought they controlled me—Stasi, the KGB, the SVR, the Mossad, the CIA, Stuart Roberts. I fooled all of them."

Frank tried to buy time.

"How did you fool them, Rado?"

Rado flew into a rage. "You journalists! Always meddling in other people's affairs! You and Viktor were getting too close to the truth. The two of you had figured out the link between Mikhail and Stuart and AmeriCon. But there are other connections that would harm my interests if they are made public. I can't permit that to happen."

Rado raised the Glock and pointed it at Frank's head. "We've talked enough! Good fortune has protected you, but this time I'll make sure the job gets done."

A voice shouted out from a corner of the lot. "Enough, Rado!"

A man stepped forward and pointed an AK-47 assault rifle at Rado. "You didn't really think we were going to let you continue your rampage, Rado, did you?"

This man was a stranger to Frank, but Rado and Svetlana knew him all too well: Nikolai Volkov, their former SVR boss when they had kept tabs on the American couple in Moscow.

Frank looked at the stranger. When would this madness end? "Who are you?" he asked.

Nikolai shrugged and gave a cold response. "You should ask your former wife. Or perhaps her father."

Frank felt like Volkov was speaking in some foreign tongue. The only thing he knew was that he was surrounded by crazy people. He had to somehow keep himself alive—and see where all this was leading.

Nikolai focused his weapon on Rado. "If you kill the American, Rado, you're a dead man. But if you cooperate, we will straighten out this business with no further complications."

Suddenly a shot rang out from behind Frank. Nikolai fell dead to the ground.

Svetlana, Glock 17 in hand, walked calmly toward Rado.

Rado trained his gun on Frank.

Lisa emerged from behind a column. She pointed a Beretta 96 pistol at Rado.

More madness. Frank had never seen Lisa hold a gun.

"Lisa? For Christ's sake, what in the hell are you doing here?"

Before his ex-wife could respond, Svetlana rushed toward her. She grabbed Lisa and threw her to the ground. The impact propelled their guns from their hands. The two women wrestled furiously, punching and using martial arts jabs as they rolled around. Frank wanted to help Lisa, but Rado's gun froze him. They were transfixed by the deadly fight at their feet. Svetlana broke free of Lisa's grip and scrambled for her gun near the edge of the well. As she grasped the weapon and swung it around, Lisa did a jiujitsu kick slide toward her. Lisa's right leg hit Svetlana and pushed her into the well. They heard her yells, then a thud, then silence.

Frank could barely comprehend what he was seeing. Lisa some kind of female James Bond? Where had she learned to fight like that?

Rado fired his Glock at Lisa, but the former Olympic gymnast did a double somersault, weaved, dove into another slide and picked up her fallen Beretta. Rising to a crouch, she fired it at Rado, but he was on the move himself. He hooked his left arm around Frank's neck and held the Glock to the reporter's head with his right hand.

"Drop the gun, Lisa, or your former husband dies!"

As Lisa released the Beretta, she looked at Frank. He saw in her eyes a glint of tenderness.

A siren pierced the air. A white unmarked van squealed into the abandoned courtyard and screeched to a halt. Its side doors slid open and a dozen figures in black fatigues and black helmets with bulletproof visors charged out, each carrying an assault rifle. They formed a semicircle around Rado, went to one knee and pointed their weapons at him. A voice that sounded American called out.

"Interpol police! We are here to apprehend Rado Weinstien for the attempted assassination of Stuart Roberts!"

Rado clutched Frank's throat tighter and pushed his gun barrel against his head. Dragging Frank, he backed away.

"Don't come any closer, or this famous American reporter will be dead!"

Lisa walked toward Rado. Two Interpol officers trained their machine guns on her, but she kept her eyes on the German-born physicist.

"Rado, Stuart is recovering and will be back campaigning soon. Right now, you're facing no worse than attempted murder. If you kill Frank in front of all these police witnesses, America will have you extradited, and I will make it my mission to secure you the death penalty. Why don't you help yourself out here? Let him go and surrender."

Rage filled Rado's response. "You Americans are so naïve! Roberts will be dead soon—and it will be pinned on me! I have nothing to lose!"

Just before Rado pulled the trigger, a tracer bullet sped from a high point far to his side beyond his field of vision. It entered his head at mid temple, an inch behind his left eye. He fell dead. The Interpol sniper stood up on a steel girder ten meters high; seventy meters from the group, the rusting beam stretched across the crumbling wall of the one-time factory.

The police sprang into action. Three officers raced over to Rado, knelt and determined he was dead. Three others found the lifeless body of Volkov at the base of a pillar.

Frank and Lisa ran toward each other and embraced.

The American Interpol captain led a small unit toward them. His officers pointed their weapons, but he motioned for them not to fire.

The captain raised his visor and spoke to Lisa. "I am United States Delta Force Captain Ron Miller on special assignment to Interpol. Who are you?"

Lisa handed him an encrypted pass.

The captain pulled a device from his pocket and scanned an ultraviolet light over the pass. He called out to the others. "She's bulletproof—senior staff CIA. Lower your weapons."

Frank tried to digest this new information. Captain Miller nodded toward him and spoke again to Lisa. "Who's he?"

"An American reporter. Frank Adams."

"The two of you seem well acquainted."

Lisa didn't want to play games. "We used to be married."

Captain Miller shook his head. "You've landed in quite

a mess here, Agent Hawkes. Why didn't you contact us for backup?"

"No one knew I was coming. I didn't tell my own people."

The captain removed his helmet. "You're free to leave. But I'm not authorized to release your ex-husband, if that's who he really is."

Lisa's voice hardened. "Captain Miller, I don't want to pull rank, so let me be clear. I will take Mr. Adams into my custody. I've had a rough day. I advise you to stand down."

Miller thought for moment and nodded curtly. "Leave now, please."

As Miller turned away, Lisa had the last word. "One more thing, Captain. You'll find the body of a Russian female named Svetlana Lutrova at the bottom of the well."

Lisa and Frank walked briskly past the white van and across the yard. They vanished around the side of the front building.

Miller went to the van and sat in the front passenger's seat. He punched a code into a satellite phone imbedded in the dashboard and dialed a number. In a secure windowless office near Langley, Virginia, Russell Talbert answered the phone. He got to the point.

"How did it go?"

"Per your instructions, we used Interpol as a cover. We included several of your Russian assets in the operation. We were able to avoid tipping off the Russian authorities, but we were unable to apprehend Rado Weinstien."

"Why?"

"One of my officers was forced to shoot him. He was holding an American reporter hostage. It was a single-shot kill."

Talbert knew who the journalist was but played along. "Who is the reporter?"

"Frank Adams."

"Ah, yes. He's been covering the presidential campaign for the *Los Angeles Register*. Where is he now?"

"We released him into the custody of one of your senior personnel. Lisa Hawkes."

Talbert smiled. He should have known that Thomas Hawkes's daughter would ride to Frank's rescue. She was just like her old man—a cowboy to the core.

"You made the proper decision, Captain Miller. I will inform your superiors of your unit's excellent work today."

"Sir, if I may?"

"Go ahead."

"Why didn't you warn us of Ms. Hawkes's presence? She was in significant danger. We barely saved her."

Talbert laughed. "Captain, I didn't know she would be there. Perhaps I should have."

Talbert wanted to make sure there were no more surprises. "I will send you our files on Rado Weinstien via secure digifax. You will note that he is former KGB and SVR. Make sure you include that in your report."

"Yes, sir."

CHAPTER 43

MOSCOW

LISA AND FRANK emerged from the industrial complex onto a side street just starting to be creased by evening shadows. Frank stopped and reached into his hip holster for the xWave. Lisa grabbed him by the arm, but he resisted.

"Lisa, wait a minute. I've got an exclusive on the Roberts hit. In a half hour, the news will be out. It's almost four in the morning in LA. I've got to wake Hudson up and get him to put a bulletin online."

Frank was surprised by how forcefully Lisa pulled him forward.

"Your story can wait, Frank. We need to disappear—now! The Russians are going to be blamed for trying to kill a US presidential candidate. Their entire law enforcement apparatus is going to hit the streets, and every American will be under surveillance. You're not exactly here on an official reporting trip, and the Russians don't know I'm in country. We are not safe."

Lisa could have used a chauffeured Cadillac DTS Platinum, part of the US Embassy's small fleet of cars, but its diplomatic license plates would have drawn attention. So when the video feed relayed by her tail had shown Frank and Svetlana leaving Gorky Park, she'd raced from the embassy and jumped into a 1995 Lada with Russian plates that was one of four battered old cars kept there for covert trips. Now she led Frank down the alley where she'd left the Lada. They got in the car and headed off with her at the wheel. When Lisa and Frank had been married, she couldn't drive a manual, or so he'd thought. As they emerged from the alley, he watched her deftly handle the Lada's stick shift.

Lisa pushed a button on the dash and spoke into an intercom. She was connected with the CIA station beneath the embassy.

"Hawkes en route in northwest Moscow sector six. I need a safe house for the night. Input the coordinates into my GPS. And please arrange a flight tomorrow morning to Los Angeles under diplomatic cover for me and another traveler. Use my standard cover name. The other traveler's handle is Henry Jamison."

A computer-modified voice responded: "Headquarters will need to know the real name."

Lisa hesitated. "Frank Adams." She added: "Send a Russian staffer to Hotel National to pick up his belongings and meet us in the diplomatic club at the airport."

The robotic voice again. "Two diplomatic passports will

be dispatched to safe house thirty-seven in southwest Moscow sector four. Mr. Adams's belongings will be delivered. The address has been transmitted to your GPS."

Amazement washed over Frank as he watched Lisa operate. How could he have been married to a phantom?

"I've got a lot of questions for you, Lisa, but I need to get this story filed."

He took out the xWave and commanded: "Hudson—home!"

Lisa looked over at the odd device. "What is that thing?"

Frank's response was half-smirk, half-smile. "You're not the only one with surprises."

Hudson's voice came through. "You woke me from a dead sleep, Frank. What's going on over there?"

"Don, we've got an exclusive! The attempted assassin of Stuart Roberts is Rado Weinstien. He was killed a half hour ago in a shootout with police here in Moscow. Get it up online now!"

"How do you know that and no one else does?"

"I was fucking there, Don!"

"Always where the action is, Frank. What else do I say in the bulletin? Do we know anything about this dead man? How do you spell his name?"

"First name R-a-d-o. Last name W-e-i-n-s-t-i-e-n. He was a German physicist. He taught at a Moscow technological institute and immigrated to Israel. He was elected to the Knesset and helped other Russian émigrés settle in Israel. I think he and Roberts went into business together—but don't put that in the story until I confirm it. And when he lived in Russia, he was a KGB and SVR spy."

"Christ, Frank, how do you know all this?"

"He played poker at our flat here."

"Jesus, Adams, what is it with your fucking poker game? Everyone in it is getting knocked off!"

Frank laughed, suddenly giddy to be alive. "You don't know the half of it, Don. Just get the story online. I'll be back in touch after we get to the safe house."

Don's confusion crossed the globe.

"Who's 'we'? 'Safe house'? What in the fuck is happening over there?"

Frank ignored the questions. "Get Robinson to call his sources at State. Have Howard reach out to someone at the White House. Ask Diaz to run his CIA lines. We need to get some US response into the story."

Frank turned off the xWave and put it into the holster. He and Lisa drove in silence. She controlled her impulse to speed and steered the car at a measured pace as the GPS delivered directions. They stopped at a light.

Frank looked at her. "I think I've figured out what should have been obvious to me a long time ago. Your AmeriCon Energy job when we lived in Moscow was just a cover, wasn't it?"

"Frank, that's a very long story."

"Give me the edited version."

Lisa glanced over. "I worked for the Agency."

After the day's events, nothing shocked Frank. "How did you hide it from me?"

Now Lisa looked straight ahead. "I was a NOC."

Frank stared blankly.

"Non-Official Cover. I had virtually no contact with our government, including the CIA and the embassy. That made it easier to conceal my covert work from you and everyone else."

"How could you keep that secret from me for so long?"

"Frank, don't you remember? We worked out an agreement. In order to protect each other, there would be parts of our work we wouldn't share."

He chuckled to himself. Frank Adams, the great investigative reporter, completely hoodwinked by his own wife. In retrospect, Lisa's covert life wasn't quite so incongruous. Her language skills were remarkable. She always asked the most intelligent questions in discussions with their friends, colleagues, politicians and business acquaintances. Despite their agreement not to reveal details of their work, Lisa had possessed a knack for getting him to divulge interesting information about stories he was working on. In a subtle way, she'd often helped him look at things from a different angle or arrive at a new avenue for his reporting.

Still, it was discomforting to realize that he'd never really known his wife.

It was almost nine. Frank had called in updates on his article and asked Hudson to reserve him 100 column inches in Thursday's paper for his enterprise article based on his reporting in Moscow and Atyrau. When Don asked what the piece would say, Frank responded: "It will be good. Just trust me." As much as Frank liked his editor, he couldn't afford risking any details about his exposé getting out in the building. He'd learned long ago that a reporter loses control of a big story the minute its secrets are divulged, even to colleagues.

Now, Lisa and Frank lay in each other's arms in the dusty bed at the safe house. They had just made love together for the first time since their divorce. Frank turned and spoke softly to Lisa. "I have something that I bought for you in Kabul."

Frank reached over to his briefcase and pulled out the package that the Afghan vendor had wrapped for him in brown paper. He'd taken it with him for the meeting with Svetlana because of the broken safe at the Hotel National. He handed the gift to Lisa. "When I saw this displayed at the merchant's stand, I realized that I still love you."

Lisa unwrapped the package and saw the necklace with the lapis lazuli stone. Tears filled her eyes. "Frank, this is magnificent! The color is such a pure blue. It's one of the most spectacular pieces of stone I've ever seen."

Frank took the necklace and placed it around Lisa's neck. "It's a spectacular stone for the most spectacular woman I've ever known."

Frank prided himself as a reporter on his willingness to ask obvious questions—questions he suspected other journalists feared asking. Holding Lisa, Frank asked her an obvious question. "How did you hook up with the CIA?"

Lisa laughed quietly. She saw no more need to withhold the truth. "Through my father."

Her answer hit Frank like a lightning bolt. "Your father?"

Lisa understood: if she and Frank were to have a true second chance, the long, elaborate cover story that was their family history had to come to an end. "The CIA took in my father after getting my mother out of the Soviet Union. Langley made it clear it was a job offer Daddy couldn't turn down. He later became a disciple of James Jesus Angleton."

Another revelation on a day filled with them. "You've got to be kidding me. The Kingfisher? He was one of the founders of the CIA!"

Frank thought before asking his next question. He felt like he was uncovering the most incredible story of all. "Is your father still with the CIA?"

Lisa gave an indirect answer. "No one ever really leaves the Agency."

Frank shook his head. "I can't believe that the publisher of the *Los Angeles Register* and the man who's been my mentor has a double life."

"My father has done a lot of good for the country." Her tone was defensive.

Newly connected with Lisa, Frank felt an odd mixture of love and betrayal. "So the *Register*'s editorial support of Stuart Roberts, its endorsement of him for president—none of that is accidental."

Lisa felt once more the skepticism with which she'd long regarded Operation Long Shadow. "My father and a few close allies of his have worked for years to get Roberts into the White House."

Frank got out of bed and pulled on his boxers. "I need a drink."

He opened his briefcase and removed two small bottles of Stolichnaya that he'd taken from the hotel in Atyrau.

Lisa swung her legs onto the floor. "Frank, think about

what you're doing. You've worked too hard to free yourself from the need to pick up a drink every time something goes wrong."

Frank faced her. "After Viktor was murdered in Atyrau, I had a couple of drinks to calm down. I handled it just fine. With what I've learned about you and your family today, I need something to help me digest the lies I've been fed all these years."

Lisa walked over and put her arms around his neck. "You know that I still love you. I promise you this: from now on, we will always tell each other the truth."

Frank put the unopened bottles on the counter. He went back to his bag and pulled out a slim reporter's notebook. "I need to start sketching out my Thursday article."

Lisa appealed to him. "Frank, what we've discussed must remain between us."

He looked her in the eyes. "I love you, Lisa, but I can't make that promise."

Lisa made one last request. "Will you at least keep Roberts's ties to Sergei Yemelin out of your article? Yemelin is a valuable asset."

This exasperated Frank. "That's one of the most important parts of my piece! Roberts keeping a foreign consultant on retainer without reporting it violates campaign-finance rules and lobbyist regulations and countless other federal laws. How can I leave that out?"

"It's a matter of national security."

Frank steadied his voice. "That's not good enough."

Lisa thought of her new vow to tell Frank the full truth about her hidden past.

"When you interviewed Sergei, he spoke to you under my instructions. Everything you know about his ties to Roberts is because of me."

Frank wondered when these bombshells from Lisa would stop. "Yemelin works for you? He's a CIA mole?"

"Not exactly. He thinks he's being paid by AmeriCon Energy. I've never told him his payments come from Langley. He doesn't know who I really work for."

Frank felt anger and admiration. "You've got all the angles covered, don't you, Lisa?" He shook his head. "Which of my other sources over here are you running?"

Lisa understood that just as Frank couldn't compromise his struggle against alcoholism, she couldn't tell him partial truths. "I've never been on board with Operation Long Shadow."

Frank felt like he was interviewing his most important source. "Operation Long Shadow?"

"That's my father's name for his plan to get Roberts in the White House. It goes back years. It's been a rogue operation from the start. Daddy wanted to insulate the Agency. I've always thought his plan was way too risky, not to mention just plain wrong. And going back to our poker games here, I've never trusted Roberts. He was deceiving everyone. I knew he'd unravel after the assassination attempt. I came to Moscow to help you get the story and save my father from himself."

When Frank remained silent, Lisa filled the void. "The man who shot Surum in the alley outside the Atyrau bar. You recognized him, didn't you?"

Now it came back to Frank: lying dazed on the ground, his head had turned sideways to see the Sheremetyevo driver holding the gun after shooting the Kazakh. Was there anything about his trip Lisa didn't know?

"Should I bother asking how you saw that?"

"I was watching live video feed at the embassy. The man—your driver—is one of our most skilled Russian operatives. I assigned him to protect you."

Lisa approached Frank again and pulled him close to her. Her eyes welled up. "The most important reason I came to Moscow was to keep you safe."

Frank thought back to the first time he'd seen Lisa, standing in front of his Russian class at the DLI. He felt like he should feel furious, yet as she held him tight, his anger dissolved.

She whispered in his ear. "Now you know all my secrets. And you've gotten the story you came here to get. There's nothing left for you to discover."

Lisa wasn't quite right.

VIII: WINNER TAKES ALL

I must complain the cards are ill shuffled till I have a good hand.

Jonathan Swift

CHAPTER 44

Los Angeles

FRANK AND LISA breezed through passport control at LAX with their black diplomatic passports. They'd left Moscow at nine, and thanks to the time difference it was only mid morning in Los Angeles. They had learned to travel light. While other passengers went to claim baggage, the newly united couple rolled trim stowaway bags to the front of a customs line, showed their forms with nothing to declare and walked through a sliding glass door. They rode an escalator upstairs and entered the international terminal with its vast skylight and large Estee Lauder ad over the check-in counters.

During the thirteen-hour flight from Moscow, they'd talked about everything except their suddenly changed relationship status. They'd held hands, and Frank caressed Lisa's hair as she dozed, her head on his shoulder. Lisa knew better than to repeat her entreaties about the content of his Thursday article. He'd written a rough draft on his laptop on the plane and would finish it when they got home. It was understood that Lisa would stay with Frank for most of the weekend before flying to Washington. He'd never left the pink stucco house they'd purchased after returning from Moscow. When they divorced and he bought her out, he'd held off selling at what he would learn was the height of the market, and the housing crash had left him stuck with it. He'd never imagined that Lisa would walk back into the single-story dwelling and share his bed again.

Frank ducked into an airport store to buy a bottle of water. Passing a newsstand on the way to the cooler, he saw a stack of Wednesday *Register*s. His spot article from Moscow was spread across the top with a six-column headline: "Roberts Would-Be Assassin Found, Killed in Russia in Police Shootout." He'd read the story on the plane, online on the screen on the back of the seat in front of him, still amazed that he could access an article he'd written scarcely fifteen hours earlier while flying at thirty thousand feet. But he was a throwback—there was nothing like seeing it splashed on the front page of the paper. He tucked a copy under his arm, took a liter of spring water from the fridge, went to the cashier and paid. He met Lisa outside the store, and the two of them headed out to the taxi stand.

Fifty minutes later they stood in Frank's living room. Lisa was amazed: the room looked just as it had the day she left, save for a large flat-screen TV in the dark-wood Gisela cabinet they'd bought at the Venice antiques flea market. Frank dropped his bag, turned to Lisa and kissed her.

"Welcome home."

Lisa almost used the tender moment as a lever to ask him again to exercise restraint in writing his exposé about Roberts.

Instead, she kissed him back and murmured, "It's good to be home." She cuffed him gently on the side of the head. "You've got a story to write, Mr. Adams," she said before disappearing into the bathroom for a shower. She would have to trust him.

Frank walked into his study, a dingy room off the kitchen with outdated paneling and a small window facing the driveway. He turned on his PC and retrieved the draft article he'd e-mailed to himself from his laptop on the plane. For the next three hours, he pored through the notebooks he'd used in Moscow and Atyrau, marking key quotes with a red pen, highlighting other important material in yellow. He turned on his digital recorder and listened to parts of his interview with Yemelin; now that he knew the Russian consultant worked for Lisa, he wanted to hear his revelations about Roberts again, as much for tone as for substance. Hudson called and e-mailed Frank a half dozen times, asking when the story would be ready, but the reporter ignored him. Finally, just before four, Frank sent Don an e-mail: "Story is in the can. Giving it a final read and will ship shortly. I have added Viktor Romanov as a second byline. As you know, he was my friend who was killed while we were reporting together in Kazakhstan. It's a matter of basic fairness that he be listed as coauthor. Without his help, I couldn't have gotten the story."

Frank printed out his piece and started for the living room. Articles always read differently on paper than on the screen, and with one this sensational he wanted to be extra careful. As he reached the couch, his cell phone rang. Frank looked for the number on his phone, but it said restricted. He answered the call and heard an unfamiliar voice.

"Frank Adams?"

"Yes."

"I know that you are on deadline with an important article, but you and I must meet before you deliver it."

Frank was annoyed. "Who are you? And how do you know about my article?"

Russell Talbert stood near the Griffith Observatory, looking down on Los Angeles.

"You did an excellent job on your trip, but your reporting is incomplete. You wouldn't want to publish anything but your best work on a story this big."

Frank sensed that this mystery man wasn't holding all the cards his confident voice suggested he held. "I'm not going to meet you unless you tell me who you are."

Talbert paused. He hadn't thought this would be easy. "I'm an active intelligence official. In your parlance, a senior intelligence source."

Frank upped the ante. "I know a lot of intelligence officials."

Talbert was ready. "You don't know any with details about Stuart Roberts's hidden past in Russia." He sweetened the pot. "And how it connects with important people here in America."

This froze Frank. It was his bluff that had been called. "Where do we meet?"

"On the south side of Morris Reservoir. Take the 210 east to Azusa, then drive north out of town on Route 39. It turns into San Gabriel Canyon Road. Just after you see the reservoir below you, the road bends to the left. There's a wide dirt trail off to the right just after the bend. Drive up the trail fifty yards. Make sure your car isn't visible from the road. Wait for me there."

Frank's line went dead. He walked back into the study and typed out another e-mail for Hudson: "New development. Need to meet a source for the Roberts story. It will miss deadline, but hold space."

Frank looked in his bedroom to see Lisa napping on his bed, his faded burgundy robe covering her shoulders and half-open in front. He wrote a note and left it on the nightstand: "Got a call from a new source on Roberts. Out to meet him. Back soon. Don't worry."

Avoiding downtown Los Angeles, Frank guided his '09 Malibu onto the 405 north toward San Fernando. He took the 210 east and drove through Glendale and Pasadena, the traffic thinning as he passed Arcadia. In a few minutes, he exited at Azusa, headed north on Route 39 and followed its twists into Angeles National Forest. As Morris Reservoir came into view below him, the road bent left and he saw the trail to his right. He down-shifted the Chevy, crept along for a minute and stopped. An hour had passed since he left home.

Ten minutes went by, then another five. Just as Frank was thinking about leaving, he heard a tap on his side window. A giant of a man with a ruddy face waved him from the car. Frank got out and started to speak, but the man walked along a barely discernible path into the woods. Frank followed him. They reached a small clearing with boulders spaced at odd intervals. The man sat on a flat portion of one boulder and motioned Frank over. Frank stopped ten feet away, off to the side and slightly in front of the man.

"I'm here."

The man studied Frank for a moment. "Thank you for coming, Frank, especially under the circumstances. I know that you've been through hell. I admire your grit."

"You didn't come here to flatter me."

The man continued as if he hadn't heard. "Congratulations on reuniting with Lisa. She is a wonderful woman. The two of you deserve a second chance."

The man took out a cigarette and lit it. Frank almost blanched at seeing someone smoke in California, and in a national forest to boot.

"I also know that Lisa told you about Operation Long Shadow." The man exhaled. "It was a doomed operation from the start—a bad idea that should have been DOA. I blame myself for not stopping it earlier."

Suddenly, all the tension of the last week hit Frank. He was bone tired. Before he could stop himself, he was raging at the man.

"Who *are* you people? Hawkes playing at publisher while working for the CIA. Lisa monitoring me on video in Moscow. You watching me from God knows where. What gives all of you the right to control others and move them around like pieces on a board?"

The man nodded. "If I were you, I would be angry too. I'm here to help you. You've done a heroic job of reporting in Russia, but you need confirmation of what you've learned. I can provide it."

The man reached into his olive-colored coat and withdrew a thick file. He tried to give it to Frank, but the reporter pulled back as if it was radioactive.

"What is this?"

"Our intelligence dossier on Stuart Roberts. I believe you will find it quite illuminating."

"You're giving me a CIA file?"

"Oh, Frank, this is not merely a CIA file. This is CIA, FBI, NSA, DIA, Secret Service—just about every intelligence agency there is. It represents, let us say, the government's comprehensive knowledge of Senator Roberts."

Frank shook his head. "I'm not accepting a file I could go to jail for taking without knowing who you are. What's your name?"

"Alright, fair enough. In the end, when you've had time to think things through, I'm sure you won't want to expose me— or your boss or . . . your wife. And you yourself have secrets that you won't wish to come out." The man stubbed his cigarette on the ground with his foot. "I am Russell Talbert. Head of science and technology for the Agency. I've known Thomas Hawkes for many years." He nodded at the folder. "Take a look."

Frank opened the file and started reading the documents inside: cables, e-mails, transcripts of intercepted calls, handwritten notes from meetings, satellite photographs, invoices, packing labels, postmarked envelopes from foreign countries, summary reports. The materials confirmed his reporting, but they also provided new details, some he had suspected, others he hadn't imagined. After five minutes, Frank closed the folder and handed it back to Talbert.

"People like you don't share something like this out of the goodness of your heart. Why do you want Roberts taken down?"

Talbert sighed before answering. "We should have vetted him better before launching Operation Long Shadow. He's like all choir boys—too good by half. I thought he would put the country's interests ahead of his own. Thought it would be a win-win for everyone—him, me, Thomas, the Agency, the nation. Of course, I made sure the Agency had no official involvement. But his psychological profile wasn't a suitable match for a mission this sensitive. And Thomas. A good man, but he's always been a cowboy. Always taking a gamble for the sheer sake of the risk." Talbert paused. "It started to become clear some time ago that Roberts couldn't be trusted in the White House. Given his secret business involvements overseas, he was wide open to blackmail. It would have been child's play for any government's intelligence apparatus. We thought if we waited, his political rivals might get the best of him without our interference. But after he started winning primaries, we realized other steps were needed."

Frank grimaced and shook his head. He didn't want to believe what he was hearing. "My God. It was you, wasn't it? You set up the Russians! You set me up. Everything I reported yesterday about the hit on Roberts was a lie."

"I wouldn't put it like that, Frank. You reported what you knew. You had good reason to believe it. A former KGB agent tried to kill you! The police came to arrest him."

It was Frank's turn to pause. He tried to slow his racing mind. "You wouldn't be telling me this if you thought I would report it. You must be desperate. You're asking me to be part of a cover-up of a major crime! I can't do it. I won't do it!"

Frank started to walk away. Talbert stopped him with a hand on his shoulder.

"Stuart is alive and well. As they say in basketball, no

harm, no foul. His own actions and decisions will do him in, and your fine reporting will bring them to light." Talbert lowered his voice. "You're in the big game, boy. It wasn't your fault that you went to work for a spook and married another one. But now you've got to play the hand you were dealt, and it's not a bad hand. Without getting into any of these other matters, you've already got the makings of a Pulitzer. I'm asking you to put your family first. I know you want to protect Lisa—and Thomas too. You and Lisa have admitted that your marriage failed because of your jobs. Now you've got another chance. Do it right this time."

Frank felt like he was being pulled deeper into a nightmare from which he couldn't wake. He understood that Talbert's apparent concern was really by way of a warning.

"You're threatening me, aren't you?"

Talbert waved his hand. "Threats! That's a rather dramatic way of putting it. We're all in this together. If the crazy notions you and I have been discussing here were ever to see the light of day, they would cause great harm to the nation. I know you're a patriot. I'm sure you'll put your country as well as your family ahead of your work."

Frank walked away from Talbert without looking back. He got in his car, turned on the engine and drove away. His article was already past deadline, and now he had more to do.

CHAPTER 45

SANTA MONICA, CALIFORNIA

THIS WAS A ritual that went back years. When the *Register* still had home delivery, each morning while the coffee was brewing, Frank opened the front door of his Santa Monica home, walked down the two steps and picked up his paper. Although he'd been a journalist for twenty-five years, it still amazed Frank, feeling the heft of the *Register*, that a thousand people could work together so frantically and produce, each and every day, a compendium of fifty, seventy-five, sometimes one hundred articles dispatched from around the world and covering so many disparate topics from a failed coup in Tanzania to a new way to cook butternut squash.

And there was a greater thrill: retrieving his paper on those days when one of his articles was at the top of the front page.

Like all the other big city newspapers, the *Register* had lost tens of thousands of print subscribers as readers migrated to the Internet or stopped reading papers altogether. Yet the

Register still had over 300,000 subscribers for its daily editions and almost 500,000 on Sundays. Frank knew it was a regrettable streak of vanity to relish the rush of excitement each time he saw his byline, "By Senior Political Reporter Frank M. Adams," over an article that so many people were reading.

Yet that thrill continued to drive him. And it helped him overcome the anxiety he still felt at the start of each assignment. Would his sources call him back in time to meet his deadline? Could he locate the holders of important information and convince them to share their secrets? Would a competitor, Jack Reynolds at the *New York Times* or Stacey Haynes Thomson of the *Washington Post*, uncover something he couldn't find? Would their story be better?

The morning ritual had been tweaked, and more than once.

After his return from Moscow, Frank found himself going first to the computer in his study, booting it up and launching his Internet browser, then waiting impatiently the few moments it took to land on his home page.

The ways of the *Register*'s "interactive media" masters were mysterious. Reading the paper online often delivered the jolting disappointment of seeing his article buried on the screen beneath the latest breathless account of celebrity scandal or a super sized photograph of an actress at last night's Hollywood gala with a generous show of cleavage.

That disappointment, having to search through the bewildering heap of headlines and photos and teasers and charts that had replaced the front page's reliable display of the day's five best stories, was offset by a new thrill born of the Internet.

The *Register* ran a supplemental wire service that sent its articles, columns, photos and graphics to six hundred subscribing newspapers, TV and radio stations, and now bloggers and websites, around the world. Sometimes Frank would sit before his computer, reading his article on the bright flat screen, and picture a New Delhi businessman or a Geneva diplomat or a Chicago commodities trader reading it on a tablet or smartphone.

Then, just a year ago, technology had changed the ritual again. For readers who still needed to feel the printed product in their hands but wanted the kind of customized, targeted read available online, the *Register* developed the latest technological marvel: the MiniPress. After Frank and a dozen others at the paper had beta-tested it for six months, the device was offered for retail use.

The MiniPress looked like a sleek descendant of the newspaper stand. Using a smartphone app, you designed your own paper. You could print the ten top stories or only business coverage. Recipes, sports scores and stock prices, plus your favorite writer's column. You could program the MiniPress to deliver the same "paper" every day or customize it each morning. You paid by the word, currently a quarter for every thousand words of print, the cost instantly charged to your credit card. You didn't have to pay extra for the ads, but neither could you choose not to print them. The digital demographic modeling selected which ads to print based on each reader's choices. An article about an NFL game carried a beer ad; a piece about the hot new diet came with coupons for organic produce; Frank's stories of political intrigue and power players were accompanied by pitches for sports cars or package trips to exotic locales.

Frank was in for a bitter surprise this morning. When the MiniPress printed out the *Register*'s front page, his thirty-two-thousand-word exclusive from Russia wasn't on it. Frank set his coffee on a counter and dashed to his study. Lisa hadn't changed in their years apart. She still left the computer on overnight.

Frank clicked away from the Hollywood column Lisa had been reading—she still loved celebrity gossip—to losangeles-register.com.

His article wasn't there.

Mystified, he typed "Mikhail Gusov" into the search window and clicked on the "go" icon. Zero results.

Frank rushed back to the MiniPress. The first section of the paper, the only place his piece would run, had printed out. He grabbed the sheaf and scanned the pages; his story was nowhere to be found.

Lisa came into the kitchen, wearing a sheer negligee, sleep in her eyes. She looked softer and sexier than before. "Did they butcher your article?"

"They didn't publish it."

Lisa draped her arms around Frank's shoulders. "This has to be my father's doing."

Frank broke away from her embrace. "He's been running our lives for too long."

CHAPTER 46

LOS ANGELES

THOMAS HAWKES KNEW who was calling when his phone rang at his home just past nine. It would be Frank, and he would be agitated. He demanded to see Thomas. Hawkes calmly agreed to meet Frank in the publisher's office at ten thirty. Thomas didn't lack for self-confidence. Thomas rarely misread people, and he had been reading Frank for a long time. The key was understanding the other person better than he understood himself and foreseeing his actions before he took them. You needed to be looking four or five moves ahead of the game. You had to see your rival's options before you made your own move.

Thomas always arrived at meetings early. One of his rules of thumb was: arrive first, speak last. So he had parked his Cadillac in the *Register*'s garage, walked up the three flights of stairs, crossed the near-empty newsroom, waved to a wire editor, unlocked his office and settled in at his desk a few minutes before hearing a knock on the door.

If it had been anyone besides Frank, Thomas would have been surprised that he hadn't come alone. Anyone else, and Thomas might have been startled to see Frank's ex-wife, his own daughter, head of the CIA's energy security section, enter the office alongside his ace reporter. If Thomas wondered why Lisa hadn't told him she would be joining Frank, he didn't let on. An explanation would be forthcoming.

Thomas beckoned Frank and Lisa over to the alcove with its high window looking out on the Los Angeles skyline. Frank and Lisa sat down next to each other on the tan leather couch.

"Why did you pull my article? I got the story I went to Moscow to get."

Thomas made himself a Bloody Mary and eased into his black leather recliner. He ate a piece of celery from his drink. Frank's fury was not unexpected. The publisher ignored the question and launched his own attack.

"Since when do you tell me which bylines to run in my newspaper? I know that Viktor Romanov was your friend and you're upset by his death. But he worked for a Russian newspaper! The *Los Angeles Register* doesn't publish work by foreign reporters."

Frank was astounded. "That's nonsense! It was thanks to Viktor's help that I got the full story about Roberts. And he paid with his life!"

Hawkes stood his ground. "I have to do what's good for the country."

"And why is a cover-up good for the country?"

"Do you reveal everything you know in your articles, Frank? Of course not. You have anonymous sources to protect. You have time and space limits. You select the most dramatic material. You leave out all kinds of interesting details. In the end, isn't the published story always just one version of the truth?"

"This isn't about leaving out details, Thomas! This is about you killing a story—the most important story of my career."

"Don't lecture me about your career. You wouldn't be where you are if it weren't for me."

Lisa stood up. "Both of you, stop it! Daddy, you know damn well Frank's the best reporter at the paper. And, Frank, you owe my father some respect."

Frank and Thomas glared at each other. The chess clock was off. The smooth covers each of them used so skillfully in life were blown. The quiet edge in Frank's voice amplified his anger. "How can I respect a man who has allowed this newspaper to become a tool of the CIA?"

Thomas looked at Lisa. She had told Frank everything. Had the two of them reunited in Moscow? Why hadn't his moles informed him?

Thomas returned Frank's steady stare, the same stare he'd first seen at Berkeley so long ago. "I will not permit your article to ruin the most important asset the Agency has ever developed just when that asset is on the doorstep of the White House."

Frank stood up. He took Lisa's hand. So Thomas was facing a team.

Lisa was silent as Frank spoke. "You've already destroyed your most important asset."

"Really? What's that?"

"The public trust."

Frank and Lisa left Thomas's office.

CHAPTER 47

LOS ANGELES

T HE ENTIRE DOWNTOWN around Staples Center had been cleansed to a sparkle for the Republican National Convention. Buildings were renovated, the homeless were temporarily resettled and brightly painted plywood covered construction sites. The city had commissioned Pasadena artist William Stout to paint a colossal mural depicting California's fabled frontier past. It was stretched across a giant billboard to greet conventioneers on their way to the conclave.

Ever since police clubbed Vietnam War protesters on live national TV at the 1968 Democratic Convention, the political poohbahs had ensured that such a spectacle would never happen again at their parties' grandest gatherings. Now, protesters exercised their First Amendment rights in fenced-off areas blocks away from the convention hall. The demonstrations—against Chinese oppression of the Dalai Lama, against

American imperialism abroad, against the use of animals in scientific research—blended into the larger pageantry and thus lost their bite.

Barricades and yellow police tape filled the streets around Staples Center. Delegates and reporters, large colorful credentials hanging on red lanyards around their necks, jostled with mimes and vendors. Uncle Sam passed by on stilts in his star-spangled glory.

Two members of a German TV crew neared an IntelliView store with a line stretching outside it for blocks. Some customers left the store with boxes. Others stood over open cartons, holding wand-like electronic devices.

One of the TV guys wondered what was up. "What are the long lines for?"

His partner explained. "That new gadget went on sale today. It's called the bioWave."

As the presidential contest neared its peak, Roberts was too busy campaigning around the country from dawn until midnight to dabble in the countless details of planning the convention that would serve as his political coronation. Instead, at the end of nightly phone talks about strategy and fundraising, he would spend a few minutes weighing convention decisions. Sometimes, as he waited backstage at a campaign stop for a governor or mayor to warm up the crowd outside, Roberts reflected that he had never allowed an event of such magnitude to be prepared by others. But then came the inevitable internal reminder: As president, he would be in charge of millions of civilian and military employees. He would have to delegate responsibilities far more than he'd ever done at IntelliView or in his diplomatic and political posts.

For two centuries, the presidential nominating conventions were the real deal. It was behind their closed doors and on their smoke-filled floors, at the bars and in the buffet lines of the corporate parties outside the convention hall, that a circle of the nation's most powerful politicians brokered deals to choose their party's nominee for the White House.

All that had changed in the last few decades. Now, a grueling grind of presidential primaries, stretched over long months across dozens of states, determined the winners. There was no longer any nominating that mattered at the big political conventions.

That didn't mean the conventions were unimportant. They fired up each party's most fervent followers—the activists who in the crucial closing months would work the phone banks, stuff the envelopes, canvass neighborhoods, distribute campaign literature and make sure their ticket's voters got to the polls. More critically, the conventions sold the candidate to Americans watching in living rooms and family rooms and hotel rooms, at airports and Laundromats and other places beyond the arena hall. They would listen to the speeches as dads loaded the dishwasher, daughters did homework, dogs curled up at their masters' feet. For many viewers, this was when they learned new things about their potential next president.

The conventions had become a political play. Each night was an act that had to be more gripping than the last in delivering its testimonials to the nominee's virtues. Each act built to the climactic final scene when tens of millions would watch for the nominee to walk onstage and deliver the most important speech of his life. With so much at stake, there was no margin for error. The last night of the convention was practiced over and over.

After spirited bidding, the Hollywood events company Perfect Productions was chosen to stage the Republican National Convention. It hired focus groups and tested political slogans, different ways of paying homage to Stuart Roberts. The winning slogans, "Roberts Nation" and "Stuart Time," were put on signs made by printers in swing states that could turn the election.

Another competition was won by Dian Prawiro, a young video director and son of Indonesian immigrants who had converted from Islam to Christianity and become loyal Republican donors. Prawiro's powerful biopics of sports stars and Iraq or Afghanistan war heroes had just the right mix of traditional values and fast-paced, cutting-edge technique for him to make the film about Roberts's life that would be shown just before his entrance to the hall.

Perfect Productions bussed in hundreds of campaign workers to fill Staples Center for rehearsals. They waved signs, stood and cheered, delivered ovations on cue.

Roberts, still recuperating from the attempt on his life, practiced his acceptance address at the podium the morning before the convention opened. Technicians tested the sound system to make sure it could handle 150 decibels of bass-heavy music. Crewmen climbed high into the Staples Center rafters to secure the netting that would hold one hundred thousand red, white and blue balloons until they were dropped as the music roared and the Roberts family joined him onstage after his speech.

Italian and French designers of past presidential wardrobes had lined up to make the suit Roberts would wear, but he'd insisted on hiring an American tailor. To his friends' surprise, the candidate had selected Jonathan Majors, a Ralph Lauren disciple who'd made a name by blending ghetto street style with suburban sensibility. Majors studied the suits of American presidents and used hundreds of photos to draw meticulous sketches of Roberts. The nominee-in-waiting had to endure four fitting sessions before the designer was satisfied.

At noon on the convention's final day, Majors helped Roberts try on his suit and hand-stitched shirt. The suit was navy blue, its traditional color and style enlivened by delicate pin stripes and an ever-so-slight jaunty cut. Roberts stood before his suite's full-length mirror, his wife at his side.

Catherine Roberts smoothed the soft fabric over her husband's shoulders. "It's perfect, Stuart," she said.

At 5:55 p.m. in Los Angeles, TV prime time on the East Coast, Roberts stood behind a curtain off the platform at the front of the hall. He had asked his aides to give him a few minutes alone before his entrance. Roberts wasn't worried about remembering the words of his speech—the teleprompter would take care of that. He was ready. Roberts had seen parts of his cinematic biography at various production stages, signed off on its use of personal photos and family videos. He peered into the hall as conventioneers hollered and clapped at the dramatic depiction of his life.

"A self-made businessman who revolutionized the telecommunications industry!"

As the crowd roared, Stuart pictured the shot of him demonstrating the first GPS device woven into a soldier's uniform at the 1994 Defense Contractors Exhibit in San Diego.

"The United States ambassador to the Soviet Union just after the end of the Cold War!" (A clip from his first Kremlin meeting with Putin.)

"The senior senator from California!" (He sat at his Senate desk, the Capitol dome rising behind him through his window.)

"An experienced statesman willing to stand up forcefully to our foes, whether Russia in Ukraine or the Islamic State in Iraq!" (Video footage of him in a command operations center with Special Forces sent back to Baghdad to secure the capital.)

"The survivor of a cowardly attempt on his life less than two weeks ago!" The crowd erupted as the screen showed Roberts, from his hospital bed, giving the thumbs-up sign.

"The next president of the United States!"

His supporters rose as one. They chanted his name and applauded in rhythm. Roberts walked onstage with crutches. He approached the podium and smiled broadly, the applause and cheers washing over him.

CHAPTER 48

LOS ANGELES

FOR REPORTERS AT a presidential convention, it's hard to avoid feeling like they're covering a circus. Delegates wear bright, outlandish clothes, silly hats, big metal buttons with photos of the nominee and slogans like "Stuart for Survival" or "The Roberts Rescue Brigade." At these conclaves, the most loyal activists put on red clown wigs and blow party horns. Patriotic mascots roam around, so you can see Uncle Sam lean down and hug the American Eagle, which wraps its fluffy wings around Uncle Sam's waist.

More than five thousand TV, radio, print and Internet reporters from around the globe were credentialed to cover the Republican Convention. Only the richest media outlets had paid the extra tens of thousands of dollars to get a separate work area with its own Internet router, TVs, phones, power outlets, microwave, refrigerator and similar essentials. The other journalists were assigned to numbered workstations—spots at long folding tables covered with white butcher paper on which the reporters periodically, when they couldn't grab a notebook in time, scribbled frantically in the clear spaces between coffee spills and pizza grease.

Rows and rows of the long tables were crammed inside the giant "media tents" that fanned out from the arena into its parking lots, magnifying the circus atmosphere. TVs hung from cables strung across the tent tops, tuned to a dozen network and cable channels. They blared a cacophony of pundits' overheated analyses, commercials, off-site protests or parties, delegate interviews, afternoon speeches from the mayors and congressmen and governors and state legislators and party operatives who preceded the keynote speaker pegged to start his address at 10:00 p.m. EDT.

Power cords from laptops, printers, chargers, iPhones and recorders entangled journalists and ran along the floor in meshed heaps behind them to metal outlet boxes. Reporters bashed their laptop keys, yelled into phones wedged between their necks and shoulders, and aimed remotes at the suspended TVs. Profanity-laced shouting would erupt when one reporter tripped over an outlet box or stumbled on the wires, wiping out stories on nearby competitors' laptop screens or sending phones flying through the air.

Many of the reporters alternated drinks—coffee for an energy boost, caffeine-free Diet Cokes to quench their thirst. Covering conventions had always been hectic, especially decades ago when the big cities had six, eight or a dozen newspapers that published special editions hawked on the street. These days, only New York had four dailies and most cities had just one. Barring a major development at the convention—a heart attack by the nominee or an unexpected challenge mounted against him—there were no special editions.

But the reporters' convention work had turned frantic in new ways. They tweeted relentlessly, running in and out of the tents as they retrieved tidbits to file. They checked their iPhones nonstop, eating sandwiches with one hand while clicking out e-mails or texts to dozens of delegates, campaign aides and party operatives. The new breed of lone-ranger podcasters were determined to update their Internet reports more often than the dinosaur TV or radio broadcasts. Every thirty minutes, they ran from the tent, dashed down three or four hallways, planted themselves in front of a banner or poster, held out their arms in front of their faces, pointed their smartphone cameras at themselves and began another "live podcast."

It didn't concern them that they had no real news to report.

By 6:00 p.m. PDT, the reporters had groaned and hooted their way through the slick video about Stuart Roberts. Many of them had covered him too closely to accept the heroic depiction of this complex, bright, often infuriating and sometimes paranoid businessman-turned-diplomat-turned-politician. As with all pols, the reporters knew the gap between Roberts's feather-brushed public persona and his actual life. The tent grew silent for his address accepting the Republican presidential nomination, save for the sound of reporters tapping notes on their laptops or turning pages as they read advance embargoed transcripts of the speech.

"The most sacred duty of an American president is to protect his countrymen against foreign threats!"

Deafening applause from the delegates.

"As your next president, I will stop at nothing to protect Americans, whether the threat comes from an Islamic State stronghold in Syria or from within the walls of the Kremlin in Moscow!"

Raucous cheers.

"As a former businessman who founded a major telecommunications company, I understand that economic power is as important as military might! As your president, I will confront our economic competitors in China, India and elsewhere around the world!"

As the cheering and clapping rose again, the picture on some of the TV screens in the media tent changed.

National News Center went to a split screen. Roberts continued speaking on one half, but with the sound muted.

NNC newscaster Wendy Hallister, whose all-American beauty accentuated her reporting skill, appeared on the other half of the screen above the banner "BREAKING NEWS." She spoke in an excited tone modulated by years of on-air experience. "We apologize for interrupting Senator Roberts's address."

Some of the reporters stopped typing or reading to focus on the TV screen.

"According to the *Los Angeles Register*, Senator Roberts has received substantial campaign funding from the recently murdered Russian oil tycoon and Kremlin opposition leader Mikhail Gusov. The illegal foreign campaign contributions were laundered through AmeriCon Energy, the Houston-based oil conglomerate."

Chaos broke out in the media tent. Reporters leapt from their chairs. They grabbed cell phones and clustered before the TV monitors, holding up digital recorders.

"The *Los Angeles Register* also reports that Gusov was building a secret oil pipeline to Pakistan with the covert aid of Taliban fundamentalists in Afghanistan and Muslim radicals in Pakistan.

"Still worse, Gusov was paying the Taliban protection money to secure the pipeline, and the Taliban were funneling aid to Islamic State fighters targeted by the US-led air campaign in Iraq and Syria.

"The story discloses that after becoming a senator and then a US presidential candidate, Roberts made a series of secret trips to Russia that he didn't reveal in subsequent required campaign and financial disclosure reports."

One reporter hollered across the room. "Dan, can you believe this shit?"

"The *Register*'s exclusive story provides more incredible details. It says that Bud Johnson, the head of AmeriCon Energy and a major contributor to the Roberts campaign, was working with Mikhail Gusov to build the oil pipeline to Pakistan. And that the two men were skimming royalties from Gusov's vast oil operations, which may account for billions of missing rubles that caused a scandal in the Russian Oil Ministry. This could justify Russian charges that American oil companies were stealing money from the Kremlin."

The sound on all the TV sets had been turned up. All TVs in the tent now showed the NNC bulletin.

"There's more in the *Register's* account. According to the paper, while Roberts was CEO of IntelliView, it formed a partnership with an Israeli defense company called NanoTek. That firm was founded by a German émigré named Rado Weinstien, who was killed by police in Moscow earlier this week while resisting arrest for the attempted assassination of Senator Roberts."

Reporters knocked over chairs and yanked laptops from power cords as they flew around the tent.

"The *Register* reports that apparently unknown to Roberts, NanoTek sold nuclear technology the two firms had developed to China and to terrorist clients as part of an international arms ring Weinstien operated."

Wendy Hallister continued broadcasting the explosive story. "Senior political correspondent Frank Adams was the *Register's* lead reporter on this bombshell expose. But in an unprecedented step, the *Register* gave a joint byline to a Russian journalist named Viktor Romanov, a reporter for the *Kapital* business weekly in Moscow. Romanov was killed in the Kazakhstan oil boomtown of Atyrau as he and Adams followed Senator Roberts's secret overseas business dealings. Adams, who narrowly escaped an attempt on his own life, wrote a first-person account that accompanied their blockbuster article about Roberts's hidden past."

Wendy Hallister held up a new electronic device, the same device customers had lined up to buy earlier that day near the convention center.

"Finally, in a brilliant marketing strategy, the *Register*

chose not to publish this exclusive on the newspaper's front page today or on its website. This sensational story is being read by thousands of Americans on something called a bio-Wave. Ironically for Stuart Roberts, the bioWave is the hot electronics device created by the company he founded. It went on sale this morning at IntelliView stores across the country."

CHAPTER 49

Los Angeles

MIDWAY THROUGH HIS speech, Roberts thought it was going well. The delegates were clapping at the applause lines, laughing at the jokes, booing at the putdowns that mocked Democrats as big spenders and weak-kneed liberals. He hadn't tried to memorize the speech, but now he barely glanced at the white lines racing across the teleprompter. His wife and children sat in the center of the front row. He leaned into the podium and focused on the cadence of his voice.

"I look forward to a vigorous campaign with my opponent. He is a good man, but one who I am sad to say is woefully ill-prepared to—"

A TV correspondent at the front of the convention hall heard an urgent message in his earpiece. A blogger was interrupted by a Tweet. A print reporter sitting among Ohio delegates read an all-caps text message. Dozens of journalists started scrambling.

Roberts continued speaking. "In today's dangerous world, we cannot afford to entrust our precious liberties and our national security to a good man with bad ideas!"

Delegates, puzzled by the sudden activity, looked around the hall. A buzz rose in the vast chamber. Thomas Hawkes sat in the second row, Lisa next to him. A note was passed down the row to Thomas. He opened it: "We need to interview you. NNC."

Thomas rose, moved across the row and walked briskly toward an exit.

Just outside the hall, an NNC reporter and his cameraman intercepted Thomas. The reporter began to speak. "We are live at the convention with *Los Angeles Register* publisher Thomas Hawkes."

A mass of other reporters and TV crews clustered around Hawkes. The NNC correspondent held a mike out to him. "How did your newspaper get this amazing exclusive about Stuart Roberts's ties to the Russian mafia, radical Muslims and an international weapons ring?" Thomas adopted his stoic posture. "As publisher, of course, I must maintain my distance from the news operation. However, given the magnitude of our investigation into the assassination attempt on Stuart Roberts, I was brought into the loop. We started getting leads about Senator Roberts through our national security sources. Our editors put our best reporters on the story."

Frank and Don Hudson sat with eight of their colleagues watching Thomas's interview on a plasma TV at the front of the *Register*'s convention workspace.

Haden Hayes, an ABC News reporter, followed up: "Why did you decide to break this remarkable story on the bioWave instead of in your newspaper?"

Thomas responded: "The newspaper industry is facing major challenges from electronic media. If we want to attract the readers of tomorrow, we need to beat our new competitors at their own game."

The other reporters and editors in the *Register*'s workspace cheered. They slapped Frank and Don on the back and offered fist bumps. Frank, who normally rejoiced at praise from his peers, felt oddly disengaged. He smiled slightly and held up his bioWave, prompting another round of cheers.

Outside, Lisa joined Thomas, and they walked quickly toward the *Register*'s workspace. Thomas ignored more interview requests, moving brusquely through the growing group of reporters, TV crews and gawkers. Applause and cheers broke out from the reporters and editors who'd just watched his TV interview as he and Lisa entered. Frank dutifully joined in the ovation but flashed a disdainful look at Thomas for taking public credit for the story the publisher had tried to kill.

Thomas knew the next move. His face beaming, he spread his arms toward his staff. "Thank you, thank you—but the applause belongs to all of you! I just pay the bills."

Thomas, still smiling, looked at Frank and Don. "I especially want to congratulate Frank Adams and his fine editor, Don Hudson."

More cheers.

As the reporters and editors broke into high-spirited conversation, Thomas approached Frank and clasped him on the shoulder. The smile was gone. Thomas leaned in and spoke in a cold whisper. "We need to talk."

CHAPTER 50

Los Angeles

A S UNFASHIONABLE AS it had become in some circles, Catherine Roberts was proud to be a stay-at-home mom. Not that many of her activities—her charity work, the volunteering, the full social calendar she managed—didn't take her outside their home in San Diego's exclusive La Jolla Country Club neighborhood. But for the better part of four decades, she had done everything in her power to ensure her husband's success. If he succeeded, she and their three children succeeded. And as Stuart rose to the top of their nation's business, diplomatic and political echelons, Catherine had come to believe that his success would help ensure the success of all Americans, those alive now and generations still to come.

Catherine had planned a reception after Stuart's acceptance speech to express their gratitude. Campaign aides told her they could use political donations to pay for four days of entertaining their friends and loved ones, but Catherine wouldn't hear of it. She and Stuart had been blessed to amass great wealth, and they could afford to host what she thought of as "their team," the hundred or so people who'd been in their corner over the years. This was personal. So Catherine had paid to fly the team to Los Angeles and put them up in VIP suites on the top floor of the Los Angeles Mirage Hotel. She had given everyone a Visa gift card with $2,000 on it to cover their costs during their stay.

Catherine spared no expense in planning the elegant reception on the final night. She had the caterers prepare dishes from five ethnic cuisines and set up serving stations in suites along the twenty-fourth floor. After a short welcome from Stuart, violinists would stroll among the suites. Bartenders would pour Dom Perignon. A friend from each phase of Stuart's career would make a toast. She would offer the last one.

As word of the *Los Angeles Register*'s sensational story spread through the convention hall, it reached Roberts's contingent in the front. While reporters rushed from the hall and delegates rose to follow them, Stuart pushed dutifully through his speech. His family and friends sat in stunned silence, determined to form a bulwark of support in the spreading chaos.

Catherine and their children remained in the first row, preparing to join him onstage for the grand finale after his address. As the buzz rose and Stuart soldiered on, Catherine told herself that this was all a horrible mistake. Everyone knew how liberal the media were—who could believe anything published in a newspaper? Her heart pounding, Catherine summoned her resolve. This wasn't the first crisis she and Stuart had faced together. When the dust settled, it would be merely their latest and most remarkable escape.

Sealed off from the outside, readying their stations for the reception, the tuxedoed bartenders and servers were unaware of the gathering storm. The music would play, the champagne would flow, the food would be served. As her guests began to arrive, Catherine saw that they were shell-shocked. They sought her out with questions. Who had spread such awful lies about Stuart? What could he possibly have to do with rich Russians and arms traders and terrorists, for goodness sake? How had all this come about?

To each friend and relative, Catherine offered a reassuring pat on the arm or a kiss on the cheek. To each guest, she murmured: "Don't you worry, Stuart and I will get to the bottom of this." As she soothed the visitors' fears and steered them toward the bars, it never occurred to her that there might be important episodes in Stuart's life she'd somehow missed. The notion that Stuart had kept secrets from her was unfathomable. Stuart and she had always shared everything. They were full and equal partners.

When Stuart arrived at their suite, Catherine knew well enough to give him some time to gather himself. She watched him drape his suit coat over a bedroom chair, loosen his tie, unbutton his shirt collar, leave the room and head for the bar. Even before the unexpected tumult, Catherine knew that this would be one of those rare occasions when he allowed himself a drink. She had already instructed the bartender how to make Stuart's special Manhattan: two shots of Canadian Whiskey, a healthy dollop of dry vermouth and just a dash of Angostura bitters. Stuart moved in silence through clusters of guests. Some tried to greet him; others offered awkward reassurances. Catherine watched as he took his drink, walked back through the suite and reentered their bedroom. It didn't surprise her that he closed the twin French doors behind him.

Catherine knew her husband: He would sit down in the armchair and take a sip of the Manhattan. He would inhale, close his eyes, exhale slowly. He would look out the window at the sunset over the downtown skyline. He would drink the Manhattan slowly as he decided on his next course of action.

What Stuart did behind the closed doors would have surprised Catherine. She was not the first person to whom he reached out amid this crisis. He sat in the armchair and stared through the window. His career was over. He held his glass tighter. He took a long drink, pulled his IntelliView WorldGate smartphone from his shirt pocket and gave it a dial command.

"Russell."

This was a name his wife would not know.

Across the continent, in a gated compound on a high bank of the Potomac River, a man in a darkened office at Langley felt his cell phone vibrate. Talbert had been waiting for the call. He had decided how he would start their talk. "I'm sorry, Stuart."

Stuart's voice was an angry whisper. "You told me this could never happen."

This first reply, too, had been practiced in advance. "Your cover is protected."

"My career is ruined."

"That was never your real career."

Stuart's interlocutor was trying to placate him, but his responses only enraged him more. "I'm not taking the fall for this alone."

"Stuart, we haven't abandoned you. We've arranged for a top-tier law firm to defend you. Discussions with the attorney general have already begun. We'll make sure you never serve prison time."

"That's not enough." A pause. "Those who exposed me must suffer the consequences."

"Revenge will be costly, Stuart."

Roberts nearly spit out his answer. "Price is no object. Or haven't you heard?" Sarcasm coated his last utterance. "I'm a visionary billionaire businessman."

CHAPTER 51

LOS ANGELES

T HOMAS, FRANK AND Lisa sat once more in the publisher's office. Reporters and editors were outside in the newsroom. Instead of reporting on Stuart Roberts's triumphant acceptance of the Republican Party's presidential nomination, Thomas's staff was covering the shocked reactions to his newspaper's exclusive.

How far back did Roberts's relationship with Rado Weinstien go? Was Weinstien's company a front for the Israeli Mossad? What other unsavory partners had Roberts done business with as head of IntelliView? How could he not have known that one of Russia's wealthiest men was funneling his campaign tens of thousands of dollars? Had military technology developed by IntelliView been used against US forces through the international arms ring? Or by the radical Muslims who were helping Mikhail Gusov build his pipeline?

Roberts's political career was certainly over. Would he go

to jail? Would he bring down others? Who would succeed him as the GOP White House candidate?

As Frank sat across from Thomas, he was surprised to see a smile on the publisher's face. Despite the praise now being heaped on his exposé, Frank was still angry over Hawkes's efforts to squelch the story. Frank had prepared himself to face the full fury of his boss and former father-in-law. Instead, Thomas went over to the liquor cabinet and pulled out the bottle of Stolichnaya that Frank had brought him from Moscow so long ago. He unlocked a side drawer and removed three of the Steuben crystal Martini glasses that he normally saved for the mayor, a senator or another visiting dignitary. He made two cocktails, walked across his office and handed one of them to Lisa. He then poured a glass of club soda and gave it to Frank. Hawkes raised his Martini.

"I would like to make a toast to a job well done by my best reporter."

The three of them clinked glasses. Frank finally spoke. "I expected you to be angry. What's going on?"

"Angry? I'm delighted! You performed just as I expected you to perform. And in the process, you cleaned up quite a mess for me."

Frank could only stammer his response. "But—but my article brought down Roberts. I thought you—"

Thomas cut him off with a wave. "Ah, you're talking about my little gambit. Operation Long Shadow was a high-risk venture from the beginning. I knew that the only way it would succeed was if everything went off perfectly without a single hitch. More than anything else, the operation depended on the reliability of Stuart Roberts."

Still stunned, Frank listened as Hawkes continued. "Stuart started going wobbly in the knees on us. I pride myself on my ability to assess people accurately, but I was wrong about him. I thought he was as tough as they come and completely cool under pressure. He could never have withstood the extraordinary rigors of being president."

Thomas was all but purring with satisfaction. "Besides, as your outstanding piece revealed, there was a whole part of Stuart's past I didn't know. From the start of the operation, he was told that he had to be completely truthful and transparent with us. This whole business with the Russian oligarch, the secret pipeline through Afghanistan, the international arms trade—I could never be associated with any of that. I'm certain that at least some of it would have been exposed between now and November. So I'm just delighted that you reported it first!"

Frank found his voice. "If you're so happy, why did you pull my article from the paper?"

Thomas reached into his briefcase and removed a bio-Wave. He fairly waved it in the air. "Marketing, my boy! I've known for a long time that Ken Nishimura over at IntelliView was your best background source on Roberts. I signed off on him giving you the xWave to beta-test on your trip to Russia. Do you think he would simply allow you, on his own authority, to run around the world with such a highly classified piece of intelligence hardware? And I counted on you to do exactly what you did—react with great indignation when I squelched your print piece, then work with Ken to get it distributed through other means. Why do you think the bioWave's release date was today? In the few hours since your story came out, bioWave sales have exploded! Ken just called to tell me they're selling a hundred units a minute on intelliview.com. It's already on back order for weeks. And all anyone's talking about is your article! IntelliView couldn't buy publicity like that, and neither could we! Some of the new bioWave customers are signing up for premium subscriptions to the *Register* delivered via the device."

Frank tried to gather his wits. How had Hawkes made him his puppet? Something about Thomas's incredible tale didn't hang together. "How could you have believed that your rogue operation to put a man in the White House would succeed?"

Thomas pursed his lips. "'Rogue' is a rather strong word, Frank. Operation Long Shadow was conducted on a need-to-know basis. And to be candid, there were very few people inside the CIA or outside who needed to know about it. Trust me, if we'd succeeded, the CIA would have been happy to make full use of Roberts once he was president. But why put Langley at such huge risk if the operation failed? No one is more committed to the Central Intelligence Agency than I am. I was willing to put that risk on my shoulders."

Frank looked at Lisa. "But you put your daughter at risk as well."

For the first time in all the years he'd known Thomas, Frank saw a blush cross the publisher's face.

"Lisa tried to talk me down from Operation Long Shadow any number of times." He looked at his daughter with sincere respect. "As it turned out, she was, as usual, right about the whole venture. I suppose I should have listened to her. But ultimately, with your help, we were able to achieve a live field test in the real world for the sort of complex but vital mission that still could prove necessary in the future."

Frank wanted to ask how a cutting-edge device like the bioWave had ended up in the hands of Thomas Hawkes, a technological caveman who could barely use e-mail. Instead, he asked his boss a more important question. "How did you know I wouldn't expose you in my article? How could you be certain I wouldn't report that your post as publisher is just a cover?"

Thomas smiled once more. "I had a little secret weapon."

Frank didn't know how much more he wanted to hear from Hawkes, so he mustered only a weak question. "What's that?"

"Romance." Thomas raised his eyes and looked back and forth from Lisa to Frank.

"It may not seem so at times, but I know my daughter well. It was apparent to me that even after your divorce, she retained strong feelings for you. And I suspected the same was true of your feelings for her. I never did understand why the two of you broke up in the first place." Thomas paused. "I knew that if I sent you on such a high-risk assignment to Moscow, she would follow you. For all our apparent differences, there's one way in which Lisa is just like her old man: she never quite trusts others' ability to do a job as well as she can. And indeed there are few who can match her at any task. So I thought that if she and you found yourselves together in Russia, alone against the world, so to speak, well . . ."

Thomas's voice trailed off. He spoke only after long moments of silence. "I knew you might be willing to see your former father-in-law go to prison. But I didn't think you'd be willing to bring down your once and future father-in-law."

As Lisa and Frank glanced at each other, seated close together on the couch, Thomas raised his glass again. "Shall we drink a toast to your reunion?"

CHAPTER 52

LOS ANGELES

S TUART ROBERTS, LIKE most politicians, avoided unscripted interviews with reporters. The days when White House correspondents would stop by the Oval Office unannounced for a chat with the president were long gone. The assassinations and shootings of JFK, Ford and Reagan, plus the 9/11 attacks, were part of the reason. But factors beyond security were at play too. The rise of political operatives to positions of extraordinary behind-the-scenes power—Lee Atwater, James Carville, Karl Rove and other pioneers of spin—had changed the rules of the game. They viewed the news media as the enemy. Most reporters were just lying in wait to ambush their bosses. Journalists were like sharks, sniffing for the faintest whiff of scandal that would bloody the waters.

Interactions with reporters were restricted as much as possible to orchestrated photo ops or one-on-one interviews with the guidelines set in advance. Even White House news conferences, which JFK had turned into comedy-laced political theater of apparent spontaneity, were now restrained affairs. Presidents limited questions to a few key issues and called on a dozen reliable correspondents who'd been tipped beforehand in silent collusion that traded access for civility. Republican officeholders were even more wary of journalists, whom they regarded as unapologetic liberals with transparent biases that marred their work.

But now Roberts had no choice. Over the last twenty-four hours, events had moved at warp-speed beyond his control. Key GOP power brokers were calling for him to end his campaign. There were backroom talks to replace him at the top of the ticket with Charles Randolph, the amiable Louisiana governor he had chosen as his running mate. Presidential candidates normally get a ratings bump coming out of their summer conventions, but the overnight polls on Roberts were devastating. He'd fallen from a virtual tie with the Democratic nominee to a fifteen-point deficit.

Overriding the advice of his aides, who assured him that his numbers had bottomed out and urged a cautious response to the scandal, Roberts decided to move quickly to tell his side of the story to the American people. Doing a live TV interview was risky, but it was necessary. He chose Wendy Hallister, the veteran National News Center anchorwoman who'd done a fair TV profile of him during the primaries and whom he'd long suspected found him attractive.

Just past 7:00 p.m., Catherine accompanied her husband to the NNC studios, sitting next to him in the backseat of the black Ford Escape as their motorcade sped through downtown Los Angeles. At Catherine's prodding, Roberts had abandoned his hand-tailored convention suit for a black Brooks Brothers outfit he'd owned for years.

NNC had preempted its normal Friday evening programming for this prime-time exclusive with the tainted White House aspirant. There was a half-hour lead-in to the interview, which would be followed by an hour of reaction from talking heads and small groups of viewers gathered in living rooms across the country.

Catherine had told Stuart the night before that he had her undying love no matter what happened. There was no need to ask him about the *Register* article; she was sure it was a pack of lies. Now, as Stuart prepared to walk onto the NNC set for his live interview, Catherine kissed him lightly on the lips. Just as he left the holding room, she winked twice, the silent gesture they'd shared to buck each other up in past crises.

The lights went up. Roberts entered the set and sat down across from Hallister. She wasted no time. "Tonight, NNC has the first interview with Stuart Roberts since the explosive *Los Angeles Register* story rocked his campaign on what should have been a triumphant close to the Republican presidential convention."

Roberts harnessed his fury as he waited for the first question. "Senator Roberts, you face allegations of serious wrongdoing in the financing of your campaign and the conduct of IntelliView when you ran the firm and afterward. What is your response?"

"Such absurd charges were a shock to me and to the nation. I am here tonight to denounce these falsehoods."

Roberts took a drink from a glass of water. Hallister bore in. "The allegations link you with the Russian oligarch Mikhail Gusov, the opposition leader who was recently killed in Moscow. What was your relationship with him?"

"I first met Gusov in the late nineties when I was ambassador to Russia. We had no business dealings. I knew of no campaign funds from him."

"The *Register* reports that Gusov contributed to your campaign through AmeriCon Energy and one of its executives, Bud Johnson."

Stuart's lips tingled. He took his handkerchief and rubbed them in a similar fashion to how Viktor Romanov had wiped his lips in Atyrau. "Again, this story is a fabrication."

Roberts struggled to continue speaking. "I suspect that the—the same people who tried to assassinate me—are behind this—this slur on my reputation."

Stuart stopped breathing. His lifeless body fell from the chair.

As the cameras rolled, Wendy Hallister yelled to off-screen aides. "Get a doctor! Something's wrong with Senator Roberts!"

Ahmad Durrani sipped an espresso with his laptop on the table in a Kabul cybercafe. The Afghan archeologist read Frank's follow-up coverage of the scandal that the American reporter's exposé had unleashed, and which he had helped his friend to document.

On the high-speed computer in his Jerusalem flat, Israeli

General Raz Gonan viewed Roberts's interrupted interview via streaming video.

Already at work early morning the next day in Moscow, momentarily unaware of the startling development in America, the Russian president sat at his cherry-wood desk in the Kremlin.

Closer to California, the new twist spurred Lisa Hawkes to rapid movement. She rose from the living-room couch in McLean, Virginia, and rushed from her condo out to a BMW 320 sports coupe. Shifting into high gear, she raced along darkened Dolley Madison Boulevard to her office at Langley.

In Los Angeles, surrounded by colleagues in a frenzied mid evening newsroom, Frank's adrenaline surged as he watched the stricken Roberts on his desk TV. The reporter quickly turned from pounding out notes on his laptop to sending rapid-fire tweets and blogging for the *Register*'s website.

Smoking a cigar in his office across the large newsroom, Thomas Hawkes stared at the bioWave's projection of the NNC interview with Roberts as this new drama ensnared his hand-picked man for the White House. Operation Long Shadow, which he'd hatched so long ago, had fallen apart. The person he so carefully groomed to be his presidential stalking horse had failed him. And yet in the end, Hawkes had contained the damage.

In his sixth floor office at Langley, Russell Talbert watched Roberts collapse with grim satisfaction. There would be no loose ends.

EPILOGUE

NEW YORK
ONE YEAR LATER

WHEN THE PULITZER Prizes were first awarded in 1917, they were given in three journalism categories: reporting, public service and editorial writing. Now, there were fourteen categories, among them photography, international reporting and feature writing. The Gold Medal for Public Service had become the most coveted award for work that went beyond exemplary journalism to compel government and social reforms. Recipients ranged from the *New York Times'* publication of the Pentagon Papers in 1972 and the *Washington Post's* exposure of the Watergate scandal in 1973 to a 1996 series by the Raleigh *News & Observer* that documented how industrial pig farming had turned the eastern half of North Carolina into a giant cesspool.

From the time the *Los Angeles Register* published its shocking exposé of Republican presidential candidate Stuart

Roberts's secret overseas business deals, the series had been a favorite to win a Pulitzer. But its receipt of the Gold Medal when the Pulitzers were announced was a surprise. The series hadn't led to any political reforms, though it did prompt three days of televised hearings at which senators demanded tougher standards for campaign-finance disclosures and stiffer fines for violating the ban on foreign contributions. In their citation, the Pulitzer judges said the *Register*'s reporting on Roberts had "performed the rare public service of reminding Americans in a visceral way that even in a strong democracy like the United States, avarice-fueled corruption is a threat."

The awards ceremony was held in Lowe Library at Columbia University. It was at the Ivy League school in Manhattan's Morningside Heights that Joseph Pulitzer had established the Columbia Graduate School of Journalism, the nation's first and still most elite master's program dedicated to the craft. Pulitzer, a Hungarian Catholic-Jewish immigrant, helped create the norms of American journalism as owner of the *St. Louis Post-Dispatch* and *New York World*. From 1878 to 1911, he published investigative articles about government corruption and rich tax dodgers. A 1909 exposé uncovering a $40 million fraudulent payment by the United States to the French Panama Canal Company prompted federal charges of libeling President Theodore Roosevelt and banker J. P. Morgan. The *World* continued reporting the scandal, and Pulitzer emerged as a hero when the courts dismissed the indictments. In advocating the creation of the Graduate Journalism School, Pulitzer echoed Thomas Jefferson in writing: "Our Republic and its press will rise or fall together. An able, disinterested, public-spirited press, with trained intelligence to know the right and courage to do it, can preserve that public virtue without which popular government is a sham and a mockery. The power to mold the future of the Republic will be in the hands of the journalists of future generations." A bronze statue of Jefferson stood outside the entrance to the red-brick journalism school.

Like so many reporters, Frank had dreamed of winning a Pulitzer since Hawkes had hired him in 1998. He had even told colleagues he would cut off an arm in order to get one. Frank sometimes felt willing to follow through on the morbid joke, but inevitably only after having consumed a fifth of vodka during that blurry alcoholic decade he had overcome. While he still had both arms, he'd cut a different deal with the devil in producing his Roberts exposé.

Adams sat at the *Register*'s round table in Lowe Library with Thomas and Lisa. She and Frank had remarried two months earlier at the Rancho Santa Ana Botanic Garden. Also at the table were *Register* political editor Don Hudson; the paper's executive and managing editors; and its CIA, White House and State Department correspondents. The foreign guest of honor was Pyotor Maximovich Vorobyov, editor of the Russian business weekly *Kapital*. Vorobyov had traveled from Moscow to accept the Pulitzer Gold Medal on behalf of his slain reporter who had shared the byline with Adams.

In addition to fourteen journalism prizes, Pulitzers were being presented for the previous year's best novel, play, poetry collection, biography, nonfiction book, historical work and musical composition. The cream of American journalism, literature, music and the arts assembled at thirty tables with white cloths crossed by silver ribbons. A jazz ensemble played in a corner of the stately library with golden ceiling-to-floor curtains covering high stained-glass windows, Roman columns made of Siena marble from Egypt, and deeply grained dark oak wall paneling.

Enrico Gonzales, a *New York Times* White House correspondent who'd been based in Moscow with Frank, came over to the table and put his arm around Adams's shoulder. "Spectacular piece of reporting, Frank! I was jealous as hell when I read it. I always told you you'd end up reporting back in Russia, but I never thought you'd win a fucking Pulitzer for it!" Other reporters followed Gonzales to the table—Elizabeth Cole of the *Washington Post*, Binh Nguyen of the *Boston Globe*, and Ben Adler of the *Miami Herald*. When no more well-wishers approached, Vorobyov clasped Adams's elbow and spoke quietly to him in Russian.

"Frank, I want to thank you personally. I understand that Viktor's byline was included because of your insistence. Viktor thought the world of your skills as a reporter, but you may not know that he also loved you like a brother. He would be so pleased to share this Pulitzer with you, and I can think of no more fitting way to honor his memory than to be here with you to accept it in his tragic absence."

For the first time today, a wave of pleasure flowed through Frank. Moved almost to tears, he gave Vorobyov a strong handshake and felt the Russian pull him forward for a brief embrace. Sarah Brewer, executive editor of the *Kansas City Star* and chairwoman of the Pulitzer Committee, approached the podium. As the room fell silent, she welcomed everyone and began the annual address on the state of American journalism. The Gold Medal for Public Service would be the last Pulitzer presented. Over the next hour, as Brewer delivered her speech and bestowed the other awards, Frank's attention waned. He was glad that Viktor would share his prize. Only Lisa knew how much in debt he was to Romanov. And he would tell no one besides her how much he had violated journalism ethics in order to get the Roberts story—hacking into Viktor's e-mail account; posing as a digital Viktor in phony messages to Vorobyov and Ahmad; reading Viktor's reporting files after his death. Frank's certainty that Viktor would have done the same thing had their roles been reversed—had Adams been killed in Atyrau instead of Romanov—gave the American little solace.

There were darker secrets that made this a bittersweet day for him. His use of the xWave with its classified technology had broken US laws, so he'd had to leave that out of the Roberts exposé and even his first-person account. As good as the published work had been, Frank knew how much else was left on the cutting room floor. The CIA, or at least some arm of it, had tried to kill a sitting senator and presidential candidate. Then, when that attempt failed, Frank suspected that the same forces had succeeded in murdering Roberts during his aborted TV interview. The autopsy had listed a heart attack as the cause of death, but Adams didn't believe it. Frank had heard the recording of Viktor's exchange with Rado in the final moments of his life in Kazakhstan. He'd watched Roberts gasp for breath and then fall dead on live television, as suddenly as Viktor had expired in the Mercedes outside the Atyrau bar.

His research had revealed everything he needed to know about tetrodotoxin. So potent was this compound from a Japanese pufferfish, a pinhead drop of it was lethal and so tiny that the most skilled pathologist would never find it in an autopsy.

Frank had rationalized his decision to exclude these pieces of the story by telling himself he would report them in subsequent articles, and Stuart's convenient death on TV had strengthened his resolve. But each time he started the work, doubts and his own secrets had stymied him. What real evidence did he possess?

Russell Talbert, the CIA's head of science and technology, had shown him an intelligence dossier filled with damning materials about Roberts's shady business dealings. That file certainly provided a motive for "removing" him, as the spies would say, but it was far from definitive proof. When Frank had listened to Talbert in their secret meeting at Morris Reservoir high above Los Angeles, he thought the gently threatening spook had admitted having been behind the bomb blast that targeted Roberts. Yet when Frank played back their conversation on the recorder he'd hidden in his shirt pocket, he heard only vague intimations. There were other secrets that prevented him from reporting the full story—secrets that hit closer to home. Even if he'd obtained proof that the CIA killed Roberts, how could he use it without reporting why the Agency had committed such an audacious crime? That, in turn, would force him to reveal Operation Long Shadow and Thomas's ties to the CIA. Outing Hawkes might even bring down the paper. Such disclosures would inevitably lead other reporters to dig deeper. They would learn of Lisa's covert status. They would no doubt discover that she'd protected Frank in Moscow and set up a CIA mole to provide crucial information about Roberts.

Frank also had been forced to confront difficult internal truths. He wasn't certain he was willing to shoulder responsibility for the fallout if he'd reported the full story. Disclosure that a US presidential candidate had been targeted and possibly even killed by his own government, no matter the justification, would have made the Watergate scandal look tame. It would have destroyed whatever faith Americans had left in Washington. Overseas it would have subjected the United States to ridicule and weakened its moral standing to influence other countries.

Lisa squeezed Frank's hand under the table to bring his attention back to the podium. Sarah Brewer was presenting the Gold Medal for Public Service Journalism.

"Officially all of the Pulitzer prizes in journalism carry the same weight, and we hail each of their recipients. However, the Gold Medal has long been first among equals. It embodies the foremost ideal that Joseph Pulitzer practiced as a publisher—and that he endeavored to honor in establishing these prizes and creating the fine journalism school here at Columbia. That ideal directs journalists to make public service their greatest ambition. It leads them to strive to promote the public good. And it makes them, certainly in the case of Frank Adams and Viktor Romanov, willing to risk their lives in order to prevent corruption from seeping into our governing institutions, our businesses or our communities. For the first time in the long history of these esteemed prizes, the Pulitzer Committee this year is honoring a foreign journalist. Viktor Romanov was an investigative reporter for the *Kapital* business journal in Moscow. He was killed while working with Frank Adams on uncovering the hidden history of Senator Stuart Roberts. That personal history, which included illegal foreign campaign contributions and secret business ties to terrorists and international arms dealers, would eventually have brought shame to our nation had Roberts succeeded in being elected president. The extraordinary work of Adams and Romanov is a rare display of personal bravery and professional achievement. It is my privilege to call to the podium Mr. Frank Adams of the *Los Angeles Register*, to be followed by Pyotor Maximovich Vorobyov, editor of *Kapital*, who will accept the Gold Medal on behalf of his fallen reporter."

As Frank rose from the table, his colleagues leapt to their feet and delivered the first standing ovation of the day.

Passing his peers on his way to the podium, Frank understood that his Pulitzer-winning article had confronted him with a stark decision: tell the entire unvarnished story with its unacceptable consequences or extend a cover-up in which he himself had broken laws, breached journalistic principles and exploited the same intelligence agency he sought to expose. For now, at least, he had no choice. The result was a work of reporting that his peers hailed today as a masterpiece, but which he knew to be badly tarnished.

Nearing the stage to accept journalism's highest prize, he felt oddly distant from the ceremony and celebration. As much as he hated to admit it, Talbert had been right: Frank was a patriot. Even harder for him to admit, Thomas had been right as well. There were always different versions of the truth, and his award was for just one of them.

ACKNOWLEDGMENTS

AS COMPLEX AS the plot of *High Hand* now is, as far-flung as are its global locales, they are simpler and more concentrated than they once were. This is largely thanks to two rounds of extremely helpful, if at times painful, revisions based on the advice of two New York editors with decades of experience at the major publishing houses. Danelle McCafferty, especially, provided an attentive, exhaustive critique that led to a slew of critical changes. Her most important of many terrific insights was to note a gaping hole at the center of the novel: "You've written a book without a villain!" she informed us. "Lots of bad guys, but not a villain who's committed murder." After much discussion, we transformed one of our bad guys into the villain. That change produced ripple effects requiring multiple adjustments throughout the novel. Hillel Black provided bracing feedback that led to tighter writing with fewer tangents snaking away from the central action. Thanks in large part to their expert editing, *High Hand* endured two fundamental restructurings that saw characters disappear, old chapters eliminated and new chapters written with less jumping around in place and time. The result, while far from simple, is hopefully a cleaner story line that is easier to follow.

Our partners put up with absences over long "creative weekends," endless animated conference calls and the occasional disconnect from family and romantic life. More important, Tance Harris, Barbara Ellenberger and Anne Salladin applied their collective high intelligence and great humor to penetrating readings of *High Hand* that helped us untangle plot knots and gain deeper insight into our characters. At several key junctures, they gently but firmly reminded us that we needed to finish writing the first book before focusing on sequels, movies or other future dreams.

Other family members and friends also kept us grounded: Jill Harris, Matt Samet, Don Ellenberger, Ernie Meloche, the Honorable Gerald E. Rosen, Mitchell Rosen. It was Jill who suggested the vehicle of the poker game. Matt schooled us in the intricacies of big-wall climbing. Mitch, not inconsequentially for a book based on a card game, pointed out that eight people can't play poker, at least not with a single deck. Ernie persuaded us that while everyone gets lost in Los Angeles, we shouldn't compound the problem with geographical errors.

Thanks also to Muriel Nellis, Jane Roberts, and Janet Fries who provided invaluable guidance.

Finally, three prominent men of government and letters took time from their own creative endeavors to give us incalculable encouragement. John Rizzo, the CIA's former top lawyer, helped prevent neophytes in spycraft from wandering too far from the particular intricacies of espionage. Joby Warrick and Kevin Giblin also lent their considerable expertise in the intelligence world to our enterprise. Without the encouragement of these three gentlemen, plus help from several others who must remain unnamed, *High Hand* would be a far less compelling read. Despite their help and the aid of others, we are solely responsible for any errors that might remain.

ABOUT THE AUTHOR

CURTIS J. JAMES is a pseudonym for the three writers who collaborated on this book. They are Curtis C. Harris, James N. Ellenberger and James Rosen.

Curtis Harris is a physician-scientist who is world-renowned in the field of cancer research. Dr. Harris has published more than 500 journal articles and 100 book chapters, has edited 10 books, and holds more than 25 advanced biotechnology patents owned by the US government. He also serves as editor-in-chief for the scientific journal *Carcinogenesis* and has held or currently holds elected offices in numerous scholarly societies and nonprofit foundations. Dr. Harris is the chief of the Laboratory of Human Carcinogenesis at the NIH National Cancer Institute. He also is adjunct professor of oncology at Georgetown University School of Medicine.

James Ellenberger worked for nearly 30 years in numerous capacities with the national AFL-CIO. Among his posts, he was responsible for Asian affairs in the organization's international affairs section and was assistant director of occupational safety and health. He later served four years as deputy commissioner of the Virginia Employment Commission under Gov. Mark Warner. A Vietnam War veteran, he has traveled extensively in Asia and the Middle East. Ellenberger has written numerous articles on international labor affairs, social insurance and medical care for injured workers.

James Rosen is a political correspondent for The McClatchy Co. based in its Washington, DC, Bureau. He previously was a news strategist and a congressional reporter for the *Miami Herald, Kansas City Star, Sacramento Bee* and 26 other McClatchy newspapers, as well as a frequent contributor to the Tribune News Service's 1,200 US and international media clients. He has received two National Press Club awards for political reporting and the McClatchy President's Award for his coverage of the 2000 post-election Florida recount. Rosen also served as a Moscow correspondent for United Press International.

The authors would love to hear from you. You can contact them via:

Website: http://www.curtisjjames.com/
Facebook: http://on.fb.me/1QXjcKE
Goodreads: http://bit.ly/1TocCuG
Pinterest: http://bit.ly/1lzOnhY
Twitter: @curtisjjames